THE TARE IN THE WHEAT

Kimberly Miller Wentworth

AmErica House
Baltimore

First printing

ISBN: 1-58851-945-7
PUBLISHED BY AMERICA HOUSE BOOK PUBLISHERS
www.publishamerica.com
Baltimore

Printed in the United States of America

Dedicated to my mother and father,

Gay and Ted Miller:

My encouragers when my strength failed,
My lamplighters when all seemed dark,
And my faithful cheerleaders

The Tare In the Wheat

Jesus told them another parable: "The kingdom of heaven is like a man who sowed good seed in his field. But while everyone was sleeping, his enemy came and sowed weeds among the wheat, and went away. When the wheat sprouted and formed heads, then the weeds also appeared.

"The owner's servants came to him and said, 'Sir didn't you sow good seed in your field? Where then did the weeds come from?'

"'An enemy did this,' he replied.

"The servants asked him, 'Do you want us to go and pull them up?'

"'No,' he answered, 'because while you are pulling the weeds, you may root up the wheat with them. Let both grow together until the harvest. At that time, I will tell the harvesters: First collect the weeds and tie them in bundles to be burned; then gather the wheat and bring it into my barn.'"

Then he left the crowd and went into the house. His disciples came to him and said, "Explain to us the parable of the weeds in the field."

He answered, "The one who sowed the good seed is the Son of Man. The field is the world, and the good seed stands for the sons of the kingdom. The weeds are the sons of the evil one, and the enemy who sows them is the devil. The harvest is the end of the age, and the harvesters are angels.

"As the weeds are pulled up and burned in the fire, so it will be at the end of the age. The Son of Man will send out his angels, and they will weed out of his kingdom everything that causes sin and all who do evil. They will throw them into the fiery furnace, where there will be weeping and gnashing of teeth. Then the righteous will shine like the sun in the kingdom of their Father. He who has ears, let him hear."

- Matthew 13:24-29, 36-43 (NIV)

Chapter 1

While everyone was sleeping, his enemy came and sowed weeds among the wheat, and went away.

-Matthew 13:25 (NIV)

The summer storm erupted suddenly, with unrestrained fury, as if God were angry at the world. Darkness covered the large, stone church as the wind mercilessly swept down followed by a torrent of rain. An unnoticed weed stretched its spiny limbs, accepting the gift of water from the sky, stealing moisture from the nearby grass. Shiny leather shoes stepped over its thorny tendrils, unaware of its creeping presence or the Georgia red clay clinging to their soles. Down the path that wound among the huge magnolias and tall hickory trees, the shoes marched, toward the back of the church, through large glass doors framed in burnished brass and into the atrium that was the entryway for all who had church business to attend to. The shoes sloppily spread brick-colored mud in their wake.

"Bill, it's a mess out there. Clean off the sidewalk before you leave tonight." A crackle of lightning racing across the sky, followed by the deafening roar of thunder, punctuated the assistant pastor's command. A trail of red, mud-splattered footprints followed him down the hall.

In a shadowed corner of the large atrium, a small woman stood, straightening her crooked body. "Doesn't Brother Cole know it's after six o'clock?" she sighed, pulling her mop out of its bucket to wipe the mud off the recently cleaned floor.

Wearily Bill shrugged his shoulders. "Don't think he cares. Not much about the time or your floor."

The older woman shook her head. "Oh, I'm used to him doing that. It'll take me just a few minutes to take care of this; then, I'll help you outside." Both of them eyed the dark sky through the large glass doors. A gust of wind swept pine straw onto the sidewalk, whipping it around carelessly. The heavy clouds obscured the sunshine that normally would have lit the June day. Large shadows covered the ground.

"That's all right, Miss Eleanor," Bill responded, a note of fatigue touching his voice. "You head on home to those cats of yours. I'm sure they're hungry."

She sighed again, relieved. Her back ached and her strength was fully taxed. It had been another long, demanding day. "Thanks Bill. Ol' Shakespeare and Dickens don't wait very patiently." She followed the footprints down the hall, the thump, thump of the mop bucket trailing behind her.

Bill hammered one more nail into the chair rail he'd been attaching to the wall. He'd have to finish this job tomorrow, he realized dishearteningly as he thought of the growing list of chores on his desk upstairs. Gathering his tools, he heard the swoosh of the wind as the atrium door opened again. His neighbor, Donald Gresham rushed into the room. Wiping his feet on the large, black indoor mat, he greeted Bill with a hint of a smile. "That's quite a storm," he said, glancing back at the dark clouds. "Think it's letting up now though." An almost imperceptible frown touched his face.

Often Bill had noticed a perpetual troubled expression that seemed to be stamped onto Donald's thin features. Unseen forces appeared to weigh the man down. Bill rose, his toolbox in hand and walked over to greet Donald. He liked this older deacon of the church.

"How's the house coming, Bill. I noticed you painted the outside. It's looking good." The slightest trace of warmth ran through the older man's words.

"It's going pretty well," Bill returned, pleased with the praise. Last winter when he and Christine had bought the house from Donald, they'd been thrilled to purchase this "fixer-upper." Hours of work had gone into the place, transforming the cottage that was sorely in need of repair into a home they could be proud of. Though it had been hard work, Bill's skills had come in handy and he'd been able to restore the house at a fraction of the cost of hiring someone else to do it. Lately Christine had been busy painting the inside trim, adding the final touches. They both were pleased with the overall results. "Stop by some time and come see it."

"I'd like to. I know Judith would love to see what you've done with the place."

Though Bill's face remained placid, internally he grimaced at the idea of Donald's wife visiting their home. She'd been against them buying the cottage, and though he didn't know the woman well, he tended to feel as if she looked down on them from some high and lofty perch of her own making and saw them as lacking.

Donald, noticing a movement outside, interrupted the conversation, relieving Bill of the need to say anything. "Good. Here's Pastor Leonard." He opened the door as the white-haired preacher hurried up the walk and into the building.

"My goodness! These Georgia summer storms can be merciless," Leonard

KIMBERLY MILLER WENTWORTH

commented. "Look at that mess out there."

"I'm fixing to go clean it up right now, Pastor Leonard," Bill said, moving his heavy toolbox to his left hand.

"Oh, no, Bill. I wasn't suggesting you do anything like that." Leonard glanced at his watch. "It's almost seven. Way past time for you to go home. Christine's probably waiting on you."

Bill smiled. "Thank you, sir. I'll take care of it first thing in the morning."

Leonard turned to walk down the hall with Donald. "I'm glad you were able to meet with Brother Cole and me tonight, Donald. I think you should be in on our discussion." His voice trailed off down the hall.

Miss Eleanor, who had reappeared to say "good-night," glanced at Bill with a light glint in her eyes. "I like those two there," she said, shaking her head in the direction of the men walking toward the pastor's office. "Look at my floor. Not a trace of mud on it."

Bill smiled. It was true. They hadn't left any red-clay tracks.

It was after ten o'clock when Pastor Leonard, Brother Cole, and Donald Gresham left the church. The grave discussion that had ensued during their meeting continued as they walked outside. The budget crisis. Too much money was being spent or too little was coming in. Leonard ran his hand through his thick silver hair as he silently listened to the others.

"We need to have a sermon series on the importance of giving," Cole reiterated for at least the third time. "You have to almost badger some people into giving. They're so tight-fisted."

"Cutting expenses where we can will help," Donald added. "We aren't that much over budget yet."

"But if things continue the way they are now," Cole sighed knowingly. "It's only June – we shouldn't be this far behind. You know how bad giving is during the summer. We could be in real trouble come September if we don't make a concerted effort to straighten out this problem."

Weariness lined Leonard's face. It was time to go home. Saying "good-night," he walked to his car. In the darkness, he didn't see the weed as he passed by. The weed that had grown imperceptibly during the day. The weed that reached deeply into the soil developing grasping roots. He didn't see its prickly little arms spreading out, choking the green grass nearby. Yes, indeed, it was flourishing quite nicely.

Chapter 2

For out of the overflow of his heart, his mouth speaks.

-Luke 6:45 (NIV)

The warm June day glittered at Christine through the dining room window, beckoning her to come join the freshly washed world outside. Instead she continued to paint the window's massive trim. Only two months had passed since she and Bill had moved into their new home, and finally this was the last room left. Soon the painting would be finished she realized with satisfaction.

Theirs was a cozy house, she decided as she dipped her brush back into the white enamel. Often she feared that she was dreaming. After spending the first eight years of their marriage in a cramped, little mobile home that seemed to shrink with the birth of each of their three children, this place was unbelievably large. Sometimes she felt afraid she would awaken to find it had disappeared; it was gone, only a wisp of the wind.

Bill had repainted the outside trim ivory and the siding a deep shade of blue. The four dormers and the high eaves had had their gingerbread trim repaired and been newly painted as well. From the outside, their home looked like a quaint cottage.

Now that the downstairs was almost finished, they could soon concentrate on building steps to the attic and renovating the space up there. Christine had been too busy to think much about the attic, but perhaps sometime this weekend she and Bill could go up and see what was to be done. After they'd bought the house, with a touch of embarrassment, Donald Gresham had informed them that he was leaving all the things in the garret for them to dispose of anyway they wanted.

"Dad insists I leave that stuff with you," he'd explained, shaking his head, as if he didn't understand his father very well. "He says it all goes with the house."

The daunting task of cleaning out the attic seemed overwhelming at the moment, but then again, it would be interesting to see what had been left up there.

Carefully she ran her brush down the right edge of trim. If she worked quickly while the children napped, she might finish this final room. A chickadee landed on the dogwood standing near the window and trilled her his song. At the top of the hill, she could see Donald and Judith Gresham's mansion. Its manicured lawns cascaded down to the white-picket fence that surrounded Bill and Christine's back yard. Their home had an austere beauty to Christine, not the quaint coziness of hers and Bill's cottage. It stood high and regal. Its massive stonework rising into four turrets at each corner and a lofty widow's walk adorned the roof. A huge chandelier could be seen through the ornate front window above the large double doors. The neighborhood had dubbed the place the Castle and the title fit.

A street of houses had built up to surround the Gresham's manor as Atlanta stretched her tentacles northeast to claim this small town near Athens. Their church, Main Street First, had also grown, tripling in membership in the last eight years since she and Bill had been going there. Bill's job as Facility Maintenance Supervisor had also tripled its workload, making him more times than not late getting home. Christine thought she wouldn't mind his late hours if she'd felt he were happy. Bill had been quieter lately. Not wanting to talk about his day. It worried her but there was little she could do about it, except pray. She did that, praying often for her husband.

BUZZZZ! The quiet of the afternoon was shattered at the strident ring of the doorbell. Christine jerked at the sound. Who could that be? Dropping her paintbrush in the bucket, she wiped her hands on a cloth rag as she rushed to the front door, hoping that whoever it was wouldn't ring again and wake the children.

BUZZZZ! BUZZZZ! Oh, they were impatient. Probably the children across the street wanting to play.

A wail from the baby made her grit her teeth. Jonathan peeked his head out of his room. "Mama, who's that?"

"I don't know. Go back to bed," she spoke harshly, irritated with herself for her impatience. At least Amanda hadn't awakened yet, but if the baby kept hollering… Christine looked out the window. There stood Judith Gresham. *Of all people, not her*, she thought as she wiped the final remnants of wet paint onto her rag before opening the door.

"Mrs. Gresham, please come in." She added a note of warmth to her voice to belie her negative feelings. As Judith came into the room, Christine excused herself to get the baby. Returning moments later, she held a red-faced eight-month-old, who, happy to be held by her mother, stopped crying and stared curiously at the stranger.

"Have a seat, Mrs. Gresham," she offered. Judith surveyed the furniture before sitting down stiffly on the edge of the rocking chair. Christine noticed her immaculate dress. Often she thought that the woman looked as if she'd

11

walked out of the pages of *Vogue*. Her own old paint clothes seemed suddenly very ragged. This older woman was lovely in many ways, but her stern expression stole most of her beauty. Christine guessed that she was somewhere in her fifties, though her clear skin was only marred by two indented frown lines between her eyes. Those eyes now gazed around the room, seeming to evaluate it, a look of a severe taskmaster stamped on her face. "Would you like a glass of ice tea?"

"No, thank you. I can't stay long. I just wanted to come see what you've done with this place. Have you refinished the floors?"

"Yes," Christine replied, pleased that the woman would notice. She explained in detail how Bill had sanded and restained the old floors before they had moved in. Mrs. Gresham didn't look at her as she talked but continued to survey the room. Christine forced herself to stop speaking, allowing an awkward, at least on her part, silence to exist.

"You know we always loved this old house," Judith said, not wistfully, but almost as if she were accusing Christine of something.

Christine remembered back to the uncomfortable day that they'd bought the house. Donald appeared happy to sell, but Judith had been angry about the whole arrangement. Christine couldn't quite figure out why. The cottage had been used for storage for several years and had fallen into disrepair during that time. It hadn't come to them well kept as a treasure usually was. She smiled politely, saying the first thing that came into her head. "We love it, too."

Judith sighed deeply before responding. Facing Christine for the first time since coming into her home, her eyes seemed to take in Christine's old clothes and smudged appearance. Christine smiled weakly. Judith Gresham smiled back, a plastic smile. "I'm glad we could help you get this nice place at such a good price. That's my Donald for you. Always giving, giving, giving."

Christine's smile faded at the words. Unsure of what to say, her automatic politeness tried to summon a "Thank you," but the grip on her heart squeezed too tight for it to come out. "Well, we're enjoying it, although we still have a lot of work to do." She hoped that this would be a gentle reminder that the house had been in awful shape when they'd bought it.

Judith stood, smoothing the wrinkles from her dress, and seeming to have brightened, spoke quickly, "It does look better. You must be some kind of little worker. And with a baby, too."

A genuine smile relaxed Christine's features. "Thank you. We have three children. This is Lauranna. Our oldest is Jonathan, and I have a two-year-old named Amanda. They're napping in their rooms."

"Well, isn't that wonderful," Judith returned in a bored voice, causing Christine to feel as if she'd said too much. "May I see the whole house?"

Caught off guard, Christine hesitated for a moment. Usually she loved to show others her new home, but she didn't really want to give Judith Gresham a tour until it was completed, and with Amanda asleep, it felt like an imposition. Briefly she considered saying that this wouldn't be a good time, but that seemed rude. She heard the words, "Certainly, except we'll have to be quiet in Amanda's room. She's still sleeping," come out of her mouth. Amanda acted like a bear if she didn't get her entire nap. Rising from her seat, Christine led Judith to the door of the master bedroom.

"You need a good window treatment to finish out this room," Judith critiqued as she walked toward the master bathroom door at the back of the bedroom. "It needs something else, even with the stained-glass windows."

"You're right," Christine said, trying to be magnanimous about the criticism. "I plan on making some curtains soon."

"Making them?" Judith turned to eye her with disbelief. "Oh, my dear, no. Don't make them. Why that would look so...so....," she moved her hand through the air as if she could find the word she searched for in it. "...homemade. I have a wonderful seamstress that I use. I'll give you her phone number. She's fairly expensive." Stopping she eyed Christine almost thoughtfully. "I suppose, what with your husband being a janitor, you're on a tight budget." The word "janitor" came out of her mouth as if she'd spit out spoiled milk. With a wave of her hand, she appeared to dismiss the idea as she rummaged through her purse before pulling out a card. "Perhaps she can give you someone who can do a fair job, more in your price range." Handing Christine the card, she turned to walk into the bathroom.

Christine didn't know what to say. She felt herself wanting to boil over and shout *Bill isn't a janitor; he's the maintenance supervisor at the largest church in North Georgia* to Judith's retreating back. Well, so what if he were a janitor. Was that so bad? Crumpling the card in her hand, she followed Judith into the bathroom.

"Now in here you need a mirror," Judith noted. "You can't have enough mirrors. I'd suggest a big brass one."

Pointing out the new floor, light, sink and tub fixtures, Christine explained that Bill had replaced them. "Since he's a certified electrician and plumber, he can do this for us," she added, boldly praising her husband.

Judith gave a dissatisfying murmured response as she left the bathroom and walked through the bedroom and down the hall to Jonathan's room.

Christine followed, feeling deflated, like a balloon from which the air was rapidly leaking.

13

In Jonathan's room, the older woman pointed out all the things still not done, commenting in the process that the rug really should be replaced. It was too worn out. "I'll look in my attic and see if I have anything there you can use."

Christine didn't want to be ungrateful, but at the same time something in her balked at the idea of using this condescending woman's hand-me-downs. All their hard work went unnoticed. Instead every flaw was pointed out. She had thought the rug in Jonathan's room looked pretty good, but well, yes, it was worn.

Walking out of Jonathan's room, Judith led the way to the hall bathroom. Ignoring the newly installed tile and cabinets, she again commented on the importance of mirrors, that she had one in almost every room of her home. How they opened a place up, making even a tiny house such as this one look bigger, more elegant.

Christine listened silently, willing herself to be polite, but wishing the woman gone. Her face, had Judith Gresham analyzed it as she did the house's interior, would have betrayed her feelings. The older woman entered Amanda's room before Christine could stop her, and for the first time Judith's criticism ceased as she eyed the sleeping child. Her gaze never searched the room but instead rested on Amanda's delicate face framed with flaxen hair. Turning without a word, Judith walked by Christine, across the hall to the kitchen. Something in her manner seemed different – almost as if an ache touched her stern features, Christine thought, but quickly the plastic smile covered whatever she had glimpsed, and Judith immediately began surveying the kitchen, even opening up cabinet doors. Her bored, "Nice, nice," didn't fit with the earlier criticism. Something in the woman's condescending attitude had changed.

Walking into the dining room, Christine knew there was still plenty to criticize and got ready for the next onslaught. The paint bucket sat on the floor on top of an old newspaper.

"Oh, so you were painting when I came in. I wondered about your clothes." Judith gave a hollow laugh as she walked through the dining room to the living room. "So now we're back where we started. Well, I'd better go – I have an appointment at the club. I'll let you get back to your painting."

Christine breathed a sigh of relief.

Pausing at the door, Judith turned toward her. "Oh, I almost forgot. My father-in-law wants you to come by and see him. So he can tell you the history of this place. That is if you care about such things. He lives out at Lanier Gardens. I'd better get going. See you in church." And like a puff of hot air, out she went.

Christine shut the door with a soft thud and locked it. Her head hurt. And she was tired. Too tired to paint any more today.

Walking back into the girls' bedroom, she put the baby, who had fallen asleep in her arms, back in her crib. Plodding back to the dining room, forgetting to be quiet for a moment, she slammed shut the paint can.

What bothered her? Perhaps the Gresham woman wasn't really such a bad sort. Perhaps she just wanted to help, and most of the suggestions she'd given were things Christine knew had to be done. But who asked her to come down and critique the place? That, if nothing else, had been rather presumptuous.

An almost sickly feeling engulfed her as she walked into the living room and sank down on the couch. Suddenly she had a word for what she felt. Shame. But what in the world did she have to be ashamed of?

Jonathan peeked around the corner. "Mama, can I get up now?"

"Sure. Come sit with me." His company would be a comfort to her wilted spirit.

He walked over and slid in beside her. His four-year-old eyes looked at her thoughtfully. "Was that a bad lady?"

A whispering voice in Christine wanted to tell him that yes indeed, he was right, Mrs. Gresham was a bad lady, but instead she answered, "I don't think she's bad, Jonathan. She's just different from us."

Jonathan cuddled closer to his mother. "I don't want her rug in my room. I want my rug. I love my rug."

He lay his head on Christine's lap. The act soothed the wound in her spirit. "Yes, Jonathan, let's keep that rug. I like it, too. I think it looks good in your room."

Sitting up, he gave her a tight hug. Together they cuddled on the couch, allowing the gentle song of the evening birds to lift their spirits.

Chapter 3

I have seen a wicked and ruthless man flourishing like a green tree in its native soil.

-Psalms 37:35

The following Sunday Christine sat by strangers in the large, crowded auditorium, trying to listen to the sermon. Bill had been asked by one of the ushers to repair something in the preschool area. Week after week this happened. If only the two of them could enjoy the sermon together, but instead Christine usually ended up sitting alone.

With effort she listened to the pastor's words. Usually his sermons captivated her, but for some reason today her concentration wandered. Maybe it was because of the heat. The sweltering June humidity seeped into the huge auditorium, making it difficult for the air conditioners to cool the large building.

Pastor Leonard wiped his brow with his handkerchief as he explained that this was the first sermon of a series on the importance of stewardship. Christine wondered if the church was experiencing financial difficulties. No, that didn't make sense. The choir had just purchased new robes, and Bill had been busy all week refurbishing the atrium. Money shouldn't be that much of a problem.

Gazing behind Pastor Leonard, she noticed a man in the choir who had fallen asleep. His head lay back in an uncomfortable position. The lady next to him kept trying to pull pieces of nit-size lint off her choir robe. Christine looked back at the pastor. His bubble words popped before being absorbed, falling on unhearing ears. If asked, she herself would be hard pressed to tell Bill what the man had said. An abnormal happening, but Leonard's words lacked their usual exuberance. He seemed slightly bored with the topic himself, as if he were trying to heat up cold words in a broken oven. It must be difficult to preach to such a distracted congregation. Out of politeness she endeavored to focus on his words.

A flutter caught the corner of her eye. Greta Odum sat at the piano, quiet as a butterfly, watching the pastor. Christine warmed at the sight of Greta. She had liked the shy, little woman from the moment she'd met her. The china-doll profile reminded her of a delicate angel she'd once seen in an expensive antique store. Greta had a gentleness about her, a quiet dignity that

Christine admired. How in the world she'd ever married that difficult man was beyond understanding. Christine's eyes inadvertently turned to the assistant pastor sitting in his high-backed, velvet throne. Yes, he was a handsome man by earthly standards. It made her stomach churn the way some of the women of the church turned to jelly whenever they were around him. Objectively she could see what the others saw, but, well, there was that smug tightness of his mouth. The way he held his head, too high. A hardness to his eye. It was all visible, too.

"My final point is...," Leonard began his conclusion. A barely audible sigh whispered through the auditorium.

Poor Pastor Leonard, Christine thought. Usually everyone was totally engrossed. What was wrong today? Her eyes again moved back to behind Pastor Leonard where Brother Cole sat on his throne, looking like a king watching an execution. A pleased, half-smile touched his square jaw. Christine wondered if he'd had anything to do with today's sermon.

Vaguely she noticed the man in front of her slumping slightly to his right, settling his head gently on his wife's shoulder. The next instant, he sat up straight, a short pig-like squeal erupting from his gut. Apparently the woman had elbowed him sharply in the ribs.

Suppressing a grin, Christine put her eyes back on the preacher to listen to his closing remarks. Thankfully soon church would be over. This afternoon, she and Bill planned on going up to the attic, and she was anxious to get to it.

Finally Pastor Leonard finished his sermon. Brother Cole's eyes surveyed the audience and a triumphant smirk flitted across his face. *Yes indeed,* Christine determined, Brother Cole Odum definitely had something to do with Pastor Leonard's sermon today.

Impatient to get home from church, the drive felt slower than usual. Rushing them all through lunch, Christine hurried the children into their beds for their afternoon naps. The baby quickly fell asleep, but Amanda seemed to take forever. With a touch of envy, Christine watched Bill climb the ladder to the attic without her. Jonathan could be trusted to stay in his room during naptime even if he was awake, but Amanda needed a more watchful eye. She'd recently figured out how to open the front door, and there was no telling what kind of trouble the adventuresome two-year-old could get into. At least once she was asleep, she slept soundly. The clock ticked away...two, two-fifteen, two-twenty. Christine cleaned the kitchen with a silent prayer that her daughter would soon fall asleep. Finally Amanda's hardy singing and laughter grew softer, till only a faint moan came from her tired mouth. Cautiously Christine peeked in on two slumbering daughters. Good. Now she could go see her attic.

Climbing the creaking ladder, her heart quickened as she poked her head into the dusty room. Two of the dormer windows stood open, letting a strong summer breeze drift through, cooling the warm room. A light rain had begun to fall outside, pattering softly on the roof. Musty smells of long-hidden secrets greeted her. Pulling herself onto the hard oak floor, she gazed around. Goodness. There were so many boxes. What could be in them all? An unexpected excitement came over her, as if it were Christmas morning and she were six years old again. Making her way over to Bill who sat in one of the dormers, she looked curiously at the box he was going through. "What you got there?"

"Books. Apparently someone liked to read a lot. Some of them look pretty good."

Turning around, Christine contemplated the cartons behind her. She pulled open the nearest one. A thick layer of dust darkened her hands and particles wafted up her nose, causing her to sneeze. She didn't care. She felt like a pirate opening buried treasure. Pulling out a pair of men's overalls, she held them up to see if they would fit Bill. They looked almost his size.

"What'd you find?" Bill asked behind her.

Glancing through the contents of the box, she answered, "A bunch of men's clothes. They look as if they might fit you."

"Great." Bill handed her a marking pen. "You can use this to write what's inside the box."

She closed the lid and wrote "Men's Clothes" in big bold letters, then looked over at the cartons Bill had marked. *Pots and Pans. Books. Tools.* He was obviously enjoying the box of books he was going through now, taking his time to thumb through each one of them.

She opened two more boxes of men's clothes, sneezing with each box. A tad disappointed in her find, she stood, wiping her face with her dirty hands, unaware of the streaks of grim she left on her cheeks. Gazing around the room, she determined that this time she would be more selective. In the far corner sat some furniture. Smiling, she hobbled around the boxes and made her way in that direction. They could use some furniture downstairs - especially dressers. She worked her way through the narrow path, shuffling near a large trunk. Stopping, she eyed it curiously. Almost everything else was stored in cardboard boxes. What could be in this? Lifting the clasps, she tried to pull up the lid. It was locked.

"Bill, could you help me open this?"

Placing the book he was reading back in its box, he rose stiffly and weaved his way over to Christine. "Maybe this will help," he said, a boyish glint in his eyes as he picked up a key attached to the side handle with a ribbon.

"Oh, I didn't see that," she laughed as Bill unlocked it.

Opening the trunk, a patchwork quilt covered whatever was inside. Christine pulled it out. Something hard and smooth touched her hand. Carefully she picked it up - a wooden stable. Reaching back into the trunk, she pulled out a large, wooden box. Its small brass latch opened easily. She glanced at Bill in excitement as she opened it. Intricately carved figurines of silver, gold, and rich burgundy looked up at her.

Bill whistled a low, awed sound as he picked up a delicately carved wooden lamb with a gentle expression on its face. "Look at that craftsmanship."

"Oh, Bill," Christine whispered, her eyes shining through the dirt and grim on her cheeks. "It's a Nativity set."

A surge of warmth toward Christine touched Bill as he looked at her childlike joy. In spite of her smudged face, when her large blue eyes danced as they were now, he couldn't help but think he'd married the most beautiful woman in the world.

"Can we bring this downstairs?" she asked.

"Sure. I'll get some rope."

As Bill left, Christine pulled out different pieces of the Nativity, examining them. For some reason memories of her Grandmother Martha came to mind, bringing a wistful longing to her heart.

Grandmother Martha would have loved this, she thought as she replaced Joseph and a donkey back in the box. It was odd how unexpectedly a longing to see her grandmother again would sometimes hit her. Out of nowhere, like a sudden downpour. A bitter sweetness would engulf her, and yet it had been almost ten years now since the dear woman had passed on.

Rain began pounding the roof. Thunder sounded outside, punctuating her find.

Bill returned. "The sky's getting pretty black," he said, walking over to a window.

Christine rose, following him. The zigzag of lightning in the distance brightened the room momentarily, surrounding them with brilliant shadows. The fresh scent of rain filled the air as lightning streaked the sky, thunder rumbling close behind, growing impatient as it advanced their way. In the valley, the little white church down the road could be easily seen. Two colts nervously ran in the direction of the barn in the Gresham's field. The

19

Gresham castle loomed above them on the hill, looking oddly foreboding. Christine eyed the large mansion as a thought occurred to her.

"I wonder if Donald Gresham knew this Nativity was up here."

"Well," Bill began, noting a hint of sadness marring her earlier joy. He knew she wanted to keep the crèche, hating to give it up, but at the same time, she didn't want to keep something that she felt wasn't rightfully theirs. "He told me his father said that all this stuff should stay with our house. It's part of it, is what he said."

Christine looked at Bill thoughtfully. "That's kind of odd, isn't it?" The heavy scent of rain lulled her thoughts. Something didn't quite make sense, but it was too much trouble to figure out. A strong breeze wafted through the window, cooling her face, playing with her hair. "Maybe we ought to mention it to them."

Bill breathed deeply, smelling the cedar as the wind carried its scent into the room. "I think," he said as merriment touched his hazel eyes, "that no one could possibly appreciate that Nativity more than you. I believe Judith Gresham would find it a little too quaint for her tastes."

A smile touched Christine's face. "I hadn't thought of that. You're right. It wouldn't quite fit the Gresham's decor." She leaned against Bill's arm.

A sudden streak of lightning followed immediately by a deafening clap of thunder woke them both from their reverie.

"We'd better go downstairs before this storm wakes the children," Bill said, closing the window.

Christine sighed, hating to abandon the other mysteries in the dusty attic. But then again she had already found her treasure. A roaring peal of thunder nearby encouraged her to agree with Bill.

In the living room, Christine cleaned each wooden figurine, humming Christmas carols as she worked. The stable had some odd holes in the roof, she noticed, as if something should fit into them. Nothing in the box matched the small, round circles. Also the baby Jesus was missing. She found a manger, but no Christ child.

"Look at this." Bill held up an old-fashioned wooden sign in the shape of a horse and buggy that he'd found in the box he'd brought down. "I bet this used to go on that post out front. It looks as if it's about the right size."

"I think you're right," Christine agreed, admiring the quaint lettering and craftsmanship. "*Friedensheim,*" she read. "What do you think it means?"

"I don't know." Bill eyed it thoughtfully. "It has a nice ring to it though." He handed it to Christine. This would look much better than the withering plant she had put out on the old post. Dusting it off, she noticed that the initials N.M. were neatly carved into its bottom right edge. Briefly wondering whom the talented N.M. was, her thoughts were interrupted by a questioning grunt from Bill.

"This is weird."

"What?"

"This Bible." He lay the book in front of her, opened to the book of Proverbs. An envelope containing a key was taped inside – a small brass key with a pink ribbon attached to it.

"Strange way to store a key. What do you think it goes to?" asked Christine.

"I don't know." Bill held the key up, examining it. "Maybe a jewelry box or a chest."

"There's a verse written on the envelope," Christine realized. "'A gift is as a precious stone in the eyes of him that hath it; withersoever it turneth, it prospereth. Proverbs 17:8.' Maybe the key or whatever it opened was a gift."

"Well," Bill studied the verse. "Either's possible...'Withersoever it turneth, it prospereth.' A key turns. I don't know. Let's hang on to this. Maybe we'll find something in the attic that it opens."

"Can you tell whose Bible it was?"

Bill turned to the front flap. "It says, 'Holy Bible presented to Nathaniel Miller by Robert Gresham on December 25, 1938.' Wow, that's pretty old. Robert Gresham? I think that's Donald Gresham's father?"

"Oh, that reminds me. Judith Gresham told me her father-in-law wants us to come by sometime. So he could tell us the history of our house. Maybe he'll tell us what the key goes to."

The idea of hearing the background of their new home intrigued Bill, especially if this older man could answer their questions about the odd key in the Bible.

Christine turned back to her chest. "I want to get more of those boxes out of the attic and see if I can find the baby Jesus."

"Next paycheck I'll buy the lumber for the attic stairs," Bill decided. "Then you'll be able to go up there any time you want."

Christine smiled. Bill worked hard at his job, and then came home and did so much. Their house was getting finished quickly, basically because of his diligence.

The soft patter of little feet coming down the hall sounded as Jonathan, looking half asleep, walked into the room and waddled over to nestle in his father's lap. Surveying the boxes and the Nativity, he said, "It looks like Christmas." He was right. It did.

Donald and his wife weren't enjoying their afternoon as were the Jamesons. At lunch, Donald had hesitantly asked Judith how they could pare back their expenses. When he'd paid their bills the night before, the checking account had been drained. He tried to explain this to Judith, hoping she would understand.

Instead Judith tersely replied that when Donald had inherited his father's company, they'd had more business than they could keep up with. Obviously he didn't manage things well, and if necessary, she would come into the office again to help get the business back on tract.

A short, unproductive argument erupted, ending with Judith stomping upstairs to her room and giving her door a resounding slam.

Plopping down on the plush pillows in the window seat, she stared out at the darkening world. The softness of the pillows irritated her. Tossing them carelessly on the floor, the hardness of the wood felt better. Stiffening her spine, she looked through the window at the dreary afternoon.

"It was my incentive program that saved that fool business years ago," she growled to herself. Each month, the electrician who had the highest billing rate received a bonus. Clearly the men were creative because profits had gone up dramatically. Donald had wondered about it, but she'd encouraged him not to ask too many questions, saying it might destroy the workers' initiative.

Judith smiled to herself. Sometimes Donald was easy to manage. All she had to do was look at him the wrong way, and he'd turn into a whipped little boy. He was probably right this very minute downstairs rethinking what he'd said to her. The thought was comforting. She relaxed slightly, her back resting against the wall of the window seat.

There was also the inventory. She was the one who kept up with the price list of the supplies. At first Donald did what his father had done, only charging for the labor, letting the parts have the same price as he'd paid for them. She suggested he add a small fee to the price of each part. After all, it cost them something to obtain and store the supplies. He liked her idea and had let her handle it. In the beginning, she'd marked up the merchandise only five percent, but when no one, not even Donald, had seemed to notice, she'd added to it. Perhaps she could add a little more to the inventory prices. That might help them through this slump.

Unfortunately rumors had spread that their business was more expensive than other electrical repair services, and a disgruntled former employee, whom Judith herself had told Donald to fire because of the man's low profits and slow work, had apparently spread all kinds of lies about the company. Their own son, Michael, had heard and believed those lies.

Michael, the thought of him tightened the knot of anger she'd been nursing, touching a sadness deep within. She closed her eyes, covering them with her hand, as if by physically blocking out the light from her pupils, she could block the pain from her heart. Why had Michael chosen to believe those vile rumors? Why had he felt it necessary to come over here and confront his father with the ugly facts? Thank goodness, she'd been home that night so she could stop him from telling all the gossipy garbage he'd heard. She'd been extremely angry, even a little afraid. Afraid that Michael would ruin their business with his unfounded accusations. Afraid that maybe she might be to blame for those rumors. Of course that was a ridiculous fear. And she'd boiled forth like a cauldron, spewing out untoward words to her son that were lost to her now. Her mouth had felt disconnected from her body as it had hurled unkind, perhaps even wicked remarks at Michael. Part of her had felt like a bystander watching. His face – that was what she remembered most – his face. Her mind's eye could see him now.

"Stop this!" she spoke sternly to herself. She couldn't afford to hurt over Michael. It was best not to think about him. She hadn't seen him since that argument last December. He'd called once and talked to the cook, telling her to tell Judith that he had called. She hadn't called back, but at least she'd had the maid take some Christmas gifts over for the grandchildren. That was enough. That was her way of apologizing. It was Michael's move again, and he hadn't made it.

A sigh deep within tore through Judith. Absently she stared back out the window, her eyes wandering down the hill to the Jameson's house. They had done a good job repainting the cottage, she noted grudgingly, encouraging her mind to wander away from painful thoughts. The Woman's Club had their monthly meeting tomorrow night. She needed to have the cook prepare some refreshments for her to take. She had plenty to keep her busy. If she guarded her thoughts carefully, she could busy herself into not thinking about any problems. That way they would simply have to evaporate.

CHAPTER 4

A crown of beauty instead of ashes, the oil of gladness instead of
mourning, and a garment of praise instead of a spirit of despair.

-Isaiah 61:3 (NIV)

Hearing a knock, Robert Gresham reached for his walker and forced his stiff
legs to stand and work their way to the front door. Surely this wasn't Mabel
again. Already twice today she'd stopped by his room.

"Got a message for ya. Bill's coming by tonight," she'd said the first time.

"Bill? Bill who?"

"Ya know, your grandson."

"I only have one grandson and his name's Michael," he'd returned,
annoyed at the old woman. She shouldn't be manning the phones. Her mind
couldn't keep up with it, and she wouldn't put the calls through to his room
as he'd asked her to. He suspected her curiosity just got the best of her. She
had to know everyone's business.

"Michael?" she looked at the note she'd written. "Oh, yeah, here it is.
Michael says he's comin' by tonight. Don't know who this Bill's visitin'.
Guess it's somebody else." She laughed lightly, dismissing the memo. "What
ya got planned for today?" her gravelly voice softened slightly, trying to turn
to pudding.

Robert sighed internally. This was another reason she didn't send his
phone calls through. She liked to stay and talk. She was as welcome as a wet,
mildewed towel after a shower.

"Got to get ready for my grandson's visit," he answered, pushing his
weight against the hard door to shut it. "See you later, Mabel." He tried not
to sound too friendly, hoping to dissuade her from any intended purpose she
might have, but later she stopped by to invite him to go down to the dining
room with her. He said he wasn't ready yet and shut the door with as much
force as his eighty-nine year old muscles would allow.

Wearily he reached to unlock the heavy, hard door. It was only six-thirty.
He'd managed to evade her at supper, but Michael usually didn't come until
seven. If this was Mabel again, he'd just have to, have to... what... what
would he do? Something. He'd just have to do something.

The cold doorknob turned easily in his rough hands. He cracked the solid
door open a few inches, glaring out into the hall, ready to take Mabel on for

one final time. A family of five stood before him. A sweet-faced young woman holding an infant, a dark-haired man, and two toddlers. The dark look on his face lightened. It wasn't Mabel, but this wasn't Michael's family either.

"Mr. Gresham, I don't know if you remember me from church, but I'm Bill Jameson, and this is my wife, Christine," the young man said.

A gruff-looking smile brightened the old face. "Of course I remember you. Come in. Come in." Why, this was an answer to his prayers. The irritation he'd been feeling flooded away, making the walk back to his favorite chair much lighter than his earlier pilgrimage to the door. Christine sat down on the couch near enough for him to take her hand in his leathered paw. "So you're Christine," he spoke warmly. "I can't tell you how glad I am to finally meet you."

Christine smiled, surprised by the older man's welcome.

"I've seen you both around Main Street First from time to time. You're the maintenance supervisor, right Bill?"

"Yes, sir."

"Call me Robert," the older man said, "or if you prefer, Mr. Robert. I know how we southerners like to put a hat on our name."

Christine relaxed as the two men began to discuss Bill's work. It surprised her how much this older man knew about them. She only had the vaguest memory of seeing Mr. Robert before, but with a church membership of over five thousand parishioners, it was hard to remember everyone.

"Mr. Robert, we found a sign in the attic that had *Friedensheim* written on it," Bill said, pronouncing the word Fried-en-sheem. "We thought it might have come off the old post in front of the house."

The smile on the older man's face could have lit up a town, Christine thought, as he answered, clearly pleased to talk about their new home. "It's pronounced Freed-en-shime," he corrected. "'Course there's no way you could know that. Nathaniel was German, and they say their vowels kind of different from us. When we built that place, things were rough in his homeland. He wanted his new house to be a place of peace. So he named the cottage that."

"Oh. So *Friedensheim* means peace," Christine said, leaning closer to Mr. Robert.

"I think its exact meaning is Freedom Shine. That's the way Nathaniel explained it to me. *Frieden* means Freedom and *sheim* means Shine. The best translation for the word is Peace. Nathaniel said it was a House of Peace."

"A House of Peace," Christine repeated. "I like that."

Mr. Robert patted her hand, a hint of wistfulness touching his eyes. "That

25

would have made Nathaniel so happy." His gentle sigh joined with hers. For a moment she felt a special connection with this older man, as if they had known each other for years and had finally reunited after a long absence.

"Nathaniel must have lived in the house before us," Bill determined.

Mr. Robert's eyes widened slightly at the question. "Yes. I need to tell you all about Nathaniel Miller. He was the caretaker of my property for ages, and my best friend. He died a few years back." The older man's voice quieted, as if old memories stole him from them for a moment, but Bill's next question, asking him to tell when they built *Friedensheim* brought words back to his lips.

"Nathaniel and I started building," Mr. Robert paused, trying to remember, "spring of thirty-eight, think it was. Took us over two years to get it done. At first I had no mind to build that cottage. I was too busy courting my Grace, but my ma kept after me. She had it in her head that Nathaniel was sweet on a girl and needed a house to live in before he'd ask her to marry him."

"How'd you meet him?" Christine asked.

"He came to work for my pa when I was sixteen. He was all of eighteen, and the big brother I'd never had. We became fast friends. He was a good listener, Nathaniel was, and I was a good talker. We got along better'n peanut butter and jelly. I was only twenty when my father died. If it hadn't been for Nathaniel's know-how, I think we'd have lost everything." Mr. Robert paused, as if he were opening a door to the past, and it had stuck for a moment. "When I started my electrical business, Nathaniel took over the dairy farm. Donald didn't care too much for farming." At the mention of his son's name, the older man's voice became quieter, less animated. "Then after I came here, Donald sold all the cows. Every last one of them." Shaking his head, he sighed, then closed the door to the topic, changing the subject. "You two enjoying *Friedensheim*?"

"Oh, yes," Christine answered, her blue eyes brightening at the thought. "We love our new home."

Mr. Robert smiled warmly at her. "I knew you would. Took Donald long enough to sell it to you." Looking over at Bill, he asked, "He did give you a good price on the place, didn't he, Bill?"

"Oh, yes, Mr. Robert. He did right by us."

"Well, I hope so." The older man eyes darkened as he shook his head, doubts clouding his mind. "Had a hard time there with Donald. Judith doesn't like to give up anything, even if it is sitting unused for ages. Hope the place hadn't fallen apart too much by the time you bought it."

"It's a solidly built house," Bill reassured the older man. "I redid some of the plumbing, and put in new floors in the bathrooms and the kitchen."

"And we've repainted the entire house, both inside and out," Christine added.

"One of these days I want to come by to see it. I knew you'd take good care of it. It's a nice place. That house has some good memories for me." His old eyes lightened slightly. "Have you found the Nativity?" He looked at Christine.

Christine's eyes widened in surprise. So, the Nativity hadn't been accidentally left there as she'd feared. "Yes, Mr. Robert. We were up in the attic yesterday. I found it in a large trunk. It's beautiful."

A clarity touched the older man's brown eyes. "Good. Good. I wanted you to have it. I never could find the Christ Child or the angels. Did you find them, Christine?"

"The angels? Christ Child?" Christine puzzled over his question for a moment. "You mean the baby Jesus that goes with the Nativity?"

Mr. Robert nodded.

"No, I haven't found him." A sadness touched the older man's eyes. "But I haven't had the chance to search through the entire attic yet. Bill and I have only gone through a few boxes."

"They have to be there somewhere. Nathaniel was always hiding stuff. Glory be," he shook his head at a distant memory, "after he died, while we were cleaning the place, we found money stashed everywhere – under rugs, inside books, in the curtains. I sure was glad Judith refused to help me clean that place up. She'd have grabbed all that money to waste on her fancies," he shook his head. Glancing at Christine, he reddened slightly. "Now that wasn't a nice thing for me to say, was it?"

Christine smiled her understanding. Something the old man had said hung in her mind. "Tell me about the angels, Mr. Robert."

"They're part of the Nativity. They fit on the stable's roof." The fog returned as the older man withdrew into the past for a moment. "I remember back, all those Christmases, Nathaniel and I would sit there, drinking coffee, and talking in front of that crèche." He smiled at Christine, coming back to the present again. "Nathaniel made it, you know. Did it all himself."

Bill, remembering the strange Bible with the key, asked about it.

"That's odd. A key?" Mr. Robert was thoughtful. "Make sure you hang on to it. I'm sure it goes to something important."

A knock sounded at the door. The older man grabbed his walker and heavily lifted himself from his chair. "Excuse me, folks. I think that's probably my grandson."

In a few minutes Mike and Nancy Gresham came in with their five-year-old, Andrew, and three-year-old, Adam. Christine immediately felt a kinship toward the soft-spoken Nancy, and Jonathan and Amanda, who had been sitting quietly, hopped up to join Mr. Robert's great-grandchildren in the corner of the room.

The conversation diverged into smaller discussions as the men began talking about Mike's construction business and Christine and Nancy got to know each other. At one point, when Nancy went over to calm an argument between her two children, Christine observed Michael Gresham, Judith and Donald's only son. Odd to imagine him as their child. He seemed so pleasant, so unpretentious. More like Mr. Robert, she decided. He laughed easily and though he resembled his mother in his dark, striking appearance, the resemblance stopped there. His pleasant, down-home boyishness encouraged her to want to pursue this couple's friendship.

Surprisingly she felt completely at home with these strangers, and when, as they were about to leave, Mr. Robert insisted that they promise to come back the next week for another visit, she enthusiastically agreed. Nancy and she exchanged phone numbers, and Christine decided that she would invite her over for lunch one day in the near future. Being without any extended relatives of her own, Christine felt herself adopting this family. An emptiness that had been in her since her grandmother's death was finally being filled.

The pleasant June days faded into the hot, humid month of July that was a part of North Georgia. As each day passed, Christine began to wish that autumn would arrive with its refreshing breezes. The cooling summer rains ceased as a dry spell besieged the area with the broiling humidity of a sauna bath, robbing the earth of its moisture, refusing to replace it. As early as ten o'clock in the morning, the air was thick with humidity that wrapped over the skin, holding in the heat. Going outside even for a few minutes was unbearable to Christine's hot nature. Even the children refused to play outdoors for any length of time, making the days seem to stretch endlessly before them. There were the breaks though when Nancy and her two boys would come to visit. Then Amanda and Jonathan ignored the heat and played contentedly in the yard with their two friends while Christine and Nancy talked in relative quiet.

Christine felt her kinship with Mr. Robert deepen as the days and weeks slid by. Unexpectedly, he had become like a grandfather to her – oh, he was nothing like the brusque, implacable grandfather she'd grown up with. But Mr. Robert was the way Christine had often thought a grandfather should be. What amazed her was the quick warmth and acceptance she felt directed toward her from the older man. Her life hadn't been easy. When she was only six years old, her parents had been killed in an automobile accident. The loss was something she hadn't quite gotten over. Though Grandmother Martha was wonderful and had blessed her life, her grandfather had been a distant, angry figure that she had hid from and avoided. He was often gone for extended periods of time. Traveling, Grandmother Martha said. Though sometimes they hadn't known where their next meal would come from, God had provided, often in mysterious ways. Christine remembered those times as especially happy. Her grandmother had a way of making darkness light and finding something good in everything. Christine missed her dreadfully at times, and now to have Mr. Robert in her life, she felt as if a piece of her grandmother had been given back to her.

Sometimes she marveled at her life now. Her blessings scared her. She held herself back from fully appreciating the moment. Fearful that she would be robbed of it. Her family, her friends. She'd lost them all at one time, yet God had replaced ashes with beauty. She needed to remember that; however, as hard as she tried, that little cloud of worry hung over her head and a whispering mist of fear would attack her with its drips of doubt and concern. She just couldn't make that cloud go away.

Chapter 5

The peace of God, which transcends all understanding, will guard your hearts and your minds in Christ Jesus.

-Philippians 4:7 (NIV)

Sunday, July 23. His eighteenth birthday. Two friends stood admiring the new truck his parents had given him. Appreciation of its fine lines was in every sigh they made. He proudly displayed it. His folks had gone all out. It had everything – air conditioning, stereo, and tape deck.

"Let's go," insisted his seventeen-year-old buddy.

The same thought was on each boy's mind. A thrill of delight coursed through them as they cruised through the neighborhood displaying the new toy. On out of town toward the neighboring countryside the eighteen-year-old drove as fast as he dared, swerving precariously on the winding roads, impressing his two friends with his adroit driving skills. The truck weaved and turned like butter. Yes sir, this was a good machine.

"Stop sign ahead!" screamed the youngest.

Screeching to a halt at the unexpected sign, they caught their breath before bursting into spasms of laughter.

"Stupid place for a stop sign," the driver scoffed between breaths.

"Yeah," agreed the others.

"Wait," said the seventeen-year-old. Flinging open the door, he jumped out, the sixteen-year-old right behind him. Excitement surged through their brains, blocking rational thought as they rocked the sign's wooden post back and forth.

"Hurry, " grunted the youngest. "Before someone comes."

No concrete held the wooden post down. The county had decided not to waste the taxpayers' money to make the signs more secure. It was easy to pull up.

"What you guys think you're gonna do with that?" the driver yelled from his position at the truck's door. He wasn't going to get out and help steal a sign.

"You can take it home for a souvenir," the ringleader responded.

"Or a birthday present," suggested the youngest.

"No way. I don't want that filthy thing." He felt uneasy with this. "Besides, if I get caught, my old man'll kill me. Put it back."

"Man, you're no fun," one of the boys gripped, while the other grunted his disapproval.

"Someone's coming!" shrieked the youngest as the sound of a heavy eighteen-wheeler was heard speeding toward them.

Dropping the sign in the tall grass beside the road, they climbed over each other getting back into the truck. With shrieks of laughter, they watched the large vehicle streak through the intersection in front of them.

"I'm hungry. You guys want to get something to eat," asked the driver as he pulled away from the downed stop sign.

"I vote for pizza," declared the seventeen-year-old.

Roaring down the road, they felt exhilarated from the rush they'd just experienced.

As soon as Bill arrived at work, Brother Cole's secretary, Margie, gave him the unpleasant news that the assistant pastor wanted to see him.

What a way to start a Monday, Bill thought as he resolutely clenched his teeth and headed toward the man's office. Perhaps this wasn't so bad though. He had something he needed to talk to Brother Cole about himself.

The previous Friday, he'd been given a memorandum that stated that the maintenance crew shouldn't use the elevator unless they had heavy equipment that they were moving. Not only was this rule another example of Brother Cole's general disrespect for the maintenance workers, but it was extremely demoralizing to his underpaid staff, as if they were all being put into their place – somewhere underneath Brother Cole's shiny leather wingtips. Miss Eleanor's stolid face had crumpled ever so slightly at the announcement. The surgery she'd had last year on her foot had not healed properly, making it difficult for her to walk. When the memo had been passed around, he'd seen her shoulders sink and a fleeting expression of despair had crossed her features. The dear woman worked long, hard hours without complaint, and Bill could see no reason for her not to use the elevator. Whatever the rationale for this memo – assuming that there was one beyond Brother Cole wanting to push his weight around – it wasn't right.

Irritably Bill remembered last Monday when Brother Cole had contemptuously pointed out a pencil that the assistant pastor himself had thrown on the high ledge of one of the windows to see how long it took Bill and his crew to notice it. Bill wondered if the man had nothing better to do than to test the maintenance staff. Two weeks had apparently gone by, and Bill was soundly condemned for his inability to pay attention to the housekeeping needs in the church. It took over an hour to get the detestable pencil down. The assistant pastor's bullying attitude was not only intimidating, but downright intolerable. It was time for Bill to confront Cole Odum, and with God's help, today would be the day.

Walking into Brother Cole's office, Bill noted the expensive furniture and artwork that surrounded the assistant pastor. The plush study accentuated the true priorities of the man. When Cole Odum had come to work at the church almost three years ago, he'd decorated his office in as lavish a fashion as possible. Last winter, he'd felt the need to refurbish it again. Bill had spent many hours painting and putting in chair molding and other accessories that Cole felt were necessary. The end result was a stately room that lacked warmth or charm. Formal and unfriendly. Opulent and cold. Lush and yet oddly barren. It mirrored the man who sat behind the desk – a strongly built, handsome man in spite of his fifty-odd years. Yet, his good looks were marred by the biting, caustic personality that was the essence of this man. The outer shell lacked warmth or friendliness, and as a result, a superficial comeliness was all that existed.

Cole was talking on the phone. His gentle base voice oozed warmth and friendliness. Maybe this meeting would turn out well for a change, Bill hoped, but there were no salutations as Cole hung up. He jumped right into his speech, using the blunt sharp-edged tone that Bill had grown accustomed to over the years. Money was tight, and Bill may need to let one of his workers go. Bill balked. He knew Brother Cole was referring to Miss Eleanor. A few weeks ago, he'd complained about how old and feeble the woman looked. At that time, Bill had quickly asserted that she got her work done and did a superior job.

"We need every worker we have, especially now that the new educational wing has been finished," Bill insisted.

Cole Odum's cold eyes grew icier. Darkness seemed to surround him, though the room was well lit. "You know, Bill, you've been here a long time, and you don't really seem to go with the program." A condescending, superior tone touched his words, as if he were talking to an unruly child. "You fight the new things we're trying to do. You're unorganized and don't plan well. After, what has it been, six, seven, eight years, it seems you should be doing a better job."

Inside Bill felt a sick stirring. Often Brother Cole attacked him with unanswerable, sweeping generalizations. He knew there was nothing he could do to please this man. He had tried at first – tried with all his might. When Brother Cole had sent him a memo of what he wanted done, Bill had added it to the burdensome list he already had from other staff members, and he made sure the tasks were finished, working a lot of overtime without any extra pay. It didn't matter. The man only demanding more. Eventually Bill had realized the assistant pastor was impossible to please. There was no answer to this sweeping attack. To defend himself was useless. He stood mute, feeling a coldness seep into the room. There was something new here today. Something he hadn't encountered before.

The assistant pastor's black eyes pierced into Bill's hazel ones. A tight smile touched his mouth. Bill felt his throat constrict. "I talked about you with the personnel committee recently." Brother Cole's voice sounded almost friendly, as if he were chatting with a neighbor. His eyes left Bill's as he spoke. "I told them about your shortcomings…, and well…, they just don't know if you're on our side."

The coldness Bill felt evaporated, being quickly replaced with heat. He'd been talked about in a meeting. Oh, he could just hear what this man had to say about him.

"I told them about the pencil incident and explained how you're not on top of things around here as a maintenance supervisor should be. They gave you a vote of – how should I put this," thump, thump. He tapped his fingers together, leaning back in his chair. "…of no confidence."

"What does that mean?"

"It means they don't know if they can trust your judgment, so they've allowed me to decide what to do about your employment."

A feeling of betrayal engulfed Bill. He didn't know everyone on the personnel committee, but the ones he did know, he thought of as friends. Not one of them had come to him with even a suggestion he should do something differently. Knowing the slant Brother Cole could put on things, they'd apparently believed the words their assistant pastor had spoken.

"We're going to retain your services for the present, but I expect to see some improvements around here. Oh, and another thing." His voice became casual, as if it was an unimportant aside he was giving. "Because of the church's difficult financial state, we're going to reduce your benefits. We'll pay for your health insurance, but if you want to continue to have family coverage, then you'll have to pay the extra portion."

Though demoralized and threatened, Bill still had some fight in him. "Does this mean you and the other staff members will also not have family coverage?"

"You know we're not suppose to talk about our salary and benefits. That's one of Pastor Leonard's requirements," Brother Cole replied, annoyed by the question. He hadn't expected any trouble from the man; after all, he'd just given him a warning. "My wife works here now anyway." He smiled, pleased with the realization that he could justify his own benefits. Without another word, he turned back to his deskwork. "That will be all," he said in an uninterested voice, not looking up. Picking up his phone, he began dialing a number.

With a heavy heart, Bill left the office and made his way toward the elevator. Oh, the elevator, he'd forgotten to say anything. A darkness surrounded him, making it difficult to think. He didn't want to think too much anyway. It was too painful. Forcing Brother Cole's words into the recesses of his mind, he numbly went through the rest of the day performing the motions of work, finding it hard to concentrate or put his heart into anything. He felt as if a main artery had been cut, and he'd been left to die. A part of him wanted to fold up, to give up, and to escape. But there was work to do. He wouldn't give Brother Cole an excuse to fire him.

Late in the afternoon, he received a message from Brother Ralph, the children's minister, asking him to take some Vacation Bible School packets by a church member's house on his way home from work. Bill agreed. Though he'd not been to the woman's home before, Brother Ralph's directions proved good, and he found the place without difficulty. Getting back into his car, he tried to figure out the best way to get home. Traveling south should get him there. He checked his watch. It was after six. Christine would have supper ready. He wished he'd called her to let her know that he was running late. Her voice would help dispel this disheartened spirit that clung to him. His mind wandered back to his discussion with Brother Cole. How much of the conversation should he share with Christine? He didn't want to worry her.

Turning south, he drove down the road. Speeding up a little, he noticed an intersection was ahead. He slowed. No stop sign. They must have one the other way.

Jonathan played with his toy cars while Amanda tugged at her mother's skirt and complained that she wanted something to eat. The baby was content as long as Christine held her, which was hard to do, as she finished preparing supper, but somehow she managed. The phone rang, someone selling vinyl siding to all the homeowners in the area. Why did they have to call at suppertime? No, she wasn't interested. Hanging up, she turned off the phone's ringer. When she finished cooking, she would turn it on again.

The lemonade tasted good. Ah – just to sit here on the porch, enjoying the slight breeze. The day had finally begun to cool off. A little car came up the road. A large pickup truck sped around the curve. Horror struck her. The car didn't stop at the stop sign. The noise. The small vehicle flew fifty feet to the right and fell apart. There had been no screeching of brakes, only the awful sound of metal hitting metal. Someone must be dead, and she'd just seen it. *Run, girl, run!* Her legs slowly obeyed. Vaguely she noticed that she'd dropped her glass. As if in suspended motion her mind took in every detail. She couldn't move fast enough.

The driver of the pickup climbed out of his truck and stalked toward the mangled car.

Maybe he knew CPR. She'd taken it years ago. "Oh, Lord, help me to remember," she prayed, unaware that she spoke aloud. The truck driver cursed at the man in the little car. Furiously he tried to open the jammed door.

"Get away from that car," she yelled with such force that it surprised both her and the truck driver.

"He didn't stop. The fool ran right into me. Look at my truck." He shook his hand, which he'd cut on the car's jagged door edge while trying to pull the idiot out.

Looking through the cracked window, all she could see was someone covered in blood. But he spoke. He was conscious. He was alive.

"Please get me out. Please. Please."

His head bent over at a funny angle. She shouldn't touch him. And the blood. All the blood. "Don't you move," her voice sounded more reassuring than she felt. "I'm going to call for help; you'll be all right. Just sit still for a minute and help will be here soon."

"Please get me out. I can't die. I have three kids. They need me."

"I'll call your wife. What's your phone number?"

The man told her. She thought he must be going to be okay. He remembered his phone number. He had to be all right.

"I'll be right back. You just stay still." Looking at the truck driver kicking the ground and muttering to himself, she demanded, "You stay away from him. You hear me."

"Yeah," he answered in a chagrined, but subdued voice.

Christine put the casserole in the oven and began feeding the baby. A darkness descended on her. A deep heaviness, a burden. For some unknown reason, she felt the urge to burst into tears. Thinking of the couple that she and Bill had chosen to be the godparents of their children, she began to wonder if they'd made the right decision. Overwhelmed, she found herself praying for God to protect her and Bill. The burden was too heavy, too dark, and totally incomprehensible. And then, just as suddenly as it was there, it strangely disappeared.

Amanda again complained that she wanted to eat. Where was Bill anyway? It wasn't like him to be so late without calling. Calling. She'd turned the telephone off. He was probably trying to call her right now. Turning the switch on, the phone immediately began ringing.

"Hello." This had to be Bill.

"Hello. Is this Mrs. Jameson?" asked an unfamiliar voice.

Oh, great. Someone selling something again. Christine considered saying she wasn't interested and hanging up, but her ingrained politeness took control. "Yes," she answered tersely.

"Hi, you don't know me, but I live in the Statham area." This was definitely one of those telemarketing people. "Now, Mrs. Jameson, the first thing I want you to know is that your husband is all right."

What did she mean her husband was all right. Of course, he was all right. Who was this? This wasn't the way these calls were supposed to be.

"Now, he's had a little accident."

A little accident. The car must have broken down, and Bill needs a ride home. "But Bill's all right," Christine stated more than asked; after all, the woman had just said he was.

"Yes. He was able to give me your name and phone number, and he told me you have three children. Now let me warn you there's a lot of blood."

Blood? Blood wasn't all right. How hurt was Bill? What did she mean "able"? That didn't sound all right. This was all wrong. Her chest tightened. "Where is he?"

"He's on his way to the hospital. I've been trying to call you for some time, and finally I decided to just let the phone ring until you got home."

Guilt, why had she turned the ringer off? That had been a stupid thing to do. She stopped herself. *Just get the details.* "What hospital?"

"They took him to Athens Regional. We thought he ran a stop sign. When you see him, tell him someone had thrown the sign into the grass beside the road. The policeman didn't even see it until the newspaper reporter said, 'What stop sign?', and when we looked around, we realized it wasn't there. Your husband was real concerned he'd caused the accident, so you tell him it wasn't his fault, but whoever pulled down that sign." The woman was warming up now. "When I saw that truck hit him..."

"A TRUCK hit him?"

"Yeah, you know one of those real big pickup trucks that they make now. I don't know what kind it was, but it had those great big wheels. When I saw that truck hit the driver's side of the car..."

"It hit his side of the car?" Christine's voice squeaked hollowly. Her head began spinning. *Bill is really hurt. He is really hurt.* She caught pieces of what the woman said. She needed to listen.

"The driver was mad, real mad. He was cursing and swearing, and if I hadn't gotten down there when I did, I think he would have dragged your husband out of the car and beat him up."

A vivid picture of a terrified Bill filled Christine's thoughts. She could hear the woman talking but had trouble paying attention. With effort she focused back on her words.

"He was out on the ground when I got back down the hill. That made me so angry. Some passers-by must have moved him. That's dangerous. You never know if someone's neck is broken in a situation like this."

Christine's mind went numb. Her brain quit hearing the words. She needed to get to the hospital right away, right now. She interrupted, saying she needed to go.

Feeling as if her world had just shattered, she placed the receiver back in its cradle.

There was no time to think. She needed to call her prayer chain. Get the baby's bag together. Hurry to the hospital. She needed to do it all. Now. Picking up the phone, she called her Sunday school teacher, Karen, asking her to put her request through to the pray chain.

"Christine, I'm coming over."

"No,no. That's not necessary." Karen lived twenty minutes away. Too long to wait.

"Yes, you can't take those kids to the hospital. You might be there for a while. I'll be over in a few minutes."

Christine didn't want to wait, but Karen was right. She reluctantly agreed.

Hanging up the phone, she began moving as if she were in fast gear. She hurriedly went through the house picking up toys, washing the dishes, just doing, doing. Her adrenaline flowing, she couldn't move fast enough. As long as she kept moving, she wouldn't have time to think. She wouldn't have time to cry. She would be in control. *The children.* The thought invaded her energy wave, slowing her down. They needed to know what was happening. They sat on the couch watching her, surprisingly quiet, sensing something was wrong. She looked at their cherubic faces. Such beautiful faces – innocent, sweet faces, expecting the best out of life. Tears reached her eyes, but she refused to let them fall. There would be time for tears later. Kneeling in front of them, her hands holding theirs, she explained that their daddy had been in an accident.

"What's an accident, Mama?" Jonathan asked.

"It's when something happens that you don't expect, and it's something that hurt Daddy."

"Like if your eyes popped out and start rolling all over the floor, would that be an accident? Because that would hurt, wouldn't it?" Jonathan did have the questions.

"Yes, that would hurt, but our eyes don't roll out very easily. God made them to stay in place."

"How do they stay in?" Jonathan asked, very interested in this discussion. Amanda also listened intently.

Christine sighed. This wasn't the way she wanted the conversation to go. "Right now you need to know that Mrs. Karen is coming here to watch you while I go to the hospital to check on Daddy. Jonathan, Amanda, we need to pray for Daddy."

The little ones' heads bowed unquestioningly. Amanda prayed, "God, let Daddy be otay and come home for supper." Christine smiled at the simplicity of her prayer, agreeing with it in her heart. *Yes, Lord. Let Bill come home for dinner.*

The children began to play lightheartedly as if everything were normal. Christine sat in the rocking chair, cuddling Lauranna's sleepy form, praying silently as she continued to wait for Karen.

Finally, after what felt like an eternity, Karen arrived. An overnight bag in her hand, just in case. Christine thanked her, kissed the children goodbye, and ran out to her car. Pushing away the urge to stomp down on the gas pedal, she forced herself to drive the speed limit.

Most of the county was hurrying home from work, clogging up the roads. The awful traffic tormented her. Drivers swerved rudely in front of her, cutting her off from the exits, slowing her down – caught up only in their own narrow worlds, oblivious to her pain.

The radio wasn't good company. The Christian station she usually enjoyed sounded too upbeat, too exuberant. She turned it off. Silence. A thousand thoughts crashed into her brain at one time. The quiet screamed at her. Unconsciously she flipped the radio on again. The irritating noise. Off it went. The quiet was better.

A multitude of silent voices began screaming at her. *What about Bill? What will you do if he's dead? He might be you know.* They seemed to mock her. Whispering shadows harassed her, making it hard to think. Somewhere in the recesses of her mind, a Still, Small Voice tried to speak. She could barely hear it as Fear, Doubt, and Discouragement continued to yell at her.

Don't listen to Him, said Discouragement. *You won't like what He says.*

Who is He to talk to you anyway, said Doubt. *He's the one who let this happen.*

He'll just tell you to give Bill to Him. See what a mess He's made of things already. There's no way you can trust Him, whispered Fear.

The light seemed to take forever to change. "Hurry up. Hurry up," she pleaded.

Yes, hurry, hurry! yelled the voices around her.

The Stillness touched her deep in her soul, subduing the other voices, whispering to her. She couldn't ignore Him. The light turned green. Tentatively, fearfully she prayed, "Will you take good care of him, Father?" The other voices hushed. Quieted by His presence. Somewhere deep inside the silence of the car, she felt a gentleness, a deep abiding love, and a touch of peace.

Yes, He whispered.

Yes. He would take care of Bill. Perhaps not in her way, but He would care for Bill. Christine grabbed the peace, hanging on to its thin rope, hoping it was strong enough to carry her over this raging river.

"Lord, You know I love him." God had to know that. She needed to remind Him. "I want my children to have their father."

Poor thing, whispered Discouragement.

For a moment, tears blurred her vision. *You're driving Christine. Get a grip*, she admonished herself.

Stopping at another red light, she whispered to her Father again, a resoluteness touching her spirit. "I don't want him to suffer through life, Father." She remembered last December when they had been so excited about buying their new home. The reality of the present came back, burdening her. She knew that she'd be with him again one day in heaven if that was what He wanted. "Oh, Lord, I'd miss him so much. But, I do trust You. I do. Your will be done." Even though a few tears slid down her cheeks, something unspeakable was released. The peace beyond understanding became hers. The first real peace she'd felt since the phone call. She hugged the peace, holding tighter to the rope of hope it gave her.

Somewhere she had read that praying the words "if it is your will" was a lack of faith. Right now in this quiet moment, she realized that it took true faith to pray that way. She felt God Himself wrap His arms of comfort around her.

Chapter 6

What time I am afraid I will trust in thee.

-Psalms 56:3

Driving into the parking lot of the hospital, she saw Ben Evans standing outside the emergency room entrance. Behind him stood Pastor Leonard and Brother Cole.

How did these men know about the accident? The hospital must have called them to hurry here and tell you the news that Bill's gone? whispered Fear.

The peace began to fade. Stopping the car in front of the emergency room, Ben came up. "Let me park for you. You go on inside."

"Ben, is he, is he...," she couldn't get the words out, but if he was, she didn't want to see anyone. If he was, she wanted to be alone.

From behind Ben, a stranger with a bandaged hand growled unsympathetically, "Aw...he's all right," as he walked by.

"That's the guy whose truck he hit," Ben explained. "Bill's hurt, but they think he's going to be all right. They even said he might be able to come home tonight. Go on inside, Christine. They'll probably let you see him now." Relief flooded her. She ran inside, half expecting Bill to be sitting in the waiting room. She looked around hastily, vaguely hearing Pastor Leonard tell a nurse that she was Bill's wife.

The young nurse walked up, blocking Christine's view. Where was Bill?

"Can I see him?" she asked, looking over the woman's shoulder. There was someone with dark hair bent over in the far corner. No, it wasn't Bill.

"Not yet. We're still cleaning him up," the nurse paused, waiting for Christine's attention. Christine, looking into the concerned woman's clear eyes, felt her frenzy dissipate. "There's a lot of blood. He cut his head very badly and heads bleed a lot. We're going to need to get a plastic surgeon to sew him up before he goes home. He may have some broken bones. We don't know yet. After we get him more presentable, you can come see him. We don't think it's too bad. He's talking and knows exactly what's going on. We hope he might even be able to go home tonight."

Christine exhaled, relieved at the nurse's words.

"Come, sit down, Christine. Let us pray with you," Pastor Leonard offered as the nurse walked away.

"How did you know he was here?"

"You have a very good prayer chain. They got the word out fast. Your Sunday school teacher called the church just as Brother Cole and I were leaving. We came right over to check on Bill," Leonard explained

Together the small group held hands as Leonard prayed. At his "amen" Christine felt that peace she'd talked to in the car speak again. *Amen means So Be It.*

"So be it, Lord," she whispered. "So be it."

The young nurse walked up again. The group still held hands. "I don't want to interrupt anything," she said, "but you can see your husband now, Mrs. Jameson."

A moment of unexpected hesitancy struck Christine as she looked up at the nurse. Pastor Leonard gave her hand a reassuring squeeze before letting go. Standing up, Christine walked with the woman – through the double doors, down the hall, and into a room with a privacy curtain. There lay Bill, covered with a blanket, his head wrapped in a bloodstained sheet, his barely recognizable face bruised and pale. Her heart leapt into her throat. He looked awful.

"I got myself into a little mess," he joked. His slight smile wavered and disappeared. He'd held his own to this point, trying to make light of his situation, but seeing his wife's concerned face took away his feigned assurance. Instead he felt like a little boy who needed his mother. "I never saw the stop sign, Christine," he confided with a tremble in his voice.

"Someone knocked it down, Bill. They found it beside the road."

"Why would anyone do that?" A deep, anguished sigh came out. A tear rolled down his cheek. "I love you, Christine. I didn't think I was going to make it."

Gently she touched his arm, hoping she wouldn't hurt him. "I love you too, Bill. The nurse said it looks as if you're going to be all right."

"In the ambulance everything started to go black. I could see the attendant as if he were way off. I kept thinking I didn't want to leave you and the kids. I begged God to let me stay. Then all the blackness went away, and I knew I'd be all right." Tears streamed down his cheeks. "I need to stop crying. They told me I couldn't move in any way until they make sure my neck is okay."

"Can you feel your arms and legs?" she asked in concern.

"Yeah, believe me, I feel everything. They aren't reassuring about the pain either. Everyone says it'll get worse before it gets better."

The nurse came through the sheet, and leaning toward Christine, she whispered, "Would it be all right with you if those two preachers came in?"

41

Christine looked at Bill. "It's Pastor Leonard and Brother Cole. Do you want to see them?" She knew he'd probably want to see the pastor, but she wasn't too sure about Brother Cole being allowed in. She didn't want his presence to upset Bill.

"Yes. Yes," Bill insisted.

Walking in, Leonard, seeing Bill, stopped abruptly. Brother Cole, following in his wake, almost stepped on the pastor. Bill's poor appearance caught Leonard by as much surprise as it had Christine. This is what the young nurse had tried to prepare them for, but words didn't match the picture of strong, robust Bill Jameson lying pale and bleeding with dark bruises staining his handsome features, swelling his face almost beyond recognition. Leonard collected himself quickly. "Hi, Bill. How you doing?"

"I've been better." Bill tried to smile, but it hurt too much. With surprising strength, he grabbed Leonard's hand. It didn't matter that it hurt to do so. He needed this godly man's prayers. But, first, so many words needed to be said. He needed to ask for forgiveness for all the petty things that he and Leonard had disagreed on over the years. His emotions were on edge. His thoughts confused. His words, asking forgiveness, seemed jumbled. Somehow he had to unfetter his mind from the emotional grief he'd been experiencing in the car on the way home.

Pastor Leonard seemed taken aback. "There's nothing to forgive, Bill. It's okay."

Brother Cole, who kept his distance from Bill, had a noncommittal, bland look on his face as if he were watching an uninteresting stage play.

Leonard spoke a few reassuring platitudes before he backed up to the curtain to leave. All the raw emotion he saw in the young man made him uncomfortable.

Bill reached out to him. "Please pray for me before you go, Pastor Leonard." He had never felt the need for prayer more strongly than he did at this moment.

Leonard hurried back. Of course, that's why he'd come. Bowing his head, he gently implored God to protect and care for this brother in Christ.

A calm settled over Bill. In a quieter voice, he expressed his thanks before Leonard left. Without a word, Brother Cole stiffly followed the pastor out of the room.

A woman walked in, explaining that she was the emergency room doctor, and for a time after her appearance, there was a flurry of activity - talk of fever, X-rays, CAT scans, Insurance. As Christine watched them wheel Bill down the hall for more tests, she felt an incredible tiredness suddenly drain her. The pretty young nurse appeared at her side.

"I'll come get you, Mrs. Jameson, when he gets back. You can go talk to your friends in the lobby. There are a number of them out there. You and your husband are clearly well loved."

"Thank you," Christine responded without understanding. Over a dozen church members greeted her in the waiting room.

Pastor Leonard's wife felt puzzled when Leonard handed her a dozen roses as he came in the door.

"What are these for?" she asked pleased.

"I just wanted to let you know I love you, Ann" Leonard explained. Bill's accident had touched him deeply. A slow awakening had stirred in him as he'd driven home from the hospital. A subtle awareness that lately his priorities had been misplaced. Though Ann rarely complained, he knew he often took her for granted. He could smell the roast that she was keeping warm for him in the oven. A nice homey smell. Somehow it made him feel better.

Sitting down in his favorite chair, he realized it had been a long time since he'd even sat there. He picked up the telephone and decided to call Sam, his oldest son, just to check on him and his daughter-in-law and the grandchildren. If he had time, he would call Daniel and Aaron, too. If not, he'd call them after dinner.

Out in the waiting room, Christine was surprised to see so many friends from the church. Many she knew quite well. Others much less so. It dawned on her that some of these individuals had a quiet ministry of sitting with people in hospital waiting rooms. Christine felt blessed. It would have been lonely to have to sit and wait here all by herself.

Her close friend, Catherine Evans, handed her a paper bag from a fast-food restaurant. "Ben got you a hamburger and French fries. We thought you probably hadn't eaten."

Christine thanked her and tried to choke down a bite. It tasted like sawdust. Her taste buds weren't working, and it was difficult for her to swallow. Her senses had gone dull. Part of her felt as if all the activity around her emanated from a movie screen, and she was an outsider watching from a distance. Her friends talked about everything. They tried to get her mind off Bill, but every so often they'd come back to the subject of the accident. The tests took a long time. Finally Christine put down the hamburger. She just couldn't eat.

If Pastor Leonard hadn't asked him to go to the hospital, Cole wouldn't have gone, but he tried to do whatever the pastor wanted. The whole display Bill had put on seemed weak. It irritated him the way the man had tried to manipulate Leonard.

Arriving home, he glanced at his watch. It was late, and he was hungry. "Greta, I'm home." Walking through the house, he saw no sign of supper being prepared. "Greta, where are you?"

A weak voice from upstairs called out, "I'm up here."

He pounded up the steps. He worked long hours and expected to be fed when he got home. But there she was, in her bedroom, in the bed.

"What are you doing in here?"

"I've been sick all day. That awful stomach virus. Can't keep anything down."

"Where's supper? What should I do about eating?"

The thought of food made Greta feel even sicker. "I think there's some stew left over from Saturday night. You can heat it in the microwave."

"I don't know how to use a microwave."

Greta pulled herself to a sitting position. She would fix it for him; then, she could go back to bed till she felt better. He usually had work to do, and he'd leave her alone once he had his dinner. Her head throbbed from the fever. Even though she felt unsteady, she managed to get down the stairs. Cole went into the living room, turned on the television, and sat down to read the newspaper. He was a stranger these days. When she'd first met him, he'd seemed so strong, independent, and caring. All those qualities she wished she had, he had. He could be quite charming when he wanted to be, but he hadn't been that way with her for such a long time that it was hard to remember.

Opening the bowl of stew, the strong smell that met her nose nauseated her. Throwing the dish down, she rushed to the bathroom as the sickness overtook her.

"Good grief." Cole stood in the doorway. "Never mind, I'll go get myself something to eat." In a moment he was gone.

Greta slowly climbed the stairs. A wave of self-pity overwhelmed her. When the children had been home, she'd had so much to live for, but now? "Dear Jesus...," she entreated, feeling sick at heart as well as physically ill.

The quiet strain of a melody whispered through her mind, comforting her. Just yesterday she had played that new piece during the offertory. What a lovely rendition it was. By Mozart. Yes, she didn't feel so sorry for herself when she thought of God's gift of music that was a part of her. Sighing, she sunk back into her bed. Becoming church pianist was a special blessing, something that she'd not confessed to Cole. These days it was her lifeline. At least she had her music. If she could just go to visit her children again. Well, her life had its blessings. It really did. There was much more to her life than Cole Odum.

Chapter 7

The Lord watches over you.

-Psalms 121:5 (NIV)

"Mrs. Jameson, your husband's back," said the young nurse, suddenly beside her.

Putting down her half-eaten sandwich that her friends had encouraged her to try to eat, Christine walked with the woman toward Bill's cubical, part of her dreading going back. The waiting room was full of pleasant words and smiles, the back room full of whispers and frowns.

The nurse slowed her pace, turning toward Christine. "Mrs. Jameson." She stopped, looking Christine in the eye. For the first time, Christine really saw this figure in white. Young, wise eyes sparkled at her. "I want to tell you how much the nurses think of your husband. He's so friendly and nice. Usually patients fuss and complain. We know he's in a lot of pain, but he even tries to make us laugh. I just want you to know we're all rooting for him."

"Thank you." This kind nurse's words encouraged Christine that Bill still had a lot of his old self in there.

Walking into his cubical, she didn't observe the same strong man that the nurse saw. Upon seeing her, he turned immediately into an unhappy, scared little boy, complaining of extreme nausea, afraid the doctor would follow through on her threat to put a tube down his throat if he did get sick. He begged Christine to help him.

Feeling inadequate to meet his needs, she left his room in search of the doctor, finding her down the hall.

"I'm one step ahead of you," the woman interrupted as Christine explained the problem. She held up a syringe. "We were able to determine he has no concussion. We can give him a shot for the nausea," she spoke quickly as she strode down the hall into Bill's room. "It'll make you sleepy," she explained to Bill. "Don't fight it. Go on to sleep if you want. The plastic surgeon should be here soon to sew you up." She paused, looking at her chart intently. "We want to talk to you about the results of your CAT scan. We've sent for a neurosurgeon to see what he thinks, but you just try to get some rest while we wait." She turned to leave, ignoring Christine's presence, avoiding the concerned expression on her face.

"A neurosurgeon?" Christine asked. The emergency room doctor didn't stop, seeming intent to get out of the room. Christine grabbed her arm, forcing the woman to notice her. "What do we need a neurosurgeon for?" She racked her brain. What did neurosurgeons do? Neurology? It had something to do with nerves. Nerve damage, maybe?

"I'm just an emergency room doctor," the woman explained with a touch of condescension, finally looking Christine in the face. She spoke as if talking to a child. "Sometimes I like to get other doctors' opinions. For instance, we'll have a plastic surgeon sew his head, and we're going to call in the orthopedic surgeon to set his broken shoulder and finger. Don't worry, this is normal." She left the room, keeping her secret with her.

Christine wasn't fooled by the woman's nonchalance. If anything, it nettled her. "But why a neurosurgeon?" she asked the retreating figure.

An authoritative, hard-faced nurse changing Bill's I.V. tube spoke abruptly to her, "Because they want to get a doctor who can do surgery if he needs it." Though her impatient, can't-you-figure-it-out-for-yourself voice stung, the word "surgery" bit into Christine's mind, terrifying her.

"Surgery!" Was that what the doctor was hiding from her? Her stomach tightened, sending acid to her throat.

The nurse frowned, realizing that she'd said too much. "Not that he necessarily needs surgery."

A sick gloom enclosed Christine. Her stomach threatened to revolt the wretched hamburger. Instinctively she rushed to the bathroom down the hall and threw water on her hot face, cooling it, slightly calming her stomach. Her pale reflection gazed back at her from the mirror. The room smelled funny, like disinfectants, like a hospital. She shook her head wearily. Of course it did. What time was it? It must be after eleven o'clock. She should be home. She wanted to go home. But Bill – she'd left him alone with that callous-looking nurse. Her irritation with the insensitivity of the woman helped straighten out her stomach problem. Hurrying back to his room, she found that he had fallen asleep. The young nurse was there, writing something on his chart.

"He still has a fever," she confided, "but it's a little lower." She smiled, patting Christine's arm as she walked out.

Christine sat on the stool beside his bed, looking at her battered husband. His breathing was calmer. His coloring a little less pale. She would be quiet so he could sleep. Resting her arms on the edge of his bed, careful not to touch his bruised shoulder, she lay her head down, praying silently, wishing she too could go to sleep. The waiting seemed endless.

Finally, the curtain opened and the pretty, young nurse walked in with a man who looked to be in his twenties, his long, brown hair pulled into a neat ponytail.

She stood as he came to her. His hand extended in greeting. "Hi, I'm Doctor Keith." Turning to Bill, he introduced himself again in the same loud, cheerful voice. "Mr. Jameson, I have some good news and some bad news. Which do you want first?"

Bill, groggy from his drug-induced slumber, answered, "I guess the bad news." He felt as if his head were full of cotton, making it hard to concentrate.

"Well sir, you have a broken neck," the doctor returned bluntly. Bill couldn't digest this. Surely he'd misunderstood; after all, he had feeling in his legs and arms. He hurt too much to have a broken neck. The doctor must have said a hurt neck. That certainly fit what he felt.

Christine heard the man quite clearly, her legs turning to jelly at the words.

Dr. Keith eyed her with concern. He tried to keep a cheerful tone to his voice, but paused to glance at the nurse and nodded his head toward Christine. The nurse took the cue. Christine vaguely noticed someone's hand touching her arm.

Turning back to his patient, who had not seemed surprised by the news, Dr. Keith's voice softened, "I should have told you the good news first." He glanced apologetically at Christine. "If you had to break your neck, you did it in the right way. There's no damage to the spinal cord. We just have to take good care of it, so the spinal cord isn't injured." He went on to explain that Bill's neck was actually broken in two places, describing where.

His words blared in Christine's ears, sounding too loud, too cheerful. The glaring lights burnt her eyes, making it hard to see. Sickly smells of antiseptics and blood nauseated her. Unconsciously she held her breath, trying to keep them away. Why had she eaten any of that hamburger? The taste of it lingered in her mouth. Strong and sickening. Everything began to feel far away. The doctor's loud voice penetrated her haze as he suggested she go into the waiting room while he examined Bill. The nurse walked her into the corridor, asking if she was all right.

Christine took a breath, easing the faintness. Her voice sounded as if it came through a long tunnel, "Yes, I'm okay." Moving made her feel better.

She walked into the waiting room, expecting it to be empty. Ben, Catherine, and most of the people she'd left earlier were still there. It amazed her that they'd stayed this long. It was after midnight. They stopped talking and looked at her expectantly. In a voice that sounded far off and unreal, she told them what the neurosurgeon had said. Suddenly, all she wanted to do was go home. She didn't want to be around anyone right now. She just wanted to be alone – someplace where no one would see her cry. Where she could scream and no one but God would hear her.

Ben Evans asked the nurse if he could see Bill. Christine hadn't realized the young woman was still with her.

"You visit with your friends a little while, Mrs. Jameson. This man can stay with your husband. Don't worry, we won't leave him alone. We'll take good care of him. I'll call you if anything happens." It was as if this young lady – this lifeline of kindness – knew the thoughts and turmoil Christine felt.

Ben followed the nurse, and Christine's friends started talking, trying to brighten her flagging spirit. It wasn't long before she missed being with Bill. As she walked back to his cubical to check on him, the insensitive nurse stopped her. "Wait, just a minute. The doctor's in there," she said in a firm, no-nonsense voice that irritated Christine. She started to tell the woman that she had no intentions of waiting when Ben came out from behind the curtain. She could hear Bill's voice saying, "Don't come in here, Christine."

"What's going on?" she asked Ben.

The nurse grunted, making a sound much as a pig might make and left them muttering as she went, "I was only doing what the doctor told me to do."

"The plastic surgeon's sewing him up," answered Ben. "It's a little gruesome. Bill doesn't want you to see it."

"How bad is it?" Christine asked, trying to decide what to do.

"Well," Ben lowered his voice and whispered, "there's a lot of blood, and I can see his skull bone."

That was enough for Christine. Her face gave Ben all the answer he needed. "I'll stay with him through it," he offered. "When it's done, I'll get you."

Christine smiled weakly. "Thanks, Ben. I appreciate it."

"Mrs. Jameson, we have some papers we need you to fill out," another nurse informed her, one that she hadn't seen before. Apparently a new shift had come on duty. She realized the pretty, young nurse was either working a double shift or was staying around to make sure Bill was all right.

They had decided to admit Bill, and she needed to fill out the myriad of forms. Christine went to the station to take care of business. There was one broken finger and his shoulder blade was shattered, whatever that meant. The orthopedic surgeon would be called in the morning. Because it was late, they were going to put Bill in a room when the plastic surgeon finished. The admission nurse, a heavy-set, middle-aged woman, was used to doing her job and asked her questions in a businesslike manner. His name, work, phone number, address, insurance card and number, does he have a Living Will?

"What?" asked Christine. Why did she ask that?

"A Living Will is a document he has signed saying the hospital should not go to any extra effort or expense in order to save or prolong his life," the woman returned in a well-rehearsed voice.

Did this woman know something that she didn't? Christine had delivered all three of her children in this hospital and had not been asked that question before. "I know what a Living Will is, but why are you asking?" She felt a little paranoid. What did this woman know that she didn't?

"It's a standard question, ma'am."

"No, he doesn't have one," she answered in a strained, tired voice.

The woman sighed, giving her a look that said "why didn't you just say so" and went on with the rest of the form.

"Mrs. Jameson, I'll be leaving now that your husband's in his room. I think you can relax. He's going to be all right." The kind, young nurse spoke gently as she walked down the hall with Christine towards Bill's room.

"Thank you for staying." She had words she wanted to say, but the evening's events had taken their toll on her mind, making it hard to put her feelings into words. "You really went beyond the call of duty." That sounded so pathetic, so platitudinous.

"Oh, I do this all the time. I just have to be certain my patients are all right. I'll check on him tomorrow to make sure he's doing okay. Good night." She walked away.

Christine turned back to see the attendant wheel Bill into his room. Why, she hadn't even gotten the sweet nurse's name. Turning back to her, she looked down the hall. The young woman was already gone. Too quickly. It was a long hall. But then again, Christine was tired. Everything went slowly for her. She wished she'd told the girl how much she'd blessed her. Briefly the thought flickered through her mind, wondering if the girl was real or had possibly been an angel there to minister to her and Bill. She didn't see the young nurse again.

Chapter 8

Your enemy the devil prowls around like a roaring lion looking for someone to devour.

- I Peter 5:8 (NIV)

Cole hung up the phone with great satisfaction. Things couldn't have gone more smoothly if he himself had planned Bill's accident. Yes, this was going to be to his liking. However, he reminded himself, he mustn't let anyone know exactly how pleased he was. He'd been smooth with Larry Herrin. The young man was easily moldable. Cole wouldn't have a hard time using him; however, he wasn't the important one. The important one was Larry's father – a wealthy businessman who had given considerable money to Main Street First Church since he'd joined two years ago. From the day Cole had met William Herrin, he'd carefully cultivated a friendship with him, and as a result, he'd learned William's biggest weakness – his son. From that moment on, he'd determined to nurture a relationship with the young man, and now – what luck – Larry had agreed to come in and do Bill's job. Cole had promised the boy a full-time position. The only problem would be to keep Bill from coming back. That shouldn't be too difficult. The groundwork for the man's dismissal had been laid. It would only be a matter of time now.

Glancing at his watch – almost noon – time to go meet William for lunch. Wouldn't the man be pleased by the news he had to offer. Cole couldn't help but smile as he left his office and breezed by Margie, his secretary. He would even pick up the tab this time

Watching the assistant pastor disappear out the door, Margie stopped her typing to look at his back. Why was he so chipper? His odd mood disquieted her, especially since she had overheard him talking on the phone with Larry Herrin. He'd been excited – too excited – as he'd hired the boy to substitute for Bill while he was out – at least she hoped Larry was only a substitute, not a full-time replacement. It was bad enough that Bill was in the hospital. Surely his job wasn't in jeopardy as well. The man didn't deserve what Brother Cole might have in mind.

The doctors were positive about Bill's progress, not realizing that there was a shadow of fear that clung to him, making him feel vulnerable and afraid. He hid his dread behind a facade of cheerfulness – apprehensive that if he ever let down his guard the hospital staff might let something bad happen to him. He'd never felt so vulnerable, so weak. His dignity was lost as he depended on strangers for even the most basic of needs. Though humiliating, his pain swallowed the embarrassment. If he'd known he'd be in this situation beforehand, he'd have been appalled. But now, he just needed to cope and get through it the best way he could. Thoughts of the accident tormented his mind. A reoccurring nightmare haunted his sleep.

What if he went home and Christine couldn't take care of him? He didn't want her to have to care for him. Deep inside a dark terrible unnamed dread wouldn't give him peace. His outward body was bruised everywhere. Each day new, ugly black, blue, and green bruises appeared, but the inward, hidden bruise on his soul was the deepest and would take the longest time to heal.

Thursday night after much arguing with herself, Christine made the phone call. She didn't want to do it. It went against her better judgment, but then again, Bill's mother should know. It was only right to tell her. Christine would want to know if it were her son. The time had come to call the woman.

Selma rolled over and looked at the clock. Only nine in the morning. Usually she slept much later than this, but so much was on her mind. Looking at her husband snoring peacefully beside her, she felt annoyed. How could he sleep so well? Without a single care in the world. Leaving her to figure everything out. "No," he'd said. He wouldn't drive her to see Billy. She couldn't drive herself. For crying out loud, he'd just have to take her. He could drop her off and come straight back home if he had to. It was only a seven-hour trip, and her only son had been hurt, badly hurt …and Christine. Christine. The woman had waited three days to call her. She, as his mother, should have been told immediately.

Sitting up, she lit a cigarette. Her head hurt. She'd drunk too much last night. Well, so what, last night was different. Her only child had been injured. She deserved to get as drunk as she wanted.

Eventually she'd get this old husband moving, and she'd get up there to check on Billy. For all she knew that girl was lying. Bill might be paralyzed or something. One way or another, the little Miss Priss would shortly have a visitor. She would get there soon, and stay just as long as she pleased.

Early Friday morning Christine brought Bill home from the hospital. Carefully guiding him out of the car, she helped him into the house, into their bedroom, into the bed. He was tired after the drive home and complained of hurting, needing medicine. She opened the bottle she had picked up at the pharmacy, giving him two pain pills. No longer would he have intravenous medication, but this was a strong medicine that should help his agony. It hurt him to swallow the pills. His bruised face ached. Everything hurt.

Nancy Gresham, who had watched the children while Christine was gone, hugged her good-bye and went out to her car to leave. Christine felt small and alone, as if she were losing her only ally. She turned back into the house, ready to brave the day. First, she needed to find Jonathan. He had run out of the room as she'd helped Bill come in. A little scared rabbit, scurrying away.

She found him hiding in his closet, a coat over his head. Sitting down next to his small form, she gently patted his back. Lauranna, following close behind, crawled up on her lap. Amanda, book in hand, sat down asking for a story. Christine began as if this were a normal everyday occurrence to sit in Jonathan's closet reading a book. Jonathan peeked his head out from under the coat, listening to the tale of David and Goliath.

As Bill lay on the bed, every part of his flesh screaming out in pain, he heard Christine's soft soothing voice, lulling him into a fitful half-awake, half-asleep world.

Darkness surrounded him. He hurried home. A loud crashing sound. No Bill. Stop. Rewind the videotape. Rewind it. The sun disappeared as he drove. Where was he? There was an intersection ahead. Someone should stop. No stop sign. The deafening sound. You idiot. You should have stopped. Stop that awful sound. Hurry. Rewind the tape. Where's the remote control? I need to rewind the tape!

Christine heard Bill cry out. "I'll be right back," she soothed the children, patting Jonathan's soft head as she got up. She put the almost-asleep Lauranna in her crib before walking to her bedroom. A terrible noise emanated from behind the door. Loud sobs racked Bill's bruised frame.

"Bill, what's the matter?"

"I hurt. I need my medicine."

"I just gave you some half-an-hour ago."

"It isn't working," he groaned. Panic engulfed him. Even though he didn't want to cry, he couldn't stop. He wondered if he was losing his mind. With his tears, he began bemoaning the fact that he hadn't stopped his car.

"Bill, try to go back to sleep."

Bill didn't know what was wrong with him. He had no control over the crying. Maybe this was part of the healing process, but no one had told him to expect it. Suddenly his stomach turned, becoming his enemy. With effort he forced himself to move quickly to the bathroom where he threw up the vile medicine. His neck ached with the exertion.

"I need another pill," he insisted dully, wearily, crawling back into bed.

"Let's give your stomach time to settle; then, you should eat something first," Christine determined.

Though he argued with her, he knew she was right. He felt a total loss of control as he lay back on the bed, telling her to leave him alone, tears flooding his face.

Christine left him. Going to the telephone, she rang the neurosurgeon's office. The hospital personnel had told her to call him if she had any questions. Well, she certainly did. Dr. Keith was with a patient and would return her call later, they informed her. A feeling of isolation surrounded her as she hung up, hearing Bill sobbing in the depths of the bedroom.

"God help him. Help me," she uttered, not knowing what to do. Maybe she should just give him time. His outburst had to be scaring the children. Lauranna had started wailing in her room too. The whole world cried out, screaming for attention.

As the minutes passed, Bill's dark emotions slowly eased. The urge to cry finally dissipated. Spent and weary, he fell into a pain-filled sleep. Though he hurt, the screaming pain didn't increase as he'd been afraid it would. He began to feel more as he had while in the hospital. When he awoke, two hours later, Christine brought him some crackers that he ate before swallowing another pain pill. Lying down to rest, he began to believe he was over the worse part, but within half-an-hour the extreme anxiety overtook him again, and the wracking sobs began echoing through the house. He couldn't sleep. If he did, the awful dreams would come back. He didn't want to remember.

Christine felt at a loss as to how to help him. The baby started crying along with her daddy, confused and scared. Jonathan, refusing to come out of his closet, buried his head under his coat. Amanda, the bravest of the lot, kept asking Christine to help her broken daddy get better. Christine left Bill alone. She needed to take care of the children and was clueless as to how to help her usually stable, strong husband. He was a stranger right now.

Bill continued sobbing. Perhaps the tears released some force he'd pent up in himself while in the hospital. Though he felt guilty to cry, he just couldn't stop. It upset Christine and the children, but his thoughts were so negative, so full of fear. Begging the Lord to help him, he finally fell into another fitful slumber.

Throughout that long hour as Bill wailed near hysteria in their bedroom,

Christine sat in Jonathan's closet with Lauranna in her arms while Jonathan and Amanda cuddled close. With great effort, she engaged them in mundane conversation. Eventually, with relief, she realized that Bill's crying had begun to lessen and finally stopped.

"Jon-Jon, you scared daddy?" Amanda asked after the house was still.

"I'm not scared of Daddy," stated Jonathan. "Noise just hurts my ears." He leaned his head against his mother's shoulder.

Amanda lay her head on Christine's lap. They sat there quietly for a few minutes. Little Lauranna's body relaxed as she fell back to sleep. The house was silent now. A few tears of relief slide down Christine's cheeks. Thank goodness Bill had stopped crying.

"How long will Daddy be broken, Mama?" Jonathan finally asked, enjoying the comfort of his mother's arm.

"Not long." That was her hope anyway. "God is fixing Daddy, but right now he hurts. You know how when you hurt yourself, you sometimes cry."

Both Amanda and Jonathan nodded their heads, and Amanda sat up to tell a long narrative of a time she'd hurt her finger. Jonathan began talking about a time he'd hurt his knee and how the bruise was still there and how he'd cried and cried.

"Well, Daddy hurt everything, and it makes him cry. He won't cry forever, just for a little while. He'll be okay soon." Wanting to change the subject, she whispered, "Now listen, if you two can be real quiet, I'm going to put Lauranna in her bed again, and we'll tiptoe into the kitchen and have some cookies."

Two whispered sounds of approval came out of the children as they followed Christine to Lauranna's bed and into the kitchen. She wondered what psychologists would have to say about her using food to get Jonathan out of his closet. She could picture herself on a talk show in twenty years. "Today we are going to have children that tell us how their mothers taught them to be fat." Well, maybe it wasn't the best way, but she was running out of options, and it worked. It was nice to see two cheerful children sitting at the breakfast table. Soon, they all were enjoying a snack. Christine had needed the food herself. She'd forgotten to eat lunch. When she looked in on Bill, he appeared to be sleeping more soundly than before.

After much cajoling, Selma convinced Jim to take her to Bill's. He would even stay for a couple of nights with her. When she got around to it, she would call Christine. Surely with both of them coming, Christine would give them the master bedroom. Jim was her third husband and the sensitive type.

She had learned early in their relationship not to provoke him. Since he'd not visited her son before, hopefully Bill and Christine would be extra friendly. They would just have to understand that Jim liked his beers in the evening. They helped him sleep. Also, they both would need to smoke in the house. She could hardly ask Jim not to. This marriage was going to work, and she wouldn't let Christine and all her quirks get in their way.

After their snack, Christine called the doctor's office again, hoping he would be there this time. Before she and Bill had left the hospital, she'd been given a minute list of symptoms to expect. Vomiting was not on the list, neither was crying. The doctor was in a meeting and would call her when he got in, they said. Irritated with their neglect, she hung up the phone.

Late in the afternoon Nancy surprised her by stopping by for a few minutes with a dinner of potato soup and homemade bread. Bill ate some, and at first it seemed to stay down, but soon after he took his medicine, it came back up. She noticed he was crying less when his medication had worn off, and her suspicion that the drug had something to do with the severe emotional anxiety he seemed to be having was growing.

By five o'clock, the doctor still hadn't called. Bill had a temperature of 100.9°. He had thrown up his small dinner, and the terrible racking sobs had begun again. Christine needed to hear from the neurosurgeon, especially since it was Friday, and it might be hard to get any information over the weekend. Calling Dr. Keith's office for the third time, she hoped that she hadn't missed him, but when the receptionist answered, she informed Christine that the doctor was at the hospital. He'd been too busy to call; however, one of the nurses was still there and could tell her what she needed to know.

The nurse listened impatiently to Christine's list of concerns. Crying was normal, especially with head injuries. It was part of the healing process. Christine explained there had been no concussion. Yes, but she didn't need to worry about the crying. Christine felt frustrated. This was not normal crying.

The nurse said a fever was anything over 101 degrees.

Well, Bill you missed that by one/tenth of a degree, Christine thought ruefully.

Throwing up was not normal, but she needed to make sure the medicine was taken on a full stomach. "I don't think you have anything to worry about," the nurse concluded easily. This woman was ready to go home and didn't want to fool with a worrywart wife.

Easy for you to say, thought Christine as she hung up the phone. She made a decision. No more pain pills. That way she would know if it was the medicine doing this; if not, Bill was going back to the hospital. Expecting Bill to balk at her plan, she was surprised when he didn't argue. He looked too worn out to complain.

By eleven o'clock that evening, the house lay quiet as Bill and the children slept. Bill's sobbing had stopped completely since the medication had worn off, and though he hurt, he said that the pain wasn't as torturous as he'd feared it would be.

Christine lay down wearily on the couch. What a long day. It felt as if a month had passed since Bill's accident, but it had only been days. At least she drew comfort from the fact that all her family was together again. Finally beginning to relax, she felt herself drift into a deep well of dreamless sleep.

Through the cobwebs of her mind, a sound broke in. Loud and unpleasant. The alarm clock? A bell? No, the phone was ringing. Christine jerked awake. Who in all of heaven and earth would be calling at this time of night? Pulling her heavy body off the couch, she made her way to the kitchen. The clock on the stove said 12:38.

"Hello," she croaked, her vocal cords still asleep.

"Christine," the caller didn't identify herself, but Christine's wakening mind immediately recognized the voice. She wanted to hang up the phone. "Jim and I will be leaving next Friday morning to come check on Billy."

"Bill's fine, Selma." Christine felt desperation creep into her being. They couldn't come now. It was hard enough as it was, but add Selma and *Oh, dear Lord, please help me. –* she needed to talk her out of it. *Let my cloudy head think.*

"He's my son," Selma responded in a voice tinged with anger. "And I want to see him." Christine felt the implied words – "and you're not going to stop me."

"All right," she heard herself say mechanically, miserably. "What time will you be getting here?"

Selma's voice, though calmer, held a strident air, "I don't know. Sometime late Friday afternoon."

"Okay," Christine responded with undisguised tiredness. "We'll see you then." Hanging up, she leaned against the wall to steady herself before walking back to the living room. Hearing Bill call out her name, she trudged to the bedroom.

"Who was that?" he questioned, looking at his worn-out wife. All the sparkle she usually possessed had been extinguished.

"It was your mother. She and Jim are coming here next Friday," she answered flatly, resignedly.

"Oh," he uttered. Did his mother really have to come now? She was a difficult houseguest to say the least, and adding Jim to the equation didn't help redeem the situation. "I'll call her tomorrow and try to talk her out of it."

Christine felt the heaviness she carried lighten. Bill appeared calm now, more his normal self. Maybe everything would be all right after all. When Selma heard her son's voice, surely she would cancel her visit.

The next day Christine noted that Bill seemed to be improving. There was no vomiting, and though his appetite was poor, his emotions were better than they'd been in a while. Calling his mother, he sounded confident and well – surely Selma would decide to stay home.

Sunday morning, July 30 dawned swelteringly hot. Pastor Leonard began sweating even before he stepped into the pulpit. With all the people in the congregation, the air conditioners weren't cooling the place down, and no one had thought to set the air conditioner's timer so that they'd be more comfortable. Bill usually did that. Leonard made a mental note to mention this to Larry Herrin himself.

Since Bill's accident, Leonard had felt his heart stirred, and though he knew the staff members expected a continuation of the series he'd been giving on stewardship, he'd felt God leading him in a different direction. The worries about the church budget seemed frivolous after his encounter with Bill the previous Monday evening. Other things were so much more important. Somehow, for some reason, he'd forgotten that these past few weeks or maybe even longer.

When the time came for him to preach, he could tell that the congregation, in spite of the heat, was also stirred. Bill's accident was the catalyst to today's sermon. His text came from Matthew 6:33-34.

"Let's stand and read these verses aloud together," he directed.

The sound of pages turning sounded like a hive of bees humming as the congregation found the scripture before standing as asked.

"But seek ye first the kingdom of God, and his righteousness; and all these things shall be added unto you. Take therefore no thought for the morrow: for the morrow shall take thought for the things of itself. Sufficient unto the day is the evil thereof."

Brother Cole sat back in his elegant, velvet chair behind the pastor where everyone could see him, smiling his blessing. This was a good choice of text. It should lead into a sermon on the importance of giving without any trouble. Soon, however, dissatisfaction marred the earlier smile as Pastor Leonard prated on about trusting the Lord and didn't even bring up the subject of stewardship. To add to Cole's irritation, Leonard referred to Bill and his accident. The congregation seemed enraptured – even Cole's wife sat there obviously absorbed in the sermon.

Greta noticed her husband glance her way. She looked at his hard face with a slight smile touching his even features. Many would think he enjoyed the sermon, but she recognized the expression of disgust that she'd come to know so well. Refocusing again on the pastor's words, she realized that she hadn't even known that Bill had been injured. Oddly Cole hadn't bothered to tell her. Usually he was so concerned with how things looked, even if he didn't care for the person, that he'd have suggested she fix a meal for the family or send a card.

The sermon touched a cord in Greta as Pastor Leonard pointed out that each day was a gift that should be treasured. She tried to endure her days, especially Saturdays when Cole was home. She didn't enjoy life very much anymore. Recently her friend, Rose, had been encouraging her to make changes. In many ways Greta felt that she'd come a long way from the shy, little mouse that she tended to be. As she listened to the pastor, she felt herself grabbing hold of each word spoken, absorbing them into her innermost being.

Observing Cole's grimace, she realized that his hard heart shut out the sermon. Sadly his life consisted of shutting out anything he didn't want to hear. Greta prayed silently, asking God to help her repair her marriage, to be a godly wife. Just for today. She would take it one day at a time.

By the end of the sermon, Leonard felt unexpectedly spent. His heart and soul had gone into this message. For a change, Brother Cole didn't comment on his talk. Usually the man would whisper words of encouragement as they shook hands before each went to stand at separate doors to bid the congregation good-bye, but Cole seemed preoccupied as the two parted today. Any of the pastor's misgivings vanished at the front door as people who usually slipped out quickly made a special point of coming to tell him how his words had inspired them.

Later, as he drove home, Ann expressed that Leonard seemed more like his old self than he had in a long time, and he began to wonder if perhaps this was true. He felt he was on a new pilgrimage, and the journey had begun well. A long-missed peace settled over him. For the first time, he had a subtle awareness of a spiritual battle being fought. At the moment, he could rejoice. He had seen the parishioners really listening as they hadn't in a long time, and today he felt confident that the Holy Spirit had led him. It had been a while since he'd felt sure of that.

Chapter 9

Knowing this, that the trying of your faith worketh patience.

-James 1:3

Even though the days crept by, the week flew past too quickly for Christine. The dreaded Friday dawned hot and muggy. A day she wasn't looking forward to, a day that threatened to bring Selma's intimidating presence. She would need to stand up to her mother-in-law, making sure that everything was as peaceful as possible for Bill and the children.

Bill's mother left later than she'd intended. First off, she overslept; then, she couldn't find a suitcase and ended up stuffing her clothes into a plastic trash bag. Jim grumbled that he had no clean underwear. Well, she didn't either, and she wasn't complaining. She told him he could've done the wash himself, and they got into an explosive argument where at one point Jim threatened that he wasn't going to go. Selma hoped Billy would appreciate the trouble she was going to in order to see him. They grabbed a couple cartons of cigarettes. The beers were gone. They would get some when they got to Bill's house. Her son didn't drink, and his wife wouldn't be polite enough to supply them with anything.

Billy had called to say that he was doing better, that she needn't come up. She knew, without a doubt, that Christine had put him up to it. Hearing his voice brought back so many memories. He'd been such a sweet kid. She'd missed out on a lot of his growing up. Her mother took over the raising of him when he was young. Selma had moved in with her mother soon after he was born, and when she'd married the second time, she let Billy stay with his grandmother. It had been the best for both of them. The second marriage lasted eight years, which she thought was pretty good considering how long most marriages last. When Billy was a teenager, she'd moved back in with her mother. What a pushover he'd been. He had just become a Christian. Selma tried to toughen him up, but he didn't have it in him. The real world would harden him though. It had her, and she was confident he'd have the same experience.

Seeing him again would be nice. And it would be great to have a break from cooking and taking care of Jim for a little while. She needed this vacation – a nice, long one.

By eleven o'clock that evening, Selma and Jim still hadn't arrived. Christine hoped they'd decided not to come. Selma did that kind of thing. She rarely informed them when she changed her mind; however, it was too early to be relieved. Still she had high hopes that Bill's phone call to his mother earlier in the week had convinced the woman to stay home.

The house lay still as everyone except Christine slept. Lying on the couch, she eventually allowed herself to relax into a quiet slumber. Perhaps her little world would remain untouched and would begin to heal. She hoped so, as much needed rest settled upon her.

A door slammed, jerking her awake. Her stomach tightened into the familiar knot she'd fought earlier in the day. Looking out the window, she saw, with a sinking heart, it was them. Both of them. They stood outside their truck, hurling remarks back and forth, arguing.

Oh, dear God, I don't want to let them in, she entreated silently, opening the sleeper couch. Maybe they would just fall into the bed right away and go to sleep.

Bill opened the bedroom door. "They're here. Sounds as if they stopped off at a bar first."

"Oh, Bill, what should we do?" Any resolve to be strong had melted away.

"I have an idea," Bill began. All week long he'd considered what to do if his mother or Jim got drunk. Perhaps this idea wasn't the best one, but it was all he'd been able to come up with. He'd at least give it a try.

Christine looked out the window. Jim stood, his back to Selma, ignoring her as she screamed at him.

Mrs. Cabiness, hearing the ruckus in the Jameson's driveway, rose from her bed, and with a racing heart, peeked out the window. A gentle woman with little to do in life except take care of her cats, she'd grown especially fond of the Jameson children as they visited her from time to time. Jonathan had begun calling her Granny as her own grandson did, stealing her heart.

It was after midnight. Who in the world were these strange, loathsome-looking people? Careful not to be seen, she eyed the unpleasant twosome. Perhaps they were lost. Their abusive speech penetrated easily into her home as they angrily disputed about what had happened to their cigarettes. The man shoved the woman, but she seemed oblivious to it as she shook her fist in his face before turning to stomp up the steps and pound on the Jameson's front door.

Mrs. Cabiness rushed to her bedside table and grabbed the phone, hastily dialing 911. The dispatcher took an inordinately long time taking her call; afterwards, she peered out the window again. That frightful couple had gone into the Jameson's house. Not knowing what to do, she crept out on her porch to wait for the police. Though she couldn't clearly hear the words, she could hear a terrible commotion coming from inside her neighbor's home. The baby was crying. The children – what was happening to the children? Bill couldn't handle this kind of encounter in his condition. Where were the police?

Almost an hour later, a patrol car lazily pulled up in front of the house. Mrs. Cabiness, angry at the slowness, sprang from her hiding place to meet it. Tomblike silence surrounded the Jameson's residence – an eerie quietness that disturbed the older woman to her very core.

"What took you so long?" she whispered fretfully.

"Sorry, ma'am," replied one of the policemen without sincerity. "Looks like all's calm here," he observed.

Mrs. Cabiness, noting the disdain in the officer's manner, felt exasperated. Being basically a soft-spoken woman, her voice didn't sound indignant, but it held a note of gravity that even the overworked policeman picked up on. "I just hope no one's hurt. This is a nice, young couple with three small children," her voice broke slightly at the thought of the young ones, "and these two people came to their door and went inside raising an awful ruckus."

The second policeman spoke gently with an element of concern in his voice that didn't escape Mrs. Cabiness' ears. "Don't worry, ma'am. You were right to call us. We'll check into it and make sure everyone's safe." He'd seen enough during his many years as a police officer to know that a mute house didn't necessarily mean all was well.

Feeling slightly reassured, Mrs. Cabiness scurried back to her porch to wait.

A short time later, when the policemen left with reassurances that everyone was safe, she realized that perhaps she might not have needed to call for help after all, but she wouldn't have gotten any sleep. Eventually she'd tell the Jamesons it was she who had called the police. Hopefully they wouldn't be upset with her.

Early the next morning, though Christine had intended to caution the children to keep their voices down, she soon realized a warning was unnecessary. Jonathan, who'd been in a fearful state off and on since Bill's accident, had refused to come near the living room where his grandmother and Jim were sleeping. Extroverted Amanda whispered her way through the morning without being asked. Of all the children, she was the only one who'd slept through the horrible events from the night before. Christine hoped this visit wouldn't add to her children's problems – especially Jonathan's. He had recently started coming out of his shell. Although he still didn't touch his father, he at least stayed in the same room with him. Now she wondered if he'd revert back into the hiding-in-the-closet state that he'd adopted earlier. She'd successfully gotten him out from under his bed, where he'd decided to sleep the night, but he wasn't going near his grandparents.

Selma awoke after eleven and felt briefly confused as to where she was. Pulling herself off the foldout couch, she stretched to get the cramps out of her body. Her head hurt. She needed some coffee. Where was the kitchen? She didn't remember seeing it last night. Actually she didn't remember much from last night. Trudging down the hall, she turned the corner to find the kitchen. Christine sat feeding Lauranna something out of a baby food jar that looked terrible.

"What you feeding that kid?" she asked.

"Carrots and broccoli." Christine felt an implied criticism as she glanced at her mother-in-law. At one time, the older woman had been fairly attractive but now her face was etched with hard lines, her skin leathered, her few teeth darkly stained, and she smelled of mildew and sweat. "Would you like a cup of coffee?"

"Yeah, hot and strong." Selma sank down heavily onto a kitchen chair. Christine arose, leaving an offended Lauranna to whine for more food.

Selma eyed her daughter-in-law critically. The girl looked awful. She used to be pretty, but now her eyes had dark circles under them, and her skin looked pasty, as if she wasn't eating right. Christine was aging badly, Selma decided with pleasure. She had often thought the girl a little too pretty.

"Cream or sugar?" asked Christine, handing her mother-in-law the mug of coffee.

"Nah," responded Selma, drinking a sip. It was hot, but not very strong. "Need to make it stronger next time."

Christine grimaced, an expression that escaped the attention of her mother-in-law. After getting very little sleep, then spending all morning cleaning up the mess that had been made the night before, the young woman's feelings were closer to the surface than usual. She really didn't care what the other woman thought right now.

Selma stretched uncomfortably. A catch in the back of her neck hurt.

"That bed's too hard." If Christine really knew how to treat company, she'd have given Selma their bed. She took another sip of coffee, then spat it out of her mouth crudely before pushing the cup away.

Christine eyes darkened with anger as she glared at her mother-in-law. A biting response formed on her lips, and at the same time her ears heard a sound that wasn't quite right. A large bang and swooshing noise came from behind her. She turned in time to see Amanda, panic written across her face, standing in a pool of milk.

"Amanda," she shrieked. Milk was everywhere – all over the floor, splashed up onto the counters, under the refrigerator.

"I try get milk." Amanda backed away from her mother. "I sorry, Mama. It accident." The tears fell down her face. "I sorry. I clean up. I sorry."

Surveying her milk-splattered little girl's mortified expression tugged at Christine's heart. With effort, she controlled her dismay. "It's okay. I'll clean it up. Next time let me get the milk out of the refrigerator."

"Otay," Amanda perked up slightly as she looked down at her dress. "I all wet."

"I'll clean you up in a minute. Don't move." Amanda obeyed.

"I'll go get some more milk," offered a gravelly masculine voice.

Christine didn't turn to look at Jim standing at the kitchen entryway. Frustrated, angry tears threatened to erupt at any moment. Everything felt too hard.

"I'll go with you." Selma stood up heavily. "I can't seem to find my cigarettes."

Christine breathed a sigh of relief as they left. At least she'd have a short respite before having to deal with that woman again.

Bill, having heard the commotion, made his way slowly to the kitchen. He saw his mother and stepfather walking out to the truck. "What happened?" he asked as he stepped toward the doorway. "Never mind, I can see what happened." He felt so useless. Slowly, painfully he lowered himself into one of the hard-backed chairs.

As the baby whined for more food, he awkwardly lifted the spoon with his right hand. In spite of his broken little finger, his other fingers worked to pick up the spoon. It felt good to get the food in the baby's mouth. A little dribbled out. He tried to catch it with the spoon and succeeded. A success. Even if it were slow, it felt good to do something useful. Lauranna grinned her appreciation, slurped down her carrots, and opened her mouth wide for more.

Christine eyed Bill with a desperate look in her usually clear blue eyes. "What are we going to do?"

Bill regarded her sadly. "I'm going to tell them that they have to go home."

Relief flooded Christine. She knew it would be hard, but it was the only answer.

They both were silent for a while. In the light of day, last night seemed like a horrible nightmare. The part of Bill that had felt fragile as a result of his accident had toughened during the night. He had slept little. Christine looked more haggard than he ever remembered seeing her. He needed to handle his mother, and he would.

Jonathan walked into the room to show his mother a picture he'd drawn.

"Let me see," Bill asked with interest. Jonathan lifted his "airplane" but didn't walk toward his father. He wanted to keep a safe distance from Bill.

Bill felt a pang of sadness for this child. Christine noticed it, too, and though she had a tendency to want to push Jonathan toward his father, she realized that wouldn't work. The child had been terrified last night and had too much for his mind to deal with right now. She prayed God would protect them all from any more problems.

An hour later, Selma and Jim drove up. Christine looked anxiously out the window. They appeared to be sober. Opening the front door, Jim handed her a heavy bag of groceries.

"That'll be thirty dollars," Selma said glibly as she walked past Christine.

Milk didn't cost thirty dollars. Was she joking? If she was, it wasn't very funny.

"Selma, Bill's in the bedroom. He wants to see you." Christine knew her voice sounded clipped and unfriendly, but she'd had enough from this woman.

She put the milk in the refrigerator and left the beer and cigarettes in the paper bag. Walking back into the living room, she handed Jim only the money for the milk.

Glancing at it, he acknowledged the money with a slight smile. Selma had said she wouldn't pay for the beer and cigarettes. His eyes showed little emotion or surprise. It had been worth the try but was nothing to worry about. He knew Selma would give the girl the riot act when she found out. In a way he felt sorry for Christine. She was a nice enough sort. He leaned back on the couch and thought about asking for one of his beers. No, he'd wait till Selma came out from talking with her son. He was ready to go home. He would definitely leave tomorrow.

Selma traipsed in to see Bill without pausing to knock. She wanted to talk to him about the sleeping arrangement, but when she saw her son, a ripple of shock stifled her intent. Here was her robust boy covered with bruises, his left arm in a sling, and some kind of splint was taped on his little finger. An ugly row of stitches stood out across his forehead down to his ear. His hair covered part of this, but right now it looked greasy. She hadn't gotten a good look at him last night, she decided.

The room was a mess. A shattered lamp, books, and papers littered the floor. A broken nightstand lay on its side. Christine obviously didn't care too much about Bill. The rest of the house was clean, but this room looked like a war zone. The idiot of a girl must leave him here to rot, she thought, then spoke the accusation aloud.

"No," Bill answered in a calm voice. "I told Christine to leave it this way. Come sit down, Mom." He motioned to a chair, but instead she sat on the bed. He winced.

"Oh, does that hurt." She got huskily off the bed, pulled the chair around and sat down. She didn't know what to say. Even though she could speak her mind to Christine, Bill was another matter. Deep inside she wanted Bill to like her.

"Mom, I need you to listen to something. Promise me you'll listen and not get up and leave."

Selma was curious. What was so hard to listen to that she'd want to get up and leave? "I don't want to hear any of that religious junk. I didn't come all the way up here from Florida to get preached at by you or nobody."

"It's not preaching. Will you listen?"

She agreed uncertainly.

"First, I need to tell you that when you and Jim got here last night, you were both drunk."

"Hold on there, Billy," she cried, pointing her finger in his face for emphasis. Her whole body raised slightly out of her chair. "I'm tired of you calling a couple of beers, drunk. You think because anyone drinks anything other than water that they're drunks. I don't push it off on you to drink, and you need to get off your high horse about me drinking."

Bill silently contemplated his mother. She couldn't understand his expression. He looked sad. Usually when they had these discussions, he seemed irritated or frustrated. That gave her a feeling of power, of control, but now he only looked sad. It disconcerted her.

Without further argument, Bill pressed the button on the tape recorder to the part he had decided to play. Selma listened. There was the sound of banging, and a loud woman's voice began whining, "Billy Boy. It's so good to see my Billy Boy. You're all okay." It sounded like a poorly made television show.

A male voice that was familiar said, "Hi, Mom." The sound of a bed squeaking.

The woman's voice fussed over "Billy Boy," and the man's voice that she could barely hear pleaded, "Be careful, Mom. I hurt easily."

The woman suddenly changed tone and asked, "What's all this goop on your head? Doesn't that wife of yours know how to take care of you?"

"Yes, Mom, she does. That's antibiotic cream so my stitches won't get infected."

Another bed squeak. "It smells like a hospital in here. I need to take you home. Jim, Jim," the voice shrilled. A baby could be heard crying in the background.

"What is it?" growled a loud, male voice that Selma immediately recognized as her husband's. Realization dawned on her, but no, surely Bill hadn't taped them.

"I want to take Billy home tonight," she whimpered before cursing the awful wife that didn't know how to care for her son.

Jim shouted, punctuating his speech with vulgarities, about how he'd come all the way up here and just wanted a good night's sleep. She should leave him alone.

Bill could be heard in the background groaning, "Mom, let go of me. You're hurting me."

Christine shouted, "Let go of him, Selma."

She heard herself yelling vulgarities at Christine, and Jim's loud obnoxious voice roared, "Get off the boy, Selma. Can't you see he's been in an accident."

More cursing, yelling, a sound of crashing followed by the tinkling of shattering glass. The ruckus became more distant, but the baby could still be heard crying, and a little boy screamed, "Mama, stop them! Make them go away!"

Christine yelled, "Get in your room. Don't come out."

Selma wanted to have Bill stop the tape but at the same time something about it drew her attention. She kept listening. The sound of banging had stopped, but she could hear the sounds of Jim and her voices quarreling with each other. An overwhelming feeling of humiliation engulfed her. She had heard enough. "Turn it off. Turn it off."

Bill stopped the recorder.

"What was all that banging?"

"That's you two having a shoving match. You started it in here and ended up in the living room. Christine cleaned up the living room, but I wanted you to see what had happened here. You broke two lamps and this table. We thought we would have to call the police to get you two to stop."

Selma rubbed her arms. She had noticed some bruises on them this morning and thought that the bed had done it. Her embarrassment quickly turned to anger. What was he thinking, taping them? Didn't he know people had a right to privacy? "How dare you tape us without even telling us," she shrieked. "Who do you think you are? The Gestapo. You had no right to do that. None at all." She stood. It felt good to be angry. This was downright humiliating. She wanted to get out of there.

Pulling the tape out of the machine, a realization struck her. "You planned this," she accused. "You and Christine planned the whole thing. No one just has a tape recorder going. What kind of son are you?" She threw the tape across the room. It landed in the broken glass and fallen books with a soft thud. "I don't want to have anything to do with you anymore. If this is how you treat folks when they come all these miles to see you, then we won't be staying."

"Mom, I love you, but you need to know that you have a problem."

She didn't listen. She was livid now. Who was this man? "I'm not the one with the problem. It's you and all your little religious friends who have the problem. If you call this love, then you have a few things to learn about love." She turned to leave. This is the way it worked best. He would try to stop her, and then she'd be able to get her dignity back and stay here as she'd planned. They had played this game before, and she knew how it worked. She began walking out, expecting to hear the pleading voice that she'd heard so often when he was little, "Mommy, don't be mad. I didn't mean it," but the voice didn't come.

Slamming the door, she tore into the living room and grabbed her bag of clothes and purse. "Come on, Jim, we're going." She glared at Christine. "And don't think we'll ever come back here again, young lady. You hear me? You hear me?" she screamed. Christine was usually the one who hated her tantrums, and Selma took a certain delight in tormenting her.

With a tight expression on her face, Christine stood without fear. She looked like a mother bear watching out for her cubs. "Yes," she answered in a precise, even, low voice. "I hear you."

It was not the reaction Selma had anticipated. Christine was supposed to beg her to come back again one day, to say she was sorry, something. Selma felt her anger deflate into a long, lost feeling, and deep inside she felt a grudging respect for the girl. Maybe Christine wasn't the marshmallow that she'd always thought she was.

"Come on, Jim," she ordered, swinging the door opened so hard that it reverberated after it hit the doorstop.

"Wait, let me get my beer."

"Forget the beer. Let them drink it if they want to."

"Well," Jim opened his hands, not knowing what to say.

"Here," said Christine, handing him the bag of beer and cigarettes.

"Thanks," he smiled slightly. She really wasn't a bad sort of girl, and she obviously had some gumption. He grabbed the other bag of clothes and followed his wife out to the car. This was going to be a long ride home.

Jonathan peeked out of his bedroom as Christine shut the front door. "Mama, I saw Grandma get in her truck from my window. Did Daddy make them go home?"

"Well..." Christine suddenly felt very relieved. Her whole body quivered slightly. Her last ounce of strength felt exhausted. "I guess you could put it that way."

"Yeah!" Jonathan cheered. If she'd had the energy, she would have cheered with him.

"Can I go see Daddy?" he asked.

"Sure," agreed Christine in pleased surprise. She followed him to the bedroom door.

"Daddy, thank you for making Grandma leave."

Bill looked at him with pleasure and smiled. "Hi there, Jonathan. You want to come in and talk to me for a minute."

"Okay. Boy, it sure is a mess in here."

"Be careful. I don't want you to cut your feet on any of that glass. Come on up here on the bed with me."

"What's that thing on your arm, Daddy?"

"It's called a sling. It keeps my arm from moving since I hurt my shoulder."

"Oh. What's that stuff on your head?"

A smile touched Christine's face. Jonathan was becoming his inquisitive self again.

Chapter 10

The Lord condemns a crafty man.

-Proverbs 12:2 (NIV)

The Thursday morning staff meeting at Main Street First Church began with an encouraging note – the offering the previous Sunday had met the weekly budget goal for the first time all year even though it was August – usually a slow month. Leonard realized that God had once again proved His power. All his sermons on stewardship had done little to help the need. There he had been relying on his own strength, but once he rested in God's, the Lord proved Himself faithful.

Since Vacation Bible School would begin next week, Brother Ralph took time to report on the schedule and the teachers. As a result of Bill's accident, Christine Jameson was unable to teach, and Patricia Herrin had willingly taken her place. "She's the wife of the man who's substituting while Bill's out."

Cole's ears perked up at the reference to Larry. This was a good time to promote his cause. "They're a helpful couple. I've enjoyed having Larry here. He's an excellent worker. Have you noticed how clean the church is lately?"

Actually Leonard had noticed the opposite.

Brother Dan spoke up. "We need to remind Larry to set the timers for the air conditioners next Sunday. It's really been hot in there these past two weeks."

A slight chorus of agreement went up. Cole felt annoyed that Dan had to point out a problem. "You need to remember this is new to Larry. I told Sam to take care of the air conditioner timers himself, but he must not have done it." Cole was irritated with Sam, Bill's right-hand maintenance man. If Sam's attitude didn't improve, Cole would have to get rid of him. This was a good time to let the staff know. "Sam hasn't had his mind on work lately, and… if it continues, we may have to find someone more reliable." Cole acted as if it bothered him to think about replacing Sam.

"Well, he probably has his nose out of joint because you didn't ask him to do Bill's job while Bill's out. Sam could have done it just fine. I don't understand why we didn't let him have the position and hire Larry to be one of the maintenance crew. We could use the extra workers." Brother Dan had a way of cutting to the heart of a matter, and at the moment, Leonard appreciated it. Though the same thought had occurred to him, he hadn't wanted to question Brother Cole's reasoning, at least not so bluntly as Brother Dan just had.

Immediately Cole was on the defensive. All in the room sensed it. All eyes, except Dan's shifted nervously to their note pads, toward the back wall, out the window, looking away from the reddening face. Dan, unperturbed by the mood shift in the room, waited expectantly for an explanation.

As Cole looked around, he realized he needed to keep calm. He had his own private agenda, and he wouldn't let Brother Dan or anyone else destroy it. He looked at his hands to give himself time to weigh his words carefully. "There are some things," he began slowly, giving himself a moment to think of just the right approach. He hadn't practiced his response to this question. Stupid of him really. He should have known it would be asked. In his pocket an envelope lay warm against his chest. The excitement of sharing it with the group had momentarily caused him to forget his cautions. But it was too early to show the envelope. No, he would do this his way, and with the adroitness he had cultivated over the years, a pained smile touched his square jaw, a look of concern etched itself on his features, but didn't quite made it into his dark eyes. "I really didn't want to burden you men with this, but…," he paused again, appearing deeply concerned over something as he tried desperately to think of exactly what to say. The words came out slowly, as if he were sharing a burden that had been on his heart for a long time. "I feel it's inappropriate for me to air a man's problems to a group of this size. The last thing I want to do is start any unchristian gossip around the church, and you all know how easily things can spread around here. Sometimes I feel that the walls have ears." Slight smiles and grunts of agreement whispered through the room. Cole relaxed, feeling emboldened to continue, cautious not to let the smile in his throat touch his lips. "I'd rather not say exactly what the trouble is, but suffice it to say, Sam has a problem."

Now everyone was curious. All eyes regarded Brother Cole as questions came to their mind.

"What kind of problem?" asked Brother Dan uncertainly.

Cole looked at him with a touch of undisguised disdain. "Dan, I just said that I didn't want to spell it out." Cole sounded exasperated, and it wasn't far from the truth. "I don't want to start rumors. If it becomes a big problem, I'll let you know. I think I've handled it for now, but I just didn't feel that I should give him Bill's job."

Everyone was silent. Brother Dan had noticed the slip of the tongue. Give him Bill's job? Bill's job wasn't for the taking. This Larry was only a substitute. No one else noticed the remark. All felt concern for Sam. They liked the young man and wondered what was going on.

"We all need to remember," Pastor Leonard began in a quiet voice, "to keep Sam in our prayers. Are there any other prayer requests?"

A few were given. Pencils and pens wrote them down, and at the top of each minister's list was Sam's name.

After the prayer, as Leonard began to dismiss them, Cole interrupted, "Oh, I forgot this." He handed an envelope to Pastor Leonard before anyone had risen from their seat. "I don't know what it is," he lied. "But William Herrin gave it to me last week. He asked me to give it to you, Pastor, at our weekly meeting." This too, was a lie, but who would know.

Leonard opened the envelope. Inside was a check made out to the church for ten thousand dollars. Cole relished the pastor's reaction. This would help give him job security for a long time.

After the meeting, Cole took the afternoon off. Something he rarely did, but today, the tenth day of August, was his birthday, and tonight he and Greta were going out to dinner with William and Carol Herrin.

Greta felt anxious as she dressed for dinner. The Herrins both seemed nice enough, but they were so wealthy, so perfect, and she wasn't. Carol seemed rather aloof. She didn't look like the mother of grown children as Greta felt she herself did. She must look her best tonight. If she looked her best, she'd feel better about herself, and then she might even have a little fun. She had taken special care with the gift that she'd chosen for Cole – a gold watch that had cost an exorbitant amount of money. Cole only wanted the best, and she knew his present would have to be something expensive. It had taken all her earnings from her job as pianist at the church to buy it, but – and this was the important thing, the thing that gave her confidence – he would love it. He often complained that his watch didn't keep good time and had stopped wearing it recently.

Looking through her closet, she fretted over what to wear. She didn't have many dressy clothes, and Cole had said to dress elegantly tonight. She would have bought a new outfit if the watch hadn't cost so much. Putting on the beautiful dark blue dress that she had worn to her youngest son's, Brad's, wedding two years ago, she examined her reflection in the mirror. It was becoming, but hung on her skeleton frame loosely. She must have lost some weight recently. Searching through her closet again, she reached for her old friend, the pink suit, but Cole would think it wasn't fancy enough. Well, the blue dress would just have to do. It was pretty, and the soft color suited her delicate skin, giving her a rosy, healthy glow.

Rose came by shortly before Cole arrived home to help Greta with her make-up. Since Greta's move to Georgia, Rose had become a good friend. Her outgoing and friendly personality contrasted with Greta's shy and reserved one. Dear Rose had become closer than a sister to Greta, a touch of sunshine in her dark world.

Cole didn't care much for Rose, saying she was too outspoken for a woman. But then again, Cole didn't care much for anyone, not really. Oh, he pretended to like the Herrins, and in his misguided way, he did, but if they'd had no money, she knew the Herrins would be stricken from his list of friends. Rose and her husband, Hal, were simply middle-class, not ritzy like the Herrins, and Cole tended not to give them a second look.

"I love the dress," Rose encouraged as soon as she arrived. "You look elegant. Wait till I make you up. You'll knock them all dead tonight."

Her words raised Greta's fragile confidence, and as Rose masterfully applied the make-up, Greta began to feel better about herself.

"Cole's probably not even going to want to go out to dinner tonight but stay home with you instead," Rose laughed.

Greta laughed with her – Cole doing that was as likely as the Georgia red clay turning rainbow colored. She only hoped he wouldn't find anything critical to say. He could so quickly knock down her self-confidence, and she needed it tonight in order to make it through this meal with the Herrins.

When Cole arrived home, Greta was ready. She'd gone all out. Her hair was pinned on top of her head, and the jewelry she'd chosen went well with her dress. Rose had done an excellent job with her makeup, giving her a natural look with her soft touch. She'd even used a small amount of eyeliner that Greta had not used before. Looking at herself in the mirror, she thought, *Not bad for a grandmother of two.*

Taking a deep breath, she walked into Cole's bedroom where he was putting on his tie. Standing quietly, hopefully, she waited for him to see her.

He glanced her way. "Good, you're ready. We need to go soon. I told the Herrins we'd meet them at 7:30."

"How do I look?" she asked, hoping for a tidbit of praise.

Cole scrutinized her with a frown. With a sinking feeling, she realized she shouldn't have asked. She had just set herself up for criticism.

"That dress is a little young for you." He turned back to the mirror to adjust his tie. "But we don't have time for you to change."

Greta's shoulders sagged. Rose had told her to stand tall. It made her look better, more confident and beautiful, but right now she just wanted to hide inside herself. She walked into the bathroom. Yes, she was sagging again, and it wasn't a pretty sight. Straightening her shoulders, she looked at herself in the mirror. With good posture, this dress looked lovely on her, she decided. She stood straight and examined herself, liking what she saw. That would need to be enough.

The Herrins hadn't arrived at the Polaris Club when Cole and Greta walked into the exquisite restaurant. The waiter seated them at their table to wait for their company. Greta had not been to this restaurant before. It was beautiful. Built on top of the Hyatt Regency in Atlanta, the dining room slowly rotated so that one could get a view of the entire city. It was still daylight, and Greta looked forward to seeing the sunset from up here. This was a rare treat for her.

"I hope you'll be friendly and talkative tonight. Don't act like a mouse," Cole cautioned.

His admonishment caused her to feel more mouse-like and didn't help her to be the friendly, outgoing person he wanted her to be. But this was his birthday. She'd try her best to be everything he wanted. She had his gift tucked into her purse. It gave her a feeling of confidence. She knew this present would impress him. It was the first time in their married lives she'd had money to spend, and she'd done a good job.

Looking around, she observed, "This is one of the nicest restaurants I've ever been in."

"And don't talk like that. I don't want the Herrins thinking you're some country hick who has never been to the big city before." His words stung. She was a country girl, and it was an embarrassment to him. "What's that awful stuff you have around your eyes?" he asked suddenly.

She stiffened as he inspected her. "I...it's eyeliner," she stuttered, shattered. She had half expected this reaction at the house but not here.

"Go to the restroom and get it off. Hurry before the Herrins get here."

She went, having to ask the way. She felt broken, as if a baseball bat had hit the tiny self-assurance she'd gained from Rose's encouragement earlier in the day, shattering the fragile emotion into a million pieces. She had hoped tonight would be different. Cole seemed so bent on pleasing the Herrins for some reason, and she'd thought his sharing them with her was his way of accepting her. But she'd obviously been wrong. Apparently Cole wanted her there because he needed her for the sake of his image. Slowly the hurt she felt was replaced by anger. The thought resounded in her mind. Tonight was important to Cole. What if she just took a taxi and went home? How would he handle that? It was the kind of thing Rose would do, but then Hal wouldn't treat Rose in such an unloving manner.

She could do it. The thought gave her a sense of self that she hadn't had in a while. But it was Cole's birthday, and he'd probably tell the Herrins that she'd gotten ill, and then she'd pay for it later at home.

She looked at the barely visible line of eyeliner. With a tissue, she tried to remove some of it. It stuck fast. Taking a little water from the sink, she tried again. Apparently it was waterproof. It wouldn't come off, but some of the makeup she and Rose had applied so carefully did. What a mess. Tears threatened to fall. Cole treated her this way all the time. For years she'd tried to convince herself that all husbands were like him and that he really did care for her in his own pushy way. She'd thought that if she were just a little smarter, friendlier, better, he wouldn't be so critical.

Something in her resolved that this wasn't the way she wanted to live the rest of her life, walking on eggshells, afraid of what mood Cole would be in.

Carol Herrin walked in. "Hi, Greta. Cole said you were in here adjusting your makeup. I thought I'd join you."

Greta gazed at Carol's obviously expensive and quite becoming outfit, immediately feeling intimidated. She reminded herself that she wouldn't be a quiet mouse tonight. She would pretend Carol was a good friend, like Rose, and talk to her as if she were. "You look beautiful," she remarked sincerely.

Her gentle words touched Carol unexpectedly, and the wealthy woman's usual reserve vanished as she felt an immediate gush of emotion. She looked at the woman who had smudged her makeup, and her initial judgmental response disappeared. Here was a person who could use a touch of kindness.

"I've made a mess of my makeup. Cole said he didn't like the eyeliner, so I tried to take it off, and, well...," Greta stopped. She'd said too much. She suddenly noticed Carol wore eyeliner, and she realized she had insulted her husband. Cole would be furious if he knew.

"Why, I think it looks good on this eye," Carol observed pointing to the eye Greta hadn't touched. "Do you have any makeup with you?"

"Yes, right here in my purse."

"Good. We'll have you looking back to your beautiful self in no time." Carol began fussing over Greta's face. By the time they came out of the restroom, they were talking as if they were old friends.

Cole was surprised and uneasy to see the two women chatting so freely. Hopefully Greta wouldn't say too much. She was being uncharacteristically friendly, and even though it was what he'd told her to be, he knew she'd probably say the wrong thing. He needed to keep an eye on her. He was disturbed that the line of eyeliner was still there. He would have to talk to her about it at home.

The dinner was delicious. Greta felt so encouraged by Carol that she decided she had misjudged the woman. Sometimes her own insecurities made her assume things that were untrue about others. When Carol suggested that they have lunch together, Greta readily agreed. She knew it would probably not happen, but in the moment it felt good that Carol would even consider it.

During dessert, William handed Cole a birthday card. Cole opened it, expressing his thanks. Greta peered over his shoulder. Inside the card was a check for a thousand dollars.

"My goodness," she exclaimed without thinking. Cole grabbed her knee and squeezed it tightly to silence her. "This is very generous of you," she said in a more subdued tone.

"You have no idea how much your husband has come to mean to us," William began. "I can't thank you enough for all you're doing to help our Larry. Also, we have a little gift for you, Brother Cole." William reached into his inside lapel pocket and pulled out a small box. Cole opened it. A beautiful watch glimmered up at him. Greta had seen it at one of the stores she'd gone to and knew it cost almost as much as the one she'd bought. "I noticed that you weren't wearing one and thought you could use it."

Cole smiled as if he were happy but not impressed by the gift. "Thank you. It's just what I needed." Taking it out of the box, he put it on.

There was an awkward silence, or maybe only Greta felt awkward. She realized she couldn't give Cole her gift. She wasn't sure what to say, and she felt herself withdrawing into her shell again.

"Thank you so much," Cole interrupted the silence. "This has been one of the best birthdays I've ever had." The waiter offered them more coffee, and soon William and Cole were talking again, and Carol and Greta began to discuss the beautiful sunset. Inside, Greta had so many unbidden thoughts. She pushed them back. She would have time to think later.

On the way home, Cole pronounced the evening a success. He was in such a good mood that he decided to overlook Greta's little mutiny with the eyeliner.

Greta was quiet most of the ride home. She listened as Cole talked about how wise he'd been to hire Larry Herrin, and what a good job Larry was doing. It made her uneasy. She liked the Jamesons. She didn't say anything though, just listened. It was rare for Cole to share much about his work with her. She tried to respond with appropriate sounds as he talked.

"Do you realize how much this watch must have cost them? This is the expensive kind. It's nice to be appreciated for a change," he sounded bitter. She wasn't sure who didn't appreciate Cole. From the staff at the church she'd heard only good things about him.

Eventually she spoke up in such a quiet voice that he had to ask her to repeat herself.

"I did get you a gift, Cole," she repeated, a little louder. He had stopped at a stop sign near their home. She opened up the watch and showed it to him. "I got you a watch, too."

"Oh, well," he said, "I guess I can take yours back."

"I thought it was a nice watch." Greta's voice held a lot of emotion, but Cole missed it. He turned into their driveway. She handed him her gift, which he quickly pocketed.

Sitting in the car while he walked to the house, her body felt heavy, too heavy to drag inside. Her emotions had slipped back into the mouse mood that felt safe and secure. Even Rose would have found it a challenge to get her out of that mode tonight.

Chapter 11

Lead a quiet life.... mind your own business...

-I Thes. 4:11 (NIV)

Daily Bill's health improved. It had been over two weeks since the car accident, and the deep black and blue bruises, though still evident, had lightened considerably, turning a yellowish-green color. His swollen face had returned to normal, and though the severe laceration across his forehead stood out red and raw, making him feel like Frankenstein's little brother, the plastic surgeon reassured him that it was healing nicely. Eventually it should disappear almost altogether into a barely noticeable scar that his hair would one day cover. Though he ached, it was the dull pain of hurt muscles, not the excruciating stabs that he'd experienced the first days after his accident. His biggest complaint was the large, bulky neck brace rubbing painful blisters into the skin of his collarbone, choking him uncomfortably. Realizing what his life could have been like at this moment without God's protective hand, he knew he had little to complain about.

The irrational fear he'd felt the first week of his recovery had dissipated, though a general disquiet often claimed his spirit. Part of this was simply due to the fact that he hurt, and after days of aching pain, his spirit had deflated, stealing the merriment he'd once had; however, as he climbed carefully into his bed, a degree of contentment crept into his being. They'd had a pleasant visit from Mr. Robert, Mike, Nancy, and their children this evening.

A smile touched his face as he remembered Mike's offer. "If you ever decide to leave the church, I could really use you helping me in my construction business."

"Right now, I don't think I could do you much good," Bill had responded in a wry voice, glancing down at his broken body.

"You'll heal," declared Mr. Robert confidently. "If it makes you feel any better, I knew a fellow who broke his neck one time, and after it healed, the doctor said the place that had been broken was the strongest part."

That did help. Bill hadn't heard anything like that before. Part of him worried he'd be this way the rest of his life. A lightness tugged at the heaviness he'd allowed to engulf him for the past two weeks, gently lifting it away. The older man's encouraging words knocked down each of Bill's fears, one by one. The realization that Brother Cole might use this accident as an excuse to finally fire him was less haunting as he thought of the possibility of working for Mike.

Painfully reaching to turn out the lamp, he eyed the handsomely built nightstand that Mike had gotten down from the attic that very evening. Mr. Robert had adamantly insisted that his grandson bring down Nathaniel's favorite piece. *Friedensheim,* as nice as Bill had made it look, wasn't complete without it, he'd explained. With amusement, Bill lay back on his pillows, remembering the scene. The older man definitely had his quirks. And he was right. The ornate piece did add a touch of character, even elegance, to their home.

Christine's eyes had lit up at the sight of the gracefully carved nightstand. Something about the sturdy piece that had endured the years well encouraged Bill. As if he too could endure. The moon's soft light gently lit the room, making the night a little less dark than usual.

Saturday dawned hot and sweltering. The August heat wave of the Georgia summer was in full force. Bill was beginning to make progress. Though he still tired easily, he could walk through the house now without any help. Christine and the children trudged off to the grocery store, promising to return with something special to make a nice dinner.

Bill realized this was only the second time he'd been alone for more than thirty minutes since his accident, and it felt strangely refreshing. The peaceful solitude of the house reassured him. They really did have a beautiful home, he decided as he walked from room to room, trying to get some much-needed exercise. It was too hot to consider going outside.

Walking into the master bedroom, next to the living room, he gazed around. This was the most finished room in their home. The antique oak dresser with the large, beveled mirror that they'd found for practically nothing at a garage sale last spring looked good in here. On the bed laid the quilt that Grandmother Martha had made. Next to it stood Nathaniel's nightstand, looking for all the world as if it had always belonged in this very room.

Bill smiled as he left, making his way slowly down the hall to Jonathan's room. He eyed the wallpaper border with trains on it that Christine had put up the week before his accident. The trim accented the colors in the wall and the rug, creating an overall attractive effect that any little boy would enjoy. Glancing at the rug, he couldn't help but remember what Christine had told him the know-it-all Judith Gresham had said. He hoped the woman would stay away from them. From the first time he'd met her, he hadn't trusted her.

Working his way down the hall, he glanced into the small bathroom as he passed by. Replacing the old floor had been a grueling job. Suddenly a feeling of thankfulness touched him. The Lord had perfect timing, allowing Bill to get all this done so that they could move into the house before he'd had his accident.

Walking past the girls' bedroom, he glimpsed the closet at the far side with the shelves that he'd built into it. God had been gracious. How easily he forgot that.

Plodding through the kitchen and dining room, back to the living room, he felt exhausted. At least he'd made it around the house one time. With God's help, his strength would come back. Slower than he might like, but he was healing. Awkwardly he lowered himself down on the couch, breathing like an old man. He would catch his breath and then trudge through the place again. Gazing up at his reflection in the mirror over the mantel, an unshaven, shirtless ruffian from an old cowboy movie met his eye. Hopefully he'd looked better last night when his guests were here. At least at that time Christine had helped him to get a shirt on. With his broken shoulder, it was too hard to wear one unless absolutely necessary.

The doorbell rang. Probably Christine wanting him to let her in. Rising heavily from the couch, he fumbled awkwardly with the doorknob. With great effort, he finally got the door open. Outside stood his neighbor from the Castle, Mrs. Judith Gresham.

Inwardly Bill braced himself. The woman had a hard, no-nonsense, businesslike look on her face that didn't sit well with him.

"Hello, Mrs. Gresham." The heat of the day streamed in fast. He needed to shut the door before the cool air in the house was replaced by this humid, hot August heat. "Would you like to come in?"

Judith, taken aback at seeing this wounded young man answer the door, hesitated. His look unnerved her. She wouldn't have forgiven Donald if he'd been so uncouth as to open the door without having his shirt on. "Actually, I came to talk to your wife. Is she home?"

"No." Bill stepped to the side so that Judith could enter the house. He didn't want this woman to bother his wife. "Please come in. Excuse the way I look. It's hard for me to get a shirt on with my broken shoulder and neck brace."

The heat drove Judith inside. Bill shut the door and offered her a seat, but the woman continued standing. Bill settled himself slowly, painfully on the couch. "How can I help you?"

She reluctantly sat on the edge of the rocking chair. "I really don't want to bother you in your um...," she searched for the right word, "your sensitive condition. I'll come back another time." She started to rise, but Bill stopped her.

"Please, Mrs. Gresham, tell me what you need." The words "sensitive condition" hit a raw spot.

"Well," began Judith uncertainly. She set her chin in the air. She had come here to say something, and she'd say it. "I was talking to one of the neighbors recently, and she told me about you having some loud, uncouth company over to your house. That it disrupted the entire neighborhood."

Bill inwardly sighed, but his face remained blank, not revealing the ache in his soul. "When did this happen?"

Judith seemed slightly nonplused by the question. "I heard about it last Saturday while I was out walking my dog. I'm sure that the woman told me because it's common knowledge that we sold you this house. We can't have that kind of goings-on in the neighborhood, you know."

Bill couldn't imagine any of the neighbors being comfortable enough to gossip with the austere Judith Gresham. "Tell me what you heard?"

"She said that some strange people were seen going into your house last Friday night, and I felt that it was my duty to talk to you about this, especially since we sold you the house. I don't want you to bring the neighborhood down by letting people like that come into it. You've upset everyone," she declared haughtily, spitting her words out as she gave her little speech.

Bill continued to appear undisturbed, reminding himself that when someone has a weak position, they tend to get louder. He wondered just how loud Mrs. Judith Gresham could get. In a mild voice that irritated Judith he asked, "And who asked you to come talk to us?"

"No one. I felt it my responsibility to speak to you. I've seen neighborhoods go downhill before, and I won't allow it to happen here. We sold you this house in good faith, and, now, after what has happened...," she stopped in the middle of her sentence, but the implication was quite clear.

Swallowing hard, Bill thought of all the witty retorts that he could make, but answers like that would probably backfire on him. He wanted to say something to this woman that would sting her the way he felt stung. This was one hardhearted lady who wouldn't change her mind easily and could quickly destroy their reputation among the neighbors with her acid tongue. Perhaps nothing would help to persuade her that they too did not want to "ruin the neighborhood." His tone was a bit icier as he spoke, "And tell me Mrs. Gresham, what did these people look like?"

"I don't know. I didn't see them."

"What did they sound like?"

"I told you. I didn't see them, and I didn't hear them. I'm just telling you what Mrs. Cabiness said." Oops, she hadn't meant to say that.

"So you're repeating gossip?"

"Why, no." She stood, holding her handbag in front of her as if to protect herself. "I don't gossip, and I don't appreciate you implying that I do. You people have no business disrupting the neighborhood."

Bill awkwardly pulled himself up from the couch – an act that would have softened a less hard heart. Rising from a sitting position was one of the hardest things for him to do, and he felt frustrated by his inability to do it with dignity. "Mrs. Gresham, the last thing we want to do is disrupt the neighborhood." Bill had little strength to argue with this woman. "I'll be sure to go over and reassure Mrs. Cabiness."

Judith didn't want this. Mrs. Cabiness had been mortified that she would even consider talking to the Jamesons and had begged her not to repeat what had been said. Judith had promised her at the time that she wouldn't. Her voice softened, "Now, that won't be necessary. I'll tell her myself. That way she won't worry anymore."

Bill perceived the truth of the situation, realizing that Mrs. Cabiness had not betrayed his family with ugly gossip. She had just been concerned for Bill and Christine and had told her worries to the wrong person. He decided to test his theory. "I'll be happy to talk to her myself."

"Oh, no. No. Don't you worry about it. It'd be hard for you to walk over there in your condition. I'll be happy to talk with her. I'm glad we had this little chat."

Bill cringed inwardly at the audacity of this woman. Letting her think she'd won might be the best way. After she left, he shut the door, thinking of how Christine would have been mortified and probably apologized all over the place to that hoity-toity Mrs. Gresham. He would keep this little discussion to himself.

When Christine arrived home, she immediately noticed a change in Bill. He seemed withdrawn and preoccupied with his own thoughts. She had just begun to believe he was past that point. Perhaps this too was part of the healing process – Bill being depressed from time to time, but it was hard for her not to take it personally. Hopefully he'd quickly bounce back to the easy-going, quick-to-smile husband that she'd always known.

Chapter 12

He will bring to light the hidden things of darkness.

-I Corinthians 4:5

Alex Haygood walked out of the bright sunshine into the dimly lit restaurant, trying to get his bearings. Following his instructions, he headed for the back right-hand booth. Three teenagers busily stuffing pizza in their mouths greeted him. Glancing around, he heard an almost inaudible voice saying his name. Looking to his left, a thin-faced man sitting in a dark corner of another booth motioned him his way.

"Are you John?" It was in Alex's professional nature to sound friendly, even though right now he faked it. His Saturday boating trip had been canceled because of this unplanned interview. This had better be a good tip. Cynthia had assured him it might prove to be the story of the year. John nodded his head quickly, his eyes darting fretfully around the room. Alex seated himself opposite the squeamish man.

"My editor called. Said you had some information for me."

The uneasy man leaned in close. "Keep it down, will ya."

"Hi, gentlemen. What can I get for you today?" asked the waitress, coming around from behind the booth. John's leg whacked the bottom of the table as he jerked at the sound of her loud voice.

"Buffet for me," responded Alex pleasantly, ignoring the man's jangled nerves, hoping the waitress would do the same.

"Just water," replied John quietly.

"Get the buffet, John. Lunch is on me," Alex spoke as if they were long-time friends. "We'll both have the buffet."

"Help yourselves. The plates are right over there."

As the woman walked away, Alex leaned toward the nervous man. "People will think you're up to something if you keep acting so tense. Pretend we're old friends out eating lunch. Come on, now. Relax."

John breathed deeply as he followed Alex to the food bar. The man was right, but he'd been tense for so long – and today, of all days, he didn't want to accidentally run into any of Gresham's goons.

"I don't want to be on television," he informed Alex as soon as they sat down with their pizza. He kept looking around the room nervously, like a mouse with a cat nearby.

"That's fine," answered Alex. "Just tell me what you know."

John exhaled a deep breath, as if he were about to bear his very soul to Alex Haygood. His cloudy eyes cleared slightly as he looked for comfort in Alex's friendly face and seemed to find it. "Two years ago I started working for Gresham Electric Company."

Alex pulled a small notebook and pen out of his shirt pocket to take notes.

"When I found out what they were doing, I should have quit, but I didn't. I have a wife and children to support, and I'm ashamed to say they fired me."

Alex felt like putting his notes away. "Fired?"

"Yeah. I'm ashamed, not because I was fired, but because I didn't have the gumption to quit first."

Alex reevaluated. Maybe this guy was worth listening to. "Go ahead."

"At first I blabbed it around what they were doing, but then some of the workers – at least I think it was them – came to me one night right before Christmas last year and beat me up. I thought I was gonna die."

"Where'd this happen?"

"At the parking lot at Georgia Square Mall. I'd been Christmas shopping for my children. I didn't have much for them since I'd been fired, but I'd gotten a couple of little things. It was dark, so I couldn't see them real good. I think they were waiting for me by my car. When I went to put my keys in the door, one grabbed me from behind, and the other one started punching me. I didn't know who they were. They just came out of nowhere. I thought maybe they were muggers, and I told them to take my money, but they laughed and said they didn't want my money. They just wanted me to keep my mouth shut. That's why I figured it was some of the men at the company. If they find out I've talked to you, I don't know what they'll do." He glanced around the room nervously, then slid back into the recesses of the booth.

"Don't remember hearing about this?" Alex couldn't, of course, remember every incident that happened in the Athens area, but the mall was close enough to his own home that he'd have remembered hearing if someone had been assaulted there, and the newsroom received all the police reports. He should have heard about this.

"I didn't go to the police. I was afraid to go to the hospital at first, but my wife finally made me. I told them I'd fallen down the stairs. I don't think they believed me, but they didn't push the issue."

"What made you decide to talk again?"

"It's not right what they're doing, Mr. Haygood. My conscience eats at me all the time. The other day I talked to an old friend who told me that her grandmother called Gresham Electric when her air conditioner went out last month. Said the woman had been charged two thousand dollars to have her entire electrical system redone in her house. The woman now thinks she might have to sell the place in order to make ends meet. I'm ashamed I ever worked for them and that I was intimidated into keeping my mouth shut." He squared his eyes on Alex. A light fire burned in them. "It isn't right what they're doing. I hoped you could look into it. Maybe that way people would know the truth and not get ripped off anymore."

Alex felt more compassionate. This didn't sounded like a vendetta. The man had a conscience and a dilemma, wanting to protect his family and wanting to stop a company from hurting old ladies. "As long as you tell me the truth, I'll keep your name out of this," he promised.

"Thanks. I'll tell you everything I know."

Contemplating John's face, Alex realized the man looked older than he probably was. He hadn't touched his pizza. "Start eating and try to relax so you won't look suspicious," Alex exhorted gently. "Tell me as specifically as you can what they did?"

His quiet professionalism was more like a therapist than a newsman. John found himself telling more than he'd planned. It felt good to get it all out.

Alex listened, and the more he heard, the more he thought this would be a good story. He needed to check it out, of course, and he would. "Here's my home phone number. I don't give this out to many people. Use it only if you have more information or if you think they know you've talked to me." Alex handed the thin man his card as they were about to leave. "You go out first. I'll pay, then follow you to make sure you get safely in your car."

John scrutinized the restaurant one more time. Everything looked clear. He picked up and ate his last bite of pizza. He loved pizza, and it did taste good. Thanking Alex, he rose to leave, a less burdened young man. At least Alex hadn't made light of his situation. If anything, he seemed to be an ally.

Alex glanced around. The only other customers were two older ladies and some high school kids. They looked innocent enough. He finished the last few bites of the food on his plate. John was getting in his car now. It looked as if their conversation had gone undetected by anyone who might be concerned. Alex mulled over what he'd just heard. If half these allegations were true, this could turn into a good news story.

Chapter 13

The tongue is a fire, a world of iniquity.

-James 3:6

Sunday morning, Greta dragged herself out of bed, wondering for the hundredth time if she were anemic. She would find out soon enough. She'd finally scheduled her annual check-up. Probably she should have told the receptionist about the lump, but she hoped it would be gone by the time her appointment came. If it wasn't, her routine examination might not be as routine as she hoped it would be.

Christine backed the car into the road and began the thirty-minute drive to church. It had been exhausting getting the children ready without Bill's help. She leaned back in her seat, wanting to relax and enjoy the sunny August weather.

Abruptly the tranquility disappeared as a distressed voice from the back seat cried, "I forgot my blankey. Mama, I forgot my blankey. Can we go back and get it?"

"No, Amanda, we're already running late."

"P'ease Mama, P'ease."

"No, we'll be late."

"I said 'p'ease'."

"No. We don't have time to go back."

The distressed voice turned into a whining cry. "I want my blankey. I want my blankey."

"Do you have my sunglasses, Mama?" asked Jonathan. Christine fumbled in the box where she kept sunglasses. Good. There was a pair. She handed them to her son.

"I want funglasses. I want funglasses," insisted Amanda loudly.

"Amanda, I don't know where yours are. Look around your seat."

"I want funglasses," came the high-pitched roar.

"Jonathan, do you see Amanda's sunglasses?"

"No. Oh, yeah, I do. They're on the floor."

"Amanda, I'll get them at the next red light." The roar settled into a sniffily whine in the back seat. Finally, they reached a stoplight. Christine undid her seat belt and leaned back to find Amanda's sunglasses. Immediately her daughter quieted down. Christine looked at the tear-stricken girl wearing pink sunglasses. As the light changed, she rebuckled her seat belt. The car behind her honked his indignation that she hadn't started immediately.

I hope this is worth it, Lord, she prayed silently.

Judith Gresham arrived at her Sunday school class earlier than usual. It was her turn to do coffee time, so she'd had her cook, Elsie, make some of her delicious cinnamon rolls. In the past, she'd received many compliments on them, and several friends had asked for the recipe, but she'd told them it was a family secret. No one knew Elsie made them. They all assumed Judith had done so, and Judith didn't correct their wrong impression.

She was looking forward to giving her class a report on the Jameson family this week. They would be intrigued to know how well her talk with Bill had gone.

Some of the church ladies came up to get a cinnamon roll, commenting as they did on how delicious they were. Judith felt good. This would be her day to shine. She enjoyed the attention.

Christine arrived later than she'd hoped. All the parking places in the main lot were full. She pulled into the grocery store parking lot across the street and found an empty spot. After helping Jonathan and Amanda out of their car seats, she picked up Lauranna. The muggy morning air wrapped itself around them. By the time they reached the church's doors, Christine and all three children were soaked in sweat. Amanda suddenly didn't want to go to Sunday school and began pulling backwards. As Christine dragged her grumbling daughter into the building, she decided that she didn't ever want to do this again without Bill. The cool blast of conditioned air helped them feel better; and after a firm word from her mother, Amanda stopped balking. Christine walked to the nursery, eager to get the children in their classes so she could attend her own.

Greta arrived a few minutes late to Sunday school. She saw the delicious cinnamon rolls that she knew were brought by Judith Gresham and made by her cook. Everyone knew Elsie made the rolls, but they didn't mention it to Judith. Greta's stomach felt a tad irritable this morning, so, to be on the safe side, she decided not to eat one. She didn't want to embarrass herself or Cole by getting sick in the middle of the morning worship service. As she sat down, she noticed that Judith seemed to have an attitude of self-importance about her. Greta would try to stay out of her way. The woman tended to snipe unexpectedly when she was in this grandiose mood. She hoped Judith wouldn't take it personally that she wasn't having one of the homemade cinnamon rolls.

Judith didn't notice that Greta sat down without any food. Eleanor Hughs, who worked at the church with Bill and was referred to by all the staff as Miss Eleanor, sat eating a cinnamon roll that she really didn't want and felt that Greta was indeed becoming quite bold these days. She hoped Judith wouldn't say anything.

Rose arrived and slid into the seat beside Greta. "How'd the birthday dinner go?"

Greta, aware of the other ladies in the class, answered, "Fine," but her face told Rose a different story. Noticing Judith Gresham listening close by, Rose decided to wait to talk to her friend about it another time. She changed the conversation, inviting Greta to go out to lunch with her later in the week. Shirley, the teacher, interrupted to say it was time to get started and asked if anyone had a prayer request.

Judith spoke up immediately, declaring she had some good news. Smugly, she repeated to the ladies her talk with Bill Jameson. A polite murmur was offered from a few of the women. Judith noticed Greta sitting quietly, examining her skirt. Rose, on the other hand, boldly stared straight at her the entire time she talked – almost glaring at her. There was no trace of a smile on her face. Judith didn't know how to take Rose and felt deeply disappointed by the basically apathetic response of the class.

Eleanor, who thought highly of Bill, was also closed-mouthed. She gave no polite murmur to Judith and wished with all her heart that she had the courage to speak up to this pompous woman.

A few minutes later, Shirley began the lesson, using as her text the third chapter of James. She had chosen this scripture especially for one member of her class who had a need to hear it. She knew they all needed to be reminded from time to time of what James said, but that the person she most hoped to reach would probably be the one to not recognize her problem. The lesson was on bridling one's tongue.

Christine felt refreshed after Sunday school. She wished she could go to the worship service that would be beginning in a few minutes, but she needed to get home to Bill. Before picking the children up from their classes, she decided to go into the restroom. As she stepped into one of the stalls and locked the door, one last young woman came out of the compartment next to Christine's and began washing her hands. The door opened as someone wearing heels that made a noticeable clicking sound on the tile floor came in.

"Oh, hi, Patricia, how are you?" exclaimed an amiable voice.

"Great," answered an excited voice. "I just heard the most wonderful news. I'll explode if I don't tell somebody. Y'all are not gonna believe what Brother Cole just told Larry." It was Patricia Herrin. Christine recognized the deep southern accent. She found it odd the way Patricia would talk to one person and call her "y'all" as if she were talking to a group of people. "I heard 'em out speakin' in the hall, and he said Larry was doin' such a fine job," she lowered her voice slightly, but Christine could still hear her perfectly. "Much better than the regular fellow." Her voice grew louder in a girlish rush, "And he says that Larry could just plan on stayin' right here and workin' as the Facility Maintenance Supervisor for as long as he wants to."

"Patricia, that's wonderful."

"I know, I just can't believe it. Oh, we better hurry, or we'll be late for church." Patricia's voice faded as she and her friend walked out of the restroom. The door closed with a hollow thud behind them.

Christine felt the thud in her heart. She couldn't believe it. After all the years Bill had worked here, to be treated this way. How could she tell him? Should she tell him? He was already so depressed and preoccupied. Surely they wouldn't really fire Bill and hire Larry in his place. She leaned her head against the door.

Lord, doesn't he know we have children to feed? she thought in desperation. The hospital bills had started coming, and they owed so much money, not to mention all the doctors' bills. What were they going to do?

Chapter 14

In the shadow of His hand hath He hid me and made me a polished shaft.

-Isaiah 49:2

Christine withdrew within herself, fearful that if she talked too much to Bill she might disclose what she'd overheard. She'd thought herself fairly transparent where her feelings were concerned, and expected, maybe even hoped, that Bill would notice her quietness and try to draw her out, forcing her to disclose the ugly secret, but he was preoccupied with his own thoughts, keeping them to himself, and after a couple of days, she realized that he wasn't too interested in talking about much of anything. She had dared to hope that this might change as Tuesday, the twenty-second of August approached, but instead the day proved to be a repeat of the past few days.

It began badly with Amanda waking in a foul mood as nothing suited her. A few weeks back Christine had thought her daughter was immune to the events that had followed Bill's accident, but the little girl had changed from the happy-go-lucky sweetheart she'd once been into an irritable, whiny child. Obviously she'd been more affected by her "broken father" than Christine had first realized. Jonathan, though greatly improved, still showed signs of being disturbed. Bill, withdrawn into himself, talked very little. The baby, who had been sleeping well for the last few months, had awakened twice during the night. The process of getting two new teeth disturbed both Lauranna's and her mother's sleep. Weariness tugged at Christine's body and soul, stealing any cheerfulness that she once possessed. A depression settled over her. The seeds of self-pity grew, engulfing her as the day progressed.

Trudging out to the dreaded mailbox at noon, she found it stacked with doctors' bills. They had started coming in with a vengeance. She would put them in her desk drawer and not show them to Bill. It only upset him to realize how much they owed.

There was a nice card from her Great-aunt Josie, the only family that she had left. A bittersweet feeling touched Christine. At least someone had remembered. The roots of self-pity deepened. She felt herself withering, drawing into a cocoon of self-protection. At one point she reached out to ask

Bill if he'd be interested in going out, maybe to a movie, with her. He looked at her with disbelief and complained that it would be too hard to sit in the theater's straight-back chairs without any support for his neck. Her head understood, but her heart ached. Christine felt her zest for life zapped, and the memory of what she'd overheard at church haunted her thoughts.

In the afternoon, one of the church ladies, a Mrs. Simper, called. Christine really didn't know the woman, having to think hard to put a face on the caller. Vaguely she remembered seeing her with Judith Gresham a couple of times.

"Christine, how's Bill doing?" she'd asked as if they were old friends. Not waiting for an answer, she'd droned on, "Thought I'd call to see how y'all are getting along since Bill's terrible accident. We were so sorry to hear about it. How dreadful for you."

"Thank you, Mrs. Simper. He's better now," Christine slipped the words in while the woman took a breath.

"I'm glad to hear it. I had a friend whose husband was in an accident – not nearly as hurt as Bill was – they thought he was all right at first, but then he got so depressed that he never did get over it. He would just go sit in his room for hours at a time. His wife finally couldn't take it, poor soul, and divorced him."

"Oh, that's terrible." Christine thought about Bill's moodiness.

"Oh, yes. It was a mercy when that miserable man finally died. Had another friend whose husband fell off his tractor. Hit his head. Caved it right in. It was a pity he even lived. He became mean as a snake. Finally they put him in an institution. He's there to this very day."

"Oh my."

"Yes, dear, count your blessings. Isn't it a mercy your children weren't with him when he had his accident."

"Yes." The thought had not occurred to Christine. Her mind's eye tried to stop the visual image that imprinted itself on her brain.

"Yes, indeed. Always count your blessings. That's what I say. Glad to hear y'all are doing better. I'll have to stop by some time when I go visit Judith. A better neighbor you'll never have than that Judith Gresham."

By the time Christine hung up the phone, she felt as if she'd lost something precious and that perhaps it was not going to come back. Mrs. Simper's call had depressed her into wondering if life would continue this way for the rest of their marriage. The fact that Bill didn't remember what day it was added to her fears. It was as if he had collapsed into his own little prison, locking her out.

Later that afternoon, Catherine called. Even she remembered what day it was. She wanted to give Christine a break. "Go to a movie," she said. "Have some fun. Do something just for yourself."

At first Christine refused. It had been a long time since she'd done anything for herself. She didn't even know where to begin, but Catherine insisted. Both she and Ben were coming over at six o'clock to watch the children and Bill – no ifs, ands, or buts. So it was a few minutes after six that Christine found herself in the car, driving to the dollar theater. The movie that she and Bill had talked about seeing played there now.

Sitting alone in the car added to the depression that she had nurtured throughout the day. God was out there somewhere – somewhere far away. "Oh, Father," she finally spoke through the wall she'd built between herself and the Lord. Unshed tears trembled in her eyes. "I wish Grandma Martha were here to talk to." She needed her. The hurt that Bill had not remembered this day had grown out of proportion, but no matter, she wanted to nurse that hurt; however, it was hard to pray and nurse a hurt at the same time. *I don't know how to pray*, she thought, feeling suddenly small and unworthy and so ungrateful. "Forgive me, Lord. Help me."

Silence filled the car. The running engine with the air conditioner's hum felt like the only friend she had. It was nice to sit quietly for a moment without anyone demanding something from her. The pain began to lessen. The tranquility helped her focus on her feelings. All day she had tried to bury them, to say it didn't matter that Bill had forgotten. Bill had enough on his mind. Lying to herself only made it worse.

"Lord, I do everything for him. Can't he even remember me for one day?"

A still, small voice spoke softly, "Did you remind him?"

"No!" she snapped at the thought aloud. "He should have remembered."

"You know he loves you." The thought went through her head and deflated the anger.

"I know," she admitted, almost grudgingly. She relaxed in that realization for a moment. A prayer started. "Father, could I ask you for something?" There were no gifts today. She spoke slowly, seeking the right words. "I could use a little encouragement right now. Please send me some, and dear Lord, heal us – this family of mine. I want it back to the way it was."

As she parked the car, a butterfly flew up from the pansies planted nearby and alighted on her windshield. Its iridescent blue outlined by black winked at her before it fluttered away. Its presence seemed to whisper a silent promise. Opening her door, a cool breeze met her. The day was beautiful as the clouds stretched high across the sky, letting the wind blow them around. A slight nip in the air hinted that Autumn would come soon – her favorite time of year – and after that Christmas. They would all be together for Christmas. God had allowed them to still be together. Suddenly she felt ashamed of the way she'd nourished negative thoughts throughout the day. Yes, as Mrs. Simper always said, she needed to count her blessings. A slight smile touched her face. Since the movie didn't begin for a while, she decided to buy a soda from the vending machine and sit on an outdoor bench, allowing the birds to sing her their melody.

"Christine? Christine Riley?" She heard the voice as if from a distance, and then it came into focus, someone calling out her maiden name. Why, It was Don McCoy – an old friend that she'd known in high school. They had dated a few times, and when he'd started seeing another girl, it had broken her heart. His thick dark hair neatly combed with only a shadow of gray at the temples shined – he still was as handsome as ever.

"What are you doing here?" he asked, sitting down beside her, disconcertingly close, smelling of some wonderful scent of aftershave. She felt her heart jump into her throat as if she were still a schoolgirl.

"I was just taking a break. I thought I'd go see a movie, but it doesn't start for a while."

"I know you're not a Riley anymore, but I've forgotten your married name."

"Jameson."

"That's right. I ran into Abbie Ross a while back and heard that your husband was in an accident."

"Yeah, it was pretty bad, but Bill's doing better. Two friends of ours came over to help him take care of the children."

He placed his hand on top of hers and asked in a concerned voice, "And how are you doing?" The touch of his hand sent many unbidden thoughts through her mind. There was a tenderness in his voice that touched the loneliness she'd felt in her heart all day. No one had asked her how she was doing in a long time. She needed to talk to someone. An inward voice of caution spoke. This is not the person to talk to. No – she was too vulnerable.

"I'm all right," she answered, pulling her hand away from his.

"I know it must be hard for you. If you'd like a shoulder to lean on, you can always use mine."

"Thank you, Don." For a moment, she thought maybe this was the encouragement she'd prayed for, but deep inside she knew that wasn't true. Her Grandmother Martha used to say that Satan sent his best before God sent His and to be careful.

Remind him that you have a husband and children. "Today was a hard day. The baby got me up twice last night. She's teething right now."

It was almost funny. She could see him visibly recoil. Inwardly she smiled to herself. He was the same old Don as in high school. He was probably disappointed that she wasn't ready to complain about her husband.

"Well, it sure was good to see you again," he exclaimed too heartily as he got up. "Hope you enjoy the movie."

"Thanks," she returned with a smile as he left.

An idea occurred to her. She needed someone to talk to. She didn't have her grandmother anymore, but Mr. Robert lived close by. Suddenly feeling excited, she finished her drink, threw the can in the trash, and walked hastily to her car.

When Catherine poked her head in the bedroom where Bill was resting to tell him she and Ben were there if he needed anything, Bill felt confused. What were they doing here? Where was Christine? She'd been quieter than usual lately for some reason. It felt awkward that friends had to come in to take care of the children, that he couldn't do it himself. He asked Catherine where Christine had gone – the grocery store had been his guess – but Catherine said she thought his wife was planning on seeing a movie. A movie. Why a movie? Why now?

He lay back deeper into the pillows on his bed, trying to get comfortable. The stabbing pain was gone, but a persistent, dull ache had taken its place, making him miserable. Closing his eyes brought little relief. Earlier in the day, Christine had asked him about going and seeing that comedy that they'd heard was so good. Nancy and Mike had raved about it during their recent visit. He had thought about taking Christine to see it on her birthday. Her Birthday.

His eyes flew open, as if he'd been slapped in the face. What was today? He didn't have a calendar. He tried to think. No, it couldn't be her birthday. Sitting up, he reached for the newspaper. There it was in black and white – Tuesday, August 22. Christine's birthday.

He sunk back into the pillows, suddenly feeling ashamed. He'd been so preoccupied with his needs, his wants, and his pains, that he hadn't thought about hers. He had noticed she looked tired lately, and he'd heard her get up with the baby during the night. She had four babies right now, and he was the biggest one of all. The least he could have done was to wish her a happy birthday. He closed his eyes again, angry with himself, trying to figure out what he could do. With a little effort, he could still do something.

Hearing Mr. Robert's walker shuffle to the door, Christine summoned a false smile to her face. As he greeted her in his hearty baritone and gave her a hug, she felt the loneliness that she'd been fighting all day begin to dissipate.

The older man was surprised to see this young woman whose family he had grown to love. Even though her voice sounded happy, her brooding eyes betrayed her. He could tell this wasn't just a friendly visit. "Something wrong?" he asked in his blunt way.

"No, no. Everything's fine. It's my birthday, and I thought it would be nice to see you."

Robert contemplated her carefully. He wasn't one for small talk, and the mention of her birthday helped him to sum up the situation. "Bill didn't remember your birthday, did he?" It was more of a statement than a question.

Bill had said she wore her emotions on her face, but to be read so easily was a little disconcerting. "No," she confessed. Looking at Mr. Robert, she felt suddenly like crying. "He's never forgotten my birthday before."

"Bill has a lot on his mind these days. I could tell that when we were over there. We men have short memories sometimes. You have to remind us. He won't always be this way."

She looked at him hopefully and nodded. A tear fell unbidden down her cheek. "I feel as if I've lost so much. Everything's all confused. I feel guilty to feel bad. God saved my husband's life, and yet, here I am feeling sorry for myself over something so stupid."

"I suppose in a way you have lost something. You've had to realize that we live in a fallen world and bad things happen to everyone, even you. Kind of a hard lesson that we all have to learn." He patted her hand, a nice hard pat. "Eventually you'll be a better person for it."

"I don't feel like a better person."

"Give it time, Christine. You're tired. Let God carry you for a while. Growing hurts. It's like a dark hole. Being a shallow person is easy, but gaining depth happens only after we've walked through the dark places."

"I'm ready to get out of that hole now, Mr. Robert." Christine felt trapped and unappreciated and plain old worn down by all the expectations of her family.

"I know it's hard. I kind of figure we're all like rough diamonds, and God works on us, sometimes with just light sandpaper, but other times He chisels those rough edges right on off, and that really hurts. See, I'm hardheaded enough that God has had to chisel me a number of times. He's had His work cut out for Him, shining me up."

Christine smiled weakly. "I don't think I'm too shiny yet."

Robert laughed, pleased to see the smile on Christine's face. "You're shining up just fine. Realize it takes time. Now, tell me what's been happening."

"Well, Mrs. Simper called me on the telephone."

"Mrs. Twila Simper?"

"Yes. She told me that often when accidents like this happen that the men are never the same. She told me some awful stories about some friends of hers."

"Mrs. Twila Simper is an old busybody know-it-all. Should call her a know-it-nothing," Mr. Robert growled in disgust. "That's another thing you may as well learn, Christine. You can't believe everything you hear." But he was getting off the track. "What else has been happening? Has Bill changed a lot?"

"He's so depressed and won't talk. He used to have fun and enjoy life. Now he hardly speaks to me."

"How 'bout you?"

"I guess I'm kind of the same way. There are a lot of things I don't want to worry Bill about. I want him to get well."

"What are you afraid to tell him?"

"Well," she paused, looking into his eyes. "I haven't been showing him all the medical bills. I've gotten where I dread going to the mailbox. We seem to get new bills every day, and I can't figure out where they all come from."

"They have doctors for everything now."

"I know. There was an emergency room doctor, neurosurgeon, orthopedic surgeon, someone who read the CAT scan, someone who made the CAT scan, it goes on and on, and…," she stopped herself.

"And," Mr. Robert prodded.

"And," Christine breathed deeply, looking at the older man's concerned, brown eyes. "I overheard a conversation at church. Patricia Herrin talking about her husband, Larry. He's the one that's working in Bill's place. Anyway, she said Brother Cole thought Larry was doing such a good job that he planned to keep him. She made some comment that Larry was doing much better work than Bill in the job. It sounded like Brother Cole might be going to fire Bill."

"Whoa, that is big. You say you haven't told Bill?"

"I couldn't. I was afraid it would hurt him too much."

The older man leaned back in his easy chair, thoughtful for a moment, not wanting to give bad advice. He eyed Christine before he leaned forward, speaking carefully. "He needs to know. I think you'll have to tell him, Christine; otherwise, he'll go back to work unprepared. I can't imagine that they'd really let him go."

Christine could image it. She knew enough about Cole Odum to know it was probably true.

"That church has a lot of politics in it," Mr. Robert continued. "If that were to happen, well, perhaps Bill is better off not working there. He's a smart young man and has a lot more potential than can be used at that church."

Mr. Robert's words were a healing salve on Christine's aching heart. "Brother Cole and Bill have had problems for a while."

"Brother Cole's an odd duck. I haven't figured him out yet. He can preach a sermon that will send your heart straight to heaven and back, but yet there's something about him. I can't put my finger on it. He and Donald are good friends, and don't get me wrong, I love my son, but I don't trust people who he's all buddy, buddy with. Do you know what Brother Cole's problem is with Bill?"

"No. I don't understand it. Bill's a hard worker."

"Brother Cole strikes me as the kind of man who likes things done his way and only his way. I really think, Christine, that Bill needs to know what he's up against. If you keep trying to bottle this whole thing up inside yourself, it's gonna explode out of you one of this days or eat you alive. Bill's stronger than you think. Trust him enough to tell him what's going on. He won't fall apart. Treating him as if he's too fragile to face up to life won't do either of you any good."

"I know you're right, Mr. Robert. I guess I just needed someone to tell me it was okay to talk to Bill, especially after all the stuff Mrs. Simper said. It got me scared to tell him anything."

Mr. Robert snorted at the name of Mrs. Simper. "Sometimes when you keep things from each other, it makes you seem distant and irritable. Maybe that's why Bill's being so quiet these days. He might have some secrets of his own he doesn't want to worry you about. My policy is to keep things out in the open as much as possible. It makes for a happier marriage. Now, I'm not saying to hurt each other with what you call the truth. I've seen people do that too, and that will destroy a marriage faster than almost anything, but if something's bothering you, tell your mate. They can't read your mind."

"That's true. I didn't even remind Bill it was my birthday. He probably doesn't remember and wonders what was wrong with me today."

"We all get forgetful sometimes." The older man breathed heavily. A moistness touched his glistening eyes, as if tears were being held back. "I want you to know I loved my Grace more than life itself," he confided, a sadness touching his words. "She was the sweetest person I ever met, and I would have died in her place if I could have, but I want you to know – and don't you ever tell a living soul that I told you this – I never could remember when that poor woman's birthday was. I know now. It was April 30th, but every April I would get so busy with my planting that I'd forget it. Bless her heart. My Grace's feelings got really hurt the first few years of our marriage, but then she started leaving clues around for me. Goodness sakes, I have a mind like a sieve, and sometimes I'd still forget. Finally she'd just come out and remind me her birthday was coming about two weeks in advance. A few days before it she'd say something like, 'Can I guess what you got me for my birthday?' and I'd tease her and say, 'If you guess what it is, I'll take it back to the store,' and she'd guess, and I'd know what she wanted then, and go out and buy it. No telling what would've happened without all the reminding. I'd probably have forgotten every year with this old mind of mine."

Christine doubted that. Even now, in his advanced years, the man's mind, though it slipped from time to time, was pretty sharp. She smiled at him. She had prayed for encouragement, and here it was or here he was. He didn't mince words, but with a loving heart gave her his honest opinion.

"Now don't you go telling nobody that. Some folks set great store in remembering stuff. I knew a man who didn't forget his wife's birthday or their anniversary, but he was cheating on her all the same. Folks thought she was so lucky to have him cause he would do a big to-do for any holiday that came along, but it was all his guilt doing the sweet stuff." The elderly man smiled. Though his weather-beaten face looked hard, when he smiled, he looked kind of like a lovable, old bulldog.

Christine's heart lifted. The sick sadness she'd nourished all day disappeared. She left with a lighter step than when she'd come.

Home much earlier than expected, she was met at the front door by a surprised Catherine who stopped her.

"What are you doing home so early? The movie isn't over till nine."

"I decided not to go to the movie. I went to visit Mr. Robert instead and had such a good…," Christine began. Why was Catherine blocking her way, and what was all that giggling? That was a sound she hadn't heard in a while. "…time," she finished a little lamely, trying to look over Catherine's shoulder.

"Come on in, Christine." It was Bill, a hopeful, almost boyish look touching his face.

"Happy Birthday," yelled Amanda and Jonathan. A fancy cake sat on the dining room table surrounded by construction paper cards saying Happy Birthday.

"Catherine, you shouldn't have."

"I didn't. It was all Bill's idea. I just looked up the phone number of the bakery for him."

"And I helped some," Ben laughed. "I picked up the cake."

Bill smiled. The children ran around like little wound up cars that had just been set off. It was a happy birthday after all.

That night, after Catherine and Ben left, Christine told Bill about the conversation she'd overheard at the church. He didn't seem the least surprised by the disclosure and in turn told her about his last conversation with Brother Cole on the morning before his accident. This was nothing new to him, painful, but not unexpected. Their talk continued late into the night as they both shared events from the previous weeks with each other. A bond was reestablished between them. Through this difficult time, they would stick together, no matter the outcome. An agreement was made that they would stop treating each other like China dolls – neither of them would break by knowing the truth. Their unity strengthened them.

Chapter 15

Be alert and always keep on praying for all the saints.

-Eph. 6:18 (NIV)

The next day Bill had an unexpected visit from Sam. His right-hand man complained that Larry Herrin sat around the office all day and didn't do a lick of work. To make matters worse, Larry was supposed to be Sam's boss while Bill was out; however, every time anything went wrong, Brother Cole blamed Sam, not Larry. Sam was tired of it. As far as he was concerned, Bill couldn't return to work quickly enough.

Something was amiss, too. Though he couldn't quite put a finger on the problem, there was something peculiar in the way Brother Cole talked to Larry. Not only was the assistant pastor polite, but he was downright friendly to the young man, even though the kid kept flubbing things up. It just didn't make sense. For a short time Sam thought that Brother Cole had experienced a miraculous change of character because the man had even acted friendly toward him from time to time, but eventually he'd come to realize this was only when the Herrin boy was around. Without Larry in immediate proximity, Cole Odum was his usual contemptuous self. Bill needed to be alerted, and he needed to hurry back to work.

Larry sat in the maintenance office, feeling alone and confused. He didn't have the slightest idea what he was doing. Though he was pretty good working with his hands – that's what he'd expected to do here – Brother Cole had explained that his job was only to oversee the work. As a result Larry had a lot of free time. He wished that he'd been hired to help Sam. He could do a job if he was told what to do, but to come in cold off the streets and be expected to tell others how to keep this monstrous church clean and maintained was beyond him.

Patricia and his father were proud of him. They wouldn't be so proud if they knew he just sat around all day bored to death. But there was no way he could tell them the truth. They probably wouldn't believe him anyway. Brother Cole bragged on him so much. He was a good man, that Brother Cole. Really took good care of his workers. Even encouraged Larry, though he wasn't doing that great a job. He felt like he'd jumped into calculus without ever taking basic math. There was one odd note to Brother Cole though, but probably the man was having a bad day since it was so unlike him. Larry had accidentally overheard him reprimanding Sam just this morning. It really should have been Larry that Brother Cole complained to. Larry thought about apologizing to Sam, but the man looked so angry when he'd stormed out that Larry hadn't said a word.

Deep inside, Larry had a sinking fear that perhaps his father had something to do with his new job, especially since he was such good friends with the kind-hearted assistant pastor. When he'd asked William about it, he'd stated emphatically that it was all Brother Cole's idea to hire him, that the assistant pastor did nothing but sing Larry's praises. That helped Larry feel better for a while, but after today's incident, he just didn't know what to think. He needed to work. He had a wife to support, and boy, could she spend the money. Twice already in their short marriage he'd gone to his father to ask for help to pay off their credit card debt. He and Patricia had a huge argument about the whole thing, ending with him cutting up all her credit cards and most of his. If he could help it, there was no way he would ever go crawling back to his father again.

Well, sitting here twiddling his thumbs wasn't doing anyone any good. He rose, stretched and sauntered over to Sam's table. A to-do list lay on top of a pile of papers. He picked it up.

1) No one except Larry is allowed to use the elevator—make this clear to the rest of the maintenance staff. Larry made a mental note not to use the elevator anymore himself. He hadn't heard this rule before.

2) Polish woodwork in the church sanctuary

3) Toilet in second floor nursery is leaking

The list continued on and on. Though a few items had been checked off, there were more instructions than Sam and his crew could ever get done.

Larry wondered why Brother Cole hadn't given him the list. Instead he'd gotten a sweet little note saying, "Good Job! Keep up the good work!" What good work? A little rankling doubt crept into Larry's mind that he shoved back into its crevice. At least he knew how to shine woodwork. He searched through the cabinets, grabbing a can of polish and some rags. Today he would earn his salary.

Bill and Sam talked a long time, too long in fact, so that Sam had to hurry back to work so that his pay wouldn't be docked. While talking to Bill his anger had cooled. Bill had a level head that had helped him over the years. Sam determined he would do for Larry what he'd want someone to do for him. He confessed his rotten attitude to the Lord on his drive back to the church.

When he arrived at the maintenance office, Larry wasn't there as usual. Searching through a few nearby rooms, Sam was unable to find the boy. Well, no matter, there was work to be done. Later he'd find Larry. Walking toward the auditorium with rags and polish in hand, he hadn't expected to stumble upon the Herrin boy working as hard as anyone else. The job was almost finished. Sam began shining the pew behind the young man. Even though it was difficult, he knew he should apologize to the kid. They worked side by side for a few minutes talking small talk.

Larry felt a change in Sam's attitude and determined that his working was a big step toward their reconciliation. After a few minutes, Sam confessed to Larry his negative feelings, asking the young man to forgive him. Larry in turn asked for Sam's guidance, to help him to know what he could do to get the job done better. Sam agreed, warming up to the boy's willing spirit. He praised Larry on how well the sanctuary looked. To be commended for a job well done, that he'd actually done, helped Larry feel better about himself. Sam's sparse approval felt so much better than Brother Cole's elaborate, unearned praise.

Alex Haygood regarded his cameraman. "You ready, Warren?"

"Yeah, stand over there, right next to the box." Warren looked through his lens. "Good." His left arm went down to signal Alex to begin.

Alex turned to face the retired electrician, Lester Ross, which he'd hired. "Tell us what you've done to the house."

"All I did," answered the older man, "is put in a bad circuit breaker. This one right here." He went on to explain how they could recognize the bad one from the good ones, and how he'd marked each breaker with dye visible only under ultra-violet light. The camera zeroed in on the mark shown under the special light. "See, I put my initials on it."

"How about the rest of the house? What kind of condition is it in?" Alex's polished, professional voice contrasted with the older man's less-sophisticated accent.

"It's all right. Fine. I checked it all out. The only thing wrong is this one circuit breaker."

Alex reiterated to the camera what Lester Ross had said before he told Warren to stop taping him.

The camera stopped. "Now remember, Lester, not a word to anyone."

"Sure, Alex, you can count on me," Lester promised before walking out to his car.

Alex smiled at Mrs. Worsham. The time had finally come. "All right, Mrs. Worsham, you ready."

"Yeah, I think so." She took a deep breath.

"Just do it like you usually would," suggested Alex a little anxiously. He dialed the number and handed her the telephone.

Mrs. Worsham drummed her fingers on the coffee table, then jumped as she heard the male voice on the other end of the line. "Hello. My name's Helen Worsham. Somethin's wrong with my electricity. My refrigerator's gone on the blink. Can you send someone out? ...Not till tomorrow?" Her voice held genuine anxiety. "But my groceries 'ill go bad by then...." Her shoulders sagged. "All right," she reluctantly agreed then gave them directions to her house before hanging up the phone.

"They can't come till tomorrow. All my food 'ill go bad."

"Mrs. Worsham," Alex smiled patiently, "we'll buy you new groceries. Remember we're paying you for this. Don't worry about it." He hoped this woman was capable of filling the need. She seemed to have a missing link in her thinking processes. Why had he listened to Warren when he had said he had the perfect lady for the job? At least she had sounded genuinely concerned and very real on the telephone. This had to work.

"I just hate to see good food go bad," she brooded.

An idea occurred to Alex. A good one, he hoped. "What time are they coming tomorrow?"

"They said they couldn't come till late afternoon. I know you guys put some dry ice in there for this morning, but it won't last all the way till tomorrow."

"Wait, let me check on something." He asked Warren for Lester Ross' phone number, then phoned the man.

"I just hate waste," she complained to Warren.

"Yes, ma'am. I know. We all do."

Alex talked a few minutes on the phone, then hung up. Lester could come back the next morning. "All right, Mrs. Worsham, let's see if another company can send a man down to repair it." He dialed a phone number that he chose out of the telephone book.

"You mean you ain't gonna have that Ross fellow come fix it?" she asked incredulously.

The phone had begun to ring. Alex had no time to answer more than a cursory "No" before handing her the receiver.

She looked at him irritably as she talked on the line. "Hi, I got a broke refrigerator and need some help today. Somethin's wrong with my electricity. Can you send someone out here to fix it?" She spoke with much more authority. Maybe if she'd done this with Gresham Electric, they'd have come out today, but then again, maybe Alex would be able to catch two businesses doing the same illegal stuff. Soon they would find out. This company was sending a man over immediately.

"Warren, let's get the hidden camera attached to Mrs. Worsham." Alex didn't envy Warren's job. Surely no one would ever suspect Mrs. Worsham of being part of a sting operation.

Two hours later, the electrician talked to an anxious Mrs. Worsham. "Only thing I can find wrong is this one burnt out circuit breaker. I've got one in my truck. Give me a minute to get it."

The man walked outside. Mrs. Worsham whispered, "How am I doing?"

"Great," came back the nervous reply. *Please don't expose us, Mrs. Worsham,* thought Alex.

A few minutes later, the electrician walked back in and replaced the bad circuit breaker. "Got it all fixed. Let's see if that refrigerator's working." It was. Mrs. Worsham breathed an audible sigh of relief. Either the woman was a good actress or she didn't understand the game they were playing. The electrician gave her the bill for forty-five dollars, parts and labor. "Here's the old circuit breaker. I'll just put it in the trash if that's all right."

"No!" Mrs. Worsham shouted.

The electrician looked surprised. "It can't be used again. See, it's burnt out."

"I don't want it burning the house down," she responded. Obviously the phrase burnt out sounded ominous to her.

"Okay. I can throw it away at the shop. Call me if you have any more trouble."

After he left, Alex breathed a sigh of relief and turned off the camera. Mrs. Worsham sat down heavily on the sofa. "I don't think I can do this again," she said wearily. "It's too hard on my heart."

"You did great." Alex felt like he'd caught some good footage on tape.

Mrs. Worsham rubbed her head where a headache was forming. "I'm not good at this cloak and dagger stuff. Can Warren do it tomorrow instead of me?"

"You need to be here because you're the one who made the phone call." Alex didn't add that anyone who wanted to take advantage of someone would find Mrs. Worsham an easy target.

"You did just fine. You don't need me. This was like a practice run. Tomorrow will be easier." Warren's reassuring voice and manner helped Mrs. Worsham to brighten. Alex decided his cameraman was probably good with animals and children, too.

"All right," said Alex, ready to leave. "We'll be back at nine in the morning." He was tired. Time to unwind. If this worked, it could prove to be the biggest story of his career so far.

The next morning was warm and sunny. Alex hurried out of bed, ready to get his day's work accomplished. Quickly eating breakfast, he hurried to his car to drive to Mrs. Worsham's house.

Lester Ross came back and installed another broken circuit breaker. Mrs. Worsham immediately began panicking about the fact that the dry ice probably wouldn't last long enough to keep everything cold. Alex didn't really like the idea of dry ice, fearful that it would arouse suspicion, but it was the only way to calm the older woman.

Finally a little before two o'clock, the Gresham Electric Company's van came up the driveway. Warren and Alex hurried to their position in the closet. Mrs. Worsham answered the door. She looked less nervous today, Alex noted with approval as he watched from his hiding place. Mrs. Worsham's hidden camera and mike were on her. Warren turned on the second camera looking through the peephole in the closet.

"Well, thank goodness you're finally here," Mrs. Worsham stated emphatically. "I've been waiting all day. The dry ice in my refrigerator's almost gone. All my food's gonna spoil if you don't hurry. What took you so long?"

Alex was disconcerted by the woman's entire approach. But perhaps this was the way someone would act in similar circumstances.

"Sorry, ma'am," the heavy-set electrician responded. "We're pretty busy with this heat wave. Tell me what the problem is."

"My refrigerator and this light," she pointed to the kitchen light above her sink, "aren't working."

"Where's your box?"

"What box?"

"Your electrical box," he replied a little annoyed.

She showed him, and he began pulling out circuit breakers.

"Looks like you've a problem here, ma'am. This whole box is out of date. All these circuit breakers are old. Look here." He showed her a circuit breaker. It was not the broken one. "See this dark color. It means it's going bad. To be on the safe side, I need to replace the entire box. If I don't your house could burn down."

"The house could burn down." Mrs. Worsham seemed genuinely shocked. "Show me that breaker thing again."

"See, right here, that little bit of darkness on it. Oh, look at this one. It's much worse." This time he had pulled out the broken one. "It's a miracle your house hasn't burnt down already. I need to fix all of it."

"You mean the whole box is bad?" she asked incredulously.

"Yes, ma'am."

"You mean my house could have burnt down?"

"That's why I'm here. I'm gonna fix it, and you won't have to worry 'bout a thing."

"How much is it gonna cost?"

"Well, these are the old kind of circuit breakers. They're harder to find. They cost quite a bit more, but if I don't do it, you could lose your home in a fire. I wouldn't trust this thing."

"All right. Do what you have to do." Mrs. Worsham sat down on the couch with her hand on her forehead. Alex was glad they had the back-up camera. The woman had obviously forgotten about the camera on her. He hoped she wouldn't accidentally break it.

"May I use your phone. I need to get someone from the shop to bring me some parts."

Mrs. Worsham nodded. Alex hoped the woman wouldn't have a heart attack right there on the couch.

"Hey, Joe. This is Greg. Listen, I need some circuit breakers." He described what he wanted. "Yeah, I know they're hard to get, but I need them right away."

Alex was suddenly dismayed as he realized Mrs. Worsham had left the room.

He motioned to Warren and took over the camera. They'd have to use their backup plan. Quietly Warren left the closet, climbed out the open window, and walked around the house to the kitchen door. As he entered, the electrician was saying, "Yeah, I know. Well do the best you can. This lady needs it fixed tonight. We don't want her house to burn down."

After Greg hung up the phone, Warren introduced himself as Mrs. Worsham's son. The electrician explained the problem and said, "I think your ma's kind of upset."

"Oh, I better go check on her."

"I'm gonna start working on this box while they bring me the right parts. The electricity to the house will be off for a while."

Warren found Mrs. Worsham in her bed. She had put a cool cloth over her forehead. "What are you doing?" he whispered.

She answered angrily, "That Lester fellow ruined my house. It could have burnt down on me without me even knowing it."

This woman was gullible. Warren wasn't sure how much he should tell her. After all, she might let on to the whole thing. "Let me have your camera and mike. I'll take care of the rest of this. You rest. Don't worry. We aren't going to let your house burn down."

She was relieved to hand over the equipment. Warren went back into the living room. An hour later, the job done, Joe and Greg got ready to leave. Warren noticed that they kept all the parts.

"Got it finished. Tell your mother that I'm sure the house won't burn down now. It's as good as new. Here's the bill."

Warren looked at it. Even he was shocked. "One thousand and seven dollars? Why's it so high?"

"Well, those circuit breakers are the old kind. They hardly even make them anymore so the parts are expensive, and then there's the labor charge. You can look around and find that we charge less for labor than any other electrical company in Athens. I had to charge you for both of us, since my partner here had to bring the parts." The two men left.

As they backed down the driveway, Alex got on his radio. "It's time, Max." He hadn't expected to have two vehicles come. Not being sure which one Max should follow, he voiced his indecision.

"I saw which van the parts were put in. I'm following it. I'm right behind them," answered Max's voice on the radio.

Alex felt pleased. Unless some of the equipment had malfunctioned, they'd gotten it all on tape, and it would be good. He hoped to get more. He wanted this to air as soon as possible.

Warren was back in Mrs. Worsham's bedroom. Alex could hear him gently trying to explain to her that she'd just been conned, that her house had not been about to burn down. The men had used that tactic to scare her into letting them fix more than was necessary and charge her all that money. He explained that they would pay the bill, and that Lester was on his way back over here to make sure that they'd really fixed her house and not messed anything up.

Lester arrived twenty minutes later to check out the work done. They taped him explaining that everything looked to be in good working order. He said that these circuit breakers could be found in any electrical store at a low price. The company had charged Mrs. Worsham triple the usual price. Alex made a mental note to take his camera crew by an electrical supply store to show the viewers how much this particular brand of circuit breaker actually did cost.

A couple of hours later, Mrs. Worsham finally calmed down, the phone rang. It was Max. Greg had stopped by two houses before going back to the shop. He gave Alex the addresses.

"Good," declared Alex. "Come on, Warren, let's go see if we got anything."

Mrs. Betty Rhodes was indignant. The large bill was upsetting enough, but then to have perfect strangers looking at her circuit breaker box only added to her displeasure.

"Oh boy, we got them," yelled Lester with glee. "Lookee here. Here's my initials."

"I don't understand," Mrs. Rhodes questioned. "You mean these came from someone else's house?"

"They took them from another lady's home, telling her they'd gone bad, and then they put two of them in your box," Lester explained.

"Do you mind if we get your story on film?" asked Alex.

"Mind! You better believe I don't mind. I want to get those creeps!"

The interview recorded and over, they went to the next house and found three more circuit breakers from Mrs. Worsham's home. This woman, embarrassed and upset by the whole episode, didn't want her face on the screen. She felt she'd been made a fool of. They recorded her voice, and what Lester had to say as he showed the camera the circuit breakers.

Alex beamed as he headed home that night. Georgia could soon say goodbye to Gresham Electric Company and their immoral practices.

Chapter 16

The Lord is nigh unto them that are of a broken heart.

-Psalms 34:18

With extreme fatigue, Greta climbed into the shower. The warm water felt good. Hopefully it would help wake her. She felt as if she were fighting off a virus, but then again, she'd felt this way for a long time. The lump was still there. Perhaps her doctor would allay her fears this morning.

Slowly she dressed, putting on the forest green outfit that her daughter had gotten her for her birthday two years ago. Cindy had good taste, Greta decided, feeling content as she thought about her sweet daughter. Pulling out the silver necklace that her son, Brad, had given her last Christmas, she felt that same contentment. The thought of the lump invaded her serenity.

"Lord," she spoke aloud as if she could see Jesus in the room with her. The house was empty and she did this often, feeling His presence. "I really look forward to living with you one day, but I hate the idea of leaving my children and grandchildren. They're such good kids." She sighed.

If she could find the earrings that Brian had given her for Christmas, she'd be wearing something from each of her children. She looked through her jewelry box. There they were. Green and silver to match her dress and necklace. She felt pleased with the overall effect.

Looking at the clock on her nightstand, she realized she needed to hurry so she wouldn't be late for her appointment. She picked up her inexpensive watch and put it on. The watch she'd so carefully picked out for Cole sat unused in the basket that he tossed coins and knickknacks into on top of his dresser. He hadn't bother to take it back yet, and he probably never would. She wished she hadn't bought it. She had foolishly tried to buy his love. Briefly she'd considered taking the watch back to the store herself, but it was his. Obviously he didn't know how much she'd spent on it, or he would have returned it by now. He probably hadn't even looked at it. Well, she wasn't going to tell him. She hurried on out to her car.

At the doctor's office, Greta waited for an hour in the expensively furnished waiting room before she was brought into a small, white, glaringly-lit room where she waited another forty minutes until the doctor came. Running

110

behind as usual, he was in a hurry until he felt the lump. Then he slowed down.

"How long have you had this?"

"I don't know."

"When did you first notice it?"

"Sometime after Christmas."

"And you waited this long to come in?"

"I thought it'd go away."

After all the information out there on breast cancer, didn't this woman know better. She was old enough. He lectured her, ignoring the withdrawn expression on her face. If women didn't take care of themselves, what did they expect from him? He wasn't God.

"We'll need to run some tests. Since you've waited this long, I think that we should do it immediately." He began rattling off tests that needed to be done, telling the nurse to go schedule the appointments necessary.

Greta froze into a small shadow, her mind squeezed tightly shut, turning off the doctor's voice, making all words noise without meaning, not accepting any of this. Finally he left, leaving her in silence. She dressed clumsily, fumbling with her buttons, willing her hands to work for her. Sitting down in the little dressing cubicle to put her stockings on, the fluorescent light bulb buzzed angrily at her.

A whispered whimper escaped her lips. *Oh, Jesus,* her agonized soul cried out, *make it go away.*

Chapter 17

Man is like a breath, his days are like a fleeting shadow.

-Psalms 144:4 (NIV)

"One, two, free, four, five, six, nine, ten. Weady or not here I come." Amanda whooped as she began searching for Jonathan. Jonathan was a good hider and sometimes hard to find. "Where Jonafan?" Amanda asked her mother after a few minutes.

"I don't know." Christine cracked the last egg into the cake mix, washed her hands, and helped the little girl find him. He was under his bed as quiet as a mouse. The two children squealed in glee when he was found.

"My turn. My turn," yelled Amanda. "I hide now."

Jonathan went into the kitchen and started counting. Amanda threw herself on the kitchen floor, covering herself with her blanket.

"...twenty-seven, twenty-eight, twenty-nine," Jonathan paused to think of the next number, then stopped worrying about it. "Ready or not, here I come," he yelled and walked over Amanda, pretending that he didn't see her. "Hm... Where's Amanda?"

Under the blanket, a giggle erupted. Jonathan picked up the edge of the blanket. "I found you."

Amanda jumped up and down. "Your turn now. You hide."

"You stay in the kitchen and count."

Amanda toddled next to Christine's leg and hid her head. "One, two, free, four, five," she began. There was an ominous crash followed by a little boy's voice saying, "Uh-oh."

Oh, great, Christine thought as she hurried toward the sound. The nightstand they'd brought down from the attic lay on its side. Blessedly Jonathan wasn't hurt.

"Sorry, Mama, I tried to hide under it, and it fell over." Jonathan looked small and contrite as he explained.

Christine took a deep breath, eyeing the beautiful nightstand lying on its side. The drawer had fallen open slightly. The lamp that rested on top of it had managed to land on the bed unbroken. "Remember never to get under it again," she scolded.

"Yes, ma'am."

Bending down, she carefully lifted it. "Well, let's make sure it's not

112

broken." She examined the backplate, top plate, spindles, and legs. The drawer slid back in its compartment without difficulty. Thankfully it had landed on a pillow one of the children must have knocked on the floor earlier.

"It looks like it's all right," pronounced Christine with relief. Amanda and Jonathan began touching it like mini-surgeons. They made appropriate sounds as they looked carefully to concur with Christine's opinion.

"Yup, it's otay," Amanda determined heartily.

"I don't know, Mama." Jonathan sounded concerned. "What are these gold things here?"

"Oh, those are some hinges that they used to hold it together," Christine answered distractedly, remembering the cake she had to finish. She put the nightstand back against the wall.

"What do hinges do?"

"Well, they're used to open things, like the door. See it has hinges on it." Her mind began clicking. Why did this table have hinges on it? They were right behind the drawer area, but the drawer pulled out. It didn't use hinges. She pulled the nightstand out from the wall. She hadn't consciously noticed them when she'd cleaned this piece with furniture polish the other night, but sure enough there were hinges hidden underneath the wooden panel on top of the drawer. "Go get your Daddy, Jonathan. I want to ask him about these. You may be right. This is kind of strange."

Jonathan darted from the room to find Bill, shouting as he went. "Daddy, we found hinges. We found hinges."

"Hinges?" Bill laughed as he walked into the bedroom; then, seeing the nightstand, a confused expression crossed his face. "Why would that little table need hinges?" He got down on the floor for a closer look.

"I don't know. It's odd, isn't it?" Christine said.

"Yeah, let me look at it." He fingered the hinges. "Looks like this top part above the drawer should open in some way."

Amanda and Jonathan poked their heads in front of their father's making it hard for him to see. Jonathan commented, "Yeah, that's it, Daddy," and little Amanda echoed, "Yeah, that's it Daddy." Even Lauranna in her walker tried to get closer for a better look.

"Kids, move so Daddy can see better," Christine directed.

Bill pulled the drawer out of its pocket and laid it on the floor. The children gathered around it as if they were inspecting a rare diamond. Reaching inside the cavity to feel where the drawer had been, Bill felt briefly frustrated. His neck brace prevented him from being able to look into the hole as he would have liked.

"There's a little catch of some kind here. I can feel it, but I can't open it with my broken finger."

"Let me try," Christine exclaimed. Bill pulled his hand out. She felt around until she found the assemblage. Gently she pushed the catch, moving it slightly. "I felt it give." There was a little sound as the latch unhooked.

Bill carefully pushed the top plate upward and the top of the nightstand lifted easily. "It has a hiding place."

"Look, Jonafan, a hiding place."

"Wow."

"Look, Bill. There's a book in here." Christine pulled it out, opening it to its first page. "It's Nathaniel Miller's journal."

They looked at each other in astonishment. "Well, who would have guessed?" Bill grinned. "After you finish your cake, why don't we sit down and read it together."

Christine grimaced, having forgotten her cake completely. Returning back to the kitchen, in less than ten minutes the cake was in the oven. She sat beside Bill on the couch, anxious to find out about this man who had once lived in their home.

The diary began on Friday, March 7th, 1919, Nathaniel's tenth birthday. He had received the journal as a present from his mother. Though the writing had an immature scrawl and from time to time the words were written in German, it was easy to read. He talked a lot about his older brother Oden, and what the two of them did together. Apparently they came from a big family because sisters and brothers as well as aunts, uncles, and cousins were frequently mentioned. The events were basically mundane things that happened to young boys – broken windows, arguments, fights, and school happenings. Nathaniel, a rather shy, slightly awkward boy grew up through the pages. Oden, his outgoing brother often helped Nathaniel deal with a crisis or a bully. The young Nathaniel Miller came to life to Christine. An odd sense of having somehow known this young boy struck her. From time to time, the stories had the vaguest ring of familiarity to them, as if she'd heard them before.

Reluctantly she stopped her reading – time to get dinner ready. With a sense of putting a treasure back into its box, Christine returned the journal back to its hiding place.

After dinner, though Christine wanted to read more about Nathaniel, when Bill suggested they take a walk, she agreed. Bill, hoping to go back to work on Monday, wanted to get all the exercise he could so he would be in the best condition possible. The August evening had cooled pleasantly, sending sweet scents of cedar their way. Echoes of summer play could be heard throughout the neighborhood.

Christine smiled as they walked, pleased that Bill wanted to get out. Ever since their talk last Tuesday night, things had been better. She knew that she felt relieved to not bear her burdens alone, but it was more than that. Somehow, no matter what happened, they would survive.

The half-mile walk to the little church down the hill went quickly. Amanda and Jonathan ran most of the way, and Lauranna encouraged her stroller to go as fast as possible by rocking in it. Christine admired the small, white chapel with the tall steeple – Deer Creek Church, Est 1881. Nathaniel had gone here as a boy. The old cemetery was large, going back over many acres of land. A couple of the grave markers were dated as early as 1882, and there were newer ones dated up to the present year. Some of the gravestones were broken. Others had been damaged by water and wind and could no longer be easily read. Christine wondered about the people buried here.

Having read part of Nathaniel's journal made her realize more fully that at one time all these people had lived and breathed as she did now. Life was but a vapor. One day her body would be buried as theirs were. It made her feel small. She was thankful that there was more than death and the grave to look forward to. There was the hope and promise of heaven. As she stood in the churchyard, the song of a whip-poor-will lovingly rose above the gentle breeze, calling her children home.

Chapter 18

Tomorrow go out against them; for the Lord will be with you.

-II Chronicles 20:17

Bill pulled himself out of bed. His muscles stiff. His joints aching. Uneasiness crept over him as he prepared to go back to work. No telling what would happen today. The morning began rather mechanically as Christine dressed the children and drove him the half-hour trip to the church. Taking the elevator to the third floor – thankfully Brother Cole wasn't around to see him do it – he felt oddly out of place.

This, the twenty-eighth day of August, made almost five full weeks since he'd worked. His office was basically the same. The only sign that Larry had been there was a mug with the young man's name on it. Late last week, Sam had called to tell him that he actually enjoyed working with the Herrin boy. Bill wondered where Larry would fit in now, and where he, himself, would fit in. He knew he could use the extra help, but what would Brother Cole have to say about it?

Glancing at his desk, all looked the same except for a few notes to Larry from the assistant pastor – downright flowery messages. A knot formed in his stomach. What was Brother Cole up to? On Sam's table, the assistant pastor had left his usual cursory to-do list. The man treated Sam with the same contempt that he had always treated Bill with. The door creaked open, tightening the knot in Bill's gut. It was Sam.

Seeing his boss and friend, Sam greeted him heartily. "This is a good week to come back. Margie just told me that Brother Cole and Pastor Leonard are going off to do a two-week revival in Columbus."

Relief flooded Bill. He would have a short reprieve.

"She gave me the list of what Brother Cole wants done while he's gone. It's the usual mile long."

Bill smiled at Sam's exaggeration. "Maybe you, I, and Larry can develop a routine, and there won't be any problems when Brother Cole comes back."

"Yeah. Bill, I really misjudged that kid. I thought he was downright lazy. Just wanting to sit around and get paid, but once I started helping him, he turned into a good worker. He really is an okay kid. He just shouldn't have been put in charge. I still don't understand why Brother Cole did that. When he brought Larry in here that first day, he carried on about how experienced

Larry was. All this stuff. The boy confessed to me he's not done anything like this before in his life. Sure is good to have you back, Bill. I prayed you'd be up to it."

"Thanks. I still have a ways to go though."

"Don't worry. What we need around here is someone to get us organized. I never realized all the stuff you had to deal with until the last few weeks."

The door opened as Miss Eleanor walked in. Seeing Bill, the usually dignified woman squealed her delight, wrapping him in a hug. Bill felt at home again. Any of the strangeness he'd been feeling disappeared.

"Well, Alex, it's good, real good." Alex could tell by her expression that his producer, Cynthia, was impressed. "We need to check it out with Mr. Brock. He'll probably want to have his lawyers look at it. If we aren't careful, we could get sued on this one. Boy, oh boy – you got 'em good."

Alex was pleased. It had turned out well. Better than he'd hoped. It still needed some editing, but he'd done a fair amount of that already. He'd wanted to present as much as he could to Cynthia before he started chopping it down for their evening news investigative report.

"There's a lot here. I think we might use the whole half hour, and really we can't let it air without getting this electric company's side of the story or at least trying to talk to them. I know Mr. Brock will insist on that."

"Yeah, but I didn't want to say anything until you told me if I needed to do more undercover work."

"Good point. I think you have enough." Cynthia smiled her enthusiasm. "I like the way you integrated the different parts, letting the store owner tell how much those goods really cost and then having the electrician explain why they're so expensive." She shook her head in disbelief. "This is good, Alex, real good. What these people are doing is wrong. They should be stopped. I have a feeling once we air this story, all of Georgia can say good-bye to Gresham Electric forever."

"I certainly hope so."

"I've a meeting with Mr. Brock at one today. Let me find out what he has to say before you interview the owner. Check with me tomorrow. Take a break now. I think you deserve one."

Alex whistled as he walked out of the building. Gresham Electric deserved to be closed down. People needed to realize these kinds of things were happening, probably not only with this one small company, but with many others throughout the state. If people wised up, these scams could be stopped. Alex hoped Mr. Brock would air his piece soon.

Greta helped Cole pack his clothes for the revival. It was unusual for both Pastor Leonard and her husband to go together, but apparently this was a large, prestigious church that wanted the two men. As they worked, she considered telling him about the tests that she was having done that afternoon, but she feared he'd pass it off as a silly woman problem that he was going to have to waste money on. Not wanting to hear that, she remained close-mouthed.

The watch she'd given him for his birthday still sat on his dresser. It hadn't been moved from the basket since the last time she'd looked at it.

"Cole, do you plan on returning this watch?"

"I don't have time to fool with stuff like that."

"Do you want me to take it back?"

"I don't care. You put my shirts too close together again. They're wrinkled."

"I'll take it back if you like."

"Why are you bothering me with insignificant stuff like that right now?" All he knew was that he would be late if he didn't hurry. "Take it back if you like. I don't care," he said as he hauled two of his suitcases out to the car. She followed him with a third one and stood to watch him drive away.

Back in the house, the clock ticked loudly, clicking the seconds away, clicking her life away. She'd wasted the last few years since her children had left the house. A tear slid down her cheek. There were so many things she still wanted to do.

"Well, what's stopping you?" The thought came to her.

Slowly her tears dried. What indeed. There still was time, and there was money. But it was all Cole's money.

"Is it?" came the voice in her head.

She thought about the watch Cole didn't want. Suddenly she felt much stronger. She looked at herself in the mirror. A new determination touching her. "I may only have a few months," she told her reflection in a steady voice, "but it doesn't matter. I'm going to do the things that I keep saying one day I'll do. That day has finally come."

A peace settled on her. Walking to the kitchen, she pulled out a pen and pad. At the top of the page, she wrote: THINGS I WANT TO DO .

1) Spend more time with the children. Oh, how she missed them, and they really didn't live that far away. It was ridiculous that she didn't see them more often.

2) A family beach trip. It had been years since she'd gone to the beach.

3) Record my music - a real record. Greta thought about erasing this one. It was too unrealistic. Oh, why not. Perhaps it was impossible, but this was her wish list. She left it there.

4) A sleigh ride at Christmas time. But Georgia was too hot. Chances of enough snow were almost nil. Cindy had snow in Asheville. They could all go together.

The more she thought, the more she came up with – ordering steak at a restaurant (and not feeling guilty), having her fingernails done, building snowmen with her grandsons. The list continued. Most of the things were easy to do, but some were harder, and a few seemed almost impossible; however, with the Lord all things were possible. The clock chimed out the hour.

As Christine drove back to the church to pick up Bill, she felt apprehensive as to how his first day back at work had gone. Throughout the day, she'd prayed for her husband. Driving into the parking lot, she saw him standing by the large glass entryway. A pleasant expression on his face. With care, he eased himself into the passenger seat of the car.

"Boy, am I tired."

"How'd it go?"

"Great."

Christine glanced at him. They had promised to be honest. "Great?"

"Yeah. Brother Cole wasn't there. He'll be out of town for two weeks. It went great."

Christine grinned, pleased to hear this. Brother Cole being gone did mean that things would go much smoother for Bill.

"Larry and I had a long talk at lunch today. He's a nice boy, Christine. He seems genuinely happy that I've come back to work. Even said he'd like to work at the church as one of my helpers."

"Really?" Christine asked, finding that hard to believe.

"Yeah. He told me that Brother Cole kept buttering him up, and he didn't know why considering that he really didn't know what he was doing. He asked me if Brother Cole was just the kind of person that was always positive."

Christine made a rather unladylike noise that sounded somewhat like a snort. Bill laughed. "I know. I made that same undignified sound that you made when he asked me."

"Undignified. I'll have you know that I'm not undignified," Christine giggled.

"You snorted," Bill declared.

"I did not snort. I don't snort, and I don't intend to ever snort, Mr. Bill

119

Jameson," she returned in a dignified voice before they both burst into laughter. It felt good to laugh again. "Anyway, what did you say?"

"Well, first I snorted, and then I said, 'No way, he's the most negative person I know.'"

"You didn't."

"I did. He seems honest, Christine, not like someone who would try to steal my job."

"Yeah, I remember Brother Cole seemed that way at first, too," Christine said cynically. She had stopped trusting people the way she used to.

"Well, right now. Larry works for me. He's a good worker. We got a lot done today. I'm exhausted." Bill tried to rub under his neck brace. "My neck hurts. I wish I didn't have to wear this stupid thing so long." He remembered the wreck every time he touched it.

"Me too," agreed Christine.

"Any bills today?"

"Thank goodness, no. After Saturday, I was afraid to go to the mailbox." Saturday had been bad news from the insurance company saying that the plastic surgeon charged too much, that they weren't going to pay a large portion of the bill.

"I called the plastic surgeon's office. They told me they'd send a special letter explaining the circumstances. I'm sure it'll work out," Bill said optimistically. "After all, it wasn't like I could go out and pick the surgeon of my choice."

Even if they had to pay the extra money, it was nice that their future was beginning to look brighter. At least they both hoped it would be. Two weeks without Brother Cole around would be a welcome relief, and Bill had managed to make it through his first day back at work. They both felt optimistic.

Chapter 19

To every thing there is a season, ...a time to be born and a time to die.

-Ecclesiastes 3:1-2

Christine read Nathaniel's journal whenever she had a spare moment. The boy grew into an insightful man that she was sure she would have liked had she known him. In some ways, his life held a bitter sweetness that was part of this world. He never married, though he fell in love with a young woman named Marta. As a teenager, he'd actually gotten up the courage to ask her if he could walk her home from church, and she'd happily agreed, but her father, perhaps unknowingly, had insisted that she walk home with another boy, Frank, that night.

Nathaniel didn't care too much for Frank. The two went to school together, and Frank was described as an extremely polite "fabricator who had trouble sticking to the truth"; however, his pa owned a lot of land, and Marta's father liked him and encouraged their relationship. Eventually, much to Nathaniel's disappointment, Marta and Frank married.

Christine felt for Nathaniel when she read that part. She'd hoped that the shy young man would overcome his bashfulness and win the kind Marta to himself, but this wasn't to be. Nathaniel had never declared his affection and probably Marta didn't know his deep love for her. At least their friendship continued throughout the years as he saw her from time to time.

When she became pregnant, Frank apparently philandered. Nathaniel himself happened to see the man one evening in a dark corner of the theater being "too friendly with a strange woman." His heart went out to Marta, and he determined to be as correct as he could be in his behavior, but at the same time, to help her anyway that he knew how.

Marta's daughter was born in December, and the beautiful Nativity that Christine had found in the attic was given as a gift to the child. Marta had loved it, but Frank had not been pleased and had made her return it. Nathaniel, embarrassed, kept a respectful distance from that time on. He didn't want to cause any problems for his friend. Every once in a while, he'd mention something he did anonymously to help Marta when Frank was gone "selling" for overly long periods of time, but less and less did he write of her.

In 1938 he and Mr. Robert started building *Friedensheim*. One entry Christine found especially intriguing.

March 16, 1939

I put in an extra wall today. Don't think anyone will notice. Hope not. Only I know about it, and I'll keep it that way. I'm going to put the angels and Christ Child in there so they'll be safe. It's fun to have a secret place. The letters from Tante Corey have stopped coming. We don't know why. Mutter's worried, especially now that Vater is gone. She's sure Corey would have answered her letters. We keep hearing bad things over the radio about Deutschland. Most people don't care much about it, but with family over there, you can't help but worry.

Christine paused in her reading to wonder about the "secret place." Could there be a hiding place in their home? It was hard to fathom. Bill knew this house backwards and forwards from all the work he'd put into it, and he hadn't seemed to notice anything out of sync. One day she would show this entry to him to get his opinion.

Aunt Corey and her family eventually made it to America, though other family members and some friends were not heard from again. This was a grieving time for Nathaniel's family, and when the war started, he apparently went off to fight, leaving his journal behind.

Years went by, and Nathaniel continued to love Marta from afar. Watching out for her welfare was one of his goals in life. Every once in a while, he would do something secretly to help her or her daughter. Apparently Frank wasn't the best of husbands and would leave the two to fend for themselves for extended periods of time. Nathaniel, careful not to get caught, did his little acts of kindness. It was doubtful that Marta ever knew that it was he.

A touching entry caught Christine's attention:

December 22, 1976

Today I ate lunch at Woolworth. While I was there, Marta and her granddaughter came in to do some Christmas shopping. When Marta saw me, she asked if they could join me. Of course I said yes. It was like old times. Marta was as gracious as ever. I don't know if a better woman has ever walked this earth. God gave me a Christmas present just to sit and talk with her. We talked about our school days, and the grandchild listened with wide-eyed fascination. Somehow I felt that if I'd had children, I would have had one just like her.

I put out the old Nativity tonight. Had to go up to the attic to get it – and then to my secret place. I'm getting too old for this. The Nativity sure looks pretty though. Wish I had someone to pass it on to, like Marta's granddaughter. I don't dare give it to her. Marta would know it was from me. So would Frank. Robert tells me Frank would get over it and not to worry. Frank don't think so good anymore anyway. I don't know. It's just not my way. I can write, but I can't talk. Wish I had me a little granddaughter.

Christine wished that she knew Marta's family so that she could give this Nativity to the granddaughter. Reading on, the entries became more sparse as Nathaniel's health began to deteriorate. He had to give up more and more of the farm work. Then suddenly the last entry came.

Nov. 7

My Marta is gone.

That was it. The empty pages seemed to symbolize that Nathaniel died with her. Surely there was more, Christine thought as she carefully thumbed through the remaining pages. In the back of the book were only some Bible verses.

Closing the diary, a single tear fell down her cheek. The whole final story struck a cord as she felt Nathaniel's loss, mixed in with some of her own pain – pain from the sudden loss of her own parents and then her grandmother. Life was hard. She would be careful to treasure Nathaniel's book. Years were reflected; a life shown in the pages. She understood better why Mr. Robert spoke so fondly of his friend, and here, she was in Nathaniel's house, in the house of peace, in *Friedensheim,* the house with a blessing.

Chapter 20

Weeping may endure for a night, but joy cometh in the morning.

-Psalms 30:5

"What were the results?" Rose noticed that Greta had ordered a steak, baked potato, and salad. A good appetite must mean good news.

Greta sipped her soft drink. "The doctors say it's malignant. They want to do surgery next week." Her voice sounded bland, as if she were talking about an everyday event.

Rose took the news hard. Tears formed in her eyes. She looked closely at her friend. Greta seemed too calm. Perhaps she was in shock.

"You don't seem upset about this," Rose spoke sharply as if it bothered her. She had lost her appetite.

"Oh, Rose," emotion touched Greta's voice. "I've done my share of crying, especially before I was diagnosed. The thought of anything being wrong upset me so much that I thought I wouldn't be able to deal with it. It's a funny thing. I was so afraid to hear that it might be something bad that I put off going to the doctor. And then when they suggested that it could be a malignancy, I cried and cried, and prayed and prayed. But oddly when I found out it was, this peace settled on me. One thing I've done is a lot of praying. I often prayed, but lately it's like the Lord's been letting me sit on His lap to talk to Him all the time." Greta ate a bite of her steak and savored the taste in her mouth. It was delicious.

Rose for a change had nothing to say. She quietly watched her friend enjoying her meal.

Greta continued, "I feel like a new person lately. I've made a decision. It may sound selfish, but I've decided that I'm going to enjoy whatever time I have left. I may have another fifty years, or I may have only months, but Rose, I realize there are so many things I want to do. If I don't do them now, I may never have the chance."

"When you ordered that big lunch, I thought everything was all right."

Greta leaned in close to Rose and confided, "I haven't ordered steak in years because of the expense, but it sounded good, so I decided to have one. It's one of the things I've always wanted to do."

Rose grinned. This was a new Greta, and it seemed like a healthy one. Instead of going around feeling sorry for herself, she was making the best of it. "You certainly know how to make lemonade out of lemons."

Greta blushed at the compliment as Rose called the waiter over. Greta's optimistic attitude had helped her appetite to return. "I'd like some sour cream for my baked potato, please."

"Certainly, ma'am, one or two?"

"Make it two. I might as well live it up also." Rose smiled at her friend. "Well, Greta, what else would you like to do?"

"I made a list, actually wrote it out." She began fumbling through her purse till she found it. "Some of the things may be impossible, but it's nice to hope." Together they discussed what she'd written down. "I've always wanted to take a family vacation with my children. I've made some money from working, and Cole said he didn't want the watch that I gave him for his birthday. I've been considering returning it and using that money for a trip to the beach."

"He told you to take the watch back?"

"Actually he told me that he didn't want to be bothered with it. Do you think it's wrong for me to return it and use the money?"

"No. I think it's a good idea." Rose was saddened with the way Cole treated his wife. She'd been afraid he wouldn't appreciate the birthday present. Greta shouldn't even have to worry about money. The church paid Cole Odum enough. Now that Rose's husband, Hal, was a deacon, she'd managed to find out all the salaries, and she'd discovered how well paid the ministerial staff was, especially Pastor Leonard and Brother Cole. She knew the man could well afford to take Greta to the beach.

The two friends discussed vacation places, lingering over their lunch. Rose finding to her delight that she had quite an appetite after all.

"This trip sounds like so much fun. Hal and I may have to join you."

"Oh, would you?" Greta was more enthusiastic than Rose had ever remembered her being before. Her talk bubbled over. Yes, indeed, there was a change, a good change in this dear friend. "That would make it perfect. I'm figuring toward the end of October. I have to check it out with my children's schedules first, but I should have recuperated by then."

"What about chemo or radiation? You might have to wait till all that's over."

"Maybe. I'll listen to what the doctors say, but I'm not going to let it rule my life if I can help it."

"Well, we'd love to come. I'll talk to Hal about it. You haven't told me yet, what did Cole say about your problem?"

Greta looked unhappy for the first time all afternoon. "I haven't told him yet. His revival won't be finished till after the surgery is over."

Rose was usually an outspoken woman, but for the second time today she was caught off guard and didn't know what to say. After a moments silence, she asked, "You're going to call him and have him come home, aren't you? He can't be gone when you have the operation."

"I've been thinking about what I want to do."

Rose thought her friend didn't want to interfere with Cole's plans. It made her angry to think that Greta was not high on his priority list. From what she knew of Brother Cole, he would make it out that he was the martyr to leave the revival and come to his wife's side, or, even worse, he would act as if he were very godly by staying at the meetings while his wife was in the hospital without him. Then again, there was the possibility that if Greta did call him, he might tell her to postpone the surgery, which definitely was not a good idea.

"You see, he doesn't know that I've even gone to the doctor, and..."

"And you don't want to worry him while he's in revival," interrupted Rose.

"No, it isn't that. I don't think he'd worry. I'll probably try to call him just to let him know." Greta's words were honest and without rancor. "I'm thinking about staying with Cindy afterwards."

"I think that's a good idea." Rose was relieved. The thought had occurred to her that Cole wouldn't know how to take care of a wife who was disabled for a short time, and he might put undue demands on Greta that wouldn't help her recovery. "You can come stay with Hal and me if it doesn't work out with your daughter. We'd have fun, too."

Rose's offer delighted Greta. The old Greta would have said, "No, that would be too much trouble. I couldn't do that to you," but the new Greta felt great love for a good friend who cared. She smiled. "You're a gem, Rose. Thank you."

Rose blossomed at the compliment. "I say, let's have dessert

Chapter 21

And there came a lion.

-I Samuel 17:34

For years Nancy Gresham had tried to keep peace with her mother-in-law. Careful to not complain or argue, she'd hidden many of her true feelings behind a smile, hoping that Judith would accept her, but it was a difficult, sometimes daunting task. Last December, when Michael told her he wanted to talk to his father about the business rumors he'd heard, Nancy cringed at the thought of her mother-in-law's reaction and tried to discourage him, saying she didn't think Donald would change anything because of what Michael had to say. Her husband agreed at first, but after hearing yet another complaint, he'd gone to talk to his dad, cautiously choosing a night when his mother was usually at her Ladies Circle Meeting. Unfortunately since it was so close to the holidays, they'd apparently canceled that meeting, and his mother overheard the conversation. As Michael talked to his father, she'd burst into the room and told her son to mind his own business and keep out of their life. A despondent Michael had come home that night, and something in Nancy, her careful-to-not-offend attitude, had changed. A black spot in her heart took over where respect for Judith's position as her mother-in-law had once been. The offense had darkened further when Judith refused to celebrate Christmas at their house. Michael's hurt and Nancy's indignation deepened. Since he was young, Adam didn't observe his grandmother's absence, but Andrew had noticed she wasn't there. Nancy had seen the questions in his tender eyes, and dear Michael, though he'd smiled through it all, she knew pain lay behind the smiles. Often she prayed that God would give her the grace to respond correctly to this self-centered, thoughtless woman.

A self-protective wall sprung up around Nancy as she determined to keep her family safe from any pain that Judith Gresham might try to inflict. After this past holiday's experience, she had no intention of inviting Judith to the children's birthday party that she and Christine were planning together. It would be a joint celebration for Adam and Amanda since their birthdays were only days apart; however, her decision was changed when Andrew asked if Gramma was coming, and then Adam had insisted she invite Judith. Michael had even gotten into the discussion, suggesting that she send an invitation. Reluctantly Nancy had agreed. She didn't want to be the one that continued the family feud. As she posted the invitation, she hoped that she was doing the right thing. At least she'd shown herself gracious.

At the time it had felt right. It had seemed easy enough, but now, three days later, Nancy had second thoughts. When she'd gotten home from the grocery store, the little red light on the answering machine blinked. The message was blunt but carried volumes. "This is Judith. Call me immediately." That was it, but it was enough to make Nancy's heart beat faster. She knew her mother-in-law was upset.

Taking her time putting away the groceries, she prayed as she worked, and as she was more irritable with the boys than she liked to be, she sent them out into the backyard to play so they could get out their robust, youthful energy, and she could think. The answering machine message was like a death knell to her – the forewarning of something awful that was about to happen. She hated it, and yet, at least she had time to think about what she would say. She didn't want to return the call. Whatever Judith had to say would probably be unpleasant, but maybe it would be best to get it over with. Finally, after arguing with herself and praying for wisdom, she picked up the phone and dialed Judith's number.

"Hello, Gresham residence." Good. It was the cook, Elsie.

"Hi, Miss Elsie. This is Nancy. I'm returning a call I got from my mother-in-law."

"Bless you, child. She's been on the warpath all day. I'll go get her."

Nancy waited, suddenly feeling irritated with Judith. This woman loved to cause problems.

"About time you called. Where have you been?"

"At the grocery store." Fleetingly Nancy thought about saying that she didn't have a maid to shop for her as Judith did. Judith would probably take that statement as a compliment.

"I need to talk to you about this birthday party thing. First off, I think it's inappropriate to have two children celebrate their birthdays together. It can make them feel unimportant, and it looks cheap," Judith paused, waiting for Nancy's response.

Nancy's old ingrained habit of peacemaker fighting with her desire to verbally attack this woman momentarily silenced her.

Hearing no reply, Judith continued, "And secondly, if you do have a party for your child with another child, it is only appropriate if they are the same sex. It's as if you're matchmaking the poor boy at such an early age. And with, of all people, those Jamesons."

This shocked Nancy. She knew her mother-in-law was something of a snob, but it had not occurred to her that Judith might dislike the Jamesons. "You don't like the Jamesons?"

"They're not our level of people. As a matter or fact they've already disrupted the neighborhood one time. If it happens again, we'll be forced to ask them to leave."

The audacity of this woman. One of Nancy's biggest faults was the fact that she hurt too much for others, her loyalty sometimes blinded her. She didn't like to step on anyone's feelings, but when one of her friends or family was attacked, the mother lion in her roared out, protecting her young. She had grown fond of Christine, and this insult hit her deeper than her mother-in-law could have expected. The unresolved hurt and frustration from the past lurked beneath the surface of her being, and suddenly like a cauldron spewing forth, the words tumbled out.

"Your first point is a good one," she said tightly, articulating her words evenly. "Children need to feel important, and my son does know that he is important, unlike your own son who you snubbed this past Christmas. You talk about love and caring, but you need to take a good look at yourself, Judith. How do you show love and caring? As for your second point, I hope that my children marry people as kind and good and Christian as the Jamesons are, and I hope my sons never marry anyone as snobbish, mean tempered, vindictive and hateful as you are. You don't show any love to my children or even to your own child, who if you haven't noticed is one of the finest individuals that I know. As for the Jamesons, they're too good for you and your neighborhood. You're a selfish, arrogant, gossiping old woman and should be ashamed of yourself for speaking so thoughtlessly about your neighbors." Nancy felt her steam run out and was suddenly afraid that she'd start crying. Conflicting feelings of relief for venting and an immediate sense of shame for speaking so boldly choked out any further words.

Totally flabbergasted by her daughter-in-law's speech, Judith felt her face begin to flame. She'd never heard mild mannered, gutless Nancy talk this way, much less to her. "Whom do you think you're talking to?" she hissed into the telephone. The word "gossiping" struck home. That was what Bill Jameson had implied that day when she'd talked to him. "I know you and the Jamesons talk about me and don't you deny it either. I'll get them out of my house if it's the last thing I do." She slammed the phone down.

Nancy was mortified. She'd somehow managed to control her temper before with Judith, but not this time. Maybe she should call and warn Christine. No, she'd wait till Michael came home from work and talk to him first. He might know what to do. She wished that he worked in an office where she could call him. Looking at the clock, it was after five. He should be home before too long. Leaning back in the hard kitchen chair, she gazed dismally out the window, watching the boys playing happily in the yard.

Oh Lord, what have I done? What have I done? The ache in her heart from the past few months bubbled up into a pain-filled sob.

Mike whistled as he walked in the door, excited to tell Nancy about the financial arrangement he and his grandfather had worked out with the lawyers that afternoon. Perhaps they could find a babysitter and he could take her out to a nice restaurant to celebrate, he thought as he walked into the kitchen, but Nancy was already busy feeding the children. That was unusual. Something was going on. He could tell by the tight expression of her mouth. "What's wrong?"

She finished putting mashed potatoes onto each boy's plate and told them that they needed to eat quietly. She and daddy would be in the bedroom talking for a few minutes. Michael followed his wife into the room where she sat down on the bed and looked miserably at her hands.

"Michael, I did something awful today. I have a confession to make to you." He knelt down on the floor in front of her. What in the world could be so bad? Was she going to say she was having an affair? He didn't ever remember seeing her look so wretched before. His heart leaped into his throat. This was going to be big, whatever it was. He took her hands in his.

"What is it, Nancy? What happened?"

She looked at him full in the face. Her eyes were red and swollen. "I talked with your mother today, and I lost my temper and said some awful things."

Michael sat back on the floor and started laughing.

Nancy, surprised and slightly relieved by his reaction, gave him a crooked smile. "What? What's so funny?"

"I thought you were going to tell me something awful. You scared me half to death."

"Well, when you hear what I said, you might not think it's so funny." She reiterated the phone conversation as well as she could remember. Michael no longer smiled, but he looked at her so gently that she cried a little as she spoke.

"Honey, that's nothing. She'll get over it, and if she doesn't, she doesn't."

"You think she can make the Jamesons lose their house?" She wouldn't forgive herself if her mouth hurt her friends.

"No way. When my folks sold them that place, they lost all say."

"Really? I thought maybe they had owner financed the house or something."

"No, Dad needed the money. The bank holds the Jameson's mortgage. My folks couldn't make them leave even if they wanted to. Now, knowing my mother, she could make it miserable for Christine and Bill if she put her mind to it."

"Should I tell Christine? I don't want to. I'm afraid it'll just make her feel bad."

"Let's wait it out a little. Mom talks a lot of talk, but I don't think there's anything that she could really do."

"You're right," Nancy realized, feeling much better.

Michael leaned in closer, grabbing her hand. "I have some good news. We're now a business. Grandfather and I have gotten all the arrangements made. I'm going to look for a good tract of land and begin building a subdivision of my own. How does 'Gresham Estates' sound."

"Nice. I like it."

"I talked to Bill the other night about being my foreman. I know he'd do a great job and that I could count on him. He's interested. I can tell. We both agreed to think and pray about it for the next couple of weeks."

Nancy smiled, feeling much better. The dark cloud that had hung over her head for the last hour dissolved. Judith couldn't do much to hurt her friends, and Michael actually might be able to work with Bill. The sunshine glittered through the window, touching the prisms on the bedside lamp. A cascade of rainbow colors danced on the wall, brightening the room.

As Donald drove home from work, his mind kept reviewing the disturbing conversation he'd had that afternoon with Alex somebody from the Action News Special Investigative Team. They said they were doing a story on electrical repair companies and had chosen him to interview. The unsuspecting Donald had, at first, put forth his best bonhomie impression, but as the newsman asked more and more incisive and belligerent questions, Donald suddenly realized he was being set up for an entrapment. Demanding that the man and his camera people leave, they refused at first. Alex continued pressing him. Finally Donald called for help in escorting them from his office.

They left, taking his peace of mind with them, leaving him sick inside. Yes, it was certain. They had something on him. Alex was too smug. Donald closed the shop and left a few minutes later, wishing that he were someone else, that he'd listened to Michael last December.

He drove into his garage, hoping that all those ugly rumors weren't true.

Judith hurried toward him as soon as he walked in the door. Looking furious, she immediately began ranting about something Nancy had said to her on the phone and how they needed to get rid of the Jamesons. Donald barely heard her as he walked upstairs to take a hot shower. He could hear her yelling, "Are you listening to me? Are you?" Their world was going to crash down around their necks. Whatever little tiff she'd had wouldn't be anything compared with what was about to happen.

It didn't occur to Judith that Donald might have had an upsetting day. She was angrier with him than she'd been in a long time. Grabbing her bewildered poodle, she snapped a leash on him and stomped out the front door and down the walk. A half-baked plan began to form in her furious mind. This was a quiet neighborhood, but news had a tendency to travel quickly. If she were to spread a nasty rumor about Bill and Christine, it might make it uncomfortable enough for them to decide to move away. That would show her daughter-in-law a thing or two.

Straightening her back, she walked purposefully down the hill to the sidewalk, hoping to find someone she knew outside working in the yard. Noticing Mrs. Cabiness sweeping her porch, Judith slowed her step, meandering toward the woman's house. This was someone who liked gossip. She often seemed to know what was going on in the neighborhood.

"Hello, Ruth, how are you?"

Ruth Cabiness looked closely at Judith. Strange how the woman carried an air of authority about her, even when she walked her dog.

"Hello, Judith." Mrs. Gresham had used her first name, and Ruth responded in kind, hoping it wouldn't seem too familiar. The woman intimidated her for some reason.

"Have you seen any more problems at the Jameson's house?"

"No, everything's fine." Mrs. Cabiness wished she'd never told Judith about the odd midnight visitors. She tended to talk too much. She paused to look closely at Judith Gresham, evaluating her. Even though the woman had a pleasant expression on her face, her dark eyes looked like steel, holding no warmth, cautioning Ruth to be careful about what she did say.

"I've heard something disturbing about them." A light glinted from Judith's eyes.

Ruth felt immediately curious, but then a little irritated. What was it about the Jamesons that made this lady want to talk? "What?" she asked with a tinge of impatience.

Judith thought carefully. She needed to make it something hard to check out. "I heard that Bill Jameson has himself a girlfriend," she whispered conspiratorially. It was the only thing she could think of right off hand, and maybe if she ruined the couple's marriage, then they'd divorce and have to move away. She felt pleased with the thought, and for all she knew, it was true.

"A girlfriend?" exclaimed Ruth incredulously. "Who in the world did you hear that from?"

"Well, the person doesn't want me to say," Judith answered in a secretive whisper. She thought about leaving it at that and letting Ruth Cabiness spread the rumor herself, but the woman looked too unsure.

"I find that hard to believe," stated Ruth as she sat down on her porch swing still holding her broom for support. The thought of it made her sick. Christine there with those three little children. Surely someone had misunderstood something.

Judith realized she needed to put a little meat onto her tale and spoke without fully thinking out what she would say. "Please don't tell anyone I told you this. I wouldn't want others to know, but," she leaned in toward Ruth and whispered, "I myself was downtown recently, and I saw the Jameson man in a car with a young girl all cuddled up next to him."

Ruth looked closely at Judith Gresham as a realization hit her. This woman came from the beautiful castle up on the hill. She was always well dressed and looked so proper. Why in the world would she lie? But suddenly Ruth knew without a doubt that this woman was lying. All the intimidation she'd felt earlier vanished. This lady was nothing more than a shameless, malicious liar who enjoyed messing in other people's lives. She decided to see just how far Judith Gresham would go, so she pretended to go along with the suggestion. "You don't say. A girl, what did she look like?"

Judith took the bait without batting an eye. She was quite pleased with herself. "Well, I couldn't see her well because he was on my side, but he looked right at me as if he was embarrassed and told the girl to sit up. She had blond hair though, not dark hair like the Jameson woman."

"My goodness, and you say you saw this recently."

"Yes, one day last week."

"And you're sure it was Bill."

"I have no doubt it was. He was in that," she glanced over at the Jameson's driveway, "green car of theirs."

If there was one thing Ruth Cabiness was, it was observant. She liked to watch her neighbors' comings and goings, and she saw Christine take Bill to work every morning and go back each evening to pick him up. This man was not having an affair. She stood again to resume her sweeping.

"And did he have that neck brace on?" she asked casually.

Judith had totally forgotten Bill wore a neck brace. Was he out of it yet? She turned a slight shade of red. "Yes, as a matter of fact, I think he was."

"Funny, isn't it." Mrs. Cabiness swept more forcefully than necessary. "How he can turn his head and look at you with that thing on. He's not supposed to be able to turn his head at all with his broken neck." She swept some of the debris from her porch straight at Judith, picked up her broom, walked into the house, and let the screen door slam shut behind her.

Judith felt indignant. Her dog sniffed Mrs. Cabiness' flowers. She let him do his business in her yard. She would be sure to not talk to that woman again.

Chapter 22

Create in me a clean heart, O God: and renew a right spirit within me.

-Psalms 51:10

Christine made a final check to see if everything was ready. Looking into the bag, she found the napkins, paper cups, plates, potato chips, and party favors. A second bag contained two large milk jugs filled with punch. Nancy was bringing the cake, ice cream, and games. Christine smiled, thinking how much fun this party would be for Amanda who had been hopping around the house excitedly for the past two days. When she had jumped out of her bed at six o'clock that morning and run into Christine's room to ask if it was tomorrow yet, Christine had reported sleepily that it was, and an excited Amanda quickly woke the rest of the household. As a result, they'd had time to stop by a donut shop before taking Bill to work.

"Is it time to go, Mama?" Jonathan was almost as excited as Amanda.

"Yes, let's get in the car." Two small children flew out of the house with one little toddler gleefully trying to follow along. Christine scooped up Lauranna and walked out the door. She would get the children in their car seats first then carry out the birthday items.

It was a beautiful day, this fifth day of September. A cool breeze ruffled the leaves, promising a pleasant afternoon. Christine fastened each child's seat belt and rolled down the car's windows so that the children would be comfortable.

She hurried back into the house, grabbed the first bag, ran out, and popped it into the trunk of the car. Hating to leave the children alone for even a moment, she rushed back to the house for the second bag, wondering as she went why she ever struggled with her weight since she ran so much. As she reached the porch, a movement down the street caught her attention. Glancing over her shoulder, she saw Judith Gresham walking her dog down the sidewalk, strolling her way. Christine darted inside and picked up the bag of punch and her purse. If she hurried, maybe she'd be out of the driveway before Judith got near them. Quickly coming out, she hastily turned to lock the deadbolt on the front door, accidentally knocking the keys from her hands. Maneuvering the heavy paper bag, she scrambled for the keys, finally locking the door. In a moment, she was at the car. But it was too late. Judith approached just as she slammed the trunk shut.

"Going to the birthday party, I see." Her voice sounded hard.

"Yes. Yes, we are," Christine answered, hoping that her face didn't reveal her dismay that her neighbor knew about the joint birthday celebration. Nancy must have told her. Somehow the fact that Judith and Nancy were related and would actually talk to each other surprised her.

"I don't believe in boys and girls having parties together."

Christine stood stunned, not knowing what to say. A strained silence lasted for a moment.

"I told Nancy that the other day. You two shouldn't be forcing young, impressionable children together at social events, but that's Nancy for you. Always ignoring good advice."

Poor Nancy, Christine thought. She wasn't even going to try to be polite. She would be late if she didn't hurry. "I need to go. Good-bye, Mrs. Gresham," she said curtly as she got into the car.

The children were unusually quiet as she backed out of the driveway and began driving down the road.

"Is that lady mad at us?" Jonathan finally asked, breaking the silence.

"I don't know," answered Christine honestly. How much do you tell children? "She's not a happy person. Now though, we're going to have lots of fun. Amanda, do you have Adam's birthday present?"

"Yes, ma'am," responded Amanda. "Can I open it for him since it's my birthday?"

"No, you'll have your own gifts to open. It's Adam's birthday, too. He'll open his."

"See, 'Manda, I got your present right here." Jonathan held up her gift. "You're really gonna like it. Mama said I can't tell you what it is, but I'll tell you that it's soft, and..."

"No hints, Jonathan," interrupted Christine, shaking her head. The children giggled in the back seat, Amanda begging for just one more clue. Christine relaxed. She wouldn't let Judith Gresham spoil one moment of this precious day.

Alex felt pleased. His news report should air tonight. He and the editor had spent the past two workdays fine tuning the program, and it was good, really good.

The phone rang. He picked it up with a touch of apprehension. "Hello."

"Alex. This is Cynthia. I have bad news."

"What's wrong?" This had happened before. There had been pieces postponed and even canceled at the last minute. Surely the station manager hadn't changed his mind.

"That tropical storm's been upgraded to a hurricane. It's supposed to hit the gulf coast soon. Mr. Brock's afraid we might have to interrupt your news report to cover it, so we're saving your piece for next week. He thinks it's too good to cut any of it. We're rescheduling yours to air on September twelfth, provided we don't have the flooding problems that we had a few years ago."

Gresham Electric would get a few more days of business before the bomb fell. Alex wished he hadn't called to inform Donald Gresham that the piece was going to air tonight.

Donald was late again. Judith sulked, studying the dining room as she ate. She felt a little lonely sitting there, eating all by herself. Lately, she seemed to be alone a lot. The door opened. Good. He was finally home. She would give him a piece of her mind.

"Well, it's about time. Supper's been on the table for half an hour. It's getting cold. You'd better hurry if you want to eat."

Without answering, his eyes distant, Donald slumped down in one of the chairs, pushing away the plate.

Oblivious to the weary, haggard expression on his face, Judith began telling him about her encounter with Christine Jameson.

"What time is it?" he interrupted. He hadn't touched his supper.

"What? I'm talking to you. What do you mean 'What time is it'?"

"It's six-thirty!"

"Donald, what's gotten into you? Why! Where are you going?" she demanded to his retreating back.

Donald, ignoring her, scrambled into the family room, turning on the television. Through the years he'd tried his best to please Judith, but now, overwhelmed by his present problems, he dismissed her, tuning her voice out, concentrating on his goal to hear the news report before it was over.

"Upcoming stories for tonight. A bank robber caught in Smyrna, a drive-by shooting in downtown Atlanta, and tonight our special news report is on...," a pretty young woman was saying as Judith walked into the room, livid with rage. Tired of Donald's strangeness, she turned the television off and faced him.

"It is time to eat dinner, not to watch television," she reprimanded, as if he were a child.

"What are you doing?" he roared, jumping from his chair, pushing her out of his way, and turning the television back on.

"You can't push me around like that," Judith declared indignantly. She had never seen him act this way. It scared her a little and insulted her a lot. "I don't know what's gotten into you, but..."

"Can't you be quiet for a moment, woman?" Donald bellowed at her. "We may lose everything. Let me listen and be quiet."

"What are you talking about? Lose everything? Have you lost your senses? Donald, you're acting like a mad man," Judith ranted as he turned up the television's volume so he could hear.

"Judith, for once in your life, please shut up."

Well, she would shut up. She wouldn't talk to him again, she determined as she stomped out of the room and up the stairs.

"...the hurricane is expected to hit the gulf coast sometime tomorrow. Our weatherman is keeping a watchful eye on it. We'll be going to Panama City to see what they're doing to be prepared. That's our special report tonight. Stay tuned." A commercial came on the air.

"He lied. He just out and out lied," Donald repeated over and over to himself as he watched the entire news show and no mention of Gresham Electric aired. "He was only baiting me all along." A choked, strangled animal sound of laughter mixed with tears overtook him for a moment. His pounding heart slowed its violent beating. Jumbled thoughts rumbled through his mind. His head ached. Maybe fresh air would help. Without actually making a conscious decision, he found himself outside, walking down the road.

If ever a man felt sorry for himself, it was Donald Gresham. He had not intentionally set out to hurt anyone. Why had everything gone so wrong?

Often in the life of a person there is a watershed moment that sweeps one along a different current, in a new direction. For Donald this moment had been at the death of his mother. He had sincerely loved her, but as a teenager, afraid of appearing weak, he'd refused to do almost anything she asked, thinking this showed that he was a real man. Now it seemed ridiculous that he'd acted that way, that he hadn't known better, but at the time it had made sense. With an ache in his heart, he thought of his mother – a soft-spoken, gentle woman – and remembered their last conversation. She didn't like the way he acted when he was around Judith. He'd resented her remarks and had gone away angry. Then, before they had settled their quarrel, his mother died unexpectedly, and Donald was left with a sea of regrets.

Turning to Judith to console him, he determined to change his ways, to do as Judith asked as much as possible, to make up to his mother for their quarrel. It wasn't entirely Judith's fault that she had turned into a snobbish, self-centered woman. He had encouraged her to be like a spoiled child and had falsely fed her ego. They had done little to keep each other honest or to help each other grow.

As if waking from a deep sleep, Donald looked around and discovered that his aimless wandering had led him to Deer Creek Church. Sitting down on the wooden bench that overlooked the graveyard, he covered his face with his hands. He needed to pray, but what could he possibly say? A nagging thought kept coming back. His business was in trouble. Somewhere in it all, he'd lost himself. He didn't like the person he saw. Head deacon – he felt a sinking feeling. The people at the church didn't know him very well. They didn't know about his corrupt business practices. They didn't know that his home was mortgaged to the hilt. Most people thought he was a successful businessman. He would, no doubt, be asked to give up his position as a deacon. This might even be a good thing. He was nothing more than Brother Cole's yes-man, anyhow.

"Your sin will find you out," Pastor Leonard had preached a few Sundays ago. Donald knew the time had come for him. Shutting his eyes, he asked the Lord for forgiveness, for grace, to give him a clean heart, to renew his wicked spirit.

Yes, these would be his, a peaceful thought spoke, but even so, God wouldn't erase the consequences. Donald was still responsible for the mess he had made. He must make things right.

Sitting there quietly, the shadows began to lengthen. One thought whirling around in his scattered thinking worried him. An uneasiness crept into his self-pity. A memory. A short conversation with two of his workers. The odd assurances they had given him that John and his rumors had been shut up. He had wondered what those men were talking about, but blindly tucked the words, the worries back into the recesses of his brain, ignoring them. Those two employees of his, had they actually hurt John?

"Please, God, don't let them have hurt John," he prayed, wishing that there was some way he could apologize to the man. But how? He didn't know where John lived now.

Lord, if you want me to talk to him, let me meet up with him someplace. Donald thought, part of him even hoped, that the chances of his prayer being answered were slim. It would be awkward to talk to John. He wanted to squeeze that memory away.

The sun began to set. The September night was cloudy and crisp. A strong breeze cooled his sweating forehead. A storm was brewing. The smell of wood smoke in the air took him back to his boyhood days. He could remember dusky evenings long ago, almost hearing echoes of "Here I come, ready or not" and his mother calling, "Donald, Donald, come on in. Bedtime." Oh, so very long ago. Donald gazed up in the sky and said ever so softly, "I'm sorry, Mama." Then he added, "I will make things right. Please watch and see." He squared his shoulders to walk home to Judith.

Chapter 23

Perfect love casteth out fear.

-I John 4:18

Greta peered into her closet. She didn't feel like packing, but tomorrow she needed to be at the hospital early. The dreaded surgery was scheduled, and she must be ready.

That afternoon, she'd taken the watch back. There had been some problem at first with the refund. The sale's clerk had rudely informed her that the store's policy was to give credit only. Greta, surprised by this since she'd been told at the time of purchase that she could return the watch for cash within thirty days, had almost left the store without arguing. The old Greta would have meekly taken the credit, but the new one insisted upon talking to the manager who refunded her money without question. She left the store feeling her faith in people a little restored. Glad that she'd spoken up.

The Traveler's Checks were neatly tucked in her purse. She smiled as she thought of them. At the bank, she'd emptied her savings. The teller had asked why she was closing the account. Apparently they needed those personal details for their records. Greta had responded that she would be moving. It was true. Cindy and Barry had both said that she could stay with them as long as she wanted. Greta had only told Cindy that she was having surgery and would like to recuperate with them afterwards. Though Cindy had asked her about the operation, Greta had hedged, and just answered that it was "female troubles." She cringed at even saying it. It sounded like something Cole would say. She hated the expression. When he had problems, which were rarely, but when he did, she didn't call them "male troubles," but this time it had sufficed and her daughter seemed content with the answer. Greta didn't want to cause undo concern.

"All right," she said to herself. "Get back to work." Concentrating on her task, she packed both a hospital bag and some things to take to Cindy's house.

The phone rang. Perhaps it was Cole. She had left a message with the hotel for him to call her days ago, but he still hadn't done so. Instead it was Brother Steve, the music director. She had already told him that she was going to have to be out for a while because she would be visiting her children. Only Rose knew the total truth, and she'd asked her not to tell anyone.

"Greta, I wanted to let you know that we'll be having our Christmas preparation retreat at the end of October. We'll be leaving Friday, the twenty-seventh and coming back Saturday night."

Greta answered slowly. "Steve, I'm sorry. I've already made tentative plans with my children to go on a family vacation." She knew she might not even be able to play for the Christmas musical in December. She loved playing but felt it wasn't fair to let Brother Steve think he could depend on her. Still, it was too early to say anything, and the thought of giving up her music was too depressing to even contemplate. Hopefully everything would be fine, and she'd be back soon. "Can I get back with you about this later, after I've talked to my children?"

"Sure." Steve felt concern, not about his music program, but about Greta. Something was unspoken between them, and he couldn't figure it out. "Greta, is everything okay?"

Greta felt her reserve fade. This was a friend, a good man who had encouraged her the past couple of years, and he should know what was going on. "Steve, I don't want to leave you hanging like this. I have something, I guess, I should tell you, but please don't tell anyone, not even your wife...." She took a breath. This was hard to say. "I have a malignant tumor. I'm having surgery tomorrow. They don't know how bad it is. It might be nothing, but it might mean that I won't be able to play for the Christmas musical. I'll be recuperating at my daughter's house after the surgery, and if everything's all right, I'll probably come home again in November, but I don't want to cause you problems. It might be best to plan on Dale playing for the Christmas program. I don't know whether I'll be up to it or not."

"Greta, I'm sorry." She could feel his concern but felt uncomfortable with it all the same. This was why she didn't want others to know her situation. It made talking awkward. "The Christmas musical wouldn't be the same without you. I'm not going to talk to Dale about this until you decide how you feel in October. Can I have your daughter's phone number so I can call you and see how you're doing from time to time?"

Greta smiled. That was a good idea. She didn't have to give up her music tonight. She gave him Cindy's number and address.

"Greta, I had an idea about two months ago that I've been toying with and somehow your telling me this makes me all the more committed to following through. That is if you like what I've been thinking about."

"What's your idea?"

"Well, I talked to a guy I know a while back about making a recording of some of your music. He said he'd be interested in doing it. What do you think?"

Inside Greta felt a warm glow. Yes, she liked the idea very much. It was one of the impossible items on her wish list, yet God was already using Brother Steve to bless her with this desire. Humbled by God's goodness, excitement filled her, replacing the fear of surgery that had haunted her day. "Oh, Steve, that would be wonderful. I've always wanted to do that."

"For now, you practice your favorites, and I'll get in touch with this man and try to plan something for the beginning of November. Maybe we should make a Christmas album too, but it probably wouldn't get out till after Christmas, being so late in the year."

"Oh Steve, thank you."

"Well, this has been on my mind for some time. I should have talked to you about it before. I'll get all the details worked out and let you know. You think you'll be up for it?"

"Yes, with God's help, I'm sure I'll be able to do it."

By the time she hung up the phone, she was so excited that she had to tell someone. She called Rose who rejoiced with her.

"See, God already knows what you desire even before you ask Him. I've been praying that everything on your wish list will come true."

"Thank you, Rose. Now you need to make out yours so I can pray the same for you."

"Good idea. I'd like to look nineteen again and be young and skinny."

"Rose!" Greta laughed with her friend. She went to sleep that night feeling fully at peace. She decided she'd try to call Cole again after the surgery. She didn't want to speak to him tonight and fret over anything that he might have to say. Her contentment of the moment lulled her into a restful sleep that surprised her. It wouldn't have surprised Rose or Steve who both prayed that she'd have peaceful slumber that night.

The next evening, Greta awoke from time to time and vaguely noticed faces talking to her, but she was too tired to listen and drifted back to sleep. When she awoke again, she couldn't tell how much time had passed, but she did know that she was in pain, and the medication made it hard to concentrate. All she wanted to do was sleep. She was thankful the surgery was over. Rose was there, she noticed, and nurses came in constantly to check on her.

The doctor also came into her room to confer with her, but again it was too hard to pay attention. She couldn't comprehend much at the moment.

The doctor left saying he would be back later. Something in his face, even in her drugged state, told her he had bad news. Some of his words had vaguely filtered in, but she needed to sleep.

By Saturday, Greta's head was clearer. One of the oncologists came in while Rose was there. Her friend started to leave, but Greta asked her to stay. Being alone to face the doctor's words scared her. She needed Rose's support.

The doctor told Greta that the cancer had metastasized, that it was a rare type and difficult to treat. Greta listened as he explained the seriousness of her situation and gave her treatment alternatives, their side effects, and the likelihood for their success. He hadn't used the ugly word "terminal" yet, but he skirted close enough to it that Greta knew without the word. He didn't seem too hopeful that the different therapies would work since the cancer had advanced so far.

"If I don't do anything at all, how long do you think I have?" Greta finally asked.

The man didn't like to give predictions. He didn't want to scare her or give her false hope. Glancing at her chart, he realized that she was only fifty-six. Only two years older than he was himself.

"I can't really answer that. People in your situation do different things," he said, avoiding her question. Sometimes he hated his job.

"Doctor, please give me the bottom line. I know you're not God, and I don't expect you to give me an exact date. I don't even know that it really matters very much, but in your best opinion, from what you have observed before, give me an estimate."

"Mrs. Odum, I've seen patients that were as sick as you live only weeks, most usually make it a few months to a year, and I've seen one or two make it for many years. One thirty-eight-year old patient I have has been fighting her cancer for seven years now and has beat all odds. Your cancer is very advanced. With treatment, there's the possibility you would have more time, but then the time you have could be worse because of it. We caught your cancer late, but to finally answer your question, if you have no treatments whatsoever, I would give you an estimate of six months to a year, possibly two." He added the two because he wanted to give her hope even though he knew it was probably not true. Most of his patients begged for anything they could have to hang on to their lives. This woman appeared different. She lay back very peacefully on her bed. He thought to himself what a pretty lady she was.

"You've given me the best answer I could hope for, Doctor. Thank you. I'd like to enjoy this last part of my life as much as possible. I'd rather not have any of the treatments."

"But, Greta," interjected a concerned Rose. "He said that the treatments might prolong your life."

"Rose, do you remember my list?"

"Yes." Rose tried to remember what there was on the list that would be applicable to their discussion.

"I said I wanted one more Christmas with my children, and the doctor has just estimated I'll have that. I was hoping for that, Rose, and I think God's going to give it to me." Greta smiled. "Why I might even surprise everyone and have two or three. Thank you, Dr. Barrow, for coming by."

"I want to see you regularly and check on you."

Greta explained that she would be moving to Asheville with her daughter for a time and promised to get an oncologist there that he could send her records to. Even though she was small and frail looking, this woman had a strength that he rarely saw. He wondered about the "list" that she'd referred to, thinking if it helped her this much, he'd like to share it with other patients. He didn't understand it was God's peace that ruled in her heart right now. The spiritual battle was in full force inside Greta, but for the moment, the perfect love of God had cast out all her fear.

Chapter 24

A quarrelsome wife is like a constant dripping.

Proverbs 19:13 (NIV)

The stormy, dark clouds threatened to drench the hard Georgia clay with torrents of rain Sunday morning as Donald drove to church. Judith sat beside him in stony silence, refusing to say a word. She'd not spoken since he'd shouted at her to "shut up" last Tuesday evening. Adding insult to her injured pride, he hadn't even bothered to come straight to her room to apologize but instead had apparently gone for a walk, and later, when he'd returned, she'd overheard him talking on the phone to Michael – apologizing to the kid – as if she didn't matter. Irked to the raw core by his behavior, she determined to punish him. He'd get the cold shoulder for a long time. When he'd finally come to her bedroom the other night, he'd tried to tell her something about business problems while making excuses for himself. She'd stormed into her bathroom, slamming the door defiantly in his face. The thought that her actions stung him helped to briefly soothe her wounded ego; however, he hadn't come back that night, and she'd found herself crying in her bed. Not even knowing exactly why – just that everything seemed wrong. She cried a lot lately. He'd really hurt her feelings, and well, Donald was the stable one, the strong one, the kind one. And lately he had been acting so strangely.

Even this morning, Judith had sat in stunned silence watching him eat a large breakfast. Usually when she was this way, he had trouble eating. It was an effort for her to remain quiet, and with dismay, she realized it wasn't as effective as it had been in the past. For the first time that she could ever remember, she felt unsure of herself around him.

During the difficult drive to church, she managed to keep her stoic silence. Donald talked little, but whenever he did, it disconcerted her. Usually he was cowed by this time into a humble silence, but he lacked that today. Something familiar was gone. It was a little scary. Perhaps he didn't care for her anymore. She stiffened her spine, lifting her head high. *Well, it doesn't matter*, she reminded herself. She didn't care for him either. A dark sadness crept into her soul, but she straightaway buried it, denying it, hiding her feelings behind an angry countenance.

A gentle drizzle started as Donald turned into the church's drive, quickly changing into a heavy torrent of unrelenting rain.

"I'll drop you off by the side door so you can slip into Sunday school while I park," he said as if there were no problem between them, confusing Judith, angering her. Getting out of the car, she slammed the door shut harder than necessary before dashing inside. In a foul mood that she didn't even try to disguise, she stomped to her Sunday school class.

Fewer women than usual were in the room. Shirley, the teacher, smiled at her as she poured herself a cup of coffee. Rose and Eleanor sat talking with Bertie, a member of Judith's country club. They laughed at some story Bertie was telling them, causing Judith's scowl to deepen. Walking over to the table, she poured herself a cup of coffee and took one of the store-bought donuts out of its box.

"Nothing homemade today, I see," she muttered as she sat down.

Rose, overhearing the comment, thought about explaining why she'd brought donuts instead of making something, but then she reconsidered. Judith had a dark expression in her eyes that Rose didn't care to encounter. She hadn't come to Sunday school to cross paths with Judith Gresham. She felt Greta's absence intently, wishing her friend were there.

Bertie, an easygoing, fun-loving person, tried to lighten up what she perceived to be a painful situation for whoever had brought the donuts. Speaking to Judith, who had sat down beside her, she exclaimed, "I could eat the whole box all by myself. Donuts are quite a treat to me. Hope no one minds if I eat more than my fair share."

"Not like my homemade cinnamon rolls, that's for sure." If Judith had been a dragon, smoke would have come out of her mouth. Bertie decided to ignore her.

"My goodness, we're a bit low this morning," began Shirley, surveying the class. "I guess the rain scared the other ladies off."

"Yeah, Rose, where's Eeyore?" Judith asked, a tight smile on her face.

Rose looked oddly at Judith, and Bertie's face suddenly shaded a deep red as she choked slightly on the bite of donut she had just popped into her mouth. One time she had jokingly called Greta "Eeyore" in front of Judith because of Greta's quiet nature. At the time it had seemed funny, but as she'd gotten to know Greta better, she'd realized the woman wasn't anything like the melancholy donkey in the Winnie-the-Pooh books. Bertie had a tendency to talk too much and could imitate other's mannerism so well that it kept everyone laughing. Usually she was careful not to offend anyone, mostly making fun of herself, but sometimes she got carried away, and it got her into trouble. She didn't want to hurt another person's feelings, and now she internally reprimanded herself, regretting having said such a thoughtless thing about Greta, especially to someone as unpleasant as Judith Gresham. She immediately admonished herself for her big mouth.

Rose didn't even notice Bertie's discomfort. She looked straight at Judith. Surely the woman wasn't referring to Greta. "Eeyore?"

Judith made a careless laugh. "Eeyore, you know, Greta." She swept her hand toward Bertie. "That's what Bertie and I call her."

Bertie wished she could disappear into her chair as Rose glanced her way. "I do not call Greta, Eeyore," she refuted vehemently.

"Sure you do," argued Judith, incensed by her denial. "I heard you myself that one time at the..."

Bertie interrupted, "One time I was stupid and didn't know Greta very well and because she was quiet I thought she was like Eeyore, so I said so, but I don't call her Eeyore. It was a thoughtless thing for me to say in the first place. I'm sorry. I should never have said it."

Rose thought of her good friend right now in a hospital room. She had promised Greta she would tell no one about her problems, but she wondered if it would chasten Judith Gresham to learn the truth. Probably not. Judith was too caught up in herself. Rose had a temper that she had battled with all her life. Often she spoke without thinking, but now she needed to answer carefully. Anger clouded her head, making it difficult to think clearly, but oh, she wanted to tell this woman what she thought. She was tired from the last couple of sleepless nights worrying about Greta. It was almost as if she'd been going through a type of mourning. Imagining Greta hearing Judith's unkind words and how it would have cut to the soul of her friend, Rose suddenly did the one thing that no one expected, that she didn't even expect. She burst into tears.

A voice spoke up, "Rose, what is it?"

Judith's voice, "I just asked her where Eeyore was. It's no big deal."

Bertie's response, "Be quiet, Judith. Don't you know anything."

Judith heated now. "You shut up, Bertie. You're the one who started this, Miss Goody-Two-Shoes."

Shirley's, "Ladies, Ladies!"

And the entire time Rose felt Eleanor gently patting her shoulder.

"Now, Rose, where is Greta?" Shirley asked with concern.

Rose wiped her eyes, glancing at Shirley. "I'm sorry." She looked at Judith. "I could just imagine how much that name would hurt Greta, who is one of the kindest, most generous friends a person could have. It broke my heart."

Judith crossed her arms in front of herself, scowling.

"We need to be careful with our words. As the Bible tells us in James, 'the tongue is full of deadly poison. We bless God with it and curse men.'" Shirley had been reluctant to take this Sunday school class basically because of Judith Gresham's presence. Sometimes she still considered resigning.

Judith sighed irritably. She didn't come to church to get preached to.

"Is Greta all right?" Shirley directed the question to Rose who had dried her tears. She was no fool. She'd never seen Rose act this way. Instinctively she felt there was something wrong.

"Greta's going to visit her children in Asheville for a while," Rose evaded Shirley's question, wishing she could tell the woman the whole story.

Shirley looked at Rose quizzically. Something had been left unsaid, but with Judith here, it was best not to pressure Rose. It was getting late. Beginning the lesson, she decided to change it slightly to fit the moment. Taking the scripture from the fifth chapter of Matthew, part of the Sermon on the Mount, she discussed the fact that Christians are to be salt and light on the earth. It disturbed her to see the scowl on Judith's face. She could tell by the woman's comments and countenance that she related the scripture to others, not to herself. Shirley felt concerned for this lost soul. God had ways of reaching people's hearts, and she prayed that He would work on this woman's proud, self-centered spirit.

After church, the Jamesons hurried home to prepare Sunday dinner for Mike and Nancy Gresham. A settled contentment rested on Christine as she enjoyed her friends' visit. When their guests left, she put the children down for a nap and went to sit on the porch swing with Bill. Though the sky was still overcast, a wee thread of light escaped through the clouds dispersing a soft glow on the afternoon. A pleasant breeze cooled them as they rocked gently back and forth. Christine breathed in the soaked smell of wet earth and cedar. Bill sat quietly beside her, looking as if his mind were miles away.

"A penny for your thoughts."

He smiled, waking from his reverie. "Mike talked to me again about working for him as his head foreman. How would you feel if I resigned at the church and went to work for him? It would mean a slight pay cut."

"I think it'd be good."

Bill leaned forward, momentarily stopping the swing, to pick up a small stone on the porch. "It's hard, Christine. I've felt as if this was my ministry. You know the church has pastors, elders, deacons, and maintenance men." He gave a wry laugh, tossing the stone in the air a couple of times before throwing it into the yard. "Let's pray that if this is God's will, He'll make it clear. I told Mike I'd give him my answer next Sunday. If I go, I'd need to give the church four-weeks notice. He's willing to wait for me." Bill leaned back, lost in thought again.

Christine put her hand in his. Together they rocked, thinking of what might have been.

Greta felt better now. Her medication had been reduced, and the fogginess that had bothered her was gone. This morning she'd enjoyed watching Sunday worship services on television. Charles Stanley had given an excellent sermon on what a person could look forward to one day in heaven, preaching straight to Greta's heart. She absorbed the words, knowing that God had blessed her with what she needed to hear.

She really should call Cole again. Even though she had left messages for him to call her at the hospital, he hadn't returned any of them. She wanted to explain what had happened before he came home tomorrow. Cindy was coming down Tuesday afternoon to take her up to Asheville, and it would be best if Cole were prepared before their daughter arrived.

Though it was still painful to move, she picked up the telephone and dialed the number. The hotel connected her to his room. The phone rang five times without an answer. He must still be out. As she began to hang up, she heard a sharp, "Hello."

"Cole, it's Greta. I've been trying to reach you."

"Oh, Greta. I was in the shower. I jumped out when I heard the phone ringing. Thought it might be somebody important like Pastor Leonard."

"No. It's just me." The barb didn't hurt. "I need to talk to you."

"Yeah, I got your messages. I just didn't have time to call. I really can't talk now. We're doing the last service tonight, and I've got to get ready."

"All right. I just wanted to tell you that I won't be home when you get there tomorrow. I'm in the hospital."

"In the hospital?"

"Yes. I'm at Emory. If you decide to visit me, I'll tell you about it then."

"All right. I'll see what I can do. I've got to go."

At least she'd talked to him. She felt suddenly very tired. Settling into as comfortable a position as possible, she drifted into a fragile sleep.

Early Monday morning Cole and Pastor Leonard left Columbus and began driving back to Athens. In spite of the rainy weather, Cole enjoyed traveling with the pastor. They both felt jubilant about how well the meetings had gone at Arrowhead First Church. Even though he was tired, Cole was careful to say the right things to Leonard. When the Pastor expressed a longing to see his wife again, Cole, responding in kind, agreed that he looked forward to seeing Greta. This was partly true. Greta lent a little order to his life; also, he knew these kinds of statements were expected, and he had no trouble telling the pastor anything he wanted to hear.

Finally arriving home, Cole opened the door to a clean but empty house. He put his dirty clothes in the laundry room for Greta to wash when she got home and lay the suitcases in the hallway for her to put away. Sitting in front of the television, he pressed the remote control, flying through the channels. Finally finding a John Wayne movie that he could enjoy, he relaxed, allowing himself to fall asleep. It had been a long two weeks.

Awaking an hour later, for the first time, he wished Greta were there. He needed something to eat. For the past two weeks, he'd eaten out so much that he found the thought of eating at a restaurant again unappealing. Searching through the refrigerator, he found nothing appetizing. The freezer held lasagna and what looked like a chicken potpie, but both were frozen solid. It would take too long to heat them up. He looked at his expensive watch – a jewel in his earthly crown. It was almost six o'clock. He needed to eat something, and though the thought wasn't appealing, he should probably drive the hour trip to Emory tonight to see Greta. He wanted to work tomorrow.

Greta kept herself from falling asleep, hoping that Cole would come visit her. Hearing the door open, she looked up to see Cole walk in. A smile formed on her lips, but quickly disappeared as she noticed his sour expression, forewarning her of his mood. "How was your trip?"

"I don't want to talk about that. What's the matter with you?"

"I have cancer," she said matter-of-factly, hoping to see an expression of remorse on his face. She had fantasized about how he might react, imagining him crying and saying he was sorry for having been harsh with her throughout the years. Instead he stood there woodenly.

"That's too bad. How bad is it?"

"It's bad. The doctor doesn't have much hope. I guess it's what you would call terminal."

Cole walked over to the window, looking out at the darkness. "I guess I should tell Pastor Leonard." He sighed as he weighed the pros and cons of such a disclosure, uncertain of what to do.

"I don't want you to tell anyone."

"Yes, but this affects me too." If people knew, they might expect him to want to be with Greta more. He might lose his edge in the church. Some would say that Greta having cancer was a sign from God that he wasn't a good man. Maybe no one should be told. It would complicate things too much.

It occurred to Greta that Cole had been more sympathetic toward Mrs. Gentry when she'd lost her parakeet than he was now being toward her. "Does anything affect you, Cole?" Her voice held no rancor but rather pity. Suddenly she saw this man as one void of feeling. "I feel sorry for you."

"What?" The statement took him by surprise. He turned toward her bed.

"I said I feel sorry for you. You value money, prestige, image more than people. Those aren't real, Cole."

Cole was shocked. His reticent, mouse of a wife didn't talk to him like this. Greta had punctured his shell, touching a painful, vital organ, but he bandaged it quickly. He most certainly did value people. Look at all those people at the church who'd he'd helped throughout the years. She was wrong. "Don't bother feeling sorry for me. What kind of medicine do they have you on anyway?" He wanted to leave. "I have to go."

"Wait, Cole."

Good, she was going to apologize. "What? I think you've said quite enough."

"I need to let you know that Cindy's going to pick me up tomorrow when they let me out of here. I'm going to her house in Asheville."

"I think you should come home."

Greta felt a glimmer of hope. Maybe she'd misjudged the man. Maybe he simply had a hard time showing genuine emotion. "You do? You'd have to help me out for a few weeks."

"Oh," he paused, rethinking the situation. "It'd be best if you went to Cindy's."

The tiny bubble of hope Greta had grabbed popped. She knew him. She needed to stop trying to fool herself. With a sense of sadness, she watched him leave. She probably wouldn't see him again before she left for Asheville.

Chapter 25

A man's heart deviseth his way: but the Lord directeth his steps.

-Proverbs 16:9

The soft rain that lulled Christine into a dreamless slumber woke her with a start as the winds suddenly picked up, increasing the storm's crescendo. Lightening hopscotched across the sky followed by loud peals of thunder. A vicious streak of lightening reached out, grabbing an oak tree's uppermost branch, thundering violently, shaking their house.

"That hit something close," said Bill, awakening beside her.

Christine snuggled closer to him. "I'm glad I have you with me."

"I'm glad I have you, too." Another zap of lightning with the immediate roar of thunder sounded nearby. Even as the storm slowly began to move away, though it quieted, the sky still sizzled with flashing lights, some close, some distant. By the time it had settled enough that they felt comfortable to go back to sleep, it was time to get up.

Christine drove carefully through the flooded, draining roads toward the church. A ubiquitous rain continued to pour, slowing her to a crawl, making it difficult to see. The church's parking lot was covered in water as she cautiously drove to the side door that Bill usually went in. Wishing him a good day, she absentmindedly waved goodbye before putting her concentration back on the road, creeping slowly away from the church, forgetting that Brother Cole would be back at work that day.

Bill hurried out of the rain, into the muggy, humid building. Apparently the air conditioner wasn't working. Taking the stairs to his office, he worried about any encounter he might have with Brother Cole. The past two weeks had gone smoothly, but there was no telling what would happen now that the assistant pastor was back.

In the quiet of his office, he took a moment to pray for the Lord's watchful care over his day. A few minutes later, Sam and Larry trudged in together. "Man, it's stuffy in here," Sam complained as he entered the tiny office. "Wonder if the air conditioner's broken?"

"It must be. We'll check into it, Sam, as soon as everyone gets here." Bill picked up his duty sheet.

"What's on our list for today, Boss?" Larry inquired.

"Brother Steve wants the risers set up in the auditorium for the children's singing tonight. Here, Larry, why don't you handle that." Bill handed him the diagram of how Steve wanted it set up.

"Got it." Larry went out the door as Miss Eleanor and Jason, a college student who helped part time, walked in.

Miss Eleanor began getting her supplies. "Thought I'd start in the bathrooms," she said as she collected her cleaning agents.

"Good, that's what I was thinking, too, and Jason, the Missionary Ladies are having a covered-dish luncheon at eleven. I need you to get the meeting hall ready. This is how they want it set up." Bill handed him the sheet. "Go ahead and put the tablecloths on the tables but put the plates and silverware on this serving table for them. Be sure to set up the coffee water so it can be hot. They need a VCR, too."

"Where do I put it?"

"Okay. Let's see." Bill studied the diagram. "I'd say here." He was acutely aware that Brother Cole had walked in as he continued to explain. "They can move it if they don't want it there."

"It's hot as blazes in this building. The air conditioner needs to be fixed right away, and the grass outside's too tall. It needs to be cut. Where's Larry? He's in charge. What are you doing here, Bill?"

"He works here, remember," joked Sam, only halfway trying to be funny, his remark hitting a dead silence.

"Sam and I are going to check out the air conditioning system as soon as I get everyone going on their jobs," Bill explained evenly. He handed Jason the diagram sheet. "Any more questions?"

"No, I got it. Thanks." Jason scooted out, passing by Brother Cole as quickly as he could. Miss Eleanor quietly followed him. As the door closed she heard the assistant pastor complaining, "We've started the nursery program and need that air conditioner fixed immediately." She shook her head sadly. Things were so much better when that man was gone.

"Bill, let me go up the ladder," Sam insisted. "You got that neck thing on. It could mess you up." The compressor was on the roof. They needed to check to see if it was working.

Bill considered. "All right," he finally agreed. It would be easier for Sam.

Sam climbed the ladder to the roof and listened for a few minutes. "Sounds as if it's working just fine," he announced as he climbed down. Bill was relieved that he didn't have to make the trip up to the roof to fix the unit. Getting on and off the ladder would be difficult.

After putting the ladder away, they trudged through the rain to the back door, walking back inside the muggy building to the basement door.

"Probably the air-handler's clogged," Bill guessed as he unlocked the door and turned on the light. They immediately saw where the problem was. At least four inches of water stood on the floor.

"This must be it. It's been flooded," Sam assessed quickly, bounding down the stairs.

"Wait, Sam! Don't step in that water. There could be a short. It could shock the daylights out of you," Bill hollered after him.

Sam stopped himself abruptly, backing up one step. "Hadn't thought of that. What we gonna do? The fuse box is way over there." He pointed across the room.

"We'll have to turn the whole building off. Let's go do it." Walking back upstairs, they left their rain gear and boots by the back door before tromping to Brother Cole and Brother Dan's office area. The main fuse box was in a cabinet in the receptionist room where Cole's secretary, Margie, worked. The young woman looked up as Bill and Sam came in.

"'Fraid we've got to cut the power for a few minutes, Margie."

"Oh. Okay. Give me a second to ring up the other secretaries so they won't lose anything on their computers?"

As Bill waited, Brother Cole came out of his office.

"All's clear," Margie said.

"Good." Bill opened the cabinet.

"What's this all about?" Cole's voice held a belligerent tone.

"I need to cut the power to the building for a few minutes," Bill explained.

"You can't cut the power to the whole building."

"Brother Cole, there's about four inches of water in the basement and something's wrong with the air handler. We can't step in that water. There might be a short in there. We need to turn off the electricity for just a few minutes so we can turn off the fuse box in the basement, then we can turn this back on."

"Forget it. You come up with another way. We have things to get done around here, too, you know, and there's a bunch of preschoolers in the kindergarten building that will go crazy if the power's turned off."

"I don't need to cut the power to the kindergarten building, only this one. It's too dangerous to do it any other way." Bill felt impatient with the man's unreasonableness.

"Well, you'll have to come up with one," he said, striding out of the room.

Bill looked at Sam and the secretary. "Sorry," he spoke to Margie. "I'm going to cut it off."

"But what if he cuts it back on," Margie whispered anxiously, "and you're down there in that water. I don't think I could stop him."

Bill sighed. He didn't know what to do.

"Bill, I have an idea." Sam motioned for Bill to follow him into the hall. "How 'bout we take one of the wooden chairs from the fellowship hall and push it with a board over to the circuit box, then we can walk on the board to turn off the box."

"I don't know. The thing could be dangerous. If that man would just let us turn the stupid power off."

"I think this should work, Bill."

"All right. Let's give it a try," Bill agreed grudgingly, wishing he'd gotten more sleep so he could think more clearly. This was probably all unnecessary anyway. Probably the water had just clogged something. They got a chair and a heavy two-by-eight. Bill ached under the weight of the board. He still couldn't lift things easily and this day had already taxed him more than any since he'd come back to work.

It took them a while to get the chair and board in position; then, they argued about who should go across it, but Bill, being the lighter of the two men, won that discussion. Prayerfully he stood on the board. It seemed to hold his weight. He wore his knee-high rubber boots so that if he did slip, hopefully he wouldn't get wet, and they would offer some protection. Cautiously shuffling across the board, he grinned at Sam when he got to the fuse box and turned off the circuit breaker.

Sam waded out to him, glad that he had on rubber boots in this murky water. He picked up the heavy outer casing, while Bill knelt in the cold water and began fidgeting with the air handler.

"They should have put a drain in this concrete floor. This building isn't all that old. Why didn't they do that?" Sam noticed that Bill was getting wet as he worked.

"Who knows? It has a sump pump that they thought would be enough. Probably trying to save a little money." Bill's voice was muffled as he searched for the problem. Unfortunately the church often saved money where safety was at sake. Instead they spent a small fortune on appearances. "Think I found what's wrong. Looks as if there's a shorted-out wire." He went to his toolbox to get what he needed.

Sam began to fathom what Bill had said. "A shorted-out wire. That's what you were afraid it was."

Bill trudged back over and knelt down to work. "I know, Sam. We'd probably be dead right now had we stepped in this water. I don't get why things are more important than people so often around here."

"Dead! I thought you said that it would shock the daylights out of me, but dead – that's a different story."

"These things carry a lot of voltage."

"Man, we should have told that Brother Cole to come down here himself and pushed him into the water to see if there was a short in it. Would have served him right."

Bill grinned as he pictured Sam's unusual suggestion. By the time he was finished, his back and shoulder ached. "You can put the cover down now. I think that should do it."

Sam put the grillwork back in its place and walked over to the steps.

Bill stood, shivering from the cold water that had gotten into his boots and on his pants while he worked. Stepping back up onto the old wooden chair, it groaned slightly under the extra weight.

"Here goes." He flipped the switch, turning on the power. They waited noiselessly to see if the air-handler would start working.

Several minutes went by. "It sure is taking a long time. You think it's still broken?" Sam asked, disappointed.

"Don't know. The compressor has to turn on first and run a little while, then this...." A buzzing sound interrupted him. He smiled at Sam.

"It's working," Sam cheered.

"Let's hope it's all right now." Bill closed the circuit breaker box. To be on the safe side, he'd walk across the board. As he turned, the wooden chair underneath him suddenly collapsed, throwing him into the cold, dirty water.

"Bill, you okay?" Sam ran to help his friend.

"I think so," answered Bill as Sam helped him up. Together they trudged to the steps. "I caught myself as I went down, but my arm's kind of sore."

"Yeah, it's all scraped up. You're bleeding."

A chilling thought struck Bill. "You know, Sam, if that chair had collapsed earlier, before I turned the circuit breaker off the first time...," he stopped, not finishing the sentence.

Sam looked at Bill, realizing what could have happened. "Bill, I'm sorry. It was a dumb idea."

"I'm just glad that what I did worked and there weren't any other shorts." Bill gave a slight laugh. "Christine would have killed me if I'd have gotten hurt doing anything so stupid."

"I'd have told Christine to sue the mess out of Brother Cole, and I'd have helped her do it, too," Sam stated vehemently, pent-up anger toward the assistant pastor raging out.

Miss Eleanor met a soaking wet Bill and an upset Sam in the maintenance office as she went to get her purse to take a lunch break. "What in the world have you two been up to?"

Sam told the whole story without leaving out a detail, and Bill knew that by the end of the day all the maintenance staff as well as most of the secretaries would know what had happened.

"Bill, let me take you home so you can get cleaned up."

"That's all right, Miss Eleanor. I have some work clothes here in the cabinet."

"But look at you – even your hair's wet. There could be all kinds of nasty stuff in that basement water infecting that scar of yours. And look here – you're bleeding."

Bill was pretty sore, and a hot shower at home would be nice. Without further argument, he accepted the offer.

"Why look, even your neck brace is wet," she realized. "Did you hurt your neck in that fall?"

"No. This brace doesn't let me move easily, and for once I'm glad that I have it on."

Bill changed into dry clothes with the realization that Miss Eleanor was right. His wet hair and neck brace clung to him like an icy hand, and now that the air conditioner was working, the stuffy building had cooled, chilling him. They walked out in the drizzle to Miss Eleanor's large car. As soon as they were inside, she turned on the heat to help Bill warm up.

During the drive, Bill found himself opening up to Miss Eleanor, even telling her about Mike's job offer.

"I don't give advice often, Bill, but it sounds like a good opportunity. I'd say, without reservation, that you should take that job. When you do, Brother Cole, Pastor Leonard, and all those bigwig staff will realize what all you do. Not everyone could fix the air conditioner, you know. They would have had to pay big bucks to do that if you hadn't been there. You've got to think about yourself and your family now. Sounds like God gave you an answer to your prayer today. Don't be so hardheaded that He has to nearly kill you again to get the message across."

Bill absorbed the woman's words. "You're right about that."

"You know, this opportunity may be the door that God wants you to take. Even though I think Brother Cole's awful hard for God to use, the Good Lord might even be able to use the likes of him to help you move on to something new that He wants you to do. He plans all our steps. It kind of gives you chills when you look behind you and can see how well everything was laid out."

Realizing that today's difficult turn of events may have been an odd answer to his prayer, Bill felt humbled. He had asked God to give him a push in the right direction, and well, today he'd received one, a hard one.

A decision cemented itself into Bill's mind. He would talk to Mike this coming Sunday and confirm with him that he wanted the new job, then he would turn in his resignation first thing next Monday morning.

"Look at that," said Miss Eleanor. "I think I see the tiniest piece of blue sky trying to break through those clouds up there."

Chapter 26

The truth will set you free.

Leonard, late for his luncheon, hurried into the Chinese restaurant and met Donald Gresham in the lobby. The troubled look on his head deacon's face stifled any lightheartedness in Leonard's mood. As soon as they'd ordered their food, he asked Donald what had happened.

"I've decided to resign as head of deacons."

"Why?" Leonard asked in genuine surprise.

Donald's gaze fell to the table. For years, he'd fooled himself into thinking he was a man of integrity. Since his talk with the Lord the other night, he'd taken time to look closely at who he was, and he didn't like what he saw. Looking at his pastor, his friend, he hated to admit the truth. He cared what this man thought of him, but he'd decided that he would begin telling the truth both to himself and to others. With candor, he explained some of his reasons – that he'd "rubber stamped" anything wanted, that he cared more about his image than people, that for years, he'd chosen to do the expedient thing instead of what was right.

Leonard tried to defend Donald. Perhaps there were times when the man had automatically approved motions that he and other staff members had wanted, but Donald was good at stopping disputes in the deacons' meetings. Leonard appreciated that. He thought church leaders ought not to argue over every little issue. He tried to explain this, but the look in Donald's eyes chastened him, silencing him.

As their meal arrived, Leonard asked Donald what he felt he'd "rubber stamped" over the years. Without hesitating, Donald expressed some specific concerns about poor decisions that he'd endorsed, pricking Leonard's heart in the process. Feeling overwhelmed by the man's candid answers, Leonard found himself wanting to argue, but a certain clarity with a hint of steel in Donald's blue eyes stopped him. Instead he asked, "Why didn't you express any of these concerns earlier in the deacons' meetings?"

"Sometimes right before an important, potentially explosive issue, Brother Cole would invite me out to lunch, and we'd discuss the problem beforehand. Often what Brother Cole said would cause me to put aside my misgivings. I wanted to please him. I knew what he wanted, and I would tend to follow his lead, putting aside my doubts."

Disturbed by Donald's words, Leonard argued, "Surely one man couldn't have that much influence."

Donald gave him a wry smile. "It shouldn't be that way, Pastor Leonard. You're right." He shook his head. "I'm not blaming this on Brother Cole. I'm the one who didn't express my doubts and concerns. I was too intent to keep the peace. I hate dissension, but I've learned recently that peace at no costs doesn't exist. Sometimes peace costs a lot."

Many times Leonard himself had felt pressure to go along with the consensus in order to preserve peace. A disturbing inner voice reminded him that God held him responsible for decisions made at the church.

Both became silent. Donald, because he wanted to give Leonard a chance to respond. Leonard, because thoughts rumbled through his head – a wall of denial shooting up, protesting Donald's words. Vaguely Leonard noticed that his meal tasted too salty; he pushed it away. This entire luncheon had become unpleasant. Donald had been fairly blunt – so unDonald-like – with him, yet there was a sincerity about the man that warded off any indignation Leonard might have otherwise felt. The thought slipped through his mind that Donald would probably be a much better head deacon now than he'd ever been before. He eyed him thoughtfully. "Donald, what caused all this."

Instead of answering directly, Donald asked him to watch the six-thirty news that evening.

"Tonight. I can't. We have prayer meeting." Leonard looked at Donald's concerned eyes. "I guess I could tape it."

"That would be good. You'll be glad I resigned when you see it. It'll explain everything. I am sorry, Pastor Leonard."

Leonard couldn't imagine what would be on the six-thirty news that would affect Donald so much.

The two parted shortly after with a perfunctory handshake. Both had some thinking to do. Donald felt empty – as if he'd just given himself away, and he didn't know what the consequences would be – at the same time something peaceful filled the void. The rain that had continued for days was only a slight sprinkle now, and he could see blue sky in the distance. Without much thought, he got in his car and drove in that direction. He could use some sunshine.

Leonard drove back to his office, feeling deeply troubled, as if a black hole were trying to swallow him. He couldn't shake the feeling that what little he had learned today from Donald was only a beginning to a battle he would need to fight.

He had a disquiet, a rumbling of a nearby storm that he needed to prepare for. A door was there to be opened, but he couldn't do it. Not yet.

The wall went back up. He felt angry with Donald Gresham for casting doubts, angry with the man for his forthcoming attitude – and deep inside afraid of the storm behind the door. At least for today he would leave that door shut.

Bill and Miss Eleanor arrived back at the church two hours after Bill's mishap. There was much to do to prepare for the evening prayer service, and Bill worked nonstop throughout the afternoon. He had promised Brother Steve that they would do their best to finish painting the choir room this week, so he, Sam, and Larry attacked the room together, passing the time with friendly bantering and story telling.

Time passed quickly. It was getting late. Two part-time helpers stopped by to say they'd gotten all the rooms cleaned and were leaving. Bill ached, wishing he could go home too.

"Bill, I thought I told you to get the grass cut today," an unmistakable voice criticized.

"Grass doesn't mow well when it's wet. Plus, it will tear up the ground." He thought to himself that Brother Cole had probably never mown anything in his life.

"I expect it done tomorrow, early," Cole's last word softened as he unexpectedly saw Larry coming out of the closet on the far side of the room. "Larry, that's looking good where you're painting," he said, honey in his voice.

Larry blushed with embarrassment. He knew that his wall didn't look any better than where Bill or Sam were working. If anything, his was worse, and he was the slowest painter of the bunch.

"Bill, I have a list to go over with you," Brother Cole directed with a friendly voice. Bill put down his brush and walked out with the assistant pastor. "I've been going through the buildings and have written down the problems I've found." The next hour was spent with Brother Cole taking Bill throughout the church and showing him the things he'd discovered that weren't as clean as he thought they should be.

As Bill drove home that evening, he knew God had thoroughly answered his prayer. "Got the message, Lord. I'm leaving. You don't have to let me see that man ever again." He might even call Mike tonight and tell him that he definitely would take the job. Sunday couldn't come fast enough.

Donald drove out from under the clouds into a few soft rays of sunlight. The peaceful afternoon calmed the disquiet that had claimed his emotions for the past week. Talking with Pastor Leonard had been hard. At lunch he'd had little appetite, and now his stomach growled its discontent, causing him to decide to stop at a Mom and Pop drug store that advertised ice cream. Walking in, he saw they had a large selection of milkshakes at an extremely low price. As a child he'd loved milk shakes. His mama could make the best ones in the whole county. Donald, transported back forty years in time, felt a childish gush of excitement as he ordered a peach milkshake. It's sweet, soft aroma reminding him of summers long ago. Sitting at a corner table, he watched people come and go – children with their mothers, a father with his little boy, high school students.

Finishing his milkshake, he felt unwilling to leave. Enjoying the ambiance of the place, an unaccustomed smile touched his face. He noticed a balding man with two children walk up to the counter.

"I want green ice cream," ordered the little boy.

"I want the kind with brownies in it," his slightly older sister said.

Donald couldn't see the man's face, but he recognized the voice immediately. The man told his children to choose a table, and he'd bring them their ice cream. He didn't see Donald until he'd sat down and begun licking his own cone. His face blanched as Donald walked over to him.

"Hi, John." Donald tried to sound friendly even though a knot had formed in his stomach. God had brought John across his path, just as he'd prayed. A prayer he'd hoped God wouldn't answer.

"Mr. Gresham!" John returned nervously, his eyes searching the room.

Donald realized he was afraid. A sinking feeling hit his stomach. "John, I didn't know where you'd moved to. I prayed that God would let me meet up with you someplace," he explained, ignoring the disbelieving look on the man's face. "I owe you an apology. I shouldn't have fired you. It was wrong. You were the one man on my staff that had integrity, but I was more interested in making money," and pleasing Judith, he thought but didn't say aloud. He then told John that two of the boys at the shop had bragged that they'd silenced him. He didn't know what they'd done, but he was glad John was all right. He explained that he'd never authorized any silencing, and that he'd been wrong not to get rid of the two on the spot.

An uncomfortable silence followed as John seemed to contemplate Donald's words. The fear in his face dissolved, replaced by indignation. "They beat me up, Mr. Gresham, last December. I don't know for sure if it was Jeff and Greg because they wore ski masks, but it sounded like them when they told me I'd better keep my mouth shut. I got a family to take care of, too. It was bad enough being fired, but to have to pay doctor bills and worry about my children was about more than we could take."

Though Donald had suspected something had happened, hearing the story felt like a blow. How had he been so blind? So stupid? How could he make it right for this man? "Look." He pulled out his checkbook. "I know this doesn't make up for all the pain that those guys put you through." He wrote out a check for every last penny he had in his account at the moment – over two thousand dollars. "But maybe this will help a little, and if you want to press charges against those men, I'll tell the judge what they told me."

John's mouth hung open in disbelieve. He stared at the check, his anger dissolving. A smile touching his eyes, then lips. "Thank you, Mr. Gresham. I do think you mean that.

"I do. And I'm sorry. I was wrong to not have better control over my employees." A breath of relief touched his heart. "I'm glad I saw you today. Like I said, I asked God to let me meet you somewhere since I didn't know where to find you. Oddly enough I've never been to this little place before." Shaking John's hand, he left with a feeling of freedom that he hadn't felt in ages.

That evening, Judith and Donald watched the Action News Investigative Report together. Donald had told Judith that she needed to see it, and her curiosity had won out over her desire to snub him. She was appalled at the slant the newscaster had put on everything and upset with Donald for not defending them better. Her stoic silence ended as she ripped him apart with words before rushing to her bedroom.

Jeff, one of Donald's workmen, who saw the report, called at the end of the broadcast. Donald asked him to inform Greg and Joe that he'd decided to close the business. They didn't need to report to work in the morning. Jeff argued that there had to be something they could do, but Donald ended the conversation.

Two more employees called, and he told them the same thing. Perhaps it would be over soon, but probably this was just a beginning. At least he had an unlisted telephone number.

He expected his father or Michael to call, but they didn't. Part of him hoped that they'd decided not to watch the program even though he'd asked them to.

Mr. Robert along with his grandson watched the broadcast in disbelief. He had tried to teach Donald better than this. A gamut of emotions attacked him. Mainly anger and shame-filled humiliation, but at the bottom of the heap was a deep sadness that swallowed him, causing him to almost physically hurt. When Donald had called him that morning to ask him to watch the show, he'd wondered what was wrong, but never would he have believed that it was this bad. He was ashamed that the business he'd begun, that held his name, had been run so unethically, and he was furious with Donald for allowing it to happen. Donald had seemed broken and repentant that morning. Well, he should be. But was it only because he'd gotten caught. Robert was disgusted with his son. What would happen now? There was no way the business would survive this.

Michael brought up a new fear. "Do you think they'll lose the house?"

"The house was paid for free and clear when I gave it to them. They shouldn't lose it. Just the business is down the tubes."

"Well, I know that they've mortgaged the house at least once," Michael revealed to his grandfather.

"My dad built that house. Why did I ever give it to Donald?" Suddenly he looked all his eighty-nine years.

Silence filled the room. Mr. Robert sat quietly digesting all he'd just learned. "Michael, you keep an eye on things, and let me know what happens. I don't want the family to lose the house." His voice was full of pain.

Michael promised to do that very thing, wishing his father had listened to him.

Chapter 27

You who pass judgment do the same things.

Romans 2:1 (NIV)

After the Tuesday evening prayer service, though Leonard was tired, he plopped himself into a chair and rewound the videotape. As he watched the Action News Investigative Report, something uncomfortable stirred in the core of his being. The story he saw on television and the Donald he thought he knew didn't fit together. Often he'd sensed a certain pliable, phlegmatic part to Donald that he'd appreciated, but now he saw it differently. The easy trust in others, Leonard tended to have, eroded, a new cautiousness taking its place.

The next two days, whispers of gossip were heard throughout the church as the news report spread. Cole came by Leonard's office to talk to him about it, saying that if they didn't act swiftly, the offering would be down on Sunday. Leonard felt briefly annoyed that Cole's primary worry was the church finance, but then again, the man was right. They were just beginning to recover from the budget crisis. Cole had every reason to be concerned. Leonard was concerned himself.

"It's been taken care of, Brother Cole. Donald and I met for lunch, and he resigned from the Deacon Board."

Cole's eyes narrowed. "I'd like to have been at that luncheon. Do you fully understand what that man did? He has no right to be a deacon or even a church member for that matter. We need to break fellowship with him. Take his name off the church roll. Oust him from the congregation."

Leonard winced at the idea. "I think he's genuinely repentant and wants to restore fellowship with us."

"Really?" Cole questioned with a hollow laugh, as if he thought Leonard rather gullible. "Well, I wouldn't trust him. He's probably just trying to get into your good graces."

Leonard listened to Cole's cautions, feeling a deep sense of sorrow. Donald's and his last conversation still resounded in his mind. He felt disturbed, not only by Donald, but also by Cole's unforgiving irate response. He was glad when their conversation ended; however, it would only be a short respite. The deacon's monthly meeting would be that evening.

Donald surprised everyone by showing up at the deacons' meeting. The men grew silent as he walked in the door, watching him, wondering what he was doing there. Some stood arms crossed, closing him out. Others looked around, uncomfortable, confused. Donald walked up to the front of the room and without formality quickly explained that he was there to resign from the Deacon Board. He asked the men to forgive him for the things that he'd done that had put a black mark on Main Street First Church. A stricken man replaced the confident man from last month's meeting.

After Donald excused himself and left, a huge argument erupted. Some of the deacons said that the man was sorry only because he'd been caught and hence should be put out of the church. Others spoke of forgiving a repentant brother. Leonard noticed that Brother Cole adamantly stood with the first group, and it troubled him. Perhaps if it weren't for the fact that Donald had come to Leonard before the news report had aired, he would have felt the same. He didn't want to judge anyone too harshly, and yet, Donald had seemed contrite. Time would only tell for sure, but Leonard understood the Bible to teach that if a brother repented, he should make restitution but also be allowed to continue to fellowship with the church. In the back of his mind some of his discussion with Donald echoed, causing Leonard to feel distrustful of Brother Cole, apprehensive that the assistant pastor was trying to outmaneuver him. Briefly he wondered how many of the deacons Cole might have taken to lunch the past two days. Perhaps that wasn't a fair assessment. After all, the person who had put doubts in his mind about Cole Odum was Donald Gresham.

Though it was difficult to listen to all the dissension, Leonard's confused mind stilled enough to quietly observe the deacons and staff members. He couldn't help but notice that the people who were Donald's worst critics tended to have similar sin problems in their own lives. Maybe not quite as clear-cut as Donald's, but problems nonetheless. Throughout the years, Leonard had noticed that the people who were the hardest judges tended to struggle with the same sin they were so quick to condemn. Perhaps they thought if they adamantly spoke up against a problem, it would help them in their own private lives. And here was Brother Cole, sounding so harsh in his assessment of Donald Gresham that Leonard began to wonder if the assistant pastor's own life was in good order. A Shakespearean saying came to his mind. "Me thinks he doth protest too much." Forgiveness was forgotten.

Finally, Leonard, tired of all the squabbling, stood and asked each deacon to pray for Donald and Judith Gresham. He heard the slightest grunt of distaste escape from Cole's tight lips. The unproductive meeting ended after a motion to review the situation at a later time. Leonard did not sleep well that night.

Sunday morning the church buzzed with the news of Donald Gresham and his business. If Leonard had thought some of the deacons were hard on Donald, it was nothing compared to what the congregation was saying. People acted as if they were talking about a sporting event. Many had self-righteous appalled looks on their faces. Leonard sat in his chair behind the pulpit, surveying the crowd. When had these people become so unloving, so pharisaical. They were a brood of vipers, ready to eat their prey. It was disheartening. He felt that he had let them down in some way. A weary-looking, slightly bent Donald walked into the auditorium and sat in the back row. The man certainly had grit. He sat alone even though the back rows were usually full.

After the special music, Leonard stood to prayerfully give his sermon. Feeling distressed by his congregation's cold-heartedness and their rejoicing over the failure of one of their brothers, he opened his Bible to the second chapter of Second Corinthians to tell the story through the apostle Paul's eyes of another man who had offended his Christian brothers and how Paul instructed the church in Corinth to respond.

Speaking about forgiveness – the supernatural forgiveness that is from God only – he discussed the devices by which Satan could take advantage of a church or a people or a person who refuses to let go of a grievance.

His sermon was deep. Most of the congregation listened attentively. Some appeared to take the exhortation to heart. Others seemed vexed by his words. Leonard's own heart felt grieved. At the end of the sermon he asked everyone to stand to sing a final hymn. A few people came to kneel at the altar, obviously touched by his words.

A figure from the back of the sanctuary made his way down the aisle. Leonard unconsciously held his breath as he prayed for God's intervention. Donald whispered to him, asking to use the microphone. Handing it to him, Leonard breathed again. This was the right thing. He could feel it. Tears touched his eyes as Donald gave a heartfelt speech, lacking his usual eloquence, it seemed to come from the depths of his soul. He told the assemblage that he'd done some things for which he was ashamed, that he was going to try to make restitution. He asked their forgiveness. Handing the microphone back to Pastor Leonard, he began descending the steps till Leonard stopped him.

"Ladies and gentlemen, our brother has asked us to forgive him. If it's your desire to do this, say Yes."

"Yes" went up throughout the auditorium.

"And if not, say No."

A few "No's" were heard. Some emphatic, most quiet. Leonard wasn't quite sure, but he thought he heard Brother Cole's voice among them.

"The yeses have it, Brother Donald." They shook hands.

Donald, who wasn't a showy man, felt awkward, embarrassed, and relieved all at the same time. With a quiet thank you, he quickly walked down the steps, wanting to escape as swiftly as possible. It had been hard coming here today. He hoped it had been the right thing to do.

No one spoke to him as he left, but a few smiles were offered, albeit uncomfortable ones. They felt better than all the whispering and accusatory looks he'd gotten earlier. Many still condemned him, and he didn't blame them. He condemned himself more than they could possibly know. Driving home, he realized he'd experienced probably the most difficult week of his adult life. Yet, oddly, he felt closer to the Lord than he'd ever felt before.

After five days at Cindy's home, Greta, even with all her health problems, felt happier than she had in a long time. She enjoyed her daughter and son-in-law, Barry, and the feeling seemed to be mutual. Her two sons, Brad and Brian, along with their wives had come by several times to visit, adding to her delight.

As Greta looked at her little family, she wondered how they had turned out so well. There was some anger toward their father that each of her children still struggled with from time to time, but now they rarely talked about him. He hadn't been around much when they were growing up, and if he ever was mentioned, it was almost as if they were speaking about a distant relative. They didn't seem to have much bitterness for which Greta was grateful. She remembered a time when Cindy had been resentful toward her dad, but now, because of God's blessing and perhaps because of a nurturing husband, Cindy seemed to have let go of that animosity. The boys had both connected with an elder in the church who had made them feel special, and Greta thought God had put him there especially for her sons when they needed someone to lean on.

None of the children knew how ill Greta was. She would eventually tell them, but it seemed too early. At the moment, she felt happy and well, plus she didn't want them to start treating her like an invalid.

Rose, who called Greta almost daily, had informed her about the Gresham's problems, and even though Greta didn't care for Judith, she hated to hear what had happened. Uncharacteristically for the tenderhearted Rose, she had sounded delighted that Judith should be having troubles. Greta was mildly surprised by this. Usually Rose wasn't the vindictive sort. She had a notion that something unpleasant had occurred between the two women. Greta liked the mild-mannered Donald and felt for him.

Bill and Christine had been at the prayer service the previous Tuesday evening and missed seeing the news report about their neighbors up the hill, but they certainly heard an earful at church that morning. The young couple wondered if the reports weren't exaggerated. Donald had treated them quite fairly, and both Christine and Bill doubted he had known what his employees were up to. Hoping that Mike and Nancy weren't overly affected by Mike's dad's problems, they drove over to their house for Sunday dinner, determining on the way that they wouldn't mention what had happened at Main Street First Church. For the first time, Christine was grateful that her friends still attended Deer Creek Church where Mike had grown up. She would hate for them to receive fall out from Donald's business problems.

The news report wasn't mentioned that afternoon, and Bill and Christine enjoyed Sunday dinner with their friends. Mike, pleased that Bill had decided to become his foreman, talked extensively about Bill's new job.

First thing Monday morning, Bill would tell Brother Cole that he would be resigning and turn in his four-week notice. By mid-October, with God's help, Bill would be working for Mike.

The following morning Christine dropped Bill off at work as usual. As he assigned the morning duties, Bill considered telling the maintenance staff of his decision to leave, but he decided to wait. If Brother Cole heard it from someone else, he'd be angry, and Bill didn't want to cause unnecessary resentment. As soon as everyone left, he went to seek the assistant pastor.

"He hasn't arrived yet, but I have a note here on my desk saying he wants to see you first thing this morning," Margie informed him.

Bill groaned inwardly. Anytime Brother Cole commanded someone's presence, it wasn't a good experience.

"I'll call you over the radio when he comes in."

"Thanks, Margie. I'll be outside trimming the bushes." Larry and Sam were already busy mowing the lawns.

As Bill worked, his thoughts kept revolving around the fact that this was probably the last time he would ever cut this bush, the last time he'd trim this tree. He laughed at himself and his melancholy outlook. It would be nice not to have to prune these bushes ever again. Hearing footsteps, he turned to see Brother Cole walking toward the front door.

"I left a note that you were to be in my office first thing this morning."

"I was there, but you weren't, so I decided to get some work done." Bill put down his tools and followed Cole into the building.

"Clean up and come straight to my office. I don't want that red clay on my carpet." Cole turned to walk to the elevator.

Bill went back outside to scrape his boots. There was no mud on them. They just were stained from so much use. Walking inside, he went to the elevator, feeling a little defiant in using it, but if Cole Odum could, so could he.

When he arrived at the outer office area, Margie announced to Brother Cole over the intercom that Bill was there. The assistant pastor responded that he would talk to him shortly. Bill waited. Miss Eleanor greeted him briefly as she came in with her vacuum, dust rags, and supplies to clean Brother Dan's office. Finally, thirty minutes later, Cole told Margie to send Bill in. Bill, who hated to waste time, especially while his boys were out there working so hard on this humid day, felt annoyed as he walked into the assistant pastor's office. Immediately Cole began talking.

"Bill, I've been thinking for a long time that I need to speak to you." He thumped his pencil on his desk, drawing out his words, as if it pained him to have to speak at all. His tone, his attitude, and the set of his jaw –ugh– Bill hated them all. Every move he made spoke arrogance. "You just aren't pulling your load around here. I've noticed that ever since your accident it's gotten worse. You don't seem to think clearly."

Bill felt himself grow hot under Brother Cole's abuse, but he stood and listened.

"After all your years working here, I still find things in a mess." Cole paused, feigning a look of sympathy – something Bill hated. "I just don't think you can do it. I've been watching you, and you don't get the work done."

Not defending himself, he stood stone quiet while Brother Cole continued his accusations. A heat growing in his chest.

"The personnel committee agrees with me. You aren't right for this job. I think we need to let you go. I'm not firing you – just letting you go. It would look bad on your record if you got fired. It would be best if you turned in your resignation."

His chest burned. His stomach knotted. Why did Brother Cole dislike him so much? At the same time, God was there. He had already supplied a new job. Bill wasn't as naive as Brother Cole believed him to be. He knew good and well that the assistant pastor hoped to bully him into quitting. If Bill hadn't had the other job lined up, he'd have entered the battle, but God had other plans. Regarding Brother Cole silently, he thought of telling the man that he had already planned to resign, but no, that might come across as petty or worse yet, unbelievable.

"It would be good to have your resignation in writing by the end of the day."

"Do you want me to give four-weeks notice?" Bill asked.

"Oh." Brother Cole smiled slightly. This had been easier than he'd thought it would be. He weighed the alternatives. His desire would be to have Bill gone immediately, but then again maybe this would look better. "Yes. That would be best."

Bill left the room. He had already written his note of resignation, but the joy he'd felt only yesterday was marred by the fact that Brother Cole had definitely planned on firing him. In the maintenance office, he looked dejectedly at the letter he had prepared. Well, he'd planned on leaving anyway, but he felt as if he were abandoning the church, letting this weed take over and suck all the life out of it. Walking down to Margie's outer office again, he handed her a copy of his resignation letter in an envelope for Brother Cole. Time to talk to his men. He didn't want Brother Cole telling them in his way.

He didn't have to tell Miss Eleanor, who continued to quietly clean Brother Dan's office, angry tears flowing down her withered cheeks. She'd overheard the discussion. She hoped Bill had accepted the other job, but no matter, she couldn't hold back the tears. What did it take to stop Cole Odum?

Sam, though disheartened with the news of Bill's resignation, said he understood. Still it was obvious that the decision grieved him. Bill had expected this response from his right-hand man who had become a valued friend over the past few years, but what surprised him was Larry's reaction. If possible, he was even more upset than Sam was.

"You don't think he'll expect me to be the maintenance supervisor, do you?" Larry asked, deeply worried.

"I don't know." Bill couldn't understand why Brother Cole did many of the things that he did.

"I'm not ready for that responsibility again. Sam could do it. He would be much better than me. Sam should be the one to do it."

"I appreciate the vote of confidence, Larry," Sam admitted, touched by the words.

"If I were in charge, I'd have Sam take my job, and you Larry, take Sam's job, but I'm not in charge. Brother Cole does his own thing," Bill asserted.

"Maybe you could suggest it?" Larry asked.

"The man doesn't listen to me. If I asked him, he'd probably do the opposite."

"Then why don't you tell him that Larry should be in charge and that I should continue as the second in command," Sam suggested seriously.

"If I thought it would work, Sam, I'd do it. The only one he listens to around here is you, Larry. You obviously have a key that unlocks a side of him that we've never seen. Maybe you should talk to him."

"I could try." Larry didn't sound too sure about the idea. "I don't understand why he's so nice to me."

"It must be your rugged good looks," Bill suggested with a laugh.

"No, it's all the money he's given the guy." Sam laughed, too, but Larry looked as if he took the remark seriously. "I was just kidding, Larry. I know you're not rolling in dough. But boy, I've seen Brother Cole talk as smooth as silk and as sweet as pie to anyone who has money." Sam and Bill had not made the connection of who Larry's father was, nor did they know how wealthy his family was, but Larry began to guess the truth. The thought troubled him. There was something very irregular about the way Brother Cole treated him, and these two had noticed it as well.

Later, when Bill told Miss Eleanor that he had decided to accept the job from Mike Gresham and would be leaving, she gave him a knowing look.

"You did the right thing, Bill. I'm happy for you. Don't forget to pray for us here in the trenches. As long as we have to work for that man, it's going to be hard for all of us. We'll miss you."

Bill did feel sad about leaving them, but he knew, not only that it was the right decision, but that in reality, he had no choice, unless he wanted to go to Pastor Leonard and the personnel committee to fight for his position. Sometimes God had a way of slamming a door shut and dead bolting it. But that way one knew he was headed in the right direction. He would pray for the maintenance staff. They would need it. He felt like a brand plucked from the fire.

Donald went to his office for the last time. A realtor had been contacted to sell the building. Personal belongings and business records were packed to bring home. A man from another company had stopped and given him a good price on the supplies that he stocked. "For Sale" signs were put on the vans. He needed to sell everything. Not surprisingly, there had not been one service call after the show had aired, but there had been plenty of irate phone calls from former customers. He had pulled out the records from each account and been appalled at the obvious markup of prices. There was no one to blame but himself, and with his newfound resolve to make things right, he wondered how he possibly could. Though he wanted to burn all the records and forget about the whole deplorable business, he knew that wouldn't be wise.

Michael arrived with his truck. Two hours later, at Donald's house, they unpacked the file cabinets and boxes. They put them in the office in the basement. It was a mess, but first the building must be cleaned so it would sell quickly; then, Donald would organize all this stuff. The two worked quietly with few words between them the entire morning. At one point, Judith began berating her husband for bringing all that trash into "her" house. It didn't matter that Michael was there. Donald quickly determined he liked the silent Judith better. Although he was used to her criticizing him in front of others, this time he recognized it as a way that she controlled him. He rarely responded to her tirades when anyone was around because he didn't want to fuel her fire, but as she ranted he told her to please go upstairs. He would talk to her later. To his surprise, she did just that, muttering as she went, but at least he had a little of his self-respect. Michael busily emptied a box, hiding a grin.

Later, Donald and Michael had lunch from the few leftovers in the refrigerator. While they ate, Donald told his son that he didn't know what else to do, but that he was considering selling the house – that should have been part of Michael's inheritance – in order to try to settle some of the debt he owed.

Donald sighed, a sigh that if put into words would have said, "If only..." If only he'd been smarter. If only he'd been wiser. If only he'd listened to God's inner cautions. If only... He would miss this house. He needed to warn his father. Later today he would go see Mr. Robert.

That afternoon, with the money he'd received from the sale of his inventory, Donald repaid some of the former customers who had called him. It was a humbling experience, but he knew that it would be nothing compared to visiting his father. This would be the most difficult visit he'd ever made.

Mr. Robert, disturbed and upset by what his son had done, was prepared to berate Donald when he arrived, but the broken man who stood before him helped soften his angry heart. This was his son. Something about this contrite Donald reminded him of the little boy from long ago. The son who had been brokenhearted when a stray kitten he'd found was stepped on by one of the cows and died; the child who loved to sit on his father's lap; the one who had earnestly promised his mother that when he grew up, he would marry her. Though Robert's heart involuntarily went out to his child, the reserve was still there.

Donald didn't try to hide any of the unpleasant facts. Without dissembling, he explained to his father that he was selling the business and would be using the money to pay back the people that had been cheated. The older man's face broke the son's heart. What a fool he had been. What a disappointment to this good man. Not wanting to say anything, but knowing he should, he explained his decision to sell the family home.

"You know, my father built that place before I was even born." Mr. Robert's voice was touched by a brokenness that grieved Donald. "That house is like a part of me. I don't want the family to lose it. Michael and his children shouldn't miss out on having the chance to live there. I think you should sell it to them."

The pain of having disappointed his father felt almost palpable to Donald. For years, he'd hidden behind a facade of aloof self-confidence that was crumbling. "I'd like Michael to have the house," was all he said, but his face conveyed his thoughts, his anguish. Looking at his father, he saw the upset look in his eyes turn to an understanding sympathy.

"I'm going to help Michael get the house. I'll pay the mortgage. Now, I don't think you and Judith should live with them, mind you." Mr. Robert regarded his son sharply.

Donald gave no indication that the idea had crossed his mind. "I agree," he replied.

As the two continued to talk, Donald felt thankful for this wise and caring man. He told his dad about his recent experience out at the graveyard with the Lord and confessed feelings that he'd not shared with anyone before about how deeply hurt he was to not have been able to tell his mother good-bye and that he loved her, how ashamed he was of the last time he'd been with her. A few tears were shed as they talked. The two continued baring their souls to each other as they'd not done before. They ate supper in the little cafeteria and continued talking into the wee hours of the morning. Mr. Robert discovered that he rather liked this boy of his after all.

Chapter 28

A heart at peace gives life to the body.

Proverbs 14:30 (NIV)

The days and weeks slid by as warm September evenings turned into cool, comfortable October nights. Brother Cole acted almost friendly toward Bill and stayed out of the maintenance staff's way the last few weeks that Bill worked.

The first week of October, Dr. Keith concluded that the neck brace could finally come off. Bill heaved a sigh of relief, feeling as if he'd been set free. Unexpectedly for a couple of days, his neck felt abnormally long and heavy, making it hard for him to hold his head up for any length of time, forcing him back into the brace for short periods. But toward the end of the first week, as his neck muscles strengthened, he eventually didn't need to depend on the apparatus anymore, and he got rid of his old, unwanted friend.

In mid-October, Bill started working for Mike. Long, tiring days began as he learned the different stages of the construction business. Each phase of a house was carefully planned, and Mike helped him as they worked together. Often the overworked Mike expressed his appreciation that Bill was there to help relieve the workload.

Bill's main difficulty these days was his financial situation. Their meager savings had dwindled to practically nothing as they tried to pay all their bills. He had worked out a minimum payment plan with each of the doctors and the hospital, but as their reserve dwindled, it became more and more difficult to make ends meet. They had learned to live on a shoestring budget years ago, but their present situation was tighter than any they had ever been through. Bill worried how they would pay their land taxes in December and the car insurance in January. There was only so much juggling that could be done.

Before Greta knew it, it was the twenty-third of October, and she and her children were traveling to Destin, Florida. She'd called Cole a couple of times to invite him but had only talked to the answering machine. He didn't returned her messages. In a way, it was a relief that he wouldn't be coming.

When they had moved to Georgia and begun listening to Pastor

Leonard's inspiring Bible studies, she'd thought that surely this would touch her husband, but it never did. Cole saw himself as above all that. For years it had confused her. How he could give such eloquent, sincere-sounding speeches, and yet devalue others so easily. He seemed more interested in climbing the church's social ladder. Often she wondered, why in a church? Perhaps it helped him to feel better about himself – a pharisaical type of pride – working his way to heaven – but gaining treasures here on earth as he went. And then again, perhaps this was Satan's way of having a foothold. Cole acted as if he did the Lord's work, but she knew where his heart was. It wasn't with Christ. She continued to pray that God would turn his heart toward Himself.

In spite of the heaviness that weighed on her from time to time as she thought about her husband, she enjoyed these peaceful days with her children. Her time with Cindy had been refreshing, almost as if a healing had happened. Often she wondered if the doctors had misdiagnosed her condition. She'd even been able to help her daughter by watching the grandchildren while Cindy took a woodworking class at one of the local Appalachian shops. Greta felt like part of the family. Early in October, Rose had surprised her by coming up for a short visit. The two had talked like schoolgirls, clearly amusing her daughter.

Arriving at the condominium – it was as nice as the brochure had promised – Greta went out to sit on the porch swing that overlooked the ocean. The cool evening breeze along with the sound of lapping waves and a salty breeze lulled her into a quiet, satisfying contentment. Humming softly to herself the song "All is Well With My Soul," she felt indeed that all was well.

October twenty-third was also Pastor Leonard's birthday. He took the day off to celebrate quietly with his wife instead of risking any embarrassing stunts that the secretaries might pull. Last year, at his fiftieth birthday, they had filled his office with black balloons and paid a man in a gorilla outfit to come to the front of the church's auditorium at the Sunday evening worship service. Even though it had been fun, he'd been embarrassed by the attention. Instead he preferred this quiet day, relaxing with his wife at the lake. Ann seemed at ease, too. Her life was full of tensions, perhaps more than his; however, she had a way of handling stress in a graceful manner that he admired. The stress had taken its toll on him the past few years. People expected a lot, more than any one man could give, and as his congregation grew, he'd been less and less able to meet all the demands.

For over three years now, Brother Cole had been at the church. At first Leonard had liked the man's protective, loyal spirit. He thought he himself was treated with more deference because of his assistant pastor, but those same strokes to his ego that he'd so appreciated at one time had begun to feel strangely awkward lately.

Sitting in the boat, his fishing line dangling in the water, Leonard had a lot of time to think. Though it was painful to realize, his values had subtly altered over the years. He remembered his first pastorship in a little country church in Tennessee. Though it had been part time and he'd been paid practically nothing, he'd been so pleased working there. Later when he'd received his first full-time placement, he'd felt relief that he didn't need to work an extra job to make ends meet. It had been a hard life for him and his young, growing family, but in a way, as he thought back on those years, they'd been the best. In some ways it had laid the groundwork for him to be more tenderhearted, but unfortunately that empathy had dissipated and was being replaced with something that he didn't like. Leonard felt this shifting of values, not only in his own life but also in the church's.

Just recently the Finance Committee had completed the new budget, giving Leonard and Brother Cole each a large pay raise, but the secretaries had received very little increase in salary. Even though Brother Cole had assured him that this was what the committee wanted to do, it disturbed Leonard. A nagging doubt continued to break into his thoughts. The still small voice of God, of wisdom spoke, trying to break through the wall Leonard had built to protect himself.

Bother – his fishing line was caught on something – a branch perhaps. He pulled at it, hoping he wouldn't break the twine.

In a couple of weeks there would be a deacons' meeting about the budget proposal. It would all need to be accepted, and it wasn't up to him to decide how the money was spent. Leonard comforted himself with that thought. Besides that, he tithed more than most people did. He'd given the entire love offering he'd received from the revival services in Columbus to Main Street First Church's building fund.

Yanking his line out of the water, a bag full of rotting trash was attached to the hook. Why did people have to throw garbage into this lake? The sun shimmered on the water, hiding the debris under its surface – much the way Leonard tucked away the thoughts from God, replacing them with his own self-assurances and platitudes.

As he and Ann drove home, they laughed and enjoyed each other's company as much as any newlyweds. When they finally reached their driveway, Leonard stopped to pull the mail out of the box, handing the letters to Ann.

"It looks as if you got a birthday card from your Aunt Minnie," she observed, as she went through each piece of mail.

Leonard smiled. Aunt Minnie was in her eighties, and every year she would send him a crisp new dollar bill. She still lived in the Tennessee mountains where he'd grown up, and she had few worldly possessions or income, but she often sent him a dollar. It touched his heart. It was the widow's mite.

"The electric bill, the water bill, some advertisements, and something from William Herrin," Ann finished.

"What did William Herrin send me?" Leonard closed the garage door with the control before getting out of the car.

"It looks like a birthday card. Want me to open it?"

"Sure. Let's go inside first." Leonard unlocked the door and followed Ann inside the house. He felt pleasantly tired as he sat in his easy chair.

"Which one should I start with?"

"Start with Aunt Minnie's." Leonard enjoyed hearing what she had to say.

"Dear Lenny," Ann read. She liked the way Aunt Minnie called Leonard, Lenny. If the church people knew, they might see the vulnerable man that her husband really was instead of expecting him to be perfect. "Hope your birthday finds you happy. Spend this dollar on something you've been wanting. I been feeling a mite poorly lately, but the good Lord's not given up on me yet. Don't you neither. We all are meeting together at Pearl's son's house for Christmas this year. I talked to your boy Daniel's wife, Sara, last week at meeting, and she says that you are planning on coming since Christmas is on a Monday this year. We'll look forward to it. Weren't the same without you last Christmas. See you then, Love you, Aunt Minnie. P.S. That grandson of yours is growing into a mighty handsome little boy. He helped me the other day. You can be proud."

Leonard smiled. He respected his Aunt Minnie. The woman often reminded him of who he really was deep down inside, not the highly respected pastor of a large church, but a young growing, redeemed sinner who needed love and approval. Aunt Minnie gave him that unconditionally. Everyone should have an Aunt Minnie in his life.

Ann opened the envelope from William Herrin, and a check fell out. "Oh, my! It's for two thousand dollars."

"What?" Leonard sat up from his reclined position. "Let me see that."

He took the card that read simply "Happy Birthday" with a little poem inside, and then a small written note. "Appreciate all you do. Hope you have a good birthday. William and Carol Herrin."

"Well, what do you know about that?" asked Leonard.

Ann regarded her husband. She loved him. He had integrity and the gift of sharing with others, but in the past couple of years, she'd seen an almost imperceptible shifting of his values that concerned her. She remembered the poor days in Tennessee. Though they had been hard days, living from hand to mouth meant trusting God to provide for the electric bill or the rent. God had shown Himself faithful. In some peculiar way she missed that. Now they lived lavishly, but sometimes she felt as if other women had a difficult time relating to her because their life style was much better than most of the congregation. She, herself, had been persuaded to buy more expensive and fancier clothes than she really liked or felt comfortable in. When had appearances become so important? She wished that she had suggested that Leonard give his love offering from the revival to the Charity Fund instead of to the Building Fund. Main Street First had just built one new building. Did they really need another one? The nursery school director had recently had her hours reduced and her health benefits cut. It was a hardship on her as she was a single mother. When Ann heard this, she mentioned it to Leonard. He said it was a result of a lull in the church's giving, but Ann noticed shortly afterwards that the library had put in expensive, new carpet and the choir bought new robes. True, the old ones had been around a while. But were new robes and carpet more important than a person?

"I have a suggestion," she offered tentatively. "It's your money, so you can do whatever you want with it, but I think you should put it into the savings account. Let's keep our eyes open for a family in need that we can help anonymously."

Leonard smiled at his wife's generous spirit. "I like that idea." He looked at Ann with an expression she hadn't seen in a long time. "To be honest, it feels kind of funny for William to send me all this money. I barely know the man. He's given a lot to the church in the past few months, but..."

His wife eyed him critically – the kind of look Aunt Minnie used to give him as a child. "How do you know he's given a lot of money to the church? I thought that you didn't look at the books so you wouldn't be influenced by what the members give."

"Well, now that you mention it, I don't." Leonard's voice held a note of defensiveness. "He's been giving Brother Cole envelopes with checks in them, and Brother Cole's brought them to me during our weekly staff meeting. I know about it that way. They've been rather large donations."

"So all the staff members know how much he gives?"

Leonard looked a little sheepish. "I guess they do. I didn't think of that."

"Maybe Brother Cole should just take them to the financial secretary so none of you would be influenced." Ann had a sudden realization. "Isn't that new maintenance guy, Larry, William Herrin's son?"

Leonard nodded. "You're right. If we're aware of what his father is giving, it might make us treat the boy differently. I just was so relieved when we met our budget."

Ann understood. She didn't want to be overly critical. Aunt Minnie probably would have lectured him. She let the topic drop but felt as if this was yet another example of how her husband had let down his standards. She determined to pray daily for Leonard.

The wind chimes began to clatter loudly outside. A storm was brewing.

Chapter 29

He that is soon angry dealeth foolishly, and a man of wicked devices is hated.

-Proverbs 14: 17

The beautiful late October afternoon contrasted greatly with Sam's consternation. He felt a disturbing undercurrent of oppression at work, especially when he dealt with Brother Cole. The man was capricious, Sam decided. If he and Larry were together, the assistant pastor acted friendly and seemingly agreeable, but let Larry be gone, and Brother Cole was a different man – critical and overbearing. He had fired one of the college students without warning last week in front of two of the secretaries, embarrassing the boy half to death. A nice kid, too – just needed some guidance. To add to Sam's apprehension was the realization that he couldn't afford to lose his job, and Cole Odum seemed to be on a firing spree. True, Bill had resigned, but rumors had it that he hadn't done so totally out of his own motivation. Sam prayed that Brother Cole would be the next one to leave the church's employment.

Again Larry had been given the maintenance supervisor position – much to both Sam's and Larry's displeasure. After all the years Sam had worked at the church, he'd once more been slighted. At least he was wise enough to know it wasn't Larry's fault. It was Brother Cole that he blamed.

Together Sam and Larry worked as a team, keeping knowledge of their partnership as obscure as possible. Larry improved daily. He was a quick learner with everything except the bookwork – he had a problem inverting numbers. Sam helped him as well as he could. Larry would do the books, then Sam would go over them and show the boy his mistakes, and they'd correct them together. Larry was careful to turn in the accounts at the scheduled time so no one would suspect that Sam helped him.

As the afternoon progressed, Sam, Larry, and Jason – one of the part-time workers – continued the tedious job of painting that they had been doing for hours. Though tired and achy, each determined to get his portion finished. Sam stood on his ladder, giving the ceiling trim boards a fresh coat.

"Larry, we got anymore of this white super-gloss? I'm getting low," he asked as he dipped his brush into the almost empty can.

Larry stretched his aching muscles before checking through the cans at his feet. "I guess that's the last one. I'll go down to the store and get another gallon before you run out. It looks like we're gonna need more blue, too." He headed out the door, relieved to give his tired arms a short break.

Jason and Sam continued to work, telling each other funny anecdotes that helped to pass the time.

"Looking good in here," praised Miss Eleanor as she peeked into the room, vacuum cleaner in hand. "I like that blue color. You boys want to paint my house next?"

The two laughed. "No, thank you, Miss Eleanor. Once we finish this room, I hope to retire from painting for the rest of my life," responded Jason lightheartedly.

"Don't count on it. Brother Cole will probably want the youth building painted next, and then the adult Sunday school building," Sam asserted dryly.

"Then it will be time for the new wing to be painted all over again," Jason added, shaking his head.

"Watch out, Miss Eleanor. This paint drips, and I'm right over your head." Sam smiled down from his ladder at the little lady. He rarely dripped, but he would hate for her to get white paint in her hair.

Miss Eleanor looked at her worn outfit. "Probably make me look better'n I do now."

They laughed and began joking about whether the blue or the white paint would look better on her outfit. Miss Eleanor was suggesting that the blue would match her eyes when an unmistakable voice, causing them to cringe, interrupted her. "Miss Eleanor, don't you have enough work to do without taking breaks all the time?"

"Sorry, Brother Cole." The older woman's meek voice tore at Sam's heart.

Cole coming into the room to survey the work, quickly noticed that Larry wasn't there. "Where's Larry?" he asked accusingly. Sam wanted to joke that they'd tied him up in the basement, but he knew the assistant pastor wouldn't be amused.

"He went to get more paint," answered Jason.

"More paint!" Cole sounded disgusted as he looked at the men's work. "You need to use a lighter touch up there, Sam."

Sam remained quiet, but inside his temper raged. The man only knew how to criticize and condemn. He sure didn't know anything about painting.

As Miss Eleanor began vacuuming the hall, Brother Cole bellowed for her to stop. "Can't you see I'm trying to talk to these men?" He narrowed his focus on the elderly woman. "I've been meaning to speak to you about something." His voice had an edge to it that Sam loathed. It was the voice of authority. The voice of an abusive parent speaking to their unloved child. This voice knew all and defied the comments of others. It was controlled, well modulated, and cold as ice. "The woodwork looks as if it hasn't been shined in weeks. Are you pulling your weight around here?"

Sam hated to see Brother Cole be unkind to Miss Eleanor more than anyone else. He saw the stricken look on the sensitive woman's features. He couldn't see the assistant pastor's face since he was standing right below his ladder, but he knew without seeing what the man looked like. He would have a satisfied smirk of one who enjoys wounding others plastered on his face. Sam had reached his limit of tolerance. He thumped the paintbrush down angrily on the ladder's paint shelf, and began climbing down the ladder, unaware that with each rumbling step, paint dripped from his brush.

"We expect more out of..." Brother Cole stopped suddenly as he felt a disconcerting, odd sensation on his head. Reaching up, touching his hair, a sticky wetness met his fingers. Looking at Sam, he accused, "You threw paint in my hair!"

"Sorry, Brother Cole." Though Sam meant his apology, the polka-dotted hair on the proud assistant pastor's head brought a hint of a smile to his face that Cole didn't miss.

Cole Odum went into an apoplectic rage. Sam had done this on purpose. He didn't realize who he was playing games with. He would wipe that smug look off that silly face. "Sam, you're fired! Pick up your things and get out. I mean right now. I never want to see you around her again."

As the glimmer of the smile vanished, Cole felt mild satisfaction. Without further word, he marched to the restroom to see how much damage had been done.

The man out of earshot, Jason started giggling – a muffled, strangled sound as he tried to hide it. In a moment Sam and Miss Eleanor joined in, very quietly. Seeing that proud man with splatters of paint in his hair had been a rich experience.

"I sure didn't expect that to happen," Sam began. "I was about to tell him what I thought of him talking to you so unkindly, Miss Eleanor. Guess I shouldn't have banged my brush down so hard."

"Oh, Sam, surely he realizes it was an accident," Miss Eleanor reasoned, sobering.

"I don't know, but if I had to get fired, this was the way to do it." The reality of the final statement, that he'd just been fired, began to sink in. He had just lost his job.

Miss Eleanor looked gently at Sam. "You did it for me. That's one of the nicest things anybody's ever done. I'm scared half to death of that man."

Sam smiled ruefully as he picked up his belongings. He'd better leave before Cole Odum came back. He hugged the sweet lady as he went out the door.

When Larry returned from the paint store, Jason told him the whole story. A panic rose in Larry. He needed Sam. Racing down the hall to the assistant pastor's office, he would somehow make amends. Help Brother Cole to forgive Sam. Smooth things over.

"I need to see Brother Cole right away," he said after bursting into Margie's office.

"He stormed out of here a little while ago, Larry. I think he was going home. He didn't say a word, but he looked fit to be tied. What in the world happened?" Margie asked.

Larry told her the episode as it had been related to him and explained that he desperately needed to talk to Cole in order to get him to change his mind about the firing of Sam.

"Well, if he'll listen to anyone, it'll be you, Larry. I'll make an appointment for you to see him first thing in the morning."

It perplexed Larry that even Margie had noticed the favoritism that had been shown to him. He wondered what he could say to dissuade Brother Cole from his decision. When he'd first met the man, he'd liked him a lot, but from time to time, he'd heard from others what a terror the assistant pastor could be. Larry only had glimpses of what others saw. When Bill had come back to work, Larry had noticed a colder side to Cole that he'd not seen before. It wasn't exactly what Brother Cole said that was so awful, but sometimes the tone he used. He hoped the man wouldn't talk to him in that manner tomorrow.

The first thing the next morning Larry went to the maintenance office to get everything in order before his meeting with the assistant pastor. He hoped Sam would come, but only the part-time workers and Miss Eleanor arrived. Thankfully Miss Eleanor knew what to do, but the young men stood there waiting for him to direct them. He was accustomed to Sam helping him get the morning duties scheduled. Feeling awkward, he gave the young men the one job he knew that still needed to be done – finishing painting the classroom that he and Sam had been working on yesterday. At least he could get these boys started; then, he'd go see Brother Cole.

As he hurried downstairs, he noticed Sam trudging dejectedly out of Margie's outer office.

"Sam, you're here."

"Well, I'm still out, Larry. Guess Jason or Miss Eleanor told you what happened."

"Yeah, I'm sorry."

"I tried to ask him for my job back."

"What'd he say?"

"He yelled at me as soon as he saw me. Told me to never come on this property again. If I did, he'd call the police and might press charges against me. Guess I really messed up."

"I'm gonna talk to him, Sam. I need you around here. I'm gonna tell him so. I can't do it without you. Maybe he'll listen to me."

Sam looked a little hopeful. "Thanks, Larry, I appreciate it." He shook his head. "I'm sorry to put you in this position. I appreciate you trying to help me."

Larry gave a weak smile. "Really, I'm selfish, Sam. I want you to have the job. Don't get me wrong, but if you're gone, they're gonna start realizing just how much I can't do. You're my coach. I couldn't have made it without you. I might just have to quit myself."

"No, you can do it without me, Larry. I'm sorry to have let you down."

"I'd better go. I'll call you as soon as we finish talking."

"Okay. Thanks." Sam walked out feeling more hopeful but still doubtful. Brother Cole had been so angry that he didn't think Larry, even with his influence, could change the assistant pastor's mind.

Larry, feeling more positive than Sam, felt certain that the man would listen to him. So far, Brother Cole had given him almost anything he'd asked for. Walking into the outer office, he told Margie he was there to see the assistant pastor.

"He's expecting you. You can go on in."

As Larry opened the door, Brother Cole smiled at him. "Well, what can I do for you, my boy?"

"I wanted to talk to you about Sam's job." As soon as Larry spoke the words, he saw an unpleasant expression touch the assistant pastor's face. His facial muscles hardened, and his mouth became tight. Though he kept the smile in place, his eyes darkened, glinting steel.

"There's nothing to discuss." He didn't care to have to explain his actions to this wimp of a kid, but he needed to be careful. Anything he said to the boy might reach the father's ears. A new game plan was in order. He would sound as if he were confiding in the young man. This tactic worked like a charm on most people. They felt honored that Cole Odum would share a secret with them. He spoke now quietly, as if this were something private to be kept between them. "The man has problems that you don't even know about, Larry. It's best that we're rid of him."

"But," faltered Larry lamely as he tried to think of the things he was going to say. His mind went blank. "He... he does so much around here. I need him."

"We can replace him," responded Cole. His face softened as he looked at Larry kindly. "Listen, Son, the man is dangerous. I know he seemed nice to you. It's an act that he puts on. Don't believe everyone you meet is as he seems. Sam has some deep problems. I've known about them for quite a while. He can be a slick one and cover them up, but they're there. He tried to hurt me yesterday. He's angry that I put you in the position as Facility Maintenance Supervisor. He thinks you shouldn't be the boss." This ought to make Larry think twice about any loyalties he might have toward Sam.

That just didn't make sense. True – Larry's first few weeks working with Sam had been difficult, but they had both talked about that. Sam even confessed his bad attitude toward him and had apologized for it. He seemed as honest as they come and didn't have any problems that Larry had noticed. He wondered what Brother Cole was talking about. He liked Sam. Perhaps Larry was a little naive and trusted others too easily, but he and Sam had worked closely together, and Sam had helped him with the books and taught him new skills. Both of them wished Sam was in charge. Probably Brother Cole misinterpreted what had happened. That was the most likely thing. But what problems did Brother Cole know about? Could his friend have duped him as Cole suggested? After all, Brother Cole was the assistant pastor and wouldn't just make up things. Maybe there was something that Larry had missed.

"What kind of problems, Brother Cole?"

"I don't like to discuss people behind their backs, Larry, but I do think you would be wise to stay away from him. He uses people, and he might try to use you, too."

Brother Cole's voice sounded so concerned for Larry's welfare that the boy felt even further confusion.

Cole was pleased with how this conversation was going. He arose from his chair and walked over to Larry. He would add a paternal touch that would strengthen their relationship and in turn his relationship with William Herrin. Giving the boy a fatherly hug around the shoulders, he asserted, "We'll find someone much better to replace him. You start interviewing to see who you can come up with, all right?"

THE TARE IN THE WHEAT

"Sure, all right," Larry agreed uncertainly as he walked out of the office. This was so confusing. Brother Cole was such a nice person. He obviously cared about people. What could Sam have done to cause the assistant pastor not to trust him?

Calling Sam an hour later, Larry felt unreasonably nervous. After he told him that Brother Cole had refused to rehire him, Sam thanked Larry for talking to the assistant pastor and even said that he'd enjoyed working with him. Larry felt more troubled than ever. He should believe Brother Cole; after all, as the assistant pastor, he wouldn't lie, and yet Sam sure was nice about it all. Things just didn't add up. Even though he wasn't good with figures, he was smart enough about people to know that something was out of place. Why would Jason tell him that the assistant pastor had been unkind to Miss Eleanor if the man hadn't been? Miss Eleanor hadn't said anything, but she'd been unusually quiet today. Larry had a hard time believing that Brother Cole would be harsh with the woman. The assistant pastor was kind to her when he was around. Maybe Jason had exaggerated. He hated to ask Miss Eleanor about it. Perhaps Brother Cole's criticism was meant to be constructive, and Jason had taken it wrong. Whatever the case, Larry wasn't going to be so trusting of anyone for a while. He would keep his eyes open. Perhaps people wanted to get rid of a good man like Brother Cole by giving him a bad name. But then again there had been times he'd overheard the assistant pastor talking rather brusquely. Those memories couldn't be easily erased from his mind. The Sam that Larry knew wasn't the same man that Brother Cole had described, and the Brother Cole that Larry saw wasn't the same one as Sam knew. Perhaps it was simply a personality conflict. That had to be the answer. He would pray for wisdom.

For at least the twentieth time since they'd arrived at the beach, David asked, "Grandmama, tell us a story about when you were little."

"Tell us one about Christmas this time," Joseph suggested. He was especially fond of Christmas stories since he had the same name as the Virgin Mary's husband.

"Well, let's see." Greta looked out at the ocean as she sat on the porch swing. "One time my brother, your Great Uncle Hans, got upset with me."

"Why?" asked both boys curiously.

"I don't remember. We used to argue all the time. We loved each other, but we'd fuss a lot. Anyway, Christmas was coming, and we always put our shoes by the front door for *Sinter Klaas* to fill."

"Whose *Sinter Klaas*?" asked David.

"That's the name we called Saint Nicholas." The boys looked at her blankly. "Santa Claus," she tried again.

"Oh," both boys exclaimed knowingly.

Joseph screwed up his little nose. "Why'd you call him *Sinter Klaas* instead of his right name?"

"My parents were Dutch, and that's what they called him. We used to speak both Dutch and English in our home when I was growing up. Anyway, we would put our shoes by the door so that *Sinter Klaas* would fill them with candy and little toys for Christmas."

"Why'd you put your shoes? Didn't you have stockings like we do?" David wondered.

"No, we used our shoes." Greta tweaked his nose. "We hoped that we'd been good because if we were good, then *Sinter Klaas* would come on his white horse and bring us..."

"White horse?" both boys broke in incredulously. Joseph put his hands on his little hips and corrected, "Grandmama, Santa Claus has reindeer, not horses."

"Well, that's true," smiled Greta ,"but in those days he rode on a white horse and came over the sea to bring us presents, and he brought someone I bet you've never heard of with him."

"Who?" the children asked, watching her intently.

"Black Peter."

"Black Peter, whose he?" Joseph questioned with wide eyes.

"He's the one who would put dirty old coal in your shoes if you weren't good, and there would be no room for *Sinter Klaas* to put candy and toys in them."

"I don't want to get old, yucky coal from Black Peter," decided David. "I'm always good."

"Well, I've only known of Black Peter coming one time," Greta continued. "It was when my brother Hans got angry with me. When I went to bed, he put coal in my shoes. The next morning when we got up to have Christmas though, I didn't have any coal in my shoes – I had candy and a little toy train, but Hans had coal in his shoes. He was really upset, and he said, 'I didn't put coal in my shoes, I put it in Greta's shoes,' and then we all knew that Black Peter had gotten angry at Hans for putting coal in my shoes, and put the coal in Hans' shoes instead, and he didn't get any candy."

"Poor Hans," sympathized David.

"I gave him some of mine."

"Good." Both boys seemed relieved.

"We have company," Cindy broke in as Rose and Hal walked out on the porch.

Greta stood, greeting her friend with a hug. Rose happily noted how well Greta looked.

Hal spoke up, smiling, "Why don't you two girls go take a walk out on the beach while I unpack the luggage. That way you can get all your talking out?"

Rose and Greta readily agreed. "But Hal," Rose qualified. "You'll probably be disappointed. It's hard for us to get all talked out."

"Well, I'll just hope for the best."

"You sure do have a nice husband, Rose," Greta determined as they walked toward the water. She knew Cole wouldn't suggest that she take a walk on the beach while he did the unpacking.

"He's a gem, all right. You seem happy."

"I am. I've had a great time. Should have done this years ago." Greta breathed in deeply. The evening was lovely. The sun seemed to stretch for miles, and the surf gently washed their feet as they walked. "Tell me what's been happening."

Rose began sharing some news from Georgia, and the two friends talked and laughed together as they strolled the sandy expanse. It was good to be together again.

"Oh, I have good news for you," Rose remembered. "Brother Steve has it all lined up for you to cut that album next week. He wants you to come back to Athens and be ready the first of November to begin taping. I told him that you'd be there. That I was going to bring you myself."

"That's just next Wednesday," realized Greta. Steve had called a couple of times about the recording session. The last time they'd talked, he'd said that he was talking to the company about doing two sets. One hymns and classical. The other a Christmas album. Greta was excited about the idea of having her music recorded, but there was one problem – a big one. She would have to go home to Cole again. "I sure hope I can do this."

Rose assumed that she was worried about the recording studio. "Oh, you can, believe me, and besides, it's one of the things on your list. I'll come pick you up Tuesday and take you in on Wednesday myself. I want to see how this thing works."

Greta was quiet – too quiet. Rose sensed an unsaid statement. She knew her friend well enough to know what was probably bothering her. "You can stay with me if you like. Cole doesn't even have to know that you came to town. I'll bring you back to Cindy's after it's all finished."

Greta gazed at her friend fondly. Rose had the uncanny ability to read her mind. "Thank you, Rose. I appreciate the offer. But no, I should probably go home."

Rose noticed that Greta's buoyant spirit had deflated and tried to raise it again by asking her what songs she planned on playing for the recording.

Immediately Greta began to perk up as she described different arrangements that she was considering. There was a piano at the condominium, and she'd brought her music with her. She offered to play for Rose and let her friend have a voice in which ones were her favorites. She had already gotten Barry and Cindy's opinion and had more pieces than she could possibly ever use.

"Well, I know which one I want you to play, *In The Garden*. I love that song and the way you play it."

"You got it. It's one of Cindy's favorites, too, so two votes and it's in. I'll dedicate it to you, Rose. Hey, is that why your name is Rose, because you like *In the Garden* so much."

"You might have something there, after all it does say, 'I walk through the garden alone, while the dew is still on the roses', and I do have a little dew on me." She pointed to her sandy, wet feet.

"Looks more like mud to me," Greta laughed. They were almost back to their condominium. Greta felt a pleasant kind of tired, not as sickly as she used to feel. She wondered if in reality she was getting better.

Chapter 30

An angry man stirreth up strife.

-Proverbs 29:22

"How was work today?" Christine asked Bill as she fixed his plate.

"Pretty good." He stretched his sore muscles. Suddenly remembering something Mike had told him earlier in the day, he tried to hide the smile that crept into his eyes. Casually he said, "We'll be having new neighbors soon. Mike and Nancy are moving into the neighborhood."

"Really? Where?" Christine racked her brain to think if any houses around them were for sale. A Cheshire cat grin appeared on Bill's face.

"They're going to move into the Castle," he replied in the same mellow voice, as if he'd said all there was to say about it. He loved it when he knew something that she didn't.

"You mean they're moving in with Donald and Judith?" She couldn't imagine Nancy having to live with Judith. "Poor Nancy." She shook her head at the thought.

"Poor Nancy, nothing," Bill laughed. "She's getting that whole, beautiful, big house."

"But to have to live with Judith Gresham. It wouldn't be worth it."

"Donald and Judith are moving out."

"What?" Christine's mouth dropped open. Judith Gresham's whole existence seemed to depend upon that house and her rich life style. "Bill, you're putting me on."

"I'm not. I'm telling you the truth. I told Mike that I'd help them move. It'll probably be sometime before Thanksgiving."

Christine was speechless. Thoughts flowed through her mind, but the main one was that it would be wonderful to have Nancy so close by.

For himself Bill was thinking how pleasant conversations around the dinner table had become now that he wasn't working at the church. Sometimes the way that he had to leave that job still stung but even that pain was beginning to fade. Sunday mornings were the hardest as he watched Brother Cole sitting on the platform in his fancy chair beside Pastor Leonard, looking so cocky. Though the assistant pastor may have thought he was proficient at hiding his true feelings from the congregation, Bill often read fleeting expressions of disapproval on the man's face. The day that

Donald Gresham had walked down the aisle to speak to the church, Bill had watched Cole Odum in fascination. A tapestry of undisguised emotion had flitted across the assistant pastor's face. When Pastor Leonard had asked who would accept Donald's apology, Bill had noticed that Brother Cole kept his mouth tightly shut, but when the "no's" were asked for, Bill had seen the man's mouth move, only slightly, but it had definitely moved. Perhaps Brother Cole was beginning to show his true self. Bill certainly hoped so.

The weekly staff meeting had been the most unpleasant one that Cole had experienced in a long time. He pulled his dinner out of the microwave and stewed over the discussion from that morning. Even Pastor Leonard, who Cole promoted wholeheartedly, had not seemed to fully support him. Something felt off-kilter. He walked into the living room with his meal as he mulled over what had gone wrong.

When he'd entered the meeting room with another large check from William Herrin, he'd felt confident that it would give him the edge he needed. He knew his dismissal of Sam was being discussed. He had even heard Margie talking to Pastor Leonard's secretary about it, and he'd tartly told her what he thought of her gossiping tongue. Her face had turned extremely red and her solemn apology didn't matter to him. He decided to give Pastor Leonard the note from William Herrin as soon as he walked into the meeting, hoping that would help win the tide of discussion more in his favor. But to Cole's dismay, the preacher had simply thanked him and pocketed it with a few words that he would give it to the financial secretary. He didn't even bother to open it.

"Shouldn't we see how much the check is – if we've met our budget goal?" he'd tried to ask innocently.

"No, it's better that we not know how much any one person is giving," Leonard had responded. He didn't say it in a preachy or chastising voice, but Cole felt reprimanded anyway. He couldn't forgive the preacher for this one-sentence sermonette. Internally he'd fumed, but on the outside, he'd tried to come across as peaceful and in control.

The meeting opened, and Leonard began by asking about old business. The first item on the agenda was a discussion about a computer program that Cole had suggested the church purchase. It was ideal for a church this size. The program itself was a group of form letters – hundreds of them – that looked as if they were personally written. There were letters for a birth in a family (choice of boy or girl); a series of sympathy letters when someone had died or was ill; a series of letters to help guide people in giving for a building program; the list went on and on, and all one had to do was to punch out the letter on the computer screen, type in the names, and fill in any needed blanks – as to who had died or who was born – and then *voilà*, a letter was ready to be printed in moments. It looked as if the staff cared personally, and it didn't take much work or time. A wonderful addition, Cole thought, to the church's computer system. "It would save hours of work. It's what the corporate business world is using, and with a church this size, it's a must," he told the staff.

"For those who want to look like they care even if they don't," Brother Dan had quipped.

Brother Steve, who was getting on Cole's nerves more and more lately, had argued against the program, and eventually the group voted it down. Cole had been the only "yes" vote. A humiliating experience. He'd thought that at least the pastor would agree with him.

Bad went to worse when Brother Dan asked Cole directly, "Exactly what happened that you had to let Sam go, Cole?"

Thinking back on that moment, Cole realized that he'd lost his suave persona a little. Not only had his idea been beaten down, but he'd felt Brother Dan accusing him of something. Cole didn't like the administrator, and today those feelings had been thoroughly cemented. To add to the irritation was the fact that the man didn't title him as Brother Cole, but was too familiar and just called him by his given name. At least Cole was prepared with what he was going to say. The entire incident with Sam was embarrassing and unforgivable. He wanted to forget about it. At the same time, he'd been given a good reason to fire the malcontent.

As he told what had happened, he felt as if he were being interrogated, as if they thought he'd done something wrong. It had been an odious discussion; however, the fact that Sam had been totally out of line finally helped Cole to receive a certain amount of sympathy.

Finally, the last straw to his unpleasant morning happened at the end of the meeting. Brother Steve caught Cole totally off guard with what he said. "I didn't want to tell anyone this until all the arrangements were hammered out, and I'm sure Brother Cole might want to share this with you himself, but if you don't mind, Brother Cole, I will."

Cole had nodded his head, as if he knew exactly what Brother Steve was going to say, but in reality he sat there wondering what in the world the man was talking about.

"Greta's going to make an album, actually two, next week. I've made arrangements with a studio and recording company. I'm hoping to get it done quickly and even possibly have the albums ready by Christmas."

As Cole sat thinking about the whole episode, he felt the same embarrassment that he'd so carefully hidden that morning as staff members looked back and forth from Brother Steve to him nodding their fool heads as if he should be happy about the entire event. Brother Steve had droned on and on. And then there was Greta. The woman hadn't said one word to him about this. Apparently she would be coming home next week. The least she could have done was leave a message on the answering machine.

He ate another bite of dinner. It was pretty tasteless tonight. Well, if Greta was coming home, perhaps, finally, he'd get a good home-cooked meal again.

Chapter 31

The Lord your God is with you...He will quiet you with His love.

-Zephaniah 3:17 (NIV)

The autumn glows of red, orange, and yellow did little to quiet Greta's misgivings as Rose drove her back to her home in Georgia. She tried to ignore the knot that seemed to have taken permanent residence in her stomach since she'd realized that she would see Cole that evening. Not one time had they talked since she'd gone up to visit Cindy, and though Greta had left many messages, Cole had not bothered to return her phone calls. Rose's effervescent presence helped make the time go quickly though, and before she knew it, they were driving down Hwy 29, passing parts of town she recognized, making the knot in her stomach tighten.

Cindy, before Greta had left, insisted that her mother come back as soon as the "recording debut" was over. Ordinarily Greta might have argued that Cole would want her to stay home, but in a very unGreta-like fashion, she grabbed at the chance to return to her daughter's cozy homestead, somewhat surprising Cindy. The girl's suspicions were aroused, and she'd asked a few probing questions that Greta carefully sidestepped. It was just too early to tell Cindy about her illness; besides, she was feeling so much better that maybe the sickness was gone. Maybe she should get a second opinion. No matter, as soon as she recorded her music, she would go back to Cindy's. Hopefully Cole wouldn't be angry with her for leaving him again. She would restock the freezer and take good care of him while she was at home. That ought to help.

Rose was delighted with Greta's plan to go back to Cindy's after the taping was finished. It hadn't surprised her that her friend had such a pleasant family since she enjoyed Greta's company so much, but she did find it amazing that those children had Cole for a father. A couple of weeks ago, she'd overheard a woman say what a godly man Brother Cole was because he put the church first. It was all that she could do not to interrupt and interject her opinion. She choked back the words she wanted to say to this misguided lady who confused "Churchiosity" with Christianity.

Arriving at Greta's house, she dropped off her friend. Watching the lone figure with her one suitcase enter the massive front doors, Rose prayed for an angel to protect Greta.

As she drove away, she felt as if she'd just dropped Daniel off at the lion's den.

For Greta, it felt strange to be home again – as if these familiar surroundings belonged to someone else. With a sinking heart, she surveyed the mess. A putrid odor met her nose. Cole hadn't bothered to throw out the trash in quite a while, his clothes were scattered everywhere, and the place hadn't been vacuumed probably the entire time that she was gone. Food crumbs were ground into the carpet, dishes filled the sink, and the stench was bad enough to kill a cat. A feeling of despair rippled through her. A nap would be so pleasant after that long, tiring drive, but that would have to wait. She had work to do.

Attacking the kitchen first, she threw out the smelly garbage that overflowed onto the floor. That done, the place still smelled sour. In spite of the cool weather, she opened some windows, hoping that the outside air would help to freshen the house. Loading the dishwasher, she tried to clean off the dried-on food stuck to the plates. Why had she left lasagna for Cole? The crusted cheese seemed permanently attached. Finally, the machine loaded, she turned it on, then washed off the counter top. As she worked, her shoes stuck to the sticky floor. Pulling out the mop bucket, she filled it and mopped up the filthy tile.

Walking into the living room, she threw away a small mountain of old newspapers and junk mail, picked up scattered clothes that lay around and put in a load to wash, then vacuumed the carpet. At Cole's bedroom door, she stopped. Fatigue tugged at every muscle, joints ached, and even her bones hurt. He could clean his own room. At least the awful smell she'd noticed earlier had dissipated.

Trudging upstairs, she hoped that her bedroom wasn't in disorder too. Gazing around, everything looked exactly as she'd left it. With a breath of thankfulness, she drew herself a bath. The warm water soothed her tired body. Shutting her eyes, she pretended that she was at Cindy's house. It helped her feel better.

Twenty minutes later, she emerged from the water, a wrinkled, but much more relaxed woman. A twinge of guilt for bathing so long tugged at her conscience. The first guilt she'd felt in a while. It would be nice to take a nap, she realized as she dressed, but it was late, and she needed to prepare something for dinner. When Cole came home tonight, he would probably expect a home-cooked meal to be ready. He would know that she was home now. The first thing she did when she arrived at Cindy's house after the beach trip last Sunday was to call him. Hopefully he heard the message on the answering machine. Old familiar anxiety squeezed at her stomach. Perhaps though, he had missed her, she thought, grabbing hold of the hope.

Back in the kitchen, a slight breeze touched her, and a new wave of guilt swept over her. The windows were still open. Cole would turn scarlet with rage if he knew that she'd let the house's heat escape through them. Hurriedly she shut them, thankful that she could do so before he arrived home.

As she searched through the almost empty refrigerator and freezer to try to find something to fix for dinner, an overwhelming wave of exhaustion unexpectedly hit her. She shouldn't have cleaned the house. It had taxed all her strength. But, she reminded herself, as soon as dinner was ready, she could relax. The freezer had only a few microwave meals and some mixed vegetables. Perhaps she could order a pizza. She looked where she kept the grocery money. Good – there was still some left. Cole preferred pepperoni, whereas she liked onions, so she asked them to make it half and half. In the past, she would have just gotten the pepperoni. It was a small, but significant success on Greta's part not to deny herself as she'd done previously. Putting together a small casserole with the mixed vegetables and some breadcrumbs that were in the pantry, she hoped that this would make the meal a little more homey, and since she didn't have salad fixings, this would have to suffice.

A little before seven o'clock the pizza arrived, but no Cole. Maybe he hadn't gotten her message, but, then again, he'd come home at varying times throughout their married life. This wasn't so unusual. She knew he'd expect her to wait to eat until he arrived home, but feeling unusually hungry, after arguing a great deal with herself, she prepared a plate and went into the living room to eat. It was good. She got herself another slice of the onion pizza, eating it hungrily. The Christian tape she'd put on earlier soothed her. Again she pretended that she was at Cindy's house, but it was too quiet. She missed the sounds of her grandsons' laughter.

Sitting alone, she realized that she was nervous. For all the years of her marriage, a tension had existed between her and Cole that as time went by, she'd become vaguely used to, basically ignoring it, living with it. But after the relaxing time in North Carolina, entering this home again with its stresses ate at her insides. An unexplainable foreboding had touched her as soon as she'd walked in the door. Perhaps it was just the mess that she'd encountered. But no, it felt more like a touch from God – His warning.

Having escaped for the last few weeks to Cindy's peaceful abode brought home the contrast. She tried to reason with herself – perhaps since she'd been gone so long, Cole would have missed her. Perhaps when he came in and saw what a clean house she'd made, he'd be pleased. But he wasn't even hurrying home to see her. She needed to stop fooling herself. It only added to her pain. Finally, just as she was finishing her second piece of pizza, she heard the keys in the door. Her stomach tightened into a familiar knot. He would probably be upset that she hadn't waited for him. Why did she have to worry about him being angry?

For a fleeting moment, she thought she saw a hint of warmth touch Cole's eyes when he saw her, but it quickly disappeared as he looked at the plate in her hand. "Why didn't you wait for me?"

"The pizza came, and I was hungry," she explained almost apologetically.

"Pizza! After all these weeks, I come home expecting a nice hot home-cooked meal, and you ordered a pizza. Do you know how many pizzas I've had while you've been gone?"

"I'd guess three." There had been three pizza boxes that she'd thrown away in the trash. He wasn't amused by her response. She tried to placate him. "There's not much food in the house, Cole. I need to go by the grocery store. I did make a vegetable casserole out of what I could find in the kitchen."

Without responding, he walked into his bedroom to change clothes. "Why didn't you vacuum my room?"

Greta shut her eyes to the criticism, wishing it away.

Walking out dressed in casual clothes a few minutes later, he said, "Don't bother yourself with making me a plate."

Greta breathed in deeply, wanting to rush back to Cindy's house as quickly as she could. She felt as if she'd come home to a nightmare. Instead she sat still, not knowing how to respond.

"What's this horrid stuff on this pizza? You know I hate onions."

"That's my side of the pizza. Your part has the pepperoni." An unexpected annoyance began to erupt in the core of her being, replacing the intimidation. Looking at him with new eyes, she saw a spoiled bratty child in a big body. Her children had been disciplined for that same kind of behavior when they were young. The knot in her stomach suddenly relaxed. She ate the last bite of her vegetable casserole.

As Cole noticed her eating, it disconcerted him. He didn't quite recognize what was different, but he suddenly felt as if he were dealing with someone other than his usual wife. "Why aren't we eating in the dining room where we're supposed to eat?"

"I didn't want to," Greta responded quietly, without the quaver in her voice that he was used to hearing when he continually berated her.

"Since when do you choose where we eat," he said loudly, a little too loudly. "I'm eating in the dining room."

Greta arose, rinsed off her plate, and put her cup in the sink. "I'm tired and going to bed. Good night," she murmured before plodding up the steps.

Cole sat alone in the formal dining room, not knowing what to say or think. Inside he felt vaguely disappointed. Perhaps he should have acted a little less overbearing.

The next morning Greta and Rose arrived early at the recording studio. Brother Steve, who was already there, immediately introduced Greta to the manager, Jason Seagraves. She smiled at him, feeling nervous and out of place in this professional, polished environment. A mouse out in the open field with the hawks flying overhead. Who was she to do this?

"Let's begin with the Christmas album," Jason directed. "Steve has high hopes of getting the recording out by the holidays. We'll have to see what we can do about that." He looked at Steve as he spoke. "Next week we'll do the religious recording."

Next week! Greta screamed internally. She'd hoped to be at Cindy's again next week.

"Sounds great," Brother Steve agreed.

It took a while to get started. They had Greta play both the expensive electronic synthesizer and the large piano to check all their monitors in the booth. Everyone but Greta went into the little room, and as she sat by herself, feeling like a speck of dust in the universe, she repeatedly played her first song until Jason was satisfied with the sound quality. This could turn into a long week, she decided. Once they got their sound control down, it went better. Most of the music she played on the piano, but some everyone agreed should be played on the synthesizer, and for those songs there was often a lot of discussion about what instrumental grouping to use. This was time consuming, but by the end of the day, the system's workers all seemed to agree that it had been a profitable time.

As Rose drove her home, Greta realized that, though she was exhausted, she looked forward to tomorrow. Rose would be coming back with her again. She wanted to put her two cents in as to the instrumentation that she liked best. Greta had noticed that Rose often did voice her opinion, and usually she was right.

"I know you sing in the choir, Rose, but have you ever play an instrument? You have such a good ear for music."

"Well, as a matter of fact, I played the violin as a child. Played might not be the best word. I moved a bow on a violin and screeched it a lot. I was horrible. My father tried to teach me and finally gave up. I do enjoy music though. I think I got on the nerves of that young man, Brandon, today."

Greta laughed. Brandon might be good with the sound equipment, but he definitely liked a different style of music than Rose, Greta, and Brother Steve did. Apparently he was fond of hearing a strong bass beat that tended to overshadow the melody. "I was glad that you were there, especially when I played *O Come All ye Faithful.* He wanted me to jazz it up a lot."

"I know. I like to think about people walking peacefully with a quiet joy to go see the Christ child when I hear that song, not sashaying to the manger as if they were being chased by a bear."

Greta giggled.

Rose continued. "How about eating supper with me tomorrow night. Hal says there's a deacon's meeting to discuss the budget, and you know how long those ones can last. Both he and Cole will probably be gone till midnight."

"That sounds wonderful. Since I've been home, I haven't even been to the grocery store or thought about supper." Greta looked at the car's clock. "It's already five-thirty."

"You have anything quick in the freezer you can pull out."

"There's some microwave dinners I could heat up. Cole won't like it, but I'm too tired to cook." Greta's back and arms ached from all the playing. Even her legs hurt, and they hadn't really done much of anything.

"You go home and eat your microwave dinners. Cole will just have to understand. They make those meals for working women, and lady let me tell you, you sure worked today. You'll have a full day again tomorrow, too. You ought to take a nice warm bath and get to bed early," Rose offered in a sensible mothering way that some people may have resented, but Greta felt cared for. Part of her needed permission to relax when she was at home. Cole rarely gave her that.

Cole wasn't home when she arrived. Greta turned on the stereo and put in a Pachelbel tape that she enjoyed before going upstairs to take her bath – a good long one. It helped to relax her aching muscles. As she shut her eyes, she felt as if she could see notes of music floating in front of her. If anyone had told her that making an album would be this much work, she wouldn't have believed them, and she was going to make two. She hoped that she would survive it.

The music on the stereo penetrated her sanctuary. Soft and lilting – something that shepherds might listen to while tending their sheep in the field. She pictured heaven being like a sheep's pasture – beautiful, green flowing hills with large oak trees. The imagine of herself sitting on a swing overlooking a village and gently swinging back and forth began lulling her to sleep. One-day people could listen to her music as she now listened to this melodious symphony. It would give her children and grandchildren something to remember her by. She hoped it would give them pleasure as this music gave her pleasure. There was a joy in her tiredness. Perhaps she would be remembered. It wasn't important, but it comforted her. Often she felt inadequate, insignificant, and yet the idea that her music might bless others gave her peace.

Unexpectedly the music cut off, waking Greta from her peaceful half slumber. She heard the television. Cole was home. Pulling herself out of the tub, she dried off. The time in her bath had been refreshing. She felt more able to meet her husband after her hard day at the recording studio. Dressing quickly, a few minutes later, she came down the stairs to greet him.

"What's for supper?"

"Well, let's see. We have lasagna, meat loaf, or roast beef, or you can have some pizza left over from last night."

Cole looked at her harshly. A look that had withered her spirit over the years. His words came out tightly, as if a timer for a bomb was ticking, gaining momentum, ready to explode. "You've been gone for weeks, and I've been stuck here being forced to eat garbage, and now, when you come home, and I think I'll finally get a home-cooked meal, you say we're going to eat microwave dinners."

She'd disappointed him again. "I'm sorry, Cole. I haven't had a chance to go to the grocery store. I don't know when I'll be able to. We'll just have to make do." His expression brought back to her mind the thought of a spoiled child. She turned and looked at the dinners. "Do you mind if I have the roast beef? It looks good to me," she asked calmly, as if he didn't have that stormy expression on his face.

Cole was floored by his wife's behavior. "Eat whatever you want," he snapped. "I'm going out." Grabbing his coat, he slammed the door as he went.

Though Greta felt the sting from his response, she also felt a degree of relief. Her appetite was gone, but she forced herself to eat. She was tired. She went straight to bed as soon as she finished her meal. She didn't hear Cole come back in. Her exhausted sleep was heavy and dreamless.

Chapter 32

A wicked messenger falls into trouble.

-Proverbs 13:17 (NIV)

The second day at the recording studio flew by as Greta played song after song. Toward the end of the final session, Jason informed her that they had room left for at the most two songs, possibly only one depending on its length.

Greta pulled out the music to *O Holy Night*. This was her son-in-law's, Barry's, favorite. She wanted to play all three verses using the synthesizer's hammer dulcimer sound – an instrument Barry loved to hear. For the first time, Greta spoke up clearly to the group about what her preferences were. The only major disagreement of the day occurred. Perhaps because it was getting late and everyone was a little tired, or perhaps because Greta, who usually bowed to the voices around her, adamantly stuck to her position.

After a great deal of discussion and Greta playing a portion of the song using different instrumentation, the group eventually agreed to begin with the lone sound of the hammer dulcimer, accompanying it with other stringed instrumental sounds for the second verse, and ending with an orchestrated effect by incorporating a variety of synthesized instruments for the final verse. This song would end the album with a touch of majesty that Christ deserved.

"All right," directed Jason. "Let's get started." Brother Steve sat beside Greta, ready to change the stops between each verse so that she could concentrate on her playing and get it perfect for the recording.

Rose, who had a tendency to hum, went into the soundproof booth with Brandon and Jason to watch from there. Jason gave the signal, and Greta began playing. Standing back from the others, Rose eyed the contented look on her friend's face. Greta, unaware of anyone as the feeling of the song flowed through her hands, played flawlessly. Rose felt herself taking an emotional picture of this special moment that she would keep with her for the rest of her life. A picture of someone that she valued and cared deeply for and possibly wouldn't have around for as long as she'd envisioned. The majesty of the music drew her in, whisking her emotions to a holy, ethereal place, as if Greta were playing for a heavenly choir. Greta was indeed gifted, and had her life gone down a different course, she might have been one of those rare individuals to grace a concert hall. Rose felt a swell of gratitude in her heart toward Brother Steve who had made her friend's wish come true, and in a way, a wish of her own. She would always have a part of Greta to remember.

Jason watched in wonder. It amazed him how this little woman could make such beautiful music. He had been somewhat skeptical of the entire recording session. There were many people that thought they had a star on their hands, but this lady was extremely talented. He wondered why he'd not heard of her before. He would have to speak to Steve about Greta doing more sittings for them. She had the ability to do anything that she set her mind to, he was sure, and he realized that he might have discovered a gold mine. Once people heard this, they'd want to buy more of her albums.

As the final strains of the chorus rang through the room and the music stopped, everyone was silent for a moment. Even the soundman, Brandon, seemed oddly touched; then, with the realization that something good had just happened, Jason began clapping. Brandon and Rose joined in as they walked out into the studio where Steve joined them. Greta absorbed the moment. Everyone began hugging everyone else, and they finally left the studio talking about the following week and the making of the Christian music album.

Greta, though she ached, felt a deep satisfaction as she rode with Rose to her friend's house. The exhilaration of the moment kept her from feeling tired. Indeed, God Himself was reaching down, patting her back, and blessing her spirit. What a gift He'd given her. With His help, she'd make it through next week also.

The deacons' meeting was a challenge to Cole. Something he relished. In his mind, he anticipated the one tonight, thinking of what he needed to say and exactly how he should word it. Anytime the meetings were about financial decisions, the men tended to be easily agitated. Cole took a certain pride in his ability to persuade them to do whatever he wanted. It was like a game to him, with the ultimate victory bringing him a high increase in salary, and perhaps eventually he would gain the highest position in the church if he played well enough.

Tonight though, there was at least one wild card. Pastor Leonard seemed different. The reason for the elusive change was something of a mystery. Cole wasn't even sure there was a change or if the pastor had just been having a few bad days.

Well, no matter what was wrong with Leonard, Cole was ready for tonight's challenge. Armand Molt and Eric Garwood, having gone out to lunch with him, each on separate occasions just this week, were swayed to his opinions. Earlier in the year, he'd taken the head of the Finance Committee, Aaron Fletcher, out to eat, and that twenty-dollar meal had gotten Cole a five thousand dollar raise for next year. Aaron made sure the Finance Committee voted in every raise that Cole suggested.

Eric and Armand were easy to win over. They both liked the idea of being a confidant to the assistant pastor. That would help tonight. Hal Boxwell apparently had been on vacation last week when Cole had called his office. He regretted that. Hal, though somewhat quiet, could probably be easily bought. Brother Davis had also been unable to meet with him, so he was kind of a loose cannon. It bothered Cole that Brother Davis, who was considered one of the forefathers of Main Street First Church, tended to keep his distance. He was polite and nice enough but always unavailable. One day Cole would mend this breach and win over this older pillar of the church.

Arriving in the conference room early, he found it empty. He liked the advantage of being the first one there. As Ben Evans walked in, Cole stiffened. Even Ben's first week as a deacon, he had voiced his opinion. The unspoken rule that the new deacons should keep quiet and listen had been unheeded by this intense young man. Last year he'd been a major opponent of the church deciding to begin another building fund program, saying there were many other unmet needs in the church family and the community that should be helped first. The man had almost defeated the idea with his negative talk.

Deacons started drifting in. Hal Boxwell, Rose's husband, came in with Marwin Simpson. Marwin was one of Cole's men. Cole didn't even need to bother to take the man out to lunch anymore. Brother Steve bounded in, shaking everyone's hands as he entered, seeming extra buoyant. With great effort, Cole feigned friendship with the music minister, but it was hard. The man was a simpleton, and his overly friendly nature made Cole suspicious, wondering what the music minister was really up to. Inwardly he sighed as he noticed Brother Steve coming toward him with a grin spread across his face.

"Brother Cole, good to see you." He shook the assistant pastor's hand. "We finally got the Christmas recording finished. You'll have a wife for a few days again, I'm happy to say. She did an excellent job. You'll have to take her out to dinner to celebrate her success."

It was presumptuous of Steve to tell him what he should do. He had no intentions of taking Greta anywhere, and he didn't want to feel as if others might be going to check on him. However, he reminded himself, this man was of no real importance to him. He didn't need to let it bother him. "Excuse me, Steve. Pastor Leonard just came in. I need to talk to him about something before the meeting begins." Cole felt the importance of his position as he strode over to the pastor.

"I have the financial proposal here," he said, showing the stack of papers to Leonard.

"Good." Leonard's voice held tension. "Let's get this show on the road."

Leonard dreaded this meeting. Usually a lot of arguing ensued when the budget was discussed. From time to time he gave his input about things that he thought were important to include; however, most of the budget was handled by separate committees. Unfortunately Aaron Fletcher, the head of the Finance Committee, had to unexpectedly go out of town. Though Leonard had thought about postponing the meeting, Cole said that as the staff representative on the committee, he should be able to field any questions asked. Leonard hoped that was true.

"If everyone would find a seat, we'll get started," Leonard announced. The murmur in the room immediately quieted. "Brother Cole, would you lead us in prayer."

Cole prayed eloquently to the God that he didn't know, then handed Marwin Simpson the financial sheets to pass out. Marwin beamed with the honor, and Cole thought how much cheaper this was than a lunch with the man.

The sheets contained the basic facts. All the nitty-gritty details had been discussed already by the Finance Committee. Cole continued to stand and began leading the discussion.

Initially Leonard felt relieved to yield the floor to Brother Cole. He noted that the man seemed to have nerves of steel, but as the evening progressed, Leonard felt slightly uneasy that Cole seemed to be so completely in charge, that he had such a good handle on the church finances. Brother Dan used to be the staff member that oversaw the Finance Committee. Since Dan was the church administrator, it was unusual that Cole was the one in charge of the meeting. Leonard couldn't quite remember why Cole had been put in the position, but when the change of duties had happened, it had made perfect sense. Dan, overwhelmed with other responsibilities, had willingly given up this demanding part of his job.

Now though, as Leonard listened, the thought crossed his mind that perhaps it hadn't been in the best interest of the church to have Brother Cole oversee the Finance Committee. The budget had soared since he'd taken over, and though Leonard was pleased to have received raises in salary each year, they'd definitely been more than he needed.

As the evening wore on, there was much discussion about each ministry of the church. The final item on the agenda was the employees' salaries. By the time they reached that part of the proposed budget, everyone was getting tired. Leonard suggested they take a short recess and then meet again in fifteen minutes. In truth, he was apprehensive about this section of the budget.

When the meeting reconvened fifteen minutes later, the deacons seemed mellower. After Leonard prayed, he asked the men to remember that they were Christian brothers working toward a common goal. The discussion on the staff salary increases began.

During the previous discussions, Hal Boxwell had sat back. He was a thoughtful man, a man who chose his arguments carefully. There were people in the world who were constantly contentious. They would debate every little thing. Hal wasn't like that. He spoke only when he felt something was extremely important, and as a result, people usually listened. So far this evening he'd quietly observed the deacons discuss the various expenses. Many of them made good points, but because of their aggressive stance, they tended to be ignored more than they might otherwise have been. Hal had been an effective manager of a computer company for a number of years, and even though he appeared reticent and unassuming, he could prove to be a formidable opponent when necessary. He was the type of man who liked to have all his facts correct before he spoke, and he would relate these facts unemotionally. As a result, there was little argument. He related the truth, and when someone did argue, it was either because they didn't understand what he'd said or because they wanted to hide what the real problems were behind an angry countenance.

Throughout the evening he'd watched the assistant pastor closely. Basically the man had run the entire deacons' meeting. Hal had his own opinion of Brother Cole – partly based on his close observation of the man, and partly as a result of what his wife, Rose, had told him about Greta and Cole. Rose was not known for having a tame tongue. The two were opposites when it came to that, but two months ago, she'd come home with a strangely closed mouth. So unlike herself. At the time he'd been careful not to pressure her to tell him anything; then, one Saturday, Rose, on her way out the door, had said she would be at the hospital if he needed her. He'd looked at her quizzically, and she'd immediately tried to backtrack but instead had managed to let him know more.

"Oh, did I say the hospital? I meant to say that I was going to see Greta."

"All right," he had replied as if he hadn't noticed the slip of the tongue.

"What time do you plan on getting home?"

"I should be back by four." She had fumbled for her car keys in her purse, and after finding them, waved good-bye and headed toward the door.

"Wait, Rose, you forgot to tell me which hospital."

"Oh, Emory," she'd answered without thinking, then stopped and looked at him. "Hal, you tricked me."

"Just needed to know where to look for you if the car broke down," he answered matter-of-factly. It was the truth. He didn't want to pry, but his Rose was a special woman, and he wanted to take care of her.

Rose had come home that night quieter than usual. He knew she'd been crying as soon as she walked in the door. Asking her what was wrong, she responded that she'd promised not to tell. He knew something had happened to Greta. Though he didn't have the details, he thought that it must be serious.

Just last week he and Rose had enjoyed a wonderful vacation at the beach with Greta and her family. He could see why Rose was so fond of her friend. On the way home, he'd asked his wife why Cole hadn't taken time off to come on the trip.

"Hal, it's so sad. The man doesn't care about her, not at all. It doesn't matter that she's dying. He just doesn't care." Rose hadn't realized what she'd said for a moment. He had felt the tension, the deep sadness, and the need for her to talk to him about it. It had come out accidentally. Suddenly realization of what she'd said struck her, and she'd begun to cry. "Oh, I told Greta I'd keep it a secret, and look at my big old mouth. Promise me you won't tell anyone."

He promised. He knew that he'd tell no one. He had already suspected the truth. This past Tuesday, Rose told Greta about her slip of the tongue when she picked her up in Asheville to bring her back to Georgia. Without hesitation, Greta had graciously forgiven her friend.

Since Brother Cole had come on staff here at Main Street First Church, Hal had taken moments to observe the difficult-to-understand man. Often Cole's cold eyes belied the smile on his face, revealing a lack of warmth in spite of his sincere-sounding words. He acted friendly, especially toward certain members of the congregation but was casually cool toward others.

As the meeting progressed, Hal watched Brother Cole continue to adroitly handle the deacons. The discussion of the pay levels of the employees had begun in earnest. Hal had completed some arithmetic during the break and had computed the actual breakdown of the salaries. They were divided into ministerial staff, associate staff, assistant staff, secretarial staff, and maintenance and housekeeping staff. Each had an amount of money listed as to the current year's amount, and then a second figure showing how much was allocated for next year. Finally, all the salaries were totaled. Tallying the bottom figure showed an overall four-percent increase in salary, but Hal had tallied each set of salaries individually. It was hard to tell exactly how much any one person made because he couldn't tell how many workers were included in each department; however, this question was somewhat answered after Ben Evans asked who made up the associate staff.

"They're all the full-time staff members except for Brother Cole and myself. We're the ministerial staff." Pastor Leonard had stood to help answer this part of the discussion much to Cole's chagrin. Leonard could have sidestepped that last question so some might assume that Brother Dan or other staff members who had been at the church a long time were also ministerial staff.

"And who are the assistant staff?" Ben continued his questions.

"They're the part-time workers, the organist, pianist, kitchen workers, our counselor, the Spanish minister...," Leonard continued to read down the list.

"Do you need to know who the secretaries and maintenance staff are, Ben?" Cole inquired, making some of the men laugh.

Ben smiled, slightly embarrassed. "No, I think I can figure that out." He sat down, which is what Cole had hoped he would do.

Hal, glad that Ben had asked these questions, now had a better idea of the breakdown of the staff himself. It was of great interest to him that all the money in the ministerial staff's column would be going to only two people. There was a discrepancy in the raises that he hoped someone else would notice and point out. If not, he would have to speak up.

"Do we have enough money in the maintenance budget? I've been noticing that things aren't as neat as they used to be around here. We may need to hire more help now that we're in the new building." Mortin Lewis asked. He had been a deacon for a number of years and wanted to keep things in good order. He didn't realize he had touched on Brother Cole's area and had accidentally insulted the man.

Cole fielded the question skillfully, but the sharp eyes of Hal noticed that the man's mouth thinned for a moment. "We've considered all of that, Mortin. We have enough money in here to hire one more part-time worker. That should be sufficient. We've had some people leave our employment recently. One has been replaced by a fine young man named Larry Herrin. You may have noticed him around here. He took Bill Jameson's place when Bill left us about a month ago. Larry's doing an excellent job, much better than was done before, but they're shorthanded right now. You can't expect everything to be perfect until they get more help. Once we replace the missing personnel, the church will be cleaned and maintained efficiently."

Hal noticed the brief look that crossed Pastor Leonard's face when Brother Cole had compared Larry Herrin to Bill Jameson. Flaws had a way of showing themselves more when people were tired, and as it got late, Brother Cole was revealing more of his true self. Though most didn't seem to notice the breach of etiquette that had been committed, Hal could almost see Ben Evans, who was sitting in front of him, bristle at the remark.

The staff salaries were not discussed in much detail, Hal noticed. Everyone respected the pastor too much, or they were too intimidated to talk about the raises. Brother Cole explained that the overall increase was far below the cost-of-living estimates that were put out by the government. Hal wondered if the assistant pastor thought they were unable to do their own arithmetic. Perhaps some hadn't bothered to, but there was an obvious injustice here, and no one seemed to want to point it out.

"If there's no more discussion, will someone make a motion that we vote on this part of the budget so we can all go home?" Brother Cole asked. There were some sighs of agreement that could be heard throughout the room.

Hal stood. "Excuse me, Brother Cole, Pastor Leonard, but there seems to be a discrepancy in the raises. By my figures we have the secretaries getting only a one-percent raise, the part-time staff and maintenance staff a three-percent raise, associate staff getting a three-percent raise, and the ministerial staff have a six-percent raise."

He could tell by the look on Cole's face that he'd just been labeled a troublemaker. His heart sank. This was one of the reasons he hadn't wanted to be a deacon. His conscience had to lead him even if it caused trouble.

"Run those figures by me again," asked Brother Davis in a tight voice.

Hal repeated the same percentages.

"We need to support our pastoral staff well," began Armand Molt. He had been a deacon for a number of years and was known for not disagreeing with the staff members. "I get tired of churches not supporting their pastors and making them live in poverty. Our men work hard and deserve good raises."

"I believe the secretaries also work hard." Hal tried to choose his words carefully. "I think they deserve and probably need a bigger raise."

"Most of the secretaries have been here only a short time and don't expect a raise. Also, considering how tight our funds are, the Finance Committee felt it was unnecessary," Brother Cole explained.

Hal didn't know any of the secretaries well, but some had been at the church for the four years that he and Rose had been here. Cole had only been here three years himself. "And how long have you been here, Brother Cole?"

The question made its point without being answered. Something in Hal had heated up, but he'd made his point for the moment. It was time for someone else to speak.

Eric Garwood stood and expressed the same sentiment that Armand had shared. He agreed with Brother Cole that the secretaries all being fairly new didn't need a larger raise.

Hal was about to stand again. No one else seemed to want to fight this battle, so he would do it alone if necessary. He knew how to stand alone. Even though he didn't care for the feeling, he had to live with himself. He had noticed another discrepancy, but before he could speak, Ben Evans, having noticed the same discrepancy as Hal, stood, taking the floor.

"I notice that the maintenance staff is getting a three-percent raise, and those young men are mostly college students, and Brother Cole you said yourself that the maintenance supervisor is new. Why are they getting a cost-of-living increase so soon and the secretaries aren't?"

Briefly Brother Cole's eyes darkened before the tightly controlled smiling mask was put back in place. "First off, Ben, it's hard to get good men around here who can work in that position. Larry's considered to be one of the best, and we don't want to lose him. You can't keep good people for nothing."

"Exactly my point," interrupted Ben. "I know that some of these secretaries have been here for many years. They deserve a good raise."

"But where will the money come from?" asked Eric Garwood, standing up to join the debate.

Hal had an idea where the money could come from, from the ministerial staff's raise, but he didn't want to suggest it.

Armand stood, hitting the table with his fist. "We can't continue to increase the budget like this. Once you give them a good raise, they'll start expecting it every year."

Ben knew that Brother Cole already disliked him, and though he hated to lose the pastor's respect, he felt he needed to give his suggestion. "What if we cut the ministerial staff salaries from six percent to four percent, and raise the secretarial salaries to three percent? I'm going to put it in the form of a motion."

Hal knew that the math didn't quite work right that way, but he respected the courage of the young man. "I second it." Hal's voice sounded loud in his own ears.

"You can't do that," Brother Cole thundered as his mask slid off completely for a moment.

Pastor Leonard stopped him. "There's been a second to the motion. Since this is such a personal thing. I don't want anyone to feel uncomfortable with Brother Cole's and my presence, I make a motion that we take a written vote."

Leonard's motion carried. The vote was taken, then collected by Brother Dan, who read them aloud. Ben's motion failed as Hal had thought that it would, but he'd been pleased to see that Pastor Leonard had continued the correct procedure and had suggested the private ballot. This was one reason why Hal respected the pastor. He was basically a man of integrity, and it wouldn't have surprised Hal at all if one of the "yes" votes had come from him.

The motion defeated, Hal and Ben were subdued. Brother Davis stood. It was late and everyone was tired, but the older man spoke his thoughts despite the hour.

"Since this is a proposed budget, and since the secretaries do work hard and deserve a decent raise, I'm going to move that we raise their salary to three percent along with the rest of the staff."

No one said anything to point out that the ministerial staff did indeed have a larger than three percent raise. The motion carried with little argument. Each was tired. It was well after midnight when they finished and went home. A cold, bone-chilling drizzle had begun to fall.

Chapter 33

There is nothing covered that shall not be revealed; and hid, that shall not be known.

-Matthew 10:26

Friday morning Greta awoke late with a deep tiredness that penetrated her entire being, refusing to leave her. Last night, when Cole had come home, she hadn't heard him, but as she looked into his bedroom, she saw signs that he'd been there. Wearily she made his bed and picked up his clothes. Hopefully she'd be going back to Cindy's by the end of next week, but for now, she could show the man a little affection by taking care of the house. Several hours later, the place was clean, and Greta felt exhausted. She used to do a weekly house cleaning and was never this tired; however, a tidy house was one of the few things that Cole had ever praised her for, and she remembered those moments with satisfaction. Now though it was getting late. She still hadn't been to the grocery store or thought about dinner. After putting away a load of laundry, she pulled out her cookbook. Tonight she would make an easy meal that was one of her husband's favorites – shrimp curry. Looking through the almost-empty pantry, she wrote down what she needed. Wanting to freeze some meals for Cole to eat while she was out of town, she searched through her recipes, adding items to her grocery list.

Five chimes from the mantle clock sounded. Goodness, it had gotten late. Scribbling the last few items down on her list, she went to get her purse. Only nine dollars and some change left from all the money that she'd carried with her to Cindy's. She needed more than that.

Looking in the coffee can where she kept the grocery money, she found three more dollars. Still not enough. Cole used to stop at the bank each payday and refill the can. She didn't deal with the family money. He didn't think she could handle it or so he said. Obviously he hadn't filled the can in a while. What should she do?

Cole's bedroom. Sometimes he kept money in the basket on his dresser. Making her body move in spite of the heaviness that slowed her down, she went to her husband's room and searched the basket. Only four dollars in change. Surely there had to be more money somewhere around here.

Gazing around the room, the large, oak desk seemed to beckon her. She pulled up the heavy scroll top to look inside the little cubbyholes. Nothing.

Perhaps he kept money in one of the larger drawers. Trying to open one, it wouldn't budge. That was odd. Why would Cole lock the drawers? Walking over to the dresser where he kept some keys in a small box, a tug of guilt nagged at her conscience. This was Cole's desk. She shouldn't be snooping. Well, she would tell him where she'd gotten the money from after she bought the groceries. He might not like it, but he certainly wouldn't like it if he had no supper.

Grabbing the wad of keys, she headed back to the desk. Thankfully Cole rarely came home this early, but still she should hurry. She had to get to the grocery store and then prepare supper. Trying each key, she found that the third one opened the top drawer. Only what looked to be stationary supplies were here. She shut and relocked it. The second and third drawer opened together and proved to be a large file drawer. Peering into it, she had a fleeting thought that she ought to close it and "leave well enough alone," but then what would she do about supper? Though this was a long shot, it wouldn't hurt to make a quick check.

In the drawer were many folders, all neatly labeled. Several were marked MUTUAL FUND with an identifying fund name in parenthesis. Curiously she pulled out one of the folders and rifled through it. At first she wondered if she was seeing the right figures. The most recent entry in the file disclosed that there was over one hundred thousand dollars in this one fund. She put the folder back in its place and pulled out a second one – eighty thousand here. The next one had ninety-two thousand dollars. There were five in all. Where had Cole gotten this kind of money? Contemplating the date of the first entry in the file – twelve years earlier – she racked her brain to remember. What had happened twelve years ago? That's right. His father had died. Roughly estimating, she added up the amounts of the original entries in each of the five mutual funds – over three hundred and fifty thousand dollars. Cole had apparently inherited at least this much at the time of his father's death. But – Greta shook her head in confusion – he'd acted so disappointed about how much he'd received.

A sick, sinking feeling hit her stomach. No wonder Clare and Julie had gotten so angry with him. His two sisters had each been given only twenty-five thousand dollars, and they'd accused Cole of cheating them. At the time, Greta had believed they were wrong and tried to defend her husband. She had trusted him when he'd said that he'd given them a fair share of the inheritance. She hadn't even questioned it. Now she felt more deceived than she'd ever felt before. At times she had wondered how he could afford expensive-looking clothes for himself and the luxury cars that he bought. The answer was suddenly painfully clear.

Putting the mutual fund files back in their proper place, she searched through the last remaining folders. Quite a number had the heading STOCK. Each was labeled by the company's name and alphabetized. For the first time in their married lives, she realized that her husband had invested a sizable amount of money in the stock market, and from what she could tell as she pulled out the statements, he had done quite well. She put the stock folders carefully back into the same place that she'd pulled them from, making sure that not even one page had been moved out of its original position in the drawer.

A touch of fear worked its way up her spine. If Cole found out what she knew, there was no telling what he would do. She should close the drawer. But there were only a few files left, and the next one, labeled "Trust Fund" caught her attention. Quickly pulling it out, she saw a stack of letters. Why! They were all addressed to her. Early in their marriage, Cole had forbidden her to go through the mail. She hadn't objected. She hadn't thought that it mattered. But now as realization dawned on her, a forlorn feeling of utter betrayal hit her, making her kneel down hard on the floor. All this time he had kept from her correspondences from the trust fund that her mother had set up over thirty years ago.

The memory of the day they'd buried her mother surfaced in her mind so close that she could almost touch it. At the time she was pregnant with Cindy and had been afraid that her grief would kill the child. The solicitor had told her something about a trust her mother had left for her, saying her mother had specified that only she was to get it, that the trust needed to stay in her name and not ever be put in Cole's name. Vaguely she recalled signing some papers. Looking at the first paper in the file, her heart leaped – her mother had left her twenty thousand dollars.

A sigh of relief touched her. Twenty thousand would be more than enough for the things she needed while she stayed with Cindy. She would be able to continue to help pay for the groceries and have Christmas money for her children. The file was thick. Looking at the next page, she saw that the fund had earned some interest. Actually quite a bit. Apparently the firm that managed it had invested it well. She turned to the last page, dated July of the current year. The account now contained more than a hundred thousand dollars. Greta let out an audible gasp, feeling like a child who'd finally found a filled-to-the-brim cookie jar even though she'd been told all her life that there was only one cookie left and that it wasn't for her.

BONG...BONG...BONG...BONG...BONG...BONG

The clock struck the hour – six, heavy, loud strikes – rattling Greta out of her reverie. Anger at his betrayal momentarily blocked the grip of dread that nagged in the back of her being, whispering for her to hurry, that Cole could be home any minute. He tended to come home early on Fridays. Without thinking out all the alternatives, she pulled out the last financial sheet from the trust fund company and put it into her pocket, then carefully put the file back in its place. Behind this folder, the next one said, WILL – COLE, and the one behind that was labeled, WILL – GRETA. She pulled out that folder. There were three copies of her will, each in a neat little sealed envelope. Tucking one into her pocket, she gingerly replaced the folder. As she reached for the file that contained Cole's will, the sound of keys rattling in the door startled her. He was home.

Slamming the drawer shut, she turned the key to re-lock it before slipping the ring of keys into her pocket. Thankfully she wore her cleaning dress with the big pockets. Standing, she reached to pull down the scroll top of the desk when Cole strolled into the room.

"What do you think you're doing?" he snapped as he walked over to the desk and pulled down the top. "You're to stay out of this desk. Nothing here concerns you. I thought you knew that."

Greta felt a momentary stab of guilt. She had known he'd be angry, but at the same time, from all the things that she'd just discovered, she realized she didn't know this man, this stranger. Though he'd often been aloof, somehow she'd thought he was above taking other people's money. He'd hidden things from her that she should have been told about. There was no telling what he would do. Anxiety crept up her spine, making her afraid to move, afraid that the keys in her pocket would jingle, and she'd be caught.

"I was looking for money to go to the grocery store." She hated the slight tremble she heard in her voice. "There were only a few dollars in the coffee can. I wanted to get groceries for meals this weekend."

"Well, you should have called me at work. I would've left a check for you to cash. Now go. Get out of my room."

Greta backed away from the desk. The keys in her pocket tinkled slightly.

"I'm going to take a shower. I want a halfway decent supper on the table when I get out." Cole dumped the mail on his bed, took his tie off and threw it on a nearby chair, then sat down to take his shoes off, tossing them and his socks carelessly on the floor. Greta stood there, still fearful to move. "What are you waiting for?"

Greta didn't have an answer, but as she surveyed Cole thoughtlessly throwing his clothes around, the fear in her dissolved. She knew he would expect her to clean up behind him. She felt suddenly exasperated as she saw mud that he'd trailed in on the newly vacuumed carpet. He could clean it up himself or hire a brigade of maids with all that money he had, she decided. Turning away from him, she started out the door, the keys jingling in her pocket.

"What's that sound?"

Suddenly Greta really didn't care if he did find out what she'd done. She paused, looking him in the eye as she replied, "Sometimes I jingle as I walk." Then without further words she left the room.

Cole stared after her. What kind of answer was that? He shook his head. He hadn't gotten much sleep last night, and he didn't want to deal with a difficult woman.

Greta walked upstairs, her heart pumping slightly harder than normal from the adrenaline she'd experienced with Cole's sudden arrival home, but in another way she was calmer than usual, not such a mouse with her husband. She put the will and trust fund statement into her dresser drawer. She would need to talk to Cole about this whole thing eventually, but first she wanted to take time to read both documents more closely. When she came back downstairs, she heard the shower running. Tiptoeing into his room, she replaced the desk keys in their box, then headed for the kitchen to cook the two microwave meals that were left. She would put them on nice china plates so that it would look more formal.

By the time Cole finished his shower and dressed, dinner was ready. It smelled good. He noticed how clean the house was, feeling as if his life was again back to normal.

Dinner looked pretty. Greta had set the table with the good china and lit the three candles in the centerpiece. Her mother had used candles at dinner, and she'd carried the tradition into their marriage. Cole sat down to a plate of meat loaf, green beans, and mashed potatoes. There was also a vegetable casserole. Greta hoped he wouldn't recognize the meal was really a heated microwave dinner and a leftover casserole. She ate her lasagna quickly so he wouldn't notice that she had something different on her plate.

Cole rather liked the candlelight setting. Though he hadn't told Greta this, a part of him had missed the homey atmosphere that she lent when she was around. Actually, if he were to admit it, he rather liked having someone to come home to.

Bill worked long hours for Mike, and as a result, they had recently finished and sold one of the houses they were working on. The two planned on taking a much needed three-day vacation. Christine and Bill celebrated by drinking hot chocolate in front of a warm blaze in the fireplace.

The frosty November weather was Christine's favorite time of the year. The hot cocoa heated the chill that tended to get into her bones during the colder winter months. She relaxed as she gazed at the crackling fire. In spite of their recent difficult financial situation that had a tendency to plague her mind with misgivings, for this moment at least as she watched the flames flicker, she felt all was right with the world.

"I thought I might go ahead and build the stairway to the attic while I'm off," Bill said. "I'm kind of tired of tripping over that wood in the hall."

Christine looked at Bill pleasantly surprised. He was much stronger now. Even though the job with Mike was sometimes hard on him physically, the work seemed to be rebuilding his sore, wounded muscles. "Sounds great. I'll help as much as I can."

"After I get it built, maybe we could have a yard sale or go to the flea market and sell some of the stuff up there that we can't use. Might help us pay off some of those bills."

Christine agreed. Selling the things in the attic might help them through this next month. Maybe they could sell enough to make ends meet at least for a couple more months. The jangling of the telephone interrupted her thoughts. It was Sam. He wanted to talk to Bill in person and offered to come over in the morning to help build the steps.

Early Saturday morning, Sam arrived. Embarrassed by his job situation, he hadn't wanted to explain to Bill about it over the phone. Perhaps though Bill knew of work for him. He needed to swallow his pride and ask his friend. By the time he arrived at the Jameson's house, Bill was in the process of setting up sawhorses outside the front door. The two immediately got busy as they went inside to carry out a pair of two-by-twelves.

Sam fired up his saw, and Bill drew the lines for the stringers. Sam started cutting. They worked, mostly talking about the project that they were engaged in. Putting the stringers in place was the hardest part. Sam climbed the ladder into the attic and nailed the top, while Bill nailed them to the floor. The oak tread boards were extremely heavy. Christine realized how much stronger Bill had become in such a short time as she helped the two men carry them out to the sawhorses. Boards were cut, nailed, and screwed into place. Studs were put underneath the stairs to add support and a closet. As the men worked quickly, a stairway began to form. The children, enthralled by the process, watched from a distance. Lauranna, who could now walk around on two sturdy little legs, had to be held back several times from waddling out the door.

Christine brought the two men peanut butter and jelly sandwiches about half-past noon when they stopped to take a break. The weather had warmed considerably since the early morning hours, and it was turning into a beautiful day. The men sat outside on the porch to eat.

"How's everything going at the church?" Bill asked between bites.

"Guess you haven't heard."

Bill looked at Sam curiously. "Heard what?"

"I got myself fired."

Bill choked on the bite he'd just eaten. "You didn't. Sam, what happened?"

Sam told the story with all the sordid details.

Bill could imagine dear Miss Eleanor cowering under the critical voice of Cole Odum. "Sam, I didn't know anything about this. Lauranna was sick last Tuesday, so I stayed home with her while Christine went to church. Christine didn't say a word. She must not have heard."

"Well, I'm glad it isn't the big gossip around church. Cathy's been crying off and on ever since."

Bill suddenly had an idea. "Sam, Mike's been wanting to hire more men. We have more work than we can keep up with. It's a lot of physical labor and sometimes long hours, but Mike's a great boss. Would you be interested?"

"Sure," Sam agreed with relief. He was very interested and pleased that Bill thought highly enough of him to want to work with him again. His ego had been bruised the past few days by all the rejections he'd gotten from other jobs he'd applied for.

Bill called Mike and received his approval to hire Sam. Sam in turn called Cathy with the good news. Coming out of the house a few minutes later, his face beamed pleasure.

Gobbling down their last few bites of lunch, they got back to work. Christine, who had overheard the conversation, wondered for the hundredth time why such a godly church did not see through Brother Cole. An air of dissatisfaction hung over Main Street First Church these days. Now that Bill and she were more like outsiders looking in, she felt as if Bill had been plucked from a hornet's nest.

Leonard struggled over his Sunday morning sermon, trying to decide what to say. All week long he had worked on it, and yet, still he came up empty.

The ideas he'd put down on paper seemed pointless. Something was wrong. Brother Cole had suggested that he prepare the congregation for the upcoming budget meeting, but Leonard wasn't satisfied with how the message was turning out.

Leaning back in his chair, he looked out the window into the backyard where Ann was throwing a ball for the dog to chase. She looked like a schoolgirl, laughing and petting the idiotic little animal as he slobbered all over her. Leonard wished he were out there, not in here working.

"Lord, I need your help," he prayed. He usually prayed before beginning his sermons, but sometimes his prayers were more ritualistic than earnest. This one was heartfelt. He looked at the clock. It was almost one. He would work for one more hour, then he was going to spend some time with his wife. As he picked up his Bible, it fell open to the thirteenth chapter of Matthew. One of the little titles written over each paragraph caught his attention. THE PARABLE OF THE TARES AND THE WHEAT. He began reading. This had nothing to do with the topic that he was working on. The thought flickered through his mind that he needed not to tarry here and waste time, but something inside his being compelled him to read these few verses. He read the parable once, then twice, then a third time, dissecting it, examining it, reviewing it. He pulled out his concordance and looked up the meaning of some of the Greek words. He checked out some cross-references. This was an interesting passage. Subtle in meaning, yet so much could be gleaned from it. He had examined it before as part of an eschatology study but hadn't related it to the present as he did now. As he took notes on what he learned, thoughts occurred to him.

Why were the tares mixed in with the wheat? Why did the enemy, Satan, bother to put weeds into the wheat? What was the end result when this happened? Leonard wrote down his thoughts. Perhaps this was a message for him to remember. Satan would use tares to try to ruin Main Street First Church. Satan was the enemy, and he worked constantly at destroying what God and His people were doing.

A little light began to flash in Leonard's head – a little red warning light. He thought back over the past couple of years. Many things had changed at church, and they weren't all for the better. Main Street First had lost the family atmosphere that it once held. Perhaps that was the natural response of its huge growth, but in the process of rapid expansion, they'd lost something intangible, something of the spirit of the place.

This disturbed Leonard. He no longer felt like a shepherd in the midst of his flock, guiding them. He was more of an orator up on the hill, leading the people, yes, but from a distance. He didn't even know his congregation that well anymore. Brother Cole had worked out a system in which if there was a problem a person was directed to call a beeper number, instead of the pastor. Members were asked not to bother him with their needs.

At the time, Leonard had felt that Cole was concerned for him and simply protective of his family time, which was too often interrupted, but now there was a distance between Leonard and the congregation. It troubled him. He still conducted funerals and weddings when asked, but those had also become less frequent, and he often didn't know the couples that he did marry or the families of those he buried. Something had changed. A shepherd ate and slept with his sheep, cared for them. He wanted to do this, but he didn't know what was happening in the lives of his flock. True, it was unreasonable for anyone to expect him to meet all the needs of every member of the congregation, but in reality, he'd swung too far in the other direction. Weeds were probably in the church, and he was so out of touch with what was happening that he didn't even recognize them.

Leonard sighed and felt God's inward comfort. No, God didn't expect him to meet all the needs of each and every person that he shepherded, but at the same time, Leonard loved these people. They were like his children. He wanted to protect and care for them.

Though he wanted to avoid something he felt was so definitely present – a truth that was real, that he didn't want to face, an awakening began to happen. A soft, still, small voice comforted him, reminding him that God graciously dealt with him. There were things wrong in the church that he pastored; however, with God's help, he would try to make them right. A small light of truth began to flicker in Leonard's heart and mind.

Glancing at the clock, he realized that it was almost two-thirty. He had been so engrossed in his study that he'd lost track of time, and he hadn't worked on his sermon after all. Or had he.

Some would be disappointed if his sermon didn't attack the subject of the budget, but that "some" might prove to be only one, Leonard realized. Brother Cole would be the one. As Leonard prayed, his heart knew that the sermon on the tares and wheat was the one that he needed to give. The other sermon had the same feeling of the corporate objective that he had begun to reject. A measure of peace, an uneasy peace, touched him. Funny, in his earlier days in the ministry, he'd naively thought that when he preached from the Bible, it would be received well because it was from the word of God and that was enough. Now he felt he had to defend his sermons to some unnamed source because of the corporate agenda that had taken over. Well, enough of that. He was sick and tired of the corporate agenda.

Walking into the kitchen, he poured two cups of coffee before he went out to join Ann on the porch swing to enjoy the beautiful November day. Only vaguely was he aware that he'd been given a gift of light. This light would grow, but as it grew, the enemy would attack. The Spirit had touched his heart, and the perseverance of the saints' prayers were beginning to be answered. God, in his graciousness, was opening Leonard's eyes, slower than some would like, but God's loving-kindness was great. He would patiently work in Leonard's heart to prepare him for the battle that was coming.

Chapter 34

When my spirit grows faint within me, it is You who know my way.

-Psalms 142:3

Greta's second week of recording proved to be easier than the first one had been because this album was composed only with the use of the very fine Steinway that was in the studio. She felt immediately at home as she began playing the keyboard. Her hands moved with the perfection of both experience and talent. Leaving behind the recording studio and the drudgery of housework, cooking, and the grocery shopping that had overwhelmed her the past few days, Greta felt herself float into her own peaceful world.

By Thursday afternoon, Jason informed Greta that there was room for only two more songs. Greta looked at her musical scores. She wanted to play *In the Garden* for Rose, and then she had one selection left that wasn't a true hymn – a relatively short composition by Beethoven called *Farewell to the Piano*. It was a piece that she'd learned as a child for her first recital and for that reason it had special meaning.

As Greta began *In the Garden*, Rose, excited to hear her favorite hymn, informed Jason and Brandon that this was her song. Watching Greta, who played as peacefully as if her fingers were walking through the flowers, Rose began to envision one day walking into her garden up in heaven and having Jesus join her. They would walk and talk together. That was going to be a wonderful day. At this point, it looked as if Greta would be there first. Rose felt tears come into her eyes as she realized with a pang that although she would sorely miss her friend, it would in reality only be a short time before she would see her again.

As the last notes of the hymn ended, Greta immediately began playing *Farewell to the Piano*. The music had a lilting quality to it, and yet the accidentals gave it a feeling of melancholy that was soft, thoughtful. Greta loved this song. She didn't know what had happened to Beethoven to cause him to write it, but perhaps it was something like what she felt herself. A peaceful solitude entered her soul as she held out the final cord a touch longer than she'd originally intended. It felt symbolic. This was her farewell to the piano, too, and like a farewell in life, she wanted to let it last as long as possible. After the notes faded, the room was quiet for a moment. No one wanted to speak and break the spell that had been cast.

"Good work," Jason broke the silence, and suddenly, it was as if everyone woke up. There were words, soft this time. The exuberance of finishing the second recording was subtle, not flashy. In a way, each was sad that it was over. Jason requested that Greta come again the following morning to hear how the demo sounded. He was sure that everything had gone well, but to be on the safe side, he needed her to make certain that it was mistake free.

On Friday, Greta left the studio for the last time. She didn't need to come back. Walking down the steps to her van, she felt a mixed sense of elation and sorrow – a rather bittersweet feeling. With God's grace, she'd had the strength and the ability to accomplish something that only a few months ago she had thought impossible. A feeling of reverent awe touched her as she realized that the Lord cared so much for her.

On the way home, she stopped by the grocery store. A number of boxes were being emptied by the stock boys, and she asked if she could have a few. They would be perfect for packing some of her family heirlooms to take to her children. She wanted to drive the van back to Cindy's house. Cole rarely used it, and it would be wonderful to have when they all got together to go out. Tonight, she would ask her husband about it. Hopefully he would let her use it and give her some money for the trip. Her meager savings were basically gone, and now since she knew how wealthy Cole actually was, she had no compunctions about asking him to cover her expenses.

So far Greta had said nothing to him about the papers that she had come across in his desk. Truly she didn't know how to broach the subject. She'd carefully studied the documents that she had secreted from the rest. Her will had him as sole beneficiary, and the trust fund, though strictly hers, sat in an account in North Carolina. She had no idea how to withdraw the money from it. Miserably she wondered if her husband would have ever mentioned the trust to her. He knew that she was dying, yet he'd said nothing. In the depths of her heart she knew why he'd been quiet. It saddened her.

Throughout their years of marriage, she had tried to obey each spoken rule and the many unspoken ones. She didn't know how Cole would react if he knew that she had stepped over the line that he had set years ago; however, a part of her – the timid part – was beginning to be replaced by something more courageous but also a little precarious. He had never hit her – she didn't think he would – but she'd seen his temper in the past. She knew how to be careful to accommodate him so that she would sidestep his wrath. Lately, she was having more trouble being as docile as he expected her to be. She could tell this irritated him, and she was, in truth, treading new paths in their marriage. Old reliable ruts that she had walked for the past thirty years were being left behind, hopefully for better places, not worse. She prayed for wisdom to step carefully in the right direction.

Cole, having hoarded away a fortune, some which was meant to be hers and some that really belonged to his sisters, was disturbing. Blindly she had been a party in Cole's cheating Clare and Julie. Oh, she could hardly think about it without wincing, feeling a sickness deep inside. Truly, somehow, she should say something to him. Try to make him realize the error in his ways. Be the helpmate that God intended her to be. Poor Clare and Julie. Especially Clare. How could Cole do that to Clare?

At the time of their father's death, Cole's youngest sister, Clare, had experienced several misfortunes – a sickly child, a deserting husband, and ill health. When she'd received the twenty-five thousand dollars of inheritance, she'd been so relieved. Things had begun to look up for her. But then there was Julie. Julie had suspected the discrepancy in the amounts of the bequests from the very beginning. Even though she didn't need the money as much as her sister did, she did have a right to it. She'd been furious as she told Cole this. Greta, thinking that Julie was being unfair and hoping to heal a rift that she saw developing in the family, had come to Cole's defense. Later, something had changed Clare. At some point in time, she came to believe Julie and had stopped talking to Cole and Greta. Greta had called her once, receiving only an icy greeting. Clare said she knew the truth. Hurt and angry, her resentment had been directed at Greta that day. Remembering that painful time, a stab of remorse hit Greta. Clearly Cole had used his position as executor of the estate to get the lion's share of the inheritance, and she, herself, had been remiss to be so easily taken in by him.

After all these years, it seemed an impossible task to make things right. She didn't know what she should or would say to Cole. She had thought about it off and on since she'd found out the truth. Once she'd almost brought it up, but old habits die hard, and she had let fear steal her determination. Afraid of seeing his temper aimed at her, afraid of the emotional hold that he had on her. The change that had begun in the last year and accelerated greatly during the past couple of months, caused Greta not to care so much what Cole thought of her. The little fearful spirit that clung to her heart didn't have quite as tight a hold as it used to.

"Cole," Greta weighed her words carefully at dinner that evening. "I'm going to need some money when I go back to Cindy's."

"Where's all the money that you earned as a pianist?"

"It's almost gone. I only have a few dollars left."

"You know, I let you keep it and never questioned what you did with it. Now you tell me that you've spent it, and you expect to sponge off me. You'll just have to use what you have left."

"I don't have enough." Greta flinched at the word "sponge." Over the years she'd worked hard to attend to her husband's requests, and he had given her little in return. "I want to help Cindy and Barry with the groceries. I know we can well afford it." There, she'd said it.

"What makes you think we can afford it? You'd spend money like water if I let you. Money doesn't grow on trees you know." He used the overworked cliches for the hundredth time in their marriage.

"Yes," she spoke softly as she tried to think out her words. "But it does grow in mutual funds and in the stock market quite nicely."

Cole looked at her quizzically. This was not the answer he'd expected. What in the world was she talking about? His eyes narrowed. This woman was so unpredictable these days. Mutual funds? Stock market? His mutual funds and stocks had grown nicely over the years, but what did she know of that?

She could see the question in his expression, then slowly she saw him ascertain the answer as his eyes widened for a moment, then narrowed into slits and darkened in rage. His look could wither a person. There was hate in those eyes. She immediately regretted her words and began to internally reprimand herself as she'd done so often in her life. He got up from the table and leaned toward her. She was afraid he was going to hit her for a moment. She had never been so bold before.

"You've looked in my desk, haven't you?" he accused with held-back fury in his voice.

Greta didn't want to say anything. She wanted to retreat into the silence that had been her companion throughout her long marriage, but it was time to speak up. Though her hands and legs began to shake, her voice sounded strong. "Last week when I had no grocery money, I looked into your desk and I found the files on the mutual funds that we own."

"That I own," he snarled, throwing his napkin on the table.

Greta felt herself shaking more. Not so much because of fear now. She felt cross with him and his greediness.

His voice sounded loud in her ears.

He was still standing, towering menacingly over her.

She stood and stared him in the face. "Yes, I did look at your papers. And yes, I did see your investments. And yes, I did figure out that you used your father's money to fund it all." Her voice softened, "Cole, some of that money should have gone to your sisters, especially Clare. Remember how hard it's been for her?" She appealed to his sense of right and wrong. Greta didn't realize how Cole had seared his conscience years before when it came to what he wanted.

Now he was angrier than he'd ever been before with this wife of his. He hated her. He wanted her gone. The usual calm, collected, able-to-charm-anyone man that the church saw disappeared. Feeling irrational, he didn't care. She was threatening years of savings that he himself had earned through careful investments. Something was wrong with her. He would step on it now and squash it out in whatever way was necessary. He slammed his hand down on the table, spilling his drink and hers. He could see her recoil. It was good to see her respond this way. He would bully her into obedience if necessary. She would learn how to talk to him from now on. Leaning on the table, he put his face into hers. Involuntarily she took a step backward.

"All these years I've continued with you. You. I've had to suffer with your stupidity, your dour looks, your intrusion in my life." His words stung. "You claim to be a Christian, and yet you snoop into a man's private affairs that you have no business looking at, and then you try to tell *me* how to live."

Fearful as she was, an unexpected calm surrounded Greta, opening her eyes to the fact that the hurtful part of his words, the attacking part, was a smoke screen to hide the real issue at hand. He felt threatened in a way that she'd never threatened him before. She needed to explain. "I want to be a good wife, Cole. As a good wife, I can't just let you do wrong without speaking up."

His eyes darkened more. What was wrong with this woman? She should be begging his forgiveness. Instead she'd just accused him of doing wrong. She looked concerned. If she had looked the least bit smug, he would have slapped that expression right off her face, but instead her gaze was intent. Something in her eyes stopped him from striking her. Instead he swiped his hand across the table, throwing nearby dishes on the floor, enjoying the satisfying sound they made as they shattered, liking the way she shrank back at his anger.

"Do you think you can do whatever you want here?" His words were low, spoken slowly, measured. "Well, you're wrong. Go pack your bags and get out of my house tonight. Right now, before I do something that you'll regret for the rest of your life." He stormed out of the dining room and into his bedroom, slamming the door as he went.

Greta slipped hastily upstairs. Her body shook so hard that she had to sit on the bed for a minute to regain her composure. She had seen Cole provoked before, but not this angry. She wished she could stop trembling. Her mind felt overloaded, as if there were too many thoughts trying to crowd in at the same time. The words "pack your bags," sunk into her brain with clarity. She stood with a feeling of numbness as she mechanically pulled out her clothes from the closet and placed them on the bed.

The movement helped calm her. He wanted her to leave. She might not be allowed to ever return. He wanted her gone. The words kept reverberating through her brain. She was a threat to him now. He wasn't thinking in his usual calculated rational way. That scared her.

Unexpectedly Cole bounded up the stairs. Her heart leapt into her throat as it tried to burst out of her chest. Shrinking back, trying to make herself dissolve into the wall, she watched him standing in the doorway with a menacing look on his face. Her stomach lurched.

"I thought I told you to get out of here." He looked at her cowering. Feeling that he'd won this battle, he began to gloat internally. He could and would control this woman.

"I…I was packing." She hated the quaver in her voice, the uncertainty. His expression changed from menacing to one of a tyrant who knew that he had power. He looked proud and haughty. This was the face she was more accustomed to, and though she disliked it, it was a relief over the other less controlled, more rage-filled look.

"I'm taking my papers to a place where you can't meddle into my business anymore. I want you gone when I get back." A smirk touched his strong features as an idea occurred to him. "Think I'll change the locks to make sure you don't ever come back into my life again. You've disrupted it enough." He stepped forward, pointing his finger in her face. "I'll tell you something else, too. If you tell anyone that I made you leave, I'll deny it. Tell them that you're a liar and how I've had to put up with your neurotic behavior all these years. Who do you think they'll believe? A mousy housewife or the assistant pastor of the church." Something in him was beginning to enjoy this. He could see the paleness in her face. She was probably getting sick. Good, let her get sick and go ahead and die. She deserved to be sick. "Don't you plan on taking anything that isn't yours either, or I'll report it to the police and have you arrested, and don't think I won't do it." He turned and ambled down the stairs. The power was in his hands again. He could feel it and see it on Greta's face. She looked whipped. Just the way he wanted her to be. He would let her pack her few worthless belongings. That way no one would say that he'd kicked her out. After all, did husbands who kicked out their wives let them pack a suitcase.

His files already in the car, he walked outside, slamming the door for effect, knowing that she would shutter when she heard it.

Something in Greta broke as the door banged shut. She went into the bathroom to wretch up the meal that she'd so carefully prepared. Sick and weak, the old tiredness that had plagued her for so long almost overwhelmed her. If she could only lie down and cry. But there wasn't time for that. No telling what he would do if she was here when he got back. How was she supposed to leave? The van was in his name only. He had said not to take anything of his.

Picking up the phone, she called Rose.

"Hello." Rose's voice sounded so pleasant, so peaceful. Any reserve Greta had left shattered. She began crying so hard that she could barely speak.

"Greta? Is that you?"

"Yes, Rose. Can you come and get me?"

"Sure, I'll come. Where are you?"

"I'm at home. He's kicking me out of the house."

"Oh, Greta, I'm sorry. I'll be right over. You hold on now. It'll be all right. I'm on my way."

Greta hung up feeling better. Friends like Rose were hard to come by. She appreciated having someone to lean on. Wiping her tears from her face, she began to pack her clothes in earnest. If she was going to have to leave, she needed to carry as much as she could with her, and she didn't have time to cry.

Throwing what she could into her old suitcase, she ran down to the van to get a box to fill. By the time Rose arrived, Greta had packed the majority of her personal belongings. Seeing her friend, the tears again began to flow, but she managed to tell Rose briefly what had happened. Pulling out the papers that now she felt as if she'd stolen from Cole's files, she showed them to her friend.

"Keep those safe, Honey, in your pocketbook," Rose suggested soothingly.

Greta felt Rose's concern and her love. She wanted to let go and start crying again, but she knew that Cole could be back any minute. She slid the papers into her purse.

"Let's put these into the car." Rose picked up the suitcase and a make-up bag. "Hal's outside waiting. I told him how upset you seemed, and he said I couldn't go without him. He'll come in and help. You get all your most valuable things as quickly as you can."

"Cole said he's going to change the locks. That I mustn't ever come back. I don't even know what to pack."

"Get what you can, Greta, quickly." Rose was afraid of Cole and didn't want to be around when he came home. "I'll unlock some windows downstairs. That way if he does get the locks changed, we can get back in. Now hurry."

Greta followed Rose downstairs with a bag full of her children's pictures and some special knickknacks that had been on her dresser. She put them in Rose and Hal's van, and then went to get another box that she'd brought home from the grocery store earlier. Taking her porcelain figurines that her mother had bought her when she was young off the bookshelves, she wrapped them in her socks and underclothes before putting them in the box. She could picture Cole breaking them to spite her. She thought of the Hummel Nativity that was in the attic. There was no time to get it. She would have to leave it here.

Hal kept after them to hurry. He didn't trust Cole at all and didn't want to see what the man might be capable of. He knew that abusers came from all walks of life, all economic classes, and unfortunately, all religious denominations. Hal hated to get involved in domestic disputes. "This is it, ladies. We need to get going now," he demanded in a voice that caused Greta to fear that Cole had already come home.

"Okay, let's go, Greta," Rose said, unlocking the laundry room window.

"Come on, Rose," Hal spoke with urgency. Rose hurried out to their van and sat in the front seat. Greta was already seated in the back, looking around nervously.

Hal backed out the driveway, thankful that Cole's car didn't pull up behind him. He began to relax more as he drove down the long road and finally turned out of the subdivision without any sign of the man.

"What were you doing unlocking that window, Rose?"

"Cole told Greta that he was going to change the locks on the doors, so I unlocked a window so that Greta and I could crawl in, if we had to."

Hal looked at her incredulously. "I hope you're kidding." He could picture his wife, who he described as a tad overweight, and skinny Greta trying to climb in the laundry room window.

"We're serious. Greta has a lot of her mother's things still in that house. We're going to go back to get them."

"Surely he won't really change the locks. People say all kinds of things in the heat of anger. I'd hate to see you two crawling through that window."

Rose looked around at Greta who was huddled in a corner in the back seat. Her friend's ashen face broke her heart. She wished that she could help her feel better. Looking at her own kind, gentle husband – he was such a dear, sweet, good man – made her feel all the sadder for her friend.

"Well, I suppose if you're going to do this," Hal continued in a thoughtful voice. "This Sunday would be the best. We're supposed to discuss the financial report right after the morning worship service, so it'll probably go a lot later than usual. I know Brother Cole won't want to miss that."

"That sounds good. Greta, what do you think?"

Greta didn't know what she thought. She was suddenly extremely tired and ached all over. "I don't know. I don't have much left. Some Christmas things, maybe a few odds and ends, and oh, I forgot to get my mother's dishes." Greta felt a sudden urgency to go back. "Do you think we can manage? I wouldn't want Cole to see us. He might call the police."

"Greta, the police wouldn't force you out of your own house," Hal declared.

"But everything's in Cole's name. That's why I didn't drive my van. He said that he would have me arrested if I took anything that was his. Can he do that, Hal?"

"My understanding is that as long as people are married, they basically own all the property between them. I think Georgia is a common-property state. I can't imagine that he would have a leg to stand on. If he did take you to court and filed for divorce, no judge is going to give him all three vehicles and the house."

The word "divorce" rung hollow in Greta's brain. Surely, Cole wouldn't ask for a divorce, but, she hadn't actually thought he would kick her out of the house either.

All three were silent. The word "divorce" sobered Rose who had been caught up in the last hour taking care of her friend. Hal pulled into their driveway, and without words they each got out of the van. Rose hugged Greta, and Hal wondered why people couldn't see through this sham of a man; however, if it hadn't been for Rose and her relationship with Greta, he might have been fooled, too.

While Rose led her friend to the guestroom, Hal brought Greta's little bag in from the car. The November night air was cold. The warmth that they'd enjoyed last week was over. A winter chill had moved in.

As Greta sat in the easy chair and sipped a cup of tea, Hal put another log on the fire. After closing the screen doors to the fireplace, he sat down on the couch next to his wife and waited for a lull in the conversation. Rose talked with Greta about her children. Greta's coloring seemed a little deeper now. She even smiled slightly from time to time.

Hal and Rose had never been able to have children, a deep sadness for both of them, but God had other plans, and they'd been foster parents off and on for years and touched many lives in a way that they otherwise couldn't have. They had also enjoyed a happy marriage. Rose had been beautiful when Hal met her, and she still was. Her hair was gray, and she'd added about sixty more pounds, but the liveliness of her face and the lilt of her voice brought happiness to others – especially to Hal. His wife had managed to help Greta relax, and he hoped he wouldn't ruin that now with what he felt he needed to ask.

"Greta, would you like me to call Pastor Leonard and tell him what has happened?" He saw her pale slightly and wondered if he should have kept his mouth shut.

"No, I don't want others to know. Cole told me if I told anyone, he would say it wasn't true. I think the truth has a way of coming out. That it will eventually, but right now I feel so, so...," she paused searching for the right word and not finding it, "...so, raw."

Hal and Rose both understood. The wound was too deep and personal for others to know about, even a dearly loved pastor.

Hal let the subject drop. It wasn't that he thought that Leonard could help this marriage, but it bothered him that this husband of Greta's had so much power at Main Street First Church and that the people, including the pastor, didn't know the man's true character. For now, Hal realized, he must give Greta the privacy that she wanted and needed in her own life. He found peace in the realization that Greta seemed to relax and enjoy the quiet ambiance of their household.

Greta herself felt, for the first time since leaving her daughter's home, safe – simply and utterly safe. Oddly enough, the house she shared with Cole had never felt like a place of refuge, of restoration, or of contentment. But here she felt something inside of her expand. She took several deep satisfying breaths. The fleeting thought that this is what it must feel like to come home touched her. The logs in the fireplace crackled softly as the three friends prayed together.

Chapter 35

He that is greedy of gain troubleth his own house.

-Proverbs 15:27

Upon awakening the next morning, Cole lay in bed hoping that the events of the previous evening were simply a bad dream, but no, they had really happened. A heavy, darkness invaded his usual complacency as he remembered arriving home last night, thinking that Greta was still there since both vehicles were in the garage. At that moment he'd felt an odd mixture of relief and fleeting annoyance. His immense relief surprised him. Part of it was that he wasn't sure how well he would be able to explain her absence to anyone bold enough to ask, but there was something else – a deep, buried feeling that if Greta was really gone, he'd have lost something of value, an elusive, precious quietness that she lent to his life. Internally he had crowed to himself that he could control this woman, and he'd decided to be the wounded but forgiving husband, a new role for him.

Searching the house, he found her gone. An upsetting, surprising discovery that troubled him much more than he would have expected, causing unwanted, perplexing feelings to rise up. Quickly he buried them, refusing to analyze or acknowledge them. Instead, he covered his hurt, his fear, and his misery with anger. Stomping through the house, he declared her a frustration to his mortal soul.

Going into the sitting room where the piano was, he half-expected to see her there, cowering in the lamplight. She wasn't, but her music was. Picking up Beethoven's *Farewell to the Piano,* he tore it in half. With a feeling of vindication, he began ripping each sheet of music he could find. As he pictured Greta's reaction to her shredded compositions, it made him tear more furiously. She wasn't supposed to have left. She should have squirmed and begged. He wondered where she'd gone. What would people think if she told? Well, she wouldn't tell. He knew her that well at least. She would be embarrassed. If anyone questioned him, he would say that the taping sessions had been too hard on her. Look what she'd done to her music. He would blame Brother Steve, be the indignant, concerned husband – maybe get that idiot fired.

Knocking the family pictures off the top of the piano, frames and glass hit the floor with shattering significance. They were gone. Out of his life.

233

Good riddance. One picture had resisted his torture. It fell, not breaking. He picked it up, preparing to smash it against the fireplace bricks, but it arrested his attention. Greta, with all three of their young children, smiled up at him. She looked beautiful, her eyes sparkling. He had to admit she was a good mother. Looking at himself, a forced smile on his face and a deadness in his own empty gaze, tried to force him to reevaluate something in his life, something he didn't want to think about. Fiercely he threw the frame down, breaking it, tearing the picture in the process.

The anger dissipated, leaving an empty, dejected, lost feeling in its wake. Tired out from the unsatisfying exertion, he stumbled out of the room to his bedroom. Why had she brought them to this point? Why couldn't she just let things be? Why? Why? Why? With each why his anger built. Furiously he threw his shoes at the wall as he took them off, accidentally hitting the mirror above his dresser. It cracked, a slow, long crack, before the large pieces fell, shattering as they hit the dresser top, splintering into tiny fragments.

The thought struck him as he lay there in his bed remembering last night that his life was like that mirror – cracked, shattered, broken. The brief realization upset him, angered him. Eventually Greta would come crawling back to him. *This broken mirror would be something for her to clean up when she did come back,* he brooded. She was weak. She couldn't make it alone, without him.

With that thought on his mind, he climbed out of bed, stepping as he did on a thin sliver of glass. Yelling out in pain, he hobbled into the bathroom to remove the splinter. *This was all Greta's fault,* he reproached angrily while doctoring his foot.

Carefully limping to his closet to retrieve his slippers, he realized with disgust that he should clean up the carpet. He went in search of the vacuum cleaner, unsure of where it was.

The bookshelf looked odd. Something was missing. The figurines – they were gone. She must have taken them with her. That lost feeling tried to touch him again, but bitter indignation covered it instantly. She had no right to take anything. This was his house. Not hers. What if she tried to come back to take more? Well, he'd make sure that didn't happen.

Grabbing the phone book, he rifled through the yellow pages, dialing the first number under Locksmiths.

"Aaron's Lock and Key, may I help you?"

"Yes, I need the locks on my doors changed. I live at 866 English Avenue."

"All right, sir. I'll put you on the roster for first thing Monday morning.

Can you give me directions to your home?"

"Monday's too late. Someone has stolen my keys, and they've broken into my house. I need someone today." Cole didn't even think twice about lying.

"Oh my, I can see why you're concerned. All our workers are out right now. It'll have to be late this afternoon."

"That will have to do, I suppose, but it needs to be done today. You make sure that they come out."

"I will, sir." The voice, though still polite, wasn't quite as pleasant as before. "Please give me directions to your home."

"I already told you. I live at 866 English Avenue."

"Yes, I have that, but could you tell me where English Avenue is?"

"I can't believe that you don't know this area. It's in Winchester Heights. Some of our most influential citizens live here."

"Yes, I know where Winchester Heights is. We should be able to find you." The voice on the phone had a definite businesslike ring to it now. "Could I have your name and phone number please?"

"Cole Odum," he said, his voice tinged with annoyance. He spit out his phone number, relieved to take some of his anger at Greta out on this unknown woman.

"Thank you. I'll have someone there by four."

Cole hung up. He didn't know that the woman he'd spoken to so rudely was in fact a member of Main Street First Church. He didn't recognize the voice of Shirley, Greta's Sunday school teacher.

On Sunday morning Rose and Greta sat waiting. Both jumped as the phone rang. Rose immediately answered it.

"He's here. Be careful. Don't get stuck in any windows, okay?" Hal whispered on the line. "I'd have trouble explaining that one."

"Okay, you got Greta's number?"

"Yes, I'll be sure to call you as soon as the meeting's over," Hal confirmed in a more businesslike tone. Someone must have walked into the room.

"Bye, Honey, I love you." Rose hung up.

The two had dressed in dark clothes that morning, which unfortunately made them look more conspicuous instead of less. They hurried over to Greta's house. It was ten o'clock.

"I figure we have two hours that are safe," Rose expressed nervously as Greta put her key in the door's lock. The door wouldn't open. The two walked to the back door and tried again without success.

"He really did it," Greta said in shock. "He actually changed the locks."

Rose looked through the laundry room window. It was unlocked as she'd hoped it would be. "Greta, here's the way to get in. Do you have anything for us to stand on?"

Greta, feeling a sense of loss almost as profound as the one she'd felt Friday night, stood lost in her thoughts. She had hoped that Cole would calm down, that they'd be able to work things out, but the changing of the locks felt as if Cole had locked his heart against her forever.

Rose pulled over a bench from the picnic table and stood on it. "Come on, Greta, don't give up on me now. We've got a lot of work to do in a short amount of time." She began struggling to push the window up. It moved slightly but was stiff, having rarely been opened in the past. Pounding on it, finally, after what seemed an eternity, the window made a loud, squeaking sound and opened.

Greta shook herself free from the thoughts that were binding her and walked over to her friend. "Rose, let me crawl through. I'll unlock the back door so that you can come in that way."

Rose steadied the bench as Greta climbed through the small window. In a minute, Greta was inside. "I'll meet you at the back door."

Scrambling around the bushes to the door, Rose noticed a deadbolt on it. Hopefully Greta would be able to open it. A moment later, she heard the cracking of the bolt unlocking. Good – the door opened. "Where to first?"

"The attic." Greta led the way. They walked up the stairs, past Greta's room, to a door at the end of the hall.

"I knew this was a big house but didn't realize it was this big," exclaimed Rose as she viewed the full-size attic.

Greta had the Christmas things packed in boxes at the far end of the large room. She went over and handed Rose a box, and she herself picked up the carton containing the Hummel Nativity. They walked back downstairs, opened the garage door, and put the boxes in the back of Rose's van, then headed up again to make a second trip.

"Cole will never miss this stuff," Greta predicted. "But Cindy and the boys always loved it when I decorated the house for Christmas. They'll want these things." Six more boxes of Christmas decorations were carried out. By the time they had hauled all the boxes down the two flights of steps and out to the van, they were perspiring in spite of the cold weather.

"What now?" Rose asked when they got back to the attic.

Greta looked around. "My mother's dishes need to be next. Cole never liked them, so I've stored them up here for years." They carried down the cartons, then came up to get other collectibles that Greta's mother had left to her. The remaining things were mostly Cole's.

Next they went to Greta's room. She grabbed her jewelry. Most of it was not particularly valuable, but there were some pieces that she'd been given that were precious to her. Rose pulled out the few dresses left in the closet, and they hurried downstairs. As Rose took the dresses and jewelry to the van, Greta walked into the sitting room. They had been going through the hall and kitchen to get upstairs and hadn't passed this way before. She gasped in shock as she saw her sheet music torn to shreds all over the floor. Her books were lying around with pages torn out.

Rose walked in carrying two empty boxes with her. "It's fifteen till twelve. We need to hurry. I'd like to be out of here way before – oh my…," she paused in mid-sentence. "Guess he did get upset."

Greta looked at the music that she'd loved. She had been in such a hurry Friday night that she hadn't remembered to get it, and now much of it was ruined. Suddenly a thought struck her as she noticed a picture of her and the children torn up among the mess. The family albums! She ran to the bookcase and opened the cabinet doors at the bottom. With relief she saw that they were as she'd left them. Putting them in a box while Rose tried to sort out pieces of music that were still intact and worth keeping, they worked solemnly for a while.

Rose carried Greta's filled box of photo albums out to the van. It was twelve-fifteen. Church had probably let out by now, but the special meeting should be in progress. Hal hadn't called yet to say that Brother Cole had left, so hopefully they were safe. She didn't like the mess that she'd seen in the sitting room – afraid of what this volatile man would do if he were to catch her and Greta. What if the meeting had been canceled? He would, if church had let out at twelve, as it sometimes did, be home in fifteen minutes. She felt her nerves jangled. But Hal hadn't called yet, she reasoned with herself. She went back in to encourage Greta to hurry.

Greta was hurrying. The same thoughts had occurred to her. She was angry to see her precious music torn to shreds. Not all of it was even hers. Some of it belonged to Brother Steve and some of it was the church's. Greta pulled things that had any value to her off shelves and out of cabinets. Cole would know that they'd been there, so there was no coming back.

Rose walked in with two more empty boxes and immediately began filling them. No wrapping breakables, just putting them in the box. They rushed. The air was tense. Rose could tell as Greta flung open cabinets, grabbing out things, that she knew it was time to hurry.

Rose left with another full box. Twelve-twenty. Still no phone call.

Coming back in, she picked up the phone. Yes, it worked. She turned the ringer up to its highest level so they'd be sure to hear it. Two more boxes were ready to go. Quickly she carried them out to the van. It was getting hard to find places to put things. She piled the boxes on top of each other.

The mantle clock chimed one time as she walked in. Twelve-thirty. Time to go! Two boxes were left. Greta filled one to full capacity. Rose started filling the second.

"I think that this is about it. Oh, wait, I need to get my Roseville vase." Greta grabbed it, placing it in her box and carried it out to the van. She dashed in. Twelve-forty-two. It was way past time for them to leave. Greta helped Rose pack the last few things that were on the floor.

The telephone blared. Both women felt their hearts skip a beat as they stared at it. It rang again. Rose reluctantly picked it up.

"Hello?" She would tell anyone calling for Cole or Greta that they had a wrong number.

"What are you still doing there?" Hal's voice exclaimed in concern. "I thought you were leaving at twelve."

"We're about to. Has he left?"

"He just went out to his car." Hal looked out the window. "He's talking to William Herrin right now. You two get out of there, you hear me?"

"We will. Thanks, Hal." Rose hung up. "Time to go."

"All right. This is the last box anyway. I've checked everywhere but Cole's bedroom, I think. Oh, wait. The quilts on the kid's beds upstairs are ones that my mother made. I need to get them." Greta raced upstairs before Rose could respond. Rose grabbed the box that was now full and heavy and carried it out to the van. When she walked back in, Greta was already downstairs with four quilts weighing her arms down. "Will you take these for me Rose? I want to make one last check."

Rose took the quilts. "We need to hurry Greta. We have at the most fifteen minutes left. I don't want to meet him at the door."

Greta agreed as she got a grocery bag and hurried back upstairs. Looking in each bedroom, she took a clock that Brad liked off the wall. He should have it. Downstairs again, she ran into Cole's room to glance around. Briefly she noted that the mirror was broken above the dresser. There were things that the two of them had gotten together, but nothing that had meaning to her. She looked one more time in the living room and dining room. Her mother's cuckoo clock hung on the wall. She pulled it off, along with the picture of the angel looking over the children walking across the bridge. That picture had been one her grandfather had loved. She'd had it framed as a tribute to his memory. Running down to the basement, she glanced quickly over the room. Dad's train set. Thank goodness it was boxed up. She carried it upstairs and out to the van, then bounded back inside.

Rose grabbed the cuckoo clock and picture and headed out. "We've got to go now, Greta," she insisted as she walked out the door. "I mean it. I'm starting the van."

"All right, you go. I'll be right there." After one last hurried look around, she locked the back door and the kitchen door before crawling out the laundry room window and shutting it. Let him wonder how she got in.

She hurried out to a worried Rose and grabbed her purse out of the van. "Greta, what you doing?"

"I'm going to take the van."

"You're going to take the van?" asked Rose, who although she was helping her friend gather her things, was beginning to feel like a thief, and a tired one at that. As her heart pounded, she tried to remember if she'd taken her blood pressure medicine that morning.

Greta had debated all weekend about whether to take the van or not. "Yes, I'll follow you," she said, shutting Rose's door.

Rose backed out of the driveway, glad that she could no longer be trapped by Cole's pulling up behind her. Greta hurried to the burgundy Sienna and pulled out behind Rose, shutting the garage door with the automatic button as she went. Driving out of the subdivision seemed to take forever. Each car that passed them made each woman hold her breath. If Cole happened to spot them, what would he do? Neither wanted to think about it. Finally they were out on the main road. Both breathed easier. Rose hoped her heart could take all this excitement. Greta began to relax, but as she did, she felt an ache in her stomach and a cold chill, as if she might have the first flush of a fever. The air was cold outside, but the heater should have warmed her by now. She was shaking.

Cole whistled as he drove home. No one seemed to know about his and Greta's estrangement. Even Hal Boxwell had simply greeted him with a "good day" to his welcome and gone on his way. He'd half expected to have an encounter with the man since it had finally dawned on him that Hal's wife had probably driven Greta to Cindy's house after their disagreement. Cole had thought about what he'd say to Hal if there was a confrontation. His decision to say that it was Greta's idea, that "she'd chosen to leave" sounded good in his ears, and well, it was true. Greta was a grown person who made her own decisions. People would believe it. She was a reserved woman. Few in the church outside of Rose really knew her. Probably Greta had simply told Rose that she was ready to go back to Cindy's. It wasn't like her to air their personal problems.

Donald Gresham had been at church that morning. Cole had no interest in the man now that the Greshams had lost their family business. As far as he was concerned, Donald hardly existed. Unfortunately Pastor Leonard didn't see it quite that way. For some odd reason he was still interested in Donald and had said something to Cole about the two of them going to visit Judith tomorrow evening. Apparently Donald had asked the pastor to pay her a call. Cole told Leonard that he thought Donald was asking a lot, that with all of Leonard's pastoral duties, he couldn't be expected to go visit Judith Gresham, but then when Leonard had given him a surprised look, he had quickly caught himself, saying that he would be more than happy to go visit her by himself. The pastor's expression had changed, and Cole knew that he'd said the right thing.

The only rather strange note to his morning had been when Greta's Sunday school teacher, Shirley Marls, had come by and said that she missed Greta being in class. Cole had answered her that Greta was out of town, visiting their daughter. Then Shirley had said the oddest thing. "Oh, I'm glad she wasn't there when your house was broken into."

"What do you mean? My house wasn't broken into." He couldn't figure out what this woman was talking about.

Shirley had seemed a little nonplused. "I mean, I thought that...."

"I don't know what you're talking about. No one broke into my home. Where did you get that idea?"

Shirley's face had turned a little red. "I'm sorry. I guess I heard wrong."

Pastor Leonard's wife had come up at that moment, and the two women had walked off together, much to Cole's relief. Now, as he drove home, he tried to figure out why Shirley thought their house had been burglarized. He had said something like that to the lady at the locksmith's place in order to pressure them to come out that same day. Had she said something to Shirley about it? Though it seemed odd for the two to know each other, that must be what had happened. He would call the locksmith business and give that woman a piece of his mind. She shouldn't be talking about other people's problems.

Turning into his subdivision, he didn't notice a burgundy van that turned out onto the busy road as he approached.

The business meeting after the church service had gone well. There were few questions. William Herrin had come up to him later to say how proud he was of the job that Cole was doing with Larry, and that he and Larry were going out to lunch together on Tuesday, and he wanted Cole to join them. Cole agreed that he'd be delighted to meet them at the restaurant.

Turning into his driveway, he opened the door to his three-car garage. The first thing he noticed was that the van was missing. Greta must have taken it. His blood pressure rose. Scrambling out of his car, he hit his knee on the steering wheel. Greta. This was her fault. The garage entrance to the house was locked. He unlocked it and checked the other doors. They were all locked. Even dead bolted. Had he accidentally left a door opened? How could she have gotten in?

Checking a few windows, he found them secure. None were broken. Looking around, nothing seemed different. Perhaps someone else had stolen the van? Walking upstairs, he looked in her bedroom. The quilt was missing from her bed. Had it been there Friday night? He walked through the other rooms. All the quilts were missing. Hurrying back downstairs, he looked in the cabinets. Perhaps some dishes were gone. It was hard to tell. There were so many things in these cabinets. Her music was still all over the floor. It didn't look much different. The wall looked blankly back at him. The picture was gone. Greta must have broken into the house.

Anger crept up the back of his neck. With effort, he reminded himself to think coolly. If he responded too hastily he might make a mistake.

Picking up the phone, he pressed the speed dial number to call Cindy.

"Hello?" his daughter answered.

"Cindy, this is your father. Is your mother there yet?" This would work. He would simply sound as if he were a concerned husband seeing if his wife was all right.

"No, Dad, she told me that she'd get here late this afternoon." Cindy sounded a little confused as to why he wouldn't know this. "I thought that she'd be home with you."

"I'm still at the church and didn't know." He patted himself on the back for his quick-thinking answer. "Is she driving the van or is Rose bringing her up?" He tried to sound nonchalant.

"I don't know. She didn't say," Cindy paused. This all seemed out of sync with his usual aloofness. "Is everything all right?"

She could immediately sense his defensiveness. "Yes, of course it is."

Wanting to patch things up, Cindy immediately regretted questioning her father. He was a hard one to figure out. If he was trying to make overtures of concern for her mother, she didn't want to embarrass him. "Mom said that she'd be here around suppertime. I'll have her call you when she gets in. Will you be home today?"

"Of course not, it's Sunday. I'll be at church at that time."

This sounded more like the father she was used to. She didn't know how to respond.

Cole didn't want Cindy to suspect anything was wrong, and he didn't want Greta to think he might want to talk to her. "I'll call at another time. Don't have her call me. I'm too hard to reach."

"Okay," Cindy agreed, feeling confused by his sudden turn around in attitude.

"Don't even tell your mother I called." He felt as if he needed to say this before he hung up.

Cindy heard the phone click down. Turning to her husband, she shook her head in bewilderment. "That was one of the strangest conversations I've ever had with my father. I can't figure it out, but I feel certain something odd is going on."

Apparently Greta still must be at Rose's house. That was the only answer. Before he picked up the phone again, he thought about what he should say. After all, Hal was a deacon, and if he wasn't careful, the man could make things difficult for him, but it shouldn't be too hard to outwit the slow-talking Hal. Dialing their number, a male voice answered.

"Hal, this is Cole Odum. Is my wife still there?" The long pause that followed disconcerted him. "Hal, you there?" Cole asked with as friendly a voice as he could muster.

"Yes, I'm here." Hal didn't know what to say. He hadn't expected Cole to call at their home. Greta and Rose were out in the garage discussing whether Rose should follow Greta to Asheville or not. Hal tried to signal to the women that Greta needed to get going, but they were too busy talking to notice him.

"Look," Cole began in a sincere voice. "Greta got really upset with me the other night and said that she was going to go stay with you and Rose and then go back to Cindy's for a while. I know that she's angry with me. She wanted some money, and things are so tight around here that I told her I wouldn't be able to give her much till next payday. She got upset about it. I just wanted to check on her and try to make it up to her. Is she there?"

Cole's voice oozed sincerity, but Hal knew Greta better than Cole gave him credit for. Greta hadn't climbed through a window because of a minor spat with her husband. Rose walked in while Cole was speaking. Hal interrupted. "Just a minute, Cole, I'll see if she's still here." He put his hand over the mouthpiece. "Get her out of here fast," he whispered almost inaudibly.

Rose mouthed the words, "Is that Brother Cole?"

Leave it to Rose to have to know all the details, Hal thought as he started using sign language for "Get out of here."

"Okay, Okay, I'm following Greta in my car. I'll spend the night and come back tomorrow," she whispered as she grabbed her purse and waved good-bye.

Fine, only hurry, Hal wanted to scream, but only thought. He was thankful that Rose had had the foresight to already pack her bag. She darted out, saying something to Greta as she went. Greta gave him a concerned look as she peered at him from her van through the living room window. He waved good-bye, then got back on the phone. "They've already gone, Cole. Sorry."

"Did Greta take the van?" Cole asked, sounding less concerned. The good husband act had worn off while he'd waited so long.

"Yes, she did." Hal hated to lie, and it was the truth.

"Good," Cole sounded genuinely relieved. "I wanted her to take it, but she said that she wouldn't. When it was gone I was afraid that someone had stolen it."

"No, no, it wasn't stolen. Sorry to have worried you." Hal couldn't figure this Cole fellow out. He sounded so genuine, so sincere. It gave Hal a sick feeling in the pit of his stomach. This guy was good at fooling people.

"I'd appreciate it if you would pray for Greta and me. We've never had such a bad argument before. I don't want it to stay like this." Cole sounded humble.

"I have been praying and will continue to do so," responded Hal. He began feeling sympathy for this man. Perhaps he'd only heard one side of the story. At times Rose tended to take up offenses for others and fight their battles, not thinking it all through. He was the logical one. He looked at Greta's house key on the table. Rose had come in after their little escapade and thrown the key down saying how Cole had changed the locks on the doors. Surely Greta didn't make that up.

"Perhaps we can play golf together sometime. Do you play?" Cole asked in a friendly way.

"Yeah, I like golf a lot. At least I used to when I had time to play."

"I know what you mean. I hardly ever get out on the golf course anymore, but it'd be fun to go out and hit a few balls again. How about I give you a call sometime?"

"Sure, that would be fine." Hal felt less confused. What was all this garbage about playing golf when the man's wife had just left him?

"All right, well, thanks for talking with me. It helps me feel better to know that I have a friend like you who understands." Cole spoke in that same sincere, genuine voice that had confused Hal only moments earlier. Something in it rang false this time. Hal liked to believe the best in people, but he was no fool. This guy was putting it on a little too thick.

"Yes, yes. Well, good-bye, Brother Cole," Hal said quietly before hanging up.

Cole felt an immediate victory. He noticed that Hal had used his "church" name this last time. It was as if he'd just won his title back.

"A delicious dinner, Ann." Leonard leaned back in his chair and rubbed his stomach to emphasize the point.

"We have ice cream for dessert if you still have room."

"Sure, I always have room." Leonard knew he should watch what he ate, but it was hard because Ann was such a good cook. He treated himself on Sundays to eating a little more than usual. The rest of the week he ate carefully, but Sundays he worked hard and wanted to relax. He needed to go over his notes for the evening sermon, but first he would enjoy dessert with his wife. "I noticed Greta was out again today. I'd hoped that she'd be back playing the piano since, I understand, she's back in town again. Think I'll ask Brother Steve about it. It seems kinda odd she's been out so long."

A puzzled expression crossed Ann's face as she handed Leonard the dish of ice cream. "I noticed the same thing. You know, I had a talk with Shirley Marls this morning. Remember – she's Greta's Sunday school teacher," Ann paused.

"And...," Leonard prodded. Ann was not one to mince words.

"Shirley told me that Brother Cole said Greta has gone back to her daughter's house again. Shirley's a little concerned. Apparently, Greta had been a faithful member of the class and then suddenly disappeared without anyone knowing the reason why. She feels as if something isn't quite right. Then she shared something kind of strange with me." Ann stopped to look at Leonard as she tried to decide whether to continue.

Leonard looked at her curiously. "Well, go on."

"It's probably nothing, but you know Shirley and her husband own that Aaron's Lock and Key place."

"Didn't know that. Why's it called Aaron's? His name's Harry."

"I think when he bought the business, he kept the original name. Anyway Shirley works there on Saturdays because their regular girl's out. She said that Brother Cole called to have his door locks changed, that someone had broken into his house. But then today, when she asked him about it, Cole said that his house had never been broken into. He didn't know what she was talking about. She felt rather bad about it. Figured she must have embarrassed him."

"Hmm." Leonard ate another bite of ice cream. "He didn't mention it this morning, but then we were so busy. Not much time to talk."

"I don't know, Leonard. Something isn't right there. I've felt it off and on for a while." She scrutinized her husband. Her look causing him to pause for a moment before putting the last bite of ice cream in his mouth.

"What? What is it?" he demanded in a voice that told her he really didn't want to know what she was thinking.

"Well, sometimes I think that you're like an ostrich and put your head in the sand. You don't want to see what's going on around you."

"And sometimes I think you're like a groundhog, digging around and sticking your nose in where it doesn't belong."

Ann smiled. "Can't argue with that. But Leonard, something isn't right. I think you need to figure out what's going on. This has to do with one of the leaders in our fellowship. I have a bad feeling."

"Lots of bad feelings going on right now." Leonard's voice sounded tired. He wanted peace in the church family and hated all the discontent.

"You talking about Sam getting fired?"

"Yeah, that, and the deacon's meeting was kind of rough, and...." He looked sadly at his wife, rubbing his neck. "Sometimes, Ann, I feel as if I've lost something. I think back to the days when I first started preaching, and I look at myself now. I don't like what I see. I hardly have time to pray anymore, let alone get my sermons done.

Ann patted her husband's back. "I think it's happened to both of us, Leonard. I get caught up in the politics of the Woman's Ministry and the Mission Society. I feel some of the same things."

"Sometimes I feel as if I've given up something very valuable for the wrong reasons. I don't want to analyze it all too closely. I'm afraid of what I'll see." They both were quiet together for a moment. Ann understood. She struggled with the same questions. Leonard lifted his head and changed the subject. "Well, that was a delicious dinner, and I enjoyed the dessert."

"You're most welcome." Ann got up from the table. "You know, I've been thinking about Sam a lot lately. Maybe you ought to talk to him and see exactly what happened from his point of view."

Leonard rubbed his temple. His head was beginning to pound. "I don't want Cole to feel that I'm doubting him or having to check up on him. I wouldn't like that if it were me."

"Yes, I know. You want to give your men autonomy."

"But they aren't my men. They're God's men." She gave him a questioning look. "You think I'm sticking my head in the sand don't you?"

"I don't know," Ann spoke slowly, not wanting to judge Leonard. "I do tend to stick my nose in where it doesn't belong. I don't want you to do that. But at the same time, God placed you in charge of that church. It seems to me that God will hold you accountable for wrong things that others do under your authority."

"Well, He might, but only for things I know about. He can't hold me accountable for things I don't know about." She eyed him with that same look that he was beginning to dislike. "All right, so God holds me accountable, too, for putting my head in the sand when I need to be in charge," he finally agreed. "I just need to be very careful to not poke my nose in where it doesn't belong. Do we have some aspirin? I have a headache trying to come on."

Ann got the aspirin. She wondered if she'd said too much. Leonard cared about the people in his congregation. He was a good man. She couldn't put her finger on it, but there was definitely a feeling of a wrong spirit that had crept into Main Street First Church unnoticed, and it was growing. Leonard's sermon last week on the tares and the wheat had caused her to think and watch things more closely. Something was wrong. She felt certain.

Chapter 36

Watch out for those dogs. Those men who do evil.

-Phil 3:2 (NIV)

"Excuse me, Brother Steve. May I talk with you?"

If it had been anyone other than Pastor Leonard, Steve might have asked him to come back at a different time. He was overwhelmed with how much work he had to do to get ready for the Thanksgiving and Christmas programs. "Yes, Pastor, what can I do for you?"

Leonard shut Steve's office door before he sat down. Deep worry lines etched his face, and, suddenly, the music minister had a moment of concern for his pastor. "I wanted to ask you where Greta's been the past couple of Sundays. I've missed her playing."

Shifting uneasily in his seat, Steve studied Leonard to see if he knew anything about Greta's illness. He'd thought that Brother Cole would have told him, but that didn't seem to be the case. Usually Steve was an open man that preferred honest communication, but he'd promised Greta he would keep her secret. "I miss Greta's playing, too."

"Will she be coming back soon?" Leonard asked, noticing that Steve, who was usually so forthright, had evaded his question.

"I don't know. She's gone to stay with her daughter in Asheville for a while."

"Why?" Leonard felt as if he were prying, but he didn't understand. Ann was correct. Something wasn't right here.

A long pause penetrated the room. Steve's personal integrity made it hard for him to even circumvent the inquiry. "I can't say," he finally replied.

"You can't say, or you won't say?" Leonard sounded confused and a tad exasperated.

Steve felt himself crumbling inside. This man whom he respected was asking him an honest question, yet he knew he shouldn't answer it. He would feel like a traitor if he did. Taking a deep breath, he reached over to his address book and opened it. "Pastor Leonard, I think you should talk to Greta yourself. She can give you her reasons." He wrote out the phone number. "You can reach her here."

Leonard felt slightly annoyed that Steve didn't trust him with whatever the problem was. Taking the sheet of paper, he rose to leave, noticing as he did that the music minister sat hunched over his work. A thought suddenly occurred to him. "Steve, did you tell Greta that you wouldn't say anything?"

Steve looked at him with a pained expression deep in his eyes. "Yes, sir."

Understanding dissolved Leonard's irritation, replacing it with a grudging, somewhat humbling respect for this man's loyalty. "Well, it's good that you kept your promise. I won't mention your name when I call." He left, wondering as he did why he didn't want to ask Cole about Greta? Tonight he and the assistant pastor were going over to visit Judith Gresham. Perhaps he could talk to the man and make some sense of this, but then again, he might call Greta to see what she had to say.

"Pastor Leonard, Miss Eleanor's in your office. Do you want to see her today or should I ask her to come back another time?"

Lanie, his secretary, wanted to please her boss excessively, and though Leonard appreciated this, sometimes her attitude was cloying. Briefly he recognized his critical mood and reprimanded himself for his negative thoughts. He knew Miss Eleanor had made the appointment almost two weeks ago, and here he'd forgotten about it. "How long has she been in there?"

"About twenty minutes," Lanie responded unconcerned. After all, Miss Eleanor was only a cleaning lady and couldn't be too important to the pastor.

Leonard regretted having kept the woman waiting. Usually Lanie reminded him of all his engagements, but when she'd gone over the day's schedule with him, she'd neglected to mention Miss Eleanor. Well, it was his fault, too. He had a calendar on his desk, and he'd failed to check it this morning.

Hastening to his office, he shook Miss Eleanor's hand. "I'm sorry I'm late. I forgot to check my appointments today."

"That's all right," Miss Eleanor replied nervously. She felt uncomfortable talking to this powerful, intimidating man. The secretary's attitude caused her to wonder if she was making a mistake, but she needed to say some things, and with God's help, she would. "I won't keep you long."

"What can I do for you?" Leonard asked as he shut the door. People with appointments normally had something they wanted him to do.

Eleanor swallowed, trying to calm her nervousness. "I came to tell you that it was because of me that Sam got fired. Brother Cole was provoked with me, and Sam got upset and slammed his paintbrush down, but he didn't mean to get paint on Brother Cole. I wanted to ask you if Sam could have his job back." She felt as if her words tumbled out too fast and didn't fit together right. She hoped Pastor Leonard understood what she was saying. His expression was inscrutable.

Leonard remembered his wife's admonition that there were always two sides to a story, and as he heard more about what had happened between the two men, the spiritual caution light that had begun to blink last week suddenly grew brighter. At the same time, he felt he should support his assistant pastor. "Brother Cole thinks Sam did it on purpose."

"No, sir. Truly it was an accident. The Bible tells us to forgive others. Sam and Bill Jameson almost died a couple of months ago here at the church and never got a word of apology from Brother Cole. They forgave him for that, and it seems only fitting that he should forgive Sam the same way."

"What do you mean they almost died?"

She hadn't meant to bring up the air conditioner incident, but all her thoughts were jumbled together. "You remember that bad storm we had last September when the air conditioner went out?" Leonard nodded, and she continued with the graphic details as he intently listened. "Bill got no thanks for it either. That man tried so hard, and I heard Brother Cole myself tell Bill that he needed to find himself another job, that he didn't want him working here anymore. He all but fired Bill. Bill's got a good job now, and he's doing fine, but Sam's not. He has two kids and a wife to support. He's a hard worker, too, and he could do everything – electrical work, plumbing, all that kind of stuff." She hesitated. Pastor Leonard didn't seem uncaring as she'd been afraid he might be. He paid close attention to what she said. A frown on his face showed her that he was taking her words seriously. "Pastor Leonard, I know I've given you an earful, but I just felt like enough was enough, that you needed to know what has been happening around here."

"Thank you, Miss Eleanor. I do want to know what's going on." Questions invaded his mind. "You actually heard Brother Cole ask Bill to leave?"

"Yes, sir. I was cleaning Brother Dan's office when it happened. The door was ajar, and I couldn't help but overhear."

"Why would he do that?" That inner light was blinking brighter than ever.

"Don't rightly know. But I meant to talk to you only about Sam. Bill's happy with his new job, but I'm worried about Sam, especially since it weighs heavily on me that he got fired."

"It wasn't your fault, Miss Eleanor. Sam shouldn't have lost his temper.

Brother Cole has told me that he has a few problems."

Miss Eleanor drew herself up to her full height of five feet two inches and unlike her usual self glared at the pastor. No longer would she soft-pedal the truth. "I know you and Brother Cole are friends, but I think you ought to know, he's not very nice to the maintenance staff. He complains and is hard to please. The fact that he would tell you that Sam has some kind of problem. Well…," she sputtered. "Sam is one of the nicest people I know. I haven't seen any problems at all. On the other hand, Brother Cole is like a Dr. Jekyll and Mr. Hyde. He can talk beautiful in church, then turns around and rips us apart. Sometimes he'll be throwing insults around, and then you'll walk into the room, and his voice and mannerisms will completely change. He treats us as if we don't have feelings. That's all except for Larry. He likes Larry."

Leonard mulled over what he'd just heard. Overwhelmed, he didn't know what to say.

The long silence caused Eleanor to feel uncomfortable. "I've kept you long enough, Pastor. I better get back to work." She stood, limping toward the door.

Leonard rose, opening the door for her, walking with her out of the office area and into the hallway. Even though his mind continued sorting through all that he had just been told, he noticed that the woman walked with difficulty.

"Did you hurt your foot, Miss Eleanor?"

"Yes, sir. I had surgery on it awhile back. It just didn't heal right."

"Well, be sure you take the elevator. Those steps can't be any good for you."

"No, sir, I can't do that. Brother Cole gave orders that we should use only the stairs unless we're moving heavy equipment."

"Nonsense." Leonard suddenly felt annoyed, annoyed with Cole and his rules, annoyed with himself for not knowing what was happening in his own church, annoyed with the awakening he was having. He walked her to the elevator. "If anyone says anything about this, you tell them that I said you could use the elevator from now on. If they don't like it, they can come and see me."

Miss Eleanor smiled for the first time. Her head nodded gently and a look of thanks brightened her eyes.

After the elevator door closed, Leonard stood there, lost in thought, staring at nothing, but seeing more clearly than before. Ann was right. He did need to get his head out of the sand. The sand was a comfortable, warm place, but people were hurting, and he'd been ignoring it for too long. He didn't know what he'd do. Just watch and listen for a while. He didn't want to overreact. First he needed to get as much information as he could and weigh it carefully.

Walking back to his office, he waited for his secretary to finish her phone call. "Lanie, make sure I'm reminded of all my appointments each morning."

"You mean even the little ones, like Miss Eleanor?"

"Especially the little ones."

"Yes sir," she responded slightly bewildered.

Leonard walked into his office and dialed Greta's daughter's number. The phone rang several times. Just as he was about to hang up, a young woman answered.

"This is Pastor Leonard. I'm from Greta's church and wanted to know if I could talk to her."

"Oh, Pastor Leonard, I've heard so much about you. I'm Cindy, her daughter. Pastor, Mom's kind of sick today. Her friend Rose Boxwell is here if you want to talk to her."

"Yes. Yes. I'd like that." It surprised him that Hal's wife was there. As he waited, he could hear voices in the background. A loud voice contended, "I think she should go to the doctor, but she's too stubborn." There was a softer murmured response that he couldn't understand, then the loud voice cried, "Pastor Leonard, you're sure it's Pastor Leonard?" A moment later the loud voice boomed in his ear, "Hello, Pastor Leonard."

"Rose, what are you doing in Asheville?"

"Came to help my friend move back here."

"Oh? How's she doing? Her daughter said that she's sick."

"Yeah, she isn't doing too well. I'm a little worried about her, but she doesn't want to go to the doctor. I think I'm gonna have to take her anyway."

"Sorry to hear that. I wanted to let her know that we all miss her around here."

"I'll be sure to tell her. It might help. Pray for her, Pastor. I don't like this at all."

"I will, and I'll let Brother Cole know that she's sick so he can check on her?"

"No!" The word was practically yelled. "Don't you let him come up here. He's the cause of all this." In the background he heard Cindy's anxious voice. Abruptly Rose ended the conversation. "I got to go, Pastor. I'm gonna take Greta to the hospital." The phone went dead.

Leonard hung his head to pray. He knew he needed to pray for Greta and for Sam and for Miss Eleanor and for Brother Cole, but he kept silent for a long time. His prayers stuck. Something in his own soul, a black spot of sin that he'd let grow over the past few years was between him and God. He needed that spot cleansed first. He had felt hit from all sides this morning, and he didn't know what to do. A short knock on the door interrupted him as Lanie walked in.

"Pastor, it's twelve o'clock. I'm gonna take my lunch break. Margie will answer the phone while I'm gone."

Leonard's head felt heavy, hard to move, as if he were coming down with a migraine. "Please ask Margie to hold my calls, except for an emergency from my wife. And when you get back, please don't let me be interrupted."

"Will do," she answered cheerfully as she left the room.

Leonard locked the door, walked over to the beautiful, crimson love seat, and knelt down. A practical voice in his head said, "This is too pretty to pray on."

Another voice spoke sharply to the first. "Why did you get this thing in the first place?"

Brother Dan's words echoed in his mind. "We don't need to waste money on things like new office furniture."

But things – weren't they a symbol of God's blessings? Didn't things mean that God approved, that one was going the right way? Suddenly all the things here in the office, in his life seemed so meaningless, so wasteful, and instead of symbolizing that he was on the right track with God, he realized that he'd been led down a beautiful path that was empty at the end. Myriads of thoughts rushed through his mind. He tried to quiet them.

A new voice spoke from the quiet recesses of his heart, "Be still and know that I am God." It was time to stop all those outside noises. Time to go to God. Time to confess this black sin that had crept into his life.

Rose threatened to call an ambulance if Greta didn't come with her. Knowing that her friend would do just that, Greta forced herself to get out of bed and walk to the car. She lay down in the back seat while Cindy drove. An anxious Rose watched her from the front. When they arrived at the emergency room, Cindy sat in the car with her mother while Rose hurried inside to get help. In a moment she returned with an attendant who helped Greta out of the car. The icy air immediately seeped into her bones, chilling her. She didn't notice Cindy drive off to park or anyone around her as she was taken through the large waiting room into a smaller room and lifted onto a hard iron bed with a thin mattress.

A nurse came in with forms that Rose helped her fill out and sign. The woman left, saying that the doctor would be in shortly. Greta, chilled to the bone, clung to the thin blanket, trying to warm her quivering limbs. Rose paced the floor anxiously as she waited.

"Maybe it's my time to go, Rose. I'm ready."

"No, you're not." Rose sounded angry. Realizing that she might be upsetting her friend, in a lighter voice, she said, "It's not over until the fat lady sings, and I'm the fattest lady around here. I thought I'd sing in the Christmas musical at church this year and that you'd play for me."

Greta looked at her with a touch of amusement that encouraged Rose. "Are you serious?"

"Serious as a heart attack." Rose remembered where she was. "Sorry, poor choice of words."

Greta gave half a smile that reassured Rose. "Remember your list, Greta. You haven't done everything yet."

Greta sighed and shut her eyes. "Rose, I'm just so tired."

"But what about Christmas and the sleigh ride?"

"I know. That would be nice, but it isn't necessary. My children can go on sleigh rides without me. I'll ride sleighs in heaven."

"But have you fixed your will yet?"

Greta eyes flew open. "No, I forgot. I need to do that."

"See, I told you it wasn't all finished yet," Rose exclaimed exuberantly. She could see that her friend seemed to suddenly have more of a will to live.

Cindy walked in. "I had to park all the way down the street. Has the doctor come yet?"

"No, not yet," Rose reported testily.

Greta looked at the worried face of her daughter. "I think I'm doing better."

"Oh, Mom, I'm so glad," Cindy said with undisguised relief. Greta shut her eyes and seemed to relax. Cindy sat down on the chair beside the bed and began to pray. Rose continued pacing the floor.

"This is getting ridiculous." Rose stomped out of the room only to return a few minutes later. "The nurse said there's been an accident that had to be attended to first. We're next on the list." She resumed her pacing. Greta appeared to be asleep, but it was a fitful slumber. She groaned in discomfort from time to time.

Finally, after another hour, a young, blond-haired doctor, who didn't look any older than Greta's youngest son, came in. "Hi, I'm Doctor Stephens."

"Well, it's about time," Rose expressed loudly. Greta opened her eyes and looked at the man. The doctor glanced at Rose briefly with a flicker of exasperation, then turned to look at the nurse's notes. "Now what seems to be the problem?" He read off the series of symptoms. "Fever, nausea, vomiting, looks as if you have a bad case of the stomach flu. It's been going around. You should be okay in a day or two," he concluded with ease.

Cindy looked relieved. Rose was livid. "Doctor, the woman has cancer. Could this be caused by that?" Rose had written it down on the sheet, but apparently this young man had missed it. Rose heard Cindy's intake of breath and immediately felt repentant.

Greta looked at her daughter. "I'm sorry, Cindy. I didn't want you to find out this way."

Cindy had wondered why calm, cool-headed, in-control Rose Boxwell had been so agitated when her mother had gotten ill. It had caused Cindy to worry more than she otherwise would have. Now she understood.

The doctor decided to admit Greta. Even though she preferred to go back to Cindy's, she agreed to stay the night.

After Leonard's prayer time, he felt drained and refreshed simultaneously – an odd combination. For the first time in weeks, he was more ready to meet the battle that he was facing. His armor was now in place.

Brother Cole came by his office a short time later. "I wanted to know what time we're leaving to visit the Greshams tonight?"

Leonard eyed Cole, suddenly feeling guilty. He'd been so immersed in his prayer life that he hadn't bothered to tell this man how sick his wife was. He realized Cole probably didn't even know. "Cole, have you called Greta today?"

An odd expression crossed Cole's face that Leonard didn't fully comprehend. "Yes, just got off the phone with her as a matter of fact. She's visiting my daughter in Asheville. They're going to see some kind of play tonight. Why do you ask?"

"Oh," Leonard was surprised. Apparently Rose had exaggerated Greta's illness. "To tell you the truth, I called up there myself because I miss your wife playing the piano in the church services. I wanted to encourage her to come on back," Leonard hesitated. There was a smile on Cole's face, but his eyes were not smiling. The eyes looked cold, even angry.

"What did she tell you?" Cole asked without any emotion.

Leonard felt ill at ease. After all the things he'd heard about the assistant pastor today, he felt confused. He had a lot of respect for this minister and didn't want to listen to hearsay. At the same time, Brother Cole was a complicated, multi-faceted man.

"Well, I didn't get to talk to her. Your daughter told me that she was sick.

I'm surprised that she's well enough to attend a play."

Cole looked uncomfortable. As he spoke, his voice retained its self-controlled quality, but also held a tone of sadness. "Pastor Leonard, I suppose there's something I should tell you. Can we sit down for a couple of minutes?"

They sat on the couch. Leonard could feel it. This was the big thing that he'd been waiting for. This would answer all his questions.

"What I'm about to say needs to stay between us." Cole didn't wait for Leonard to agree but continued. "Greta has this problem. It's a ...," he paused, glancing around as if someone would hear, then whispered, "a drinking problem. We got into an argument about it on Friday night, and she packed up and left me." He stopped to take a deep breath. It seemed hard for him to talk. "Cindy just didn't want to let you know that Greta was probably drunk or suffering from a bad hangover that makes her ill. It's an embarrassment for the whole family."

"Cole, I'm sorry. I had no idea." The man trusting him with this extremely private, even painful part of his life explained so much, causing Leonard to feel guilty for all the things that he'd been questioning about his assistant pastor. The poor guy had to live with a wife like that. This must be why Rose had told him not to tell Cole about Greta's illness. Rose knew her problem. They both sat in silence for a minute. "Look Cole, don't feel as if you have to go with me tonight. If you want to go to Asheville and try to work things out with your wife, I fully understand. Maybe you can get her into some kind of program."

"No. My work keeps me going. We've tried programs, but she refuses to stay in them. I need to give her room for a while." Internally Cole smiled, though his face remained somber. He could tell he'd gotten the pastor hooked, and the beauty of this story was there was little Greta could do to prove him wrong.

"Do you want me to talk to her?"

"Pastor, there's nothing you can do. She won't talk to you about it. She'll tell you she's never drunk a drop in her life. She can't even face her own problem. The children deny it, too."

Leonard felt for the first time as if he were really getting to know his assistant pastor.

"Now, enough of this," Cole interrupted the quiet. "How about you and I getting something to eat before we head over to the Gresham's house. I'll treat."

Leonard wasn't as quick to change gears as Cole seemed to be. He realized that the man had dealt with this problem for years and could let it go more easily, but Leonard felt the need to continue his fasting and praying a little longer. "You go on ahead, Brother Cole. I'm going to stay here for a while."

Cole felt a sense of glee as he left Leonard's office. All his fears of how the pastor would react to Greta's leaving him had been unfounded. He was a master of deception.

For the past two months, Judith had talked little to Donald. Instead she'd spent a good bit of time in her room pondering her options. Her parents were gone. She didn't get along with her sister, and this husband of hers was acting idiotic by giving away all the proceeds he'd made in selling the business. To top it all off, she was losing her home.

Secretly she blamed Mr. Robert. The man disliked her, and now he was giving their house to Michael. Among the few words that she'd spoken to Donald in the past few weeks were the ones stating that if Michael and his family were moving in, then she would just live with them.

Tonight, Donald had informed her that Pastor Leonard and Brother Cole were coming for a visit. She didn't trust them. She knew their kind. Only interested in people who had money. They probably intended to see how much Donald still had left so they could try and squeeze it out of him.

The old cook, Elsie, who had been there from the beginning of time as far as Judith was concerned and who Donald had refused to let go because she had helped raise him, knocked timidly on the door and informed her mistress that their company had arrived. Judith stood and shook the wrinkles out of the hostess gown that she'd decided to wear. She had taken great pains in dressing tonight. They may not have much now, but no one would know it by looking at her. As she descended the staircase, she saw the men in the living room drinking coffee. Pastor Leonard was the first to notice her. Smiling, he walked over to greet her.

"Judith, it's good to see you again."

Judith smiled a thank you and sat next to Donald on the divan.

"A beautiful home you have. I've never been here before. Donald was telling me that the local folks call it the Gresham Castle. I can see why." Leonard had come here because of Donald's request, but he didn't know quite how to approach this woman. She smiled slightly and seemed friendly in a distant, austere sort of way.

"It was nice of you to visit us," she returned formally.

"Thank you. We've missed you at church, Judith. Brother Cole and I wanted to stop by to make sure you were doing all right."

Judith ascertained quickly that Donald must have asked them to come. Well, she wouldn't let them know anything about anything. She explained briefly that she'd been busy working on a project with her country club. Leonard encouraged her to come back to church one more time, and then, trying to seem friendly asked if anyone from Main Street First also lived in the neighborhood.

"The only church members I know of," Donald began, relieved to change the subject, "are Bill and Christine Jameson. They live in the house down at the bottom of the hill on the right side of our driveway. They bought their home from us last year." Donald felt he'd said something wrong as an unpleasant expression crossed Brother Cole's face.

Judith spoke up. "The Jamesons. Surely they don't go to Main Street First anymore. I mean since Brother Cole fired Bill." Judith knew she herself would leave the church under those circumstances.

"Fired him? I didn't fire him." Brother Cole choked on his coffee and almost didn't get the words out. What could this woman know?

"It's all right, Brother Cole. That Jameson man has finagled his way into working for my son. I heard Michael tell Donald that you fired him. Nothing to be ashamed of. I thought that was one of the brightest things that has happened at that church in a long time."

"Judith," Donald tried to clarify, sensing Cole's discomfort. "Michael didn't exactly say that Brother Cole fired Bill."

Judith looked at Donald with anger flashing in her brown eyes. She hated to be contradicted, especially in front of others. "You know good and well that Michael told you Brother Cole would fire Bill if he didn't decide to quit that job himself. I heard you two talking right in this room. Now, don't act like I'm lying." Donald mutely agreed. In truth, that was what Michael had said.

Leonard rose to leave. Cole hastily followed. He couldn't get out of there fast enough. Judith had no idea of the havoc that she had just caused.

Cole drove too fast for Leonard to feel safe on the way back to the church. An uncomfortable silence permeated the car as Leonard waited, praying silently about what to say. Finally, when they stopped at a light, he asked, "What did happen to make Bill quit?"

Cole knew the question would come. He had been thinking up answers and trying to decide what Pastor Leonard's response might be. It was like playing chess in his head, and the options were too many at the opening of the game to second-guess his opponent. "I honestly don't know what Judith

Gresham was talking about. Sounds as if Bill is telling untruths about me. Sour grapes, I guess."

Leonard considered this statement, and at the same time, he remembered his conversation earlier in the day with Miss Eleanor. His personal sense of honesty found it difficult to believe that Cole would out and out lie to him. "Why sour grapes?"

Cole kicked himself internally for using the expression. He needed to be more cautious about what he said. "I don't know. Sometimes when people leave a job, they want to feel good about having left, so they justify it. Maybe this new job isn't going well and he feels as if he needs to justify having left the church by being negative. People do odd things."

That sounded plausible. Leonard had not talked to Bill about his resignation. Perhaps he should visit the man himself and see what he had to say about it.

The silence lengthened. Now Cole felt uncomfortable. He spoke as if half to himself. He might be moving his queen now, but he needed to do so, and to do it carefully, in this verbal game he was playing. "You know, Bill was a good worker for a long time, but after his accident, he started acting really strange."

"What do you mean?"

"Well, for instance, he just didn't use common sense." Cole decided to make his move and hoped it would work. He had heard some of the gossip that had gone around, and if Pastor Leonard had heard any of it, this might help him win his game. "One time the air conditioner broke because the basement was flooded. He and Sam had to turn the fuse box off and didn't want to walk through the water on the basement floor in case there was a short. They didn't think to ask me if they could turn off the entire building. I would have let them had they asked, but no, they go put a chair in the room, and put a board on it to walk across. Apparently the chair fell and no one was injured, but Bill went around telling people he would have sued the church if he'd been hurt. It was as if Bill couldn't think clearly after the accident. He went around blaming other people for his poor decisions."

"Did Bill tell you about this himself?"

"No, he didn't come talk to me about anything."

"So how do you know?"

Too many questions. Cole felt agitated, and it was beginning to show, but maybe that was appropriate, too. That was the next move to make. "I heard some of the secretaries talking about it." Actually that was true enough. "And it really bothers me that people blamed me when Bill did something so stupid." He needed to be careful not to move too quickly. "I want to do what's best for the church. At one point, I told Bill that I thought maybe something had happened to his judgment because of the accident. He got really upset. That was when he told me he was going to resign, that he'd found a better job anyway. He said some other things that I don't even want to repeat."

Leonard felt confused. This was a different story from what Miss Eleanor had told him, and the two versions didn't fit together very well. He needed more information, and he was going to get it. He had let this go on for far too long. Either Bill had been spreading lies and trying to stir up problems, or Brother Cole – he stopped himself. He didn't even want to think of that alternative. Probably Bill had caused all this. He would find out. "I didn't realize this had happened." His voice was sympathetic. Checkmate. Cole was pleased with himself.

Chapter 37

Be still and know that I am God.

-Psalms 46:10

The following day, Leonard called Lanie into his office. Before the day was out he wanted to put to rest the misgivings he had concerning the situation with Bill and Sam. The secretary sat down with a grin on her fresh, young face. "Lanie, what do you know about why Bill Jameson left?"

She looked at him with a knowing smile. Her voice lowered to a confidential level. "I ran into Margie in the bathroom last, oh, let me see, I think it was sometime in September. She looked real depressed. I asked her what was wrong, and she told me that Bill and Brother Cole had a big argument. She wouldn't tell me what it was about, but it had something to do, I think, with Bill's job, because he turned in his resignation soon after that. Margie seemed all broke up about the whole thing. I heard that Bill has a great new job now working for Donald Gresham's son. I don't know why Margie got so upset. It made me wonder if, well, you know."

"If what?" Leonard prompted.

"If maybe she had a crush on him or something like that, you know, and was upset about his leaving."

Leonard dismissed the idea and ended the interview. He would see Margie at lunchtime when he hoped Cole would be out.

Larry looked forward to meeting his father for lunch. He wanted to get some counsel about his work. In many ways, this job suited him. He was learning how to work with his hands – something he usually was able to do fairly well, and that felt good, but he didn't have the expertise to handle all the requirements of the position, especially the bookwork. Just this morning he'd overheard Brother Cole talking roughly to Margie because of mistakes that he'd made. He'd tried to tell Brother Cole that it was his fault, that he wasn't good with numbers, but the man had said it was Margie's responsibility to make sure it was done correctly, that he need not defend her. Larry had walked out of the office feeling bad, really bad. It wasn't right for Margie to be blamed for his ineptitude.

"Margie, is Brother Cole in?" Leonard looked at the secretary's red-rimmed eyes.

"No, sir. He's gone to lunch."

"Would you mind if we talked for a few minutes?" Margie nodded, but a look of dismay crossed her features. It occurred to Leonard that this was an unusual request. He suggested that they go into Brother Cole's office.

Margie followed. She wondered if this was it. She was also going to get fired. Brother Cole had gone to the pastor and complained about her.

"Here, come sit down." Leonard had been in Cole's office before, but it had been a long time. It was basically a facsimile of his own. One difference though was that these bookshelves contained only leather-bound matching volumes that looked distinguished. From his brief assessment, he decided that Brother Cole must have had some of these volumes specially bound for his office.

He turned to look at Margie, who was the picture of misery with her puffy eyes and the reserved way in which she stood. He tried to put her mind at ease. "Margie, have a seat. I wanted to talk to you for just a minute and get some information. Nothing for you to worry about. I haven't talked to you in a while. How's your family?"

"Fine." Actually they weren't fine, but she felt as if he'd only asked a polite question, and she would give a polite answer.

"Is something wrong?" Leonard sounded so kind that she was afraid she might start crying again. She pulled nervously at her skirt to straighten out the creases. Leonard sat in a chair across from her. Even if he wasn't the most sensitive person, it was clear to see that something was off-kilter. Her red-rimmed eyes had the glassy appearance of one trying hard not to cry. "What's happened?"

"I can't afford to lose my job right now, Pastor Leonard."

"You aren't going to lose your job. What makes you think that?"

"Brother Cole was pretty angry with me because of what a mess the maintenance books are in."

"I thought maintenance did their own bookkeeping."

"I did, too. They always have before. All I had to do was give the finished reports to Brother Cole and Brother Dan. But apparently I was supposed to check them, yet no one told me. The books are in a mess from when Sam left. Brother Cole says it's my fault. If I don't improve, he's going to have to let me go."

As Leonard looked at her, something sparked in him. This woman had a quiet dignity about her that inspired respect. "You haven't had to keep the maintenance books before now?"

"Never. Bill did them, and then, I suppose, Sam did them after Bill left, and I assumed Larry would do them now."

Why did Cole expect her to know something he'd not told her, and why did he threaten to fire her? That seemed extreme. "Have you ever heard Brother Cole fire anyone?"

"Yes." She looked uncomfortable, and Leonard prodded her to continue. "I overheard him one time. I try not to pay attention to what I hear coming out from his office, but sometimes, Brother Cole talks so loudly that I can't help but overhear."

"Who was he letting go?"

"Bill Jameson."

"What did he say?"

"He told Bill that he wasn't doing a good job and that he could either quit or that he would be let go, but that it would probably go easier on Bill if he left of his own accord. Next thing I knew, Bill resigned."

Leonard had a dark expression on his face as he sat back in the chair to think this through. "Did anyone else overhear that conversation?"

"I don't think so. I was alone in the outer office. I think Brother Dan was out that day."

Leonard was thoughtful for a moment. "I need to ask you about something else. Tell me what you know about the time the air conditioner was broken in the basement."

"That was a couple months ago. In September. Bill came by my office to turn off the electricity to this building. The box to the air conditioner was in the flooded basement, and he was afraid he'd get electrocuted."

"Bill came up here?"

"Yes, but Brother Cole refused to allow him to turn off the breaker switch."

"You yourself heard Brother Cole tell Bill *not* to turn the power off?"

"Yes, sir. He said Bill needed to come up with another way to handle the problem. So Bill and Sam rigged up a chair and board to walk across to turn off the box. Bill repaired the air conditioner, but when he started back across the board, the chair broke, and Bill fell. Thankfully the short he'd repaired was indeed fixed or he might have been electrocuted."

"Did Bill threaten to sue the church?"

"No, not that I know of. Now Sam went around saying he would have sued Brother Cole if Bill had been electrocuted, but I didn't hear Bill talk about it."

Leonard cradled his head in his hands for a moment, then smiled a little wanly at Margie. "Thank you, Margie. I may need to talk to you again.

KIMBERLY MILLER WENTWORTH

Please don't leave us."

"Oh, I won't. Kevin's having some back problems. He's out of work for a while. Like I said, I really need this job."

"I'm sorry to hear that. I've heard that backs can be painful."

"It's been awful for him," and for herself too, but she didn't share that part.

"What kind of work does Kevin do?"

"He works with computers. Doesn't sound that hard, but right now, he can't do much of anything."

"How long will he be out of work?"

"I don't know. I pray not very long. He started doing a little better last week."

"So this has been going on for a while?"

"Yes. He hurt it about a month ago. He's been on various therapies since then. It takes time for backs to heal."

"I'll pray for the two of you. Don't you worry about your job. It's safe."

She thanked him with a feeling of relief.

"Let's keep our talk confidential, if you don't mind."

"Yes, sir, I was planning on that anyway." Leonard felt he could trust Margie's word. They rose to leave.

"One more thing." He briefly glanced back into Cole's office. Everything looked the same as when they'd entered. He turned off the light and shut the door. "How would you feel if Sam worked here again?"

"Oh, I think it'd be wonderful. Most of us around here think a lot of Sam and were sorry to see him go," she paused. Leonard waited, knowing that she had more to say. "I don't think Brother Cole would like it."

Leonard knew that was true, but right now he didn't know what to think of Cole Odum.

Larry drove back to the church feeling disappointed. He had hoped to talk to his father alone, but unfortunately Brother Cole had been there. His father had apparently invited him on an impulse. It had been pleasant enough, but not what Larry wanted. He needed to talk to his Dad confidentially. To make matters worse, Brother Cole praised Larry to the point that if he did relate all that was really going on at work, his father might see him as a complainer. Patricia didn't seem to understand what the problem was. Perhaps he wasn't being appreciative of a good thing. His mother had invited them over for Thanksgiving. He would just have to talk to his father then.

The phone rang several times. Leonard hoped that someone would be there to answer. This was the third time today that he'd tried to get in touch with Greta.

"Hello." It was Cindy. She sounded breathless.

"Cindy, this is Pastor Leonard. I was calling to check on Greta?"

"Oh, hi, Pastor. We just got home from the hospital. She's a little better. The oncologist is going to send her home tomorrow."

"She had to stay at the hospital? I had no idea she was that sick."

"Well, it was kind of scary. I thought she just had the flu or something, and the doctor said that she probably did have a virus, but that she'll get sicker as her illness progresses. I guess you know that she has cancer. I just found out yesterday. She was trying to keep it from me," she faltered, a catch in her voice. "She wanted to protect us, I guess."

"Cindy, I had no idea."

In the background he could hear Rose interrupting the girl. "Just a minute, Pastor Leonard, Rose wants to talk to you."

"Pastor Leonard, listen, don't tell anyone about the cancer," Rose insisted. "Greta doesn't want it all spread around. Just pray for her, okay?" Rose's voice cracked a little. "She gave us quite a scare yesterday. I'm going to stay here a day or two more, then I've got to get back to Hal."

"Rose, I think I should send Cole up there."

"No!" she snapped the word out like a whip. "He's part of the reason for all this. He kicked her out of the house last Friday night, and it half broke her heart."

"He told me about the fight, and Rose, he also told me about her drinking problem."

"He told you what?" If the phone could have exploded in his hand from the shrill voice, it probably would have. "What other lies did that man tell you? Why I would bet that Greta has never drunk a drop of anything in all her life. You better watch yourself, Pastor. That man's no good. If you knew half the things that I know, you'd get rid of him in a heartbeat."

Leonard was caught off guard by the rebuke. "Rose, did Cole call there yesterday?"

"If he did, no one was here. We took Greta to the hospital, and Cindy didn't come home till late. The kids stayed the night with Barry's mother. Nobody mentioned him calling."

The truth glared painfully at Leonard. "Thank you, Rose. Obviously, you're a good friend to Greta."

"She's been a good friend to me, Pastor Leonard," Rose spoke softly now. "I don't ever want to lose her. She means a lot to me."

As Leonard hung up the phone, he had a sinking feeling in the pit of his stomach, as if he'd eaten something rotten. The confusion surrounding him for the past two days began to clear, and reality stared him boldly in the face. Yesterday he'd prayed that God would open his eyes to help heal the ills in the church so that he could better serve the Lord. Today, he felt as if his eyes were unable to shut. The truth stared at him with painful, blinding clarity. He wanted to look away from it. But he couldn't. He must take some time to think. Now, though, he had the midweek service to prepare for. Tonight the children were singing their Thanksgiving Special, and he was expected to speak only a short message. Right at the moment, he wasn't sure what he would have to say.

Christine dressed Jonathan and Amanda carefully. Tonight the two were singing. Amanda was the youngest in the three-year-old choir, but she loved to sing and gave each song all the gusto her little lungs would carry. Jonathan, who was almost five, sang songs quietly in a soft little voice that carried a melody of its own and only the words resembled any known tune.

When they arrived at the church, it was rapidly filling up. She and Bill tried to sit as close to the front as possible. The auditorium darkened slightly, and the choir teacher came in with the three-year-olds. Bill slipped out into the aisle to take a picture of Amanda looking around at the crowd. She smiled from ear to ear. The teacher moved her hands and the only voice that could be heard was that of the woman. The children's mouths moved, but they sang too softly for the microphones to pick up their voices. No one minded. The tots were moving and swaying to the piano and from time to time waving at the audience. They looked so precious that nothing else mattered.

Halfway through the second song, Brother Steve knelt beside Bill and whispered something. Getting up, her husband handed Christine the camera. "The microphones aren't working. Brother Steve asked me to try and figure out what the problem is. You take Jonathan's picture if I don't get back in time."

Christine sighed. This was like the old days. The three-year-olds finished their final song and filed out of the sanctuary. Brother Steve asked the congregation to stand to sing. Christine noticed Jonathan's group waiting in the entryway. Apparently they had expected to come in immediately. Both the children and teachers looked somewhat nonplused. Hearing some whimpers, Christine hoped that Jonathan wouldn't be afraid. The lights had been turned back on, and the group of children could see how big the auditorium was. The crying grew louder, but as a mother knows her own child's cry above everyone else's, she was thankful it wasn't Jonathan that she heard. She would have been torn about whether to go over and get him or not.

Carolyn moved out of her seat and walked down the aisle to where the children stood. It must be Kate who was crying. In a minute, Carolyn returned, carrying Kate in her arms with the little girl's head buried in her mother's shoulder. More wails had started now, too many different voices of tears mixed together to be sure which children cried.

As the congregation continued to sing, Bill walked down the aisle and touched the microphone. It screeched an ear-piercing sound that could be heard above the music. He waved to Brother Steve who looked relieved and a little overwhelmed. The song ended. Everyone sat down, and a group of tearful four-year-olds got up on the stage. Christine waved at Jonathan who looked around nervously. He didn't see her. The congregation lights again went down, and the spotlights turned onto the children. This time the assemblage had no trouble hearing the mournful youngsters – some sang, some cried. After the first song, the teacher whispered something to the group. Whatever it was helped perk them up, and then the second and third songs came out much better than the first one had.

After church was over, Christine asked Jonathan what the teacher had said that made them sing so much better.

"She told us that if we sang real pretty, she had a surprise waiting for us."

"What was the surprise?"

"We had a Thanksgiving Party. There was cake and ice cream."

"We had tookies," Amanda chimed in. "I like singing in church."

Christine liked it, too, though part of her felt for Brother Steve. He looked so weary after it was finished. She was glad Bill had been able to fix the microphones for them, but she had noticed Larry and Patricia sitting in the audience. She wondered privately why Brother Steve hadn't gone to Larry about the equipment problem. Probably the music minister didn't see the young man.

Chapter 38

Let every man be swift to hear, slow to speak, slow in wrath.

-James 1:19

Since Thanksgiving was only a week away and Leonard wasn't prepared to confront Cole Odum yet, he canceled the weekly staff meeting; nevertheless, Friday morning, he had separate visits from Brother Steve and Brother Dan. Both men were concerned about maintenance problems, and it became clear to Leonard that Larry was unable to handle all the responsibilities passed his way. Steve, anxious about the upcoming Thanksgiving Program, wanted to bring in special sound technicians to train the young man. Dan expressed concern about the soaring maintenance expenses detailed in the most recent report. Leonard realized that Larry needed a mentor - a Bill or a Sam - to help him. All agreed that though Larry was a willing worker, he simply didn't have the expertise needed to handle the position he was in.

During Leonard's meeting with Brother Dan, the administrator looked at his pastor thoughtfully before continuing. "I think we ought to ask both Sam and Bill to come back to work at the church. I know it might upset Brother Cole, but we need to do something. I'll be happy to be in charge of maintenance and housekeeping instead of Brother Cole if either of them do agree to return. I've found it easy to work with both men."

"I've been thinking the same thing myself," Leonard agreed. "Give me some time to talk with both Bill and Sam. I don't want to act too quickly. Cole won't like this."

A troubled look crossed Dan's face. "In all honesty, Pastor Leonard, I can't figure Brother Cole out. He preaches inspiring sermons and is dedicated to the church, but I sense a problem. Something has felt wrong for a while."

Leonard leaned back in his chair, breathing deeply. There was that phrase again that kept running through his mind. *Something is wrong.* As they talked, Leonard realized that the mental image he had of Brother Cole was being altered drastically by not only his own recent experiences with the man, but also by the reports of others. Their view of Cole Odum seemed similar, whereas his former view now felt askew.

"Oh, Dan. Before you leave," Leonard suddenly remembered as the administrator arose, "how much money do we have in our Charity Fund?"

"None, I'm afraid. We ran out of funds last July. It was only fifteen hundred dollars to begin with. Do you know of a need?"

"Yes, I heard of one recently. I was hoping that the church might be able to help."

The Charity Fund was a sore spot to Brother Dan. It disturbed him that a church of this size designated such a small portion to helping others. When the Finance Committee chose to cut the budgeted amount for the coming year, he'd argued against it but had basically stood alone. He was glad to see the look of concern cross his pastor's face.

Slowly Greta began to feel more like her old self. Thankfully she was out of the hospital, and Rose, her beloved and weary friend, had finally been able to leave early that morning. Poor Rose hadn't planned on staying but for one night, so she'd been wearing the same outfit all week long. Greta had said a somber good-bye, but then stiffened her spine. She had business to take care of.

Reaching for the phone on the nightstand, she called the number listed on the trust fund letter she'd taken from Cole's desk. The call turned out to be easier than she'd thought it would be. The people investing her trust, after verifying who she was through the use of a variety of personal questions, said that in order to get the money all she had to do was sign certain papers and instruct them where to send the check. They promised to send the forms immediately since the Thanksgiving holidays were quickly approaching.

The second call was more difficult. Opening the phone book, she turned to the yellow pages. Under Lawyers, it directed her to see Attorneys. She turned to pages and pages of attorneys. Apparently they specialized. Reading down the list, at the bottom of the final page, she saw the word "Wills." Nine were listed. She decided to call the only one without the dark bold print, that didn't have an ad attached to his name. She would talk to him first – Henry Adams. She dialed the number.

A young man answered, "Adam's Legal Services."

Greta informed him of her need to have a new will drawn. "I'd like to get this done as soon as possible. I've just come home from the hospital and am too weak to leave the house at the moment, but I can make an appointment to come in next week if that would be all right."

"Where do you live?" He planned to go home and visit his family for Thanksgiving next week, but he didn't want to lose this client. He needed the money.

"I'm at my daughter's home in Black Mountain."

"Oh, I live nearby. Why don't I stop by on my way home from work?" He hoped he wasn't being too aggressive. He'd only been out of law school for a year and was still trying to pay off his student loans. There were too many lawyers out there, and it was a hard business. He was glad when she sounded relieved and gave him directions to the house.

At four o'clock, the doorbell rang. When Cindy answered it, a thin, young man greeted her and explained that he was there to see her mother. Although Cindy knew Greta had said she would be having a visitor, she couldn't figure out why this young man was here. In spite of her misgivings, she led him to her mother's room and quietly listened at the door for a moment. All she heard were the introductions before the phone started ringing. Annoyed she went to answer it.

"Cindy, this is Rose. I wanted to let Greta know that I got home safely. How's she doing?"

"She seems much better. As a matter of fact she has a young man in her room visiting her right now."

"Really! Well, good! Sounds like she's taking care of business. Tell her I called. I'll call again tomorrow."

Cindy hung up feeling even more confused. Usually her mother was careful with strangers. This was out of character for her.

Bill sighed as the warm shower began to soothe his aching muscles. It was after seven o'clock before he'd been able to get home every night this week, and even though tomorrow was Saturday, there would be no rest because he'd promised to help Mike and Nancy move.

Stepping out of the shower, he noticed that the house was full of good smells. Black bean soup, he decided. One of his favorite cold weather meals, especially after being out in the harsh elements all day. It hadn't been a bad day. The temperature had been in the high forties, which was perfect working weather, but a new cold front was moving their way. He dressed and headed to the dining room. Because it was late, the children and his wife had already eaten; however, Christine sat with him while he enjoyed his meal.

"Pastor Leonard called today," she informed him.

"Oh, what about?"

"All he said was that he wanted to talk to you when it's convenient."

"Wonder what he wants."

"I'm not certain. He sounded friendly, not as if he were upset about anything. I have a feeling he wants to ask you to come back to work at the church." Christine had no desire for Bill to return to that job. She was still saddened about the way Brother Cole had treated him. Just last Sunday after the business meeting, she'd overheard the assistant pastor praising Larry Herrin to some man named "William" in the parking lot. Why Brother Cole felt the need to brag so much on Larry, she didn't know. All she knew was that it felt like a knife in her own soul.

Bill spoke thoughtfully, "I don't want to go back there. I think I'm right where God wants me. I'd feel as if I was letting Mike down if I quit on him now. He's counting on me."

"You don't have to convince me."

Bill smiled at her. "Even if Pastor Leonard needs me, I don't want to ever work with Cole Odum again if I can help it."

Without argument Christine agreed that she felt the same way.

A similar conversation was taking place at Sam's house. Sam was slightly concerned that the pastor was upset about the paint incident and felt the need to rehash the matter with him. He and his family hadn't been back to church since that time. In truth, he had no desire to meet with the pastor and wanted to forget the whole thing. "We're helping Mike move tomorrow, and I can't take off work. Bill and I need to get that house dried in before Thanksgiving. I don't know when I'll be able to talk to him."

"Well, I guess you'll just have to make the time," Cathy responded unsympathetically. She was afraid of what the preacher wanted, and she didn't trust any of them right now. The pressure felt enormous. The time between jobs hadn't been long. She should be grateful, but there was a huge invisible weight on her shoulders. Whatever the problem was, she wanted it dealt with promptly.

"I'll call him," Sam agreed.

As Donald moved boxes into the two-bedroom house he'd rented, he felt an unexpected excitement. He hadn't wanted to live in his father's home. In some odd way, it felt as if he'd finally grown up enough to have a place he could call his own. He hoped that the Gresham Castle wouldn't change Michael and Nancy. It hadn't had that effect on his father or mother, but it had seemed to work that way on Judith, and, to be honest, on himself.

Judith hadn't packed – not one thing. She refused to go and said that if Michael and Nancy didn't like it, it was just too bad. Even though Donald felt that in some ways he had let his wife down, the time had come for them to start over. He was ready to do that. His new job was going well. At this company, the electricians were honest, hard working, family men that he could respect. They didn't seem to care about his past. They were more concerned about his actions now, which he tried to keep honorable. Two of the men from work even had come to help him move. He and Elsie had packed everything that they would need. It wasn't much really. He knew Judith would have chosen to take more if she'd gotten herself involved. Tomorrow Michael and Nancy were moving in. Somehow he would have to convince Judith to come with him.

Nancy stood in the bathroom, wiping away the tears that she couldn't stop from coming. While packing, one of her little bells that she collected had broken. She cried over it as she tried to figure out if it was salvageable. The broken bell had stimulated tears that the tension in her had been wanting to release for days. She loved this house. Yes, it was small, but it was theirs. They had bought it with their own money and worked lovingly and hard to make it into a nice home. She should be excited about moving to the big Gresham Castle. It was Michael's inheritance, but the circumstances ruined the joy that she would have otherwise felt. She was a girl with simple tastes. How could she make this showplace of the community into a home for herself and her family? Plus, and this was the bottom line, what about her mother-in-law? As it was, the woman was difficult, but now Michael had said that his mother refused to move. Was she going to end up having to live with Judith?

Last night the thought had become a nightmare. She had dreamed that she was in the new house, and Judith had snuck into their bedroom with a hateful grin spread across her face, hissing, "You can have the house, but I have the children." Nancy awoke with a foreboding that she couldn't shake. Even though Michael assured her that his mother would not live with them, Nancy remained unconvinced.

Recently Mr. Robert said that Judith had used the mansion to hide from the real world all these years. Somehow Nancy knew what he meant. Now all the woman's guards were being taken away from her. Her wealth was gone. Her reputation was in shambles. Her servants and family weren't there to do things for her. She was a woman alone.

Taking a deep breath and wiping away her tears, Nancy went back to her packing. If she could turn this little place into a special home, she could definitely have fun taking on the formidable castle. Michael had said she could make any changes that she wanted. She would enjoy it as long as Judith wasn't around.

Darkness descended as the workers ate a late supper. Everything was moved to the small house – everything but Judith. Donald had talked with Miss Elsie about what he should do if his wife adamantly refused to come to their new home with him. He knew that time was getting short. Elsie listened as he discussed different alternatives. Drastic as it sounded, calling the police or picking her up and bodily carrying her out of the house were the only two options he could think of. As he ate, Elsie slipped up the stairs and tapped gently on Judith's door.

"What do you want?" Judith snarled from the window seat where she sat.

Elsie, for the first time in memory, felt a tad sorry for the woman. "I just don't want you to be embarrassed."

"Embarrassed? Why should I be embarrassed?"

"Well, there's talk about calling the police to take you out of here."

"I'd like to see them try. I'll give them the fight of their lives."

Elsie knew one of Judith's blind spots, and she decided to touch on it. "Well, see ma'am, you're a woman of dignity. I don't want any of those press people that follow the police around to get a picture of that."

Dignity? Judith stood and looked at herself in the mirror. She used to think of herself as a woman of dignity. Was she even going to throw away the little bit of self-respect that she did have to try and stay in this house - her house? Something in Judith folded. She couldn't keep up the charade anymore. In spite of the pain, it was time to move on. This was the hardest thing she had ever done, but she would do it, and do it with dignity. That would be her new byword, dignity. No one could take that from her.

"Would you ask Donald to come up here for a minute. I'd like to tell him what I want taken to my new home."

"Yes, ma'am." Elsie hurried down the stairs to inform an amazed Donald, who wondered how she'd accomplished such a miracle.

Chapter 39

Sorrow is better than laughter; for by the sadness of the countenance the heart is made better.

-Ecclesiastes 7:3

By Thanksgiving Day, Greta's new will had been drawn and copies were in safekeeping. The papers about her trust had arrived, and she'd worked out the arrangements to have the money transferred. Though she still struggled with fatigue and a general malaise, she'd encouraged Cindy to begin taking the hammer-dulcimer-making class straightaway so that the instrument would be ready for Christmas.

Leaning back against the soft, downy pillow on her bed, she allowed her mind to wander. These days her thoughts often drifted to the past – as if she were trying to sort something out. This habit had started a couple of nights ago as she'd remembered incidents from her childhood.

As she relaxed, her memory drifted to her teenage years. She was a junior in high school, and to her surprise and delight, Alan – the captain of the baseball team – had started paying attention to her. Unexpectedly along with him came a whole new popularity. Suddenly she was being invited to parties and social events where she'd been virtually an outcast before. She remembered him telling her that she was beautiful. She'd never felt particularly pretty, and she flourished under his praise. She had liked this tall, blond boy from afar but hadn't thought that he would be interested in her. She was a nobody. They didn't actually date. After class, he would get her books and walk with her to her next class, and then one day he came to her church and drove her home afterwards. That time he'd given her a little kiss – her first kiss. Feeling a gush of emotion, her shyness had fallen away for a moment. Without thinking, she'd blurted out that she loved him. His uncomfortable look made her wish she could take the words back. She didn't know what love was, and she'd spoken too quickly. He had driven away and avoided her after that – no longer meeting her after class or walking with her. He didn't come to church again, and when she did see him, he pretended not to notice her. He was soon seen with another girl, and all the friends that she'd suddenly become popular with ignored her again. It had been a painful, lonely time.

For years after that, she avoided boys. At a little college nestled in the mountains of South Carolina she'd majored in music and successfully fended off anyone who invited her out. Then Cole had come along – handsome Cole Odum, whom every girl wanted to date. When he asked Greta out, she'd refused him, something that probably had not happened to him before. Without knowing it, she drew him to herself. She hadn't understood at the time why he seemed interested in her, but in truth, Cole liked a challenge. All the other girls were too easy. Greta wasn't. She didn't want a man in her life. She wanted to pursue her music quietly and be left alone.

She remembered, and the memory brought a smile to her lips, the day that she'd come up to her dorm room, and it'd been covered in flowers. Her roommate had said that the flowers were all for her and that she needed to at least let the poor guy take her out. She had agreed to just one date, and then cautiously to another and another. He was charming and quite the flatterer as he told her that she was beautiful and that she played the piano like an angel. Slowly she was pulled under his spell, and soon, though somewhat reluctantly, she agreed to marry him. Others couldn't understand her hesitation at the time, and in spite of her doubts, she'd begun to hope that he was the perfect mate for her; however, as soon as they were married, she began to feel like a trophy that he'd won, and as such, she was placed on a shelf.

The one thing that protected their early marriage was that he wanted children – three, in fact. People of the world have two children, Christians have three, and fanatics have four or more. She wasn't sure where he got this logic, but with Cole, things were set. He knew what he wanted. She wanted children, too, and Cindy was born during their first year, Brad was born twenty months later, and Brian quickly followed after that. Because she was so busy with the three small ones, she barely noticed how lonely she was. Cole finished seminary, and then began working part time at a small country church. From there he'd moved to bigger and bigger churches. When he'd gotten the job in Asheville as pastor of education, Greta had rejoiced. It seemed to have everything needed to make him happy. By this time her children were in their late teens, and she was suddenly, unexpectedly pregnant again, but a fourth child was not in Cole's plans. He blamed her and complained throughout the pregnancy. Tears formed in her eyes as she recalled the day that she went for her monthly check up – eight months along. The doctor listened for a heartbeat. He kept trying and trying to find one, but couldn't. Finally, he sent her home, saying that perhaps he needed a new stethoscope.

Two weeks later, the baby was born – a girl – stillborn. Greta named her

Hope. Cole wasn't there. He said he couldn't come. Never had she felt so alone. She stayed in the hospital for a week, then went home to try and explain to her children what had happened. Cole didn't mention the baby, pretending that she hadn't existed. Something in Greta died along with that child for a time, but then one day she realize that she was dwelling so much on her loss that she was losing the gifts she still had – three precious children. She began to do what she could for them.

Now that she was sick, it was a comfort to know that there would be a child, perhaps twelve years old if children grew up, in heaven that would be waiting for her. She would probably be beautiful like Cindy. Greta would enjoy seeing Hope again. Clinging to that thought, she began to fall asleep. This afternoon they would all enjoy Thanksgiving together – all except for Cole. He had been invited by a tentative Cindy a couple of days earlier, but he'd said that he would be unable to make it. He had other plans.

Cole's other plans apparently flopped. Throughout Thanksgiving Day, he sat at home watching one football game after another on his television set. The microwave meal of turkey and dressing was dry. He ate it alone. Since he'd made a point of telling the Herrins that his wife was out of town, he'd hoped they'd ask him over for Thanksgiving dinner, but William must not have taken his hint. It didn't matter. He'd received a nice Thanksgiving gift from the man – a generous bonus for having to put up with the kid.

Leonard helped Ann set the table. It would only be the three of them this year, but they were thankful that Aaron didn't have other plans. Leonard put the napkins down while Ann placed the silverware on top. Even though the family group was small, they would eat in the dining room and enjoy a traditional Thanksgiving meal.

"You never told me how Margie reacted."

"Oh, it would have warmed your heart." Leonard smiled at the memory. "You know I told you I wanted to give the money anonymously but didn't want to use cash since it could get lost or stolen?"

"Uh-huh, how'd you handle it?"

"Well, yesterday morning, I went by the post office and purchased a money order. Didn't have to put my name on it, only Margie's."

"Oh, that's great. Did you leave it in her church box?"

"No, I did better than that. I put it in an envelope and addressed it and then, after Lanie put the day's mail into the boxes – my that girl is slow – I gathered up everything belonging to Brother Dan and Margie and took it all upstairs. Problem was, when I handed Margie her letters, she looked as if I had just eaten a frog. Guess I overdid it a little there, but I covered it pretty well, I think. Said I had to talk to Brother Dan, and it just seemed logical to deliver their mail and messages at the same time."

Ann started laughing.

"Now, really I was very controlled and tried to act as normal as possible. I took Brother Dan his mail and talked to him for a few minutes about nothing. If anyone got suspicious, it was Dan."

"Why didn't you let her get her own mail?"

"Because I wanted to make sure it wasn't mislaid. I couldn't ask her about it later. Anyway, there I was listening and expecting, oh, I don't know exactly what – a squeal or something. Instead, I didn't hear anything. Finally I figured I'd better get on back downstairs, and as I was leaving, there she was holding the check with tears falling down her cheeks. I asked her if anything was wrong, and she looked up at me and said, 'Pastor Leonard, I've just had an answer to my prayers.'" Leonard's voice became a little husky as he repeated what Margie had said.

"It felt good, Ann, really good. Just as I used to feel a long time ago. To be an answer to someone's prayer. Well….," Leonard spread his hands out at a loss for words for a moment, "thank you for encouraging me. If you hadn't I would have missed a blessing." He looked around the dining room. "Look at all we have, and I take it for granted. I thought I'd write William Herrin another thank you note and tell him what I did with the birthday check he sent me, not specifically, but in general let him know. He has so much that he could use to help others. He doesn't need to give it to people like us but to those who really need it."

"Oh, that reminds me. You got some mail from the Herrins yesterday." Ann left the room to retrieve the letter.

Opening William's note, Leonard found another large check, and a card that said, "Thank you for all you do. Happy Thanksgiving. The Herrins."

He shook his head. "He probably won't be so thankful when I replace Larry."

"You going to have to let the Herrin boy go?"

"I don't know what to do. I'm not planning on firing him, but he doesn't need to be in charge. At least not yet. He's inexperienced and something has to change. Brother Dan thinks the boy doesn't really want the job. Larry apparently admitted to him that he doesn't know what he's doing. Brother Dan said Brother Cole got furious with him for even suggesting that Larry was doing anything but an excellent job." Leonard picked up the Herrin's check off the table. "I think I know why Cole is so determined to keep Larry at all costs. I don't like what I see."

After Thanksgiving dinner, Larry finally found his opportunity to ask his father if they could talk. Once the library door was closed, he looked at William for a moment. He wanted to please this man but knew what he had to say would probably cause concern. "Dad, I need your help in deciding what to do about my job."

"What do you mean? Do about your job? Brother Cole gives you nothing but the highest praise."

Larry began pacing the room. "I don't know. I'm no good at it. Brother Cole's lying to you when he says I am. He knows it, too."

"Now hold on, Son. Brother Cole's a good man."

"You must be giving him money or something to keep me there. It makes no sense. I mess up all the time. It's embarrassing how much I mess up."

"You think I'm paying Brother Cole to keep you working there?" William asked incredulously.

"I don't know. I can't figure out why he keeps telling you all this garbage about how wonderful I am at my work. He criticizes other workers who are doing a much better job, and then, he goes and praises me. To make matters even worse, half the time, I think that they're being blamed for mistakes I've made. Brother Cole's secretary got yelled at last week because I fouled up the books."

"Seems as if you did a good job keeping the books until now, Larry. Every month can't be perfect. Sounds as if you're expecting too much out of yourself."

"No, Dad. You don't understand. Bill and Sam took care of them before. I can't do bookwork. I don't even know how. Sam tried to teach me, but it's all a jumble. Now that he's gone, I realize all the things I can't do. I've had to call plumbers and electricians to repair things since Sam left. I'm costing the church a lot of money."

"Well, we can help the church with any budget problem."

"You don't understand. I'm in way over my head. Sam should be the one in charge. I was learning so much from him and felt good about myself for the first time in years, and when Brother Cole let him go, well...," Larry wished he were better with words, "it just messed up everything. I can't figure out why Brother Cole brags on me so much."

A long silence followed as William mulled over what his son had said. "It can't be as bad as you think, Larry."

"Dad, you know how I've always had trouble with figures. Well, last Tuesday for the Thanksgiving banquet, I miscounted the reservations and didn't set up enough tables and chairs. People were left standing with no place to sit and eat. Everyone was grumbling, complaining, and asking, 'Whose in charge anyhow?' I felt terrible. I knew it was my fault. I'd have felt better if Brother Cole had bawled me out – yelled at me – anything. But he didn't. Instead he lit into the cooks and the college students who were helping out." Larry sat on the couch and breathed deeply. "I can't have you believing everything is going well when it isn't. I'm sorry, Dad. I wish I could do the perfect job that Brother Cole makes it sound like I do."

William sat on the corner of his desk. "What do you want to do?" His question had a resigned quality to it.

Larry faced his father. "I'd like to continue working there if I could work for someone like Sam. Sam knew I couldn't do numbers, and he never put me down for it. I want to have someone teach me. I can't learn from all those books, but I can learn if someone will show me. I've been thinking about it. I saw Sam at the hardware store recently. He told me that he's doing carpentry work for Bill Jameson. He says it's hard, but that I would be good at it, and if I ever left the church, to call Bill to see if he'd give me a job. I think Bill would."

"But a carpenter, Son. You're the Facility Maintenance Supervisor at the biggest church in town."

"And I'm lousy at it!" Larry looked his father full in the eyes and asked the question he'd alluded to earlier. "Dad, are you paying Brother Cole to keep me there? I saw you give him an envelope the other day."

"No, I'm not paying Brother Cole to keep you there. That was only a Thanksgiving gift I gave him because I'm thankful that he likes you."

"Oh, Dad!" Larry sat down on the couch and put his head in his hands. He wasn't too smart about numbers, but he was smart enough about people to know that Brother Cole was pulling the strings.

William's voice was gentle. "Son, I wasn't thinking of it as a payoff. I just was trying to show my appreciation."

"I know." He knew his father had a giving heart. "Just don't give Brother Cole any more money. Okay?"

"All right, I won't. And whatever you do, Larry, I'm sure it will be the right thing. Jesus was a carpenter himself. Perhaps it's the most honorable of professions."

Larry smiled. Part of him felt sad because some crucial learning hadn't taken place in him. He wanted to please this good man. Maybe one day, he would.

His father reached out, grabbed him around the neck, and hugged him. "I'm proud of you, Larry. You could have pretended that everything was going smoothly and ridden this train a long way, but instead, you have the integrity to face the situation honestly. There aren't many people your age with that much courage."

His words were like a salve on a wounded heart.

Christine lay in bed, pleasantly reviewing her day. The family had eaten dinner at the Gresham Castle with Mike, Nancy, Miss Elsie, and Mr. Robert. Donald had also joined them a little late. Apparently Judith had refused to come which was a relief to Christine. Donald had an unusual serenity about him that radiated throughout the afternoon. Christine found that she liked the man.

At one point, she told Nancy that she had been busy cleaning out the attic and hoped to find the angels that had been mentioned in Nathaniel's journal. Nancy, fascinated by the fact that Christine had found the old diary, began asking a lot of questions. With uneasiness, Christine suddenly realized that Mr. Robert was listening to their conversation. It occurred to her that he might disapprove of her reading something that was so personal and had belonged to his closest friend; but instead of being upset, he'd simply smiled and eventually asked her if she'd noticed the Bible verses at the end of the book, pointing out that Nathaniel had asked him to help write that part. She hadn't paid much attention to them but told Mr. Robert that she would look them up when she got the chance, probably after she had cleaned out the attic and had her garage sale.

The thought of the garage sale led to less pleasant thoughts. Their finances were stretched so thin that it would be a miracle if they ever got their medical bills paid off. Bill had sent each doctor and the hospital a smaller payment than they'd expected this month. There had been a few irate phone calls, but there was no choice. There just wasn't enough money. With great difficulty, they had managed to pay their other bills. The house was a little chilly tonight as they tried to conserve on electricity. Between paying their taxes and utilities next month, there would be no extra money for Christmas. It wasn't as if they spent much for gifts anyway, but somehow the realization that she couldn't buy her children even a small present felt sad to Christine. She and Bill had talked about one of them taking on a part-time job, but Bill worked all the time as it was, and Christine would probably only make enough to cover child-care costs. Perhaps though – just maybe – the yard sale would make enough money so that they could splurge and buy a turkey for the holidays. Clinging to that hope, she fell asleep.

Chapter 40

Walk humbly with thy God.

-Micah 6:8

Sam left the work site early. Today, this chilly last Monday in November, he had an appointment with Pastor Leonard, and he was anxious to get it over with. Unfortunately they'd been unable to meet before Thanksgiving, and though Sam tried to tuck the thought of this meeting into the recesses of his mind, it had taken some of the joy out of his holiday.

When he walked into the receptionist's outer office, Lanie gave him a disgusted look as she eyed his stained work clothes. Without acknowledging his presence, she pressed the intercom button and told Pastor Leonard that his four-thirty appointment had arrived; then, without a word, she went back to her typing. Sam felt his apprehension escalate.

The pastor's door opened, and Leonard greeted him with a warm handshake as they walked into his office. "Have a seat, Sam."

"Might be better if I just stand. I didn't have time to change before coming over here."

"Don't worry about it. Sit right here." Leonard pointed at a handsome burgundy upholstered chair that was near his desk.

Awkwardly Sam sat on the edge of it, wishing he were back at the work site, at home – anywhere but here. Pastor Leonard seemed friendly, but sometimes, Sam thought warily, Brother Cole had the same affectation before he stabbed a person in the back. After a few minutes of small talk, Leonard asked him to give his side of the story about his dismissal. This is what he'd been afraid of. In spite of his anxiety, he detailed what had happened – including the fact that Larry was gone and the concern he'd felt for Miss Eleanor as Brother Cole spoke harshly to her. He finished his narrative with an apology that felt inadequate.

"Apparently Brother Cole thought you did it on purpose."

"No, it was an accident. Though if I'd held my temper in check it never would have happened."

Leonard believed Sam. He didn't seem to be trying to excuse himself. The next question was about the air conditioner incident that had happened in September. Though almost three months had passed, Sam remembered each detail with clarity and shared everything that had occurred, adding to his version the feelings and fears he'd had for Bill. The uneasiness he'd felt earlier faded as he realized that Leonard was a concerned pastor, not an enemy who wanted to hurt him.

Leonard listened attentively, absorbing what Sam said. His story matched both Miss Eleanor's and Margie's. Deep furrows lined his face. An unconscious sigh escaped his lips. He had made a decision that would definitely upset Cole Odum. "Sam, would you be willing to come back and work here?"

Sam thought for a moment. He worked long, hard hours at his new job and missed seeing his family, but, in truth, with all the hard work and all the time away from home, it was so much better than having to work for Brother Cole. He didn't ever want to work for that man again.

"I don't think so, Pastor Leonard." Sam weighed his words, realizing that he had little to lose by telling Leonard the truth. It was time the pastor knew. "I don't ever want to work for Cole Odum again. Money and position are more important to him than people, especially the maintenance staff. The only one he's nice to is Larry. Don't take me wrong, but he acts like the rest of us aren't worth the air we breathe. I've heard him preach wonderful sermons, but he doesn't live what he says." Sam wondered if he'd said too much and stopped himself. Leonard didn't appear angry, but his face held a deep sadness that disconcerted Sam. He wished he could say something to comfort the man.

"Sam, if you didn't have to work under Brother Cole, would you consider coming back?"

Yes, Sam readily agreed. He would work here again if he didn't have to deal with Cole Odum. As they shook hands goodbye, he felt a glimmer of hope – not only for himself, but also for Main Street First Church.

With the aid of an old blanket, Christine lugged the heavy trunk down the stairs and into the living room. Cleaning out the attic was proving to be great fun. So far she'd found books galore, some old magazines and records, a few boxes of clothes, and an assortment of tools, kitchen utensils, and dishes.

Opening the weathered lid of the trunk, she lifted out a handsome quilt done in the wedding ring pattern. It was in excellent condition, having been used very little. Probably Nathaniel's mother had made this for him, and he'd wanted to save it for his wedding day – a day that never came to pass.

Underneath it was an exquisitely quilted piece that Christine recognized as Job's Troubles made from deep blue and dark green material. It would look good in Jonathan's room. The last quilt, done in the Drunkard's Path design, had a couple places where the cloth was slightly worn, but overall, it was in good shape. She pulled it out to add with the others in her laundry basket. Up in the attic, she had seen several trunks and boxes containing quilts and comforters, many that appeared to be in excellent condition. Nathaniel had commented in his journal each Christmas about the quilt his mother made for him, and they had added up to be more than she had expected. Perhaps, after she aired them out, she would take a few to that antique store she'd seen in Stone Mountain City. They probably would give her a good price for them. They certainly charged enough, being one of the more elite shops in the area.

At the bottom of the trunk was a lace tablecloth. For some reason, it was difficult to pull out. Christine's heart quickened as she realized a box was wrapped in it. The angels and baby Jesus! Remembering how she'd so casually pulled the trunk down the steps, she cringed and prayed that she hadn't broken anything. Slowly, almost fearfully, she opened the box. No, it wasn't what she expected, but another treasure – some of the prettiest bells that she'd ever seen. Thankfully none had broken. Each was wrapped in a crocheted doily. The first one was white ceramic with a hand-painted picture of a windmill. The second was similar, but instead of a windmill, it had a little Dutch girl – Catherine Evans would love these. They would match the collectible plates she had hanging on her wall. A thrill of delight touched Christine. The third and fourth bells were beautifully cut glass. One was dark red, the other pale pink. Perhaps Nancy would enjoy these. Christine suddenly remembered that Nancy collected bells. A grin spread across her face. This was fun. She'd have something special to give her friends for Christmas.

Opening the last crocheted doily, the final bell had a picture of the Virgin Mary holding baby Jesus. It had a simple beauty. It would fit in perfectly with her collection of Nativity ornaments. Sighing, Christine felt as if God had given her a special Christmas present too.

Opening his mail, William read the first letter written on a small note card:

William,
Thank you for the gift of two thousand dollars. I have much to be thankful for this Thanksgiving season. At the top of my list are you and your son and the fine work that he's doing here at Main Street First Church.
Sincerely yours, Brother Cole

William winced. Larry's talk with him on Thanksgiving Day had been eye opening. Without enthusiasm, he opened a second letter written on the church's stationery.

> *Dear Brother Herrin,*
> *Last month you blessed me with a generous gift for my birthday. On my wife's advice, I put the money in my savings account and prayed for God to show me how to use it wisely. Recently I learned of a woman whose husband had a back injury that prevented him from working. I was able to anonymously give her the money and had the delight of realizing that this gift was an answer to her prayers. This money, that you blessed me with, and I was able to bless them with, is helping them through this difficult time. I can't express how wonderful it felt to help this young family, and I wanted you to share that joy with me since it was your gift that encouraged me to do this.*
> *Before I even had an opportunity to tell you about my experience, you've again generously sent me another check for Thanksgiving. I have done nothing to deserve your gifts, but I thank you for your kindness. I plan on saving it for a need that the Lord presents to me. My wife and I are blessed beyond measure, and through your gifts, the Lord is teaching me how to become more generous myself. I intend to add some of our own money to the next burden that the Lord leads me to help.*
> *I wanted to share with you a concern that I have about the Charity Fund in our church. Unfortunately, the recent proposed budget has cut this fund to a bare minimum, which saddens me. There are many unmet needs, not only in the city, but right in our very own church family, and I would encourage you to give your well-earned money to this fund so that Brother Dan can administer it to those in need. I've been honored by your gifts to me personally, and I thank you for your generosity, but they may be perhaps more wisely used here than in my own meager efforts. Thank you for your kindness and your loving heart.*
> *In Christ's Love, Leonard*

Though Pastor Leonard's letter was gracious, there was a message in it that William could not overlook. Perhaps if Larry hadn't been so forthright, William would have missed it. If he were truly honest, he'd have to admit that he'd hoped the gifts would help Larry's situation. The boy often seemed so wayward, so lost, and yet in a strange way he was the most stable of their four children. Mark was on his third marriage, Caroline had numerous broken relationships, and Jeff was defending such questionable characters in his law practice that William sometimes wondered about him. Then there was Larry, working hard at a job that had no future, that he wasn't even good at. Larry, who could at least admit when he was in over his head or had made a mistake. William loved all his children fiercely, but there was something special about his youngest son. Though he'd experienced hard times, the boy had a certain resilience that kept him going.

The Christmas gift that William had planned on sending to Brother Cole and Pastor Leonard would instead be given to the Charity Fund. He would send Leonard and Cole each a note telling them that he'd given the fund five-thousand dollars in each of their names as a gift. That way, Larry couldn't accuse him of paying anyone off, and if either of the men didn't like it, it would show William their true character in a hurry.

Judith looked around this new place called home. For the first time since her marriage, she had absolutely no help. Donald had unpacked most of their belongings, but boxes still lay scattered here and there. The clutter unnerved her, but she'd refused to clean up. Instead, she figured that Donald would soon realize that he needed to hire someone. No help, however, had been forthcoming, and she had stayed in this cramped little dwelling without venturing out for, what was it now, ten days? She hadn't even gone to Michael's for Thanksgiving dinner. Basically she felt stripped naked and left to die. She didn't have anything now, and the worst part was that everyone knew it. She couldn't even pretend she had anything.

The one thing she did have, however, was a lot of time to think – too much time to think. There was nothing else to do. She slept and thought and ate. As a result, she was gaining weight – something that she'd not allowed herself to do in the past.

That morning to help curb her boredom, she'd watched an eye-opening talk show on television. A woman who constantly berated her husband was questioned by a psychologist as to why she felt it necessary to nag and criticize her spouse. The lady admitted to feeling afraid that if she were nice to her husband, he'd take advantage of her or ignore her. When the psychologist asked if this had ever happened to her before, Judith thought about her own past. As a child, she had felt unimportant. Most of her parents' attentions went to her sickly younger sister. It wasn't until she married the rich and handsome Donald that she began to feel, for the first time in her life, like somebody. She vowed that never again would she be a nobody, never again would she be ignored. The television psychologist had explained that each person should analyze how effectual or ineffectual his or her behavior was, and she'd pointed out to the woman on the talk show that her past experiences had made her respond in a manner that was ineffectual. The woman wanted to develop closeness with her husband but only pushed him away. That was food for thought.

Judith shook herself out of her reverie and went to the kitchen to fix a cup of coffee. It was almost gone. Being able to make coffee was the one big accomplishment that she'd achieved since moving here. She had watched Donald and learned how to do it herself without him being any the wiser. She hated to admit that she didn't know how to do something. Fixing dinner was something she could probably do too, if she wanted. Since their move here, Donald had made all the meals, and he wasn't talented in the kitchen. Often the food was burnt or tasteless. Last night she'd told him that she'd rather starve than eat any of his cooking again. A pained look had passed over his face. That look used to give her a sense of power, but somehow now it worried her that she had hurt him. She couldn't afford to lose Donald too. He was all she had left, but she was losing him – to Michael on Thanksgiving, to Mr. Robert during his frequent visits to the old man, even losing him to the church where he went faithfully Sunday after Sunday. She hadn't really meant to hurt him last night, but it was true. The food was awful. Her acid tongue had been quick to tell him this. Perhaps she should make dinner tonight, but the scary thing was that she might do a worse job than Donald, if that were possible. Even though she didn't want to take on the cooking, two things worked against her. One was that she was hungry and the second was that, if she were willing to admit it, part of her wanted to win Donald back. The constant backbiting that she'd done the past few months was failing miserably.

A decision made – she would go get groceries and try her hand at cooking dinner. Besides, she'd been cooped up in this house for too long. It would be nice to get out. Since she could read, she ought to be able to cook. Pulling out the one cookbook they had, she began looking through recipes. Everything sounded hard, and she wasn't sure how to do some things. What was "parboil"? How do you "brown meat"? How were you to know when it was done? She needed more information. The grocery store sold food so surely they would have books that would help her understand. An unexpected excitement began to build in her. She hadn't been inside a supermarket since her college days, but she loved to go shopping. This might be fun.

Walking into the bedroom, she looked in her closet. How did one dress to go grocery shopping? Elsie wore her maid outfit, but when Judith did things, she did them with style. She put on her black skirt with a silk shirt and wore a stunning gold jacket, then topped it off by wearing black-suede high heels. Putting on her winter coat, she headed out the door to her car. A stray gray cat that had begun hanging around their rented house, tried to rub its thin, cold body against her leg. She pushed it out of her way, annoyed with the fuzzy creature. Donald kept feeding it leftovers. Even his awful cooking hadn't scared it away.

Quickly backing down the driveway, she began driving the short distance to the supermarket. As she glanced at the houses on the unfamiliar street, she noted that most of them were slightly larger than the one she and Donald lived in. The realization was humbling.

A few minutes later, she turned into the parking lot at the grocery. The store was gigantic. In her youth, grocery stores had been family-run and much smaller. Walking in she immediately felt out of place and intimidated by the crowd of activity – an unaccustomed feeling and one she didn't like. Taking a deep breath, she reminded herself that she was a Gresham, and she could do this. Straightening her shoulders, she tried to pull a cart from the rack. It stuck to the one in front of it. Mortified, she gently tried to wrestle it free, hoping that no one would notice her efforts, but an older gentleman thinking he was coming to her rescue, gave the cart a hearty shove, loosening it from the rest. Feeling utterly incompetent – but hiding it successfully behind a snobbish look – she began walking away without a word of thanks.

"Lady, you should know that when a person helps you do something, it's only polite to say a nice 'Thank you.'"

Judith stopped. Her face reddening. She wasn't used to being spoken to this way. Perhaps the store was full of ill-bred people, but then again, she had been rude. It had just been so embarrassing. In trying to hide her discomfort, she'd acted ill mannered herself. With the memory of the talk show discussion still on her mind, she realized that she had two choices. She could slam out of there and show that man what she thought of his attitude toward her, or she could apologize. Her instinctual response was to turn and leave with her nose in the air, but she did need some groceries, and she might have to come back here again someday. Perhaps – just this once – she would try something different, and if it proved ineffectual, she would revert back to her usual response. Tightly, tensely, she heard herself say, "You're right. I should have said 'Thank you.' Thank you for your assistance."

"You're very welcome. I tend to be brusque at times myself. I apologize for being rude to you."

Judith found herself smiling. This was much better than the other way. She would have hurried home with no food and fumed for days over the incident. A peculiar sense of relief touched her.

Pushing her cart through the aisles, she found the books and magazines. To her dismay, there wasn't one cookbook. Well, no matter, she'd seen advertisements on television for freezer meals. She would get some of them. First, though, she needed coffee.

Noticing that other women had their carts filled to the brim, she wondered how they would get all their groceries out to their car by themselves. She would be careful to get only one bag full. Already she wished she hadn't worn her high heels. The concrete floor hurt her feet.

Walking down the beverages aisle, she found an assortment of coffees – too many to choose from. Picking up one that said "Almond Chocolate," she began reading the information on the label. It sounded good.

"Oh, that's one of my favorites," a cheerful, overweight lady with a teenage girl said to Judith. This was the kind of woman Judith had always looked down on, but somehow, she felt oddly attracted to the friendly face.

"How do you fix it?"

"Same as usual. It's easy and good." She picked up one and put it into her full cart.

"How do you intend to get all that food out to your car?"

"Oh." The woman looked slightly surprised at the question. "I usually roll my cart out myself and put the groceries in the car, but you're so nicely dressed that you might get one of the bag boys to help you. They're real nice and usually offer to do it. This your first time here?"

"Yes." Judith didn't want to admit anymore than that.

"Thought I hadn't seen you around before. My name's Emma. I live right down the road."

"I'm Judith. I live on Oak Drive."

"Well, we're practically neighbors then. I live one road over on Park. It's nice to meet you, Judith."

"Thank you." Judith found herself liking this woman.

"Oh, listen, you'll have to go check out the deli." Emma picked up some pizza crusts from her cart. "I just got these there. They're buy-one-get-one-free today."

"What do you do with them?"

"Well, I don't make my own pizza sauce. I use this stuff." She showed Judith a jar of sauce. "You find it over near the canned vegetables. Then I put some of this shredded cheese on it and some toppings and cook it. It's a great meal when you're in a hurry."

288

"Tell her about the onions," her daughter prompted.

"Jessica likes the way I fix the onions. I just sauté them till they're clear in a little butter and put them on top."

"That's my favorite pizza," the small imitation of her mother commented.

They said a friendly good-bye and walked on down the aisle. Judith determined that she would make homemade pizzas for supper that night. She would buy some onions, too, and look up in the dictionary what "sauté" meant. It was time that she developed her vocabulary.

Two hours later, Donald walked into a house full of pleasant aromas. He was tired. Lately he'd been trying to do everything, and it was too much. He couldn't clean the house, cook, and work. He noticed that the place was still a mess, but the sight of Judith setting the table encouraged him.

"Good. You're just in time. I was afraid it would get cold before you got home. Sit on down."

Why, Judith almost sounded cheerful. Donald washed his hands and sat down expectantly. Judith pulled a big pizza out of the oven. She must have ordered out. As she brought a salad to the table, he noticed that the lettuce was in huge chunks, the carrots hadn't been peeled, and the tomato was hard to recognize, but at least she'd tried. The pizza didn't look like any brand that he'd seen before. After the blessing, he took a bite. It was delicious. "Oh, whose pizza is this? It's great. I love the onions."

Judith grinned. She realized she deserved this compliment. It felt good. She had often claimed Elsie's cooking for her own, but those compliments weren't hers to accept. This was one that she'd earned all by herself. It had been a long time since that had happened. "I made it myself."

Donald's reaction made her laugh in satisfaction. "You made this? Come on, Judith. Where'd you get it?"

"Honest. I really made it. I met a lady named Emma at the grocery store who told me how to do it. I think it turned out well, too!"

Donald watched this wife of his. She animatedly began telling him all about how there were fellows who would push your cart out of the grocery store for you and how big the place was and that she'd learned to never wear high heels there again. He could tell she was proud of herself, but it wasn't the false, know-it-all pride that she usually had. This was genuine satisfaction that comes from worthwhile achievement. His wife had been robbed of that during their years of marriage. He felt as if he were meeting a new person. It was the first time since the terrible television revelation about his business that he and Judith talked about normal everyday things and even laughed together.

The pizza finished and the salad half eaten, Judith got up and poured Donald a cup of "the most wonderful coffee I've ever had." Donald grinned and enjoyed coffee with his wife.

Chapter 41

There was silence and I heard a still, small voice.

-Job 4:16

After the Tuesday evening prayer service, Bill walked to Pastor Leonard's office, passing Brother Cole on his way. As he hesitated at the door, he noticed Cole eyeing him. The man still could make him uncomfortable. Trying to shake off the unpleasant emotion, he entered the empty office area. Sam had told him about his discussion with the pastor, and as Bill sat down on the couch opposite the secretary's desk to wait, he hoped that his prayer that Leonard's eyes be opened had finally been answered.

A moment later, Cole walked in and put a paper on Lanie's desk. "What's your business here?" His voice was pleasant, even friendly, but his cold eyes betrayed him.

"I'm meeting Pastor Leonard," Bill answered truthfully, wondering if Cole knew about Sam and the preacher's earlier conversation.

"Oh, what about?" Cole asked, nonchalantly, as he eyed the document he had placed on Lanie's desk. He seemed only vaguely interested in their conversation.

Bill wasn't deceived by Cole's seeming indifference. "I don't know. Pastor Leonard wants to talk to me."

Leonard came in, his heart dropping at the sight of Cole Odum. Well, he had some things that needed to come out between them soon anyway. "Hi, Bill, sorry to keep you waiting. Come on into my office. Cole, did you need to see me?"

"No, just passing the time with Bill here," Cole returned amiably as he began to leave. "See you later, Bill. Glad all's going well with you."

"Come into my office," Leonard repeated as soon as the assistant pastor was gone. "Have a seat." He pushed a chair toward his desk and as far away from the door as possible in case anyone walked into the outer office and accidentally overheard, or worse yet, tried to listen. That thought caused him to hesitate. "Just a minute, Bill." Walking to the outer office, he locked the door. That should take care of any eavesdroppers. With a deep sigh, he returned to his office. A church shouldn't have to be this way.

"Bill, I wanted to get your view of what happened when you left here."

Even though certain memories were painful, Bill determined that he'd be as honest and open as possible. He began with his job offer from Mike and his uncertainty, how he'd prayed for clear direction, the accident in the basement, and his final decision.

Leonard asked many of the same questions that he'd asked the others. Bill's account fit together with what Miss Eleanor, Margie, and Sam had told him, whereas Brother Cole's view of the situation was totally different.

"Did Brother Cole fire you, Bill?" Leonard knew he was being aggressive, but he wanted to ferret out the truth.

Bill looked at the pastor as if he were in pain. His answer came out haltingly. "Yes and no. He told me that if I didn't quit, he'd let me go. I'd already decided to take the new job but hadn't told him yet when he gave me that ultimatum. He said it would look better on my record if I resigned." Bill had tried to forget this conversation. The memory still humiliated him.

Leonard looked sorrowfully at this man, not wanting to prolong or add to his agony. "From what I've seen in all the years that you've worked here, I see no reason for anyone to find fault with you. I don't understand why Brother Cole would doubt your ability. You did an excellent job and are sorely missed. I'd like it if you would come back."

The dejection Bill felt vanished with Leonard's healing words. "Thank you, Pastor, I appreciate the offer," he paused briefly, considering his answer. "I couldn't do that."

"Because of Brother Cole?"

"That's part of it. I don't want to work for him again, but also I like what I'm doing, and the fellow I'm working for is counting on me. I can't let him down."

Even though Leonard understood, a feeling of remorse for the turn of events that had caused them to lose Bill touched him. This shouldn't have happened.

Bill felt the remnants of unresolved pain over his past job situation melt away.

Leonard asked Bill if he thought Sam would be a good maintenance supervisor, and Bill highly recommended him with only one reservation – he didn't want to see Larry booted out like day-old bread.

"No, no. We'll keep Larry here if he wants to stay. He's a hard worker, but to be honest, I'm not sure he could ever do the complete job."

"You'd be taking my right-hand man at my new job. I might just take Larry under my wing if he wants to come." Bill grinned.

Leonard smiled back. "We'll do right by Larry whatever the case." Rising heavily from his chair – he felt like an old man these days – he reached out to shake hands. "Thanks for talking to me, Bill. I've got a lot of thinking to do. Don't say anything to anyone yet. I want to handle this right."

Bill left the pastor's office, an unseen weight having been taken off his shoulders.

Unfortunately that weight now lay on Leonard's back. Driving home, he felt in a quandary. Cole would probably come by his office first thing in the morning for an explanation as to why he'd talked to Bill. Leonard dreaded tomorrow. He still wasn't sure how to best approach the situation or Brother Cole. When he arrived home he told Ann what he'd learned. Together they discussed and prayed about the problem until it became late. Leonard spent a troubled night trying to sleep and awoke feeling exhausted. His hot shower did little to alleviate his anxiety.

Seemingly insignificant events that he had given little credence to at the time kept popping into his head. Times when Cole had been evasive or when Leonard had walked into a room and sensed a sudden change in a conversation. As the scenarios played through his head, he couldn't seem to stop them. He felt downhearted for the role he'd played. For this he needed to ask forgiveness and be careful, no matter what the outcome of the decision about Cole, to not let things slip by unnoticed again. He had allowed himself to overlook events that now seemed so clearly wrong, and the reason for ignoring those things shamed him to the core – his pride, his desire to have more: more people in the church, more money for himself, the most beautiful church in Georgia. It all boiled down to pride, and another sin – the sin of the lack of contentment.

That sin had often plagued him. He was frequently seeking more, not content with what God had given him. It was part of the original sin. Eve, there in the garden, was told by the serpent that she could have more if she wanted it, that she really could have the fruit if she chose. Eve lived in the most beautiful place ever made, and yet she wasn't content with that. She also wanted and finally took the fruit. Perhaps there was a sermon in this for one Sunday morning. His sermons were getting fairly personal lately as God worked in him.

Dragging himself to the kitchen for breakfast, Ann looked at him with concern. The usual lighthearted smiling face was overshadowed with a forlorn, defeated expression. Dark circles hung under his eyes. Worry seeped into her heart as she thought about many young pastors who had experienced heart attacks. She didn't want anything to happen to this good man. "Leonard, why don't you call Lanie and tell her that you're going to stay home today? You can study here if you want. You look worn out."

The idea was a good one. Part of him wanted to get the inevitable meeting with Cole Odum over with, but he wasn't sure what he should say. After breakfast he took Ann's advice and called his secretary, then trudging to his study, he knelt down to pray. This was what he needed to do.

Miserably he thought back to when he'd had his head stuck in the sand. He chastised himself for not controlling it from the beginning and prayed for forgiveness. He prayed for Brother Cole, begging for wisdom to know what to do.

Inside the still, small voice of God spoke above his thoughts. *The decision is not yours alone.* That was true. There were others who would need to be part of this. It was doubtful that they knew the truth about Brother Cole.

I have everything worked out. The second thought came. God knew what He wanted. He was in charge. If He could open Leonard's eyes after they'd been shut for so long, He could have prepared others as well. A decision made, Leonard picked up the phone and called Lanie. "I need the names of those on the Personnel Committee."

Lanie pulled up the file on her computer screen. "All right. I've got it. Harry Marls is the head and Hal Boxwell is the deacon on the committee, then there's Sarah Norwing, Cal Schift, and Jackie Cisrow." Leonard wrote down each name.

"By the way, Brother Cole came by to see you. Will you be in later so I can tell him a good time that he can talk with you?"

Leonard felt tension at Cole's name. "Tell him I'll be back tomorrow morning. Do I have any morning appointments?"

"No. Just the regular nine o'clock staff meeting."

Right. Leonard had forgotten that tomorrow was Thursday. "Tell Cole that we can meet in my office at one-thirty tomorrow."

Cole banged out the phone number his secretary had written down. He was in a foul mood. It troubled him that Pastor Leonard was out today. Something felt terribly wrong. True, Leonard usually studied on Wednesdays – but in his office – not at home. To top it off, Leonard's meeting with Bill Jameson the evening before was extremely disturbing. At least now Cole had his eyes open. He would be careful. The phone was ringing. A pleasant female voice answered, naming the business that he had contacted. "Hello. This is Cole Odum, returning Howard Barbin's call."

"Yes, just a minute. I'll connect you to Mr. Barbin."

There was a brief pause. Some music came on the line. Cole tried to remember who Barbin was. The business didn't ring any bells for him. The phone number had a west-Georgia area code. Hopefully this wasn't someone trying to sell something.

"Brother Odum, Howe Barbin here. I'm sorry to bother you at work, but I didn't know any other way to reach you."

"Yes, what can I do for you, Mr. Barbin?"

"Well, I don't know if you remember me, but I'm a deacon at Arrowhead First Church here in Columbus where you and Pastor Leonard did the revival last summer."

"Oh, yes, I remember you." Cole recalled the man now and prided himself on his quick memory. "We went out to dinner together with your pastor."

"That's right. I know that you're a busy man, so I'll get right to the point. Reverend Leas resigned a few weeks ago, and I'm the head of the pulpit search committee. The entire committee has agreed that we'd like you to consider becoming our pastor. We were impressed with your sermons. We're all praying that you'll accept our offer."

The foul mood Cole had felt all morning dissipated into a warm, luscious gush of glee. This was a nice-sized church, a church of his own where he wouldn't have to be told what to do, where he would be the boss, and there wouldn't have to be any more placating those above him. This would be an excellent opportunity for him. "I'd be interested in considering your offer. What did you have in mind?"

"Since we've already heard you preach – this would be more of a formality than anything else – we'd like you to come, if possible, one Sunday before Christmas, and bring your wife and family."

"I think I could arrange that, but I'm not sure my wife could come. She has a busy schedule."

"Oh, we'd really like to meet her, too. Perhaps after Christmas would be better."

Cole thought quickly. Perhaps the truth would be an advantage for him this time. "Howard, to tell you the truth, my wife is a bit under the weather these days. She's been ill. I think the trip might tax her too much. She's planning on visiting my daughter during the Christmas holidays. It would probably be best if I came while she was there." Hopefully he came across as a caring husband, something that would be demanded of him in this new position.

"Oh, I'm sorry to hear that." A slight pause followed, then, "Sure, that would be fine."

Cole looked at his calendar. He shouldn't appear too eager. "Let's see. The earliest I could do it would probably have to be the seventeenth. How's that look to you?"

"That would be great. Why don't you come down the sixteenth. I'll arrange a dinner with the pulpit committee so that we can get to know you better; then, Sunday afternoon, we'll have the deacons meet with you after lunch."

The arrangements sounded good. Cole hung up the phone feeling smug satisfaction. A church of his own.

As Hal Boxwell drove up the pastor's driveway, he speculated about what could have happened to cause Leonard to need to see him so urgently. It seemed odd that they were meeting here instead of at church, but it might be the late hour. Parked outside the house was a van labeled "Aaron's Lock and Key." Apparently someone else was joining them. Ann promptly answered his knock and led him to Leonard's study. Harry Marls was in the room along with the pastor.

"Good to see you, Harry," Hal expressed pleasantly. He liked the easygoing, good-natured Harry. There was some small talk between Leonard, Harry, and Hal for a couple of minutes – something Hal was not good at. He was relieved when Pastor Leonard suggested they get down to business.

"I have something important I need to talk to you about. This morning I spent hours in prayer trying to figure out what to do. I felt God lead me to call you and get your counsel since you're both on the Personnel Committee." Leonard began by telling them what he'd learned recently about Bill and the maintenance staff situation; then, he told of his concern for Greta, and knowing that Hal's wife, Rose, was good friends with the woman he asked Hal to give his assessment of what was happening there.

Hal felt an unaccustomed openness coming from the pastor and the freedom to voice what he knew about the situation; however, at the same time, he knew that Greta's privacy should be honored. "I don't want to say anything that would embarrass Greta," he spoke circumspectly, "but Pastor Leonard, if you're asking me about my thoughts regarding retaining Cole Odum as the assistant pastor of our church, then I would have to say that I have concerns about this man."

The usually loquacious Harry sat back listening intently to what was said. He had his own part to add, something that had been bothering him for a while. When Leonard asked him to voice his thoughts, Harry was quick to reply. "Something odd happened at the shop a couple weeks ago. Brother Cole called and asked us to change the locks on the doors of his house. He said it had been broken into, and he didn't want it to happen again. It was a Saturday, so Shirley took the call – my wife works on Saturdays – and we sent a truck out to his home.

"A couple days later, my regular girl, Amy, gets this irate call from a customer named Cole Odum who wants the girl who worked on Saturday to call him back immediately. After she told me, I went home and asked Shirley to call him while I listened in on the extension line. You wouldn't believe how abusive he was. He sounded so different from his normal self that it occurred to me there might be two Cole Odums in town, but then he started raving about how he was a highly-respected assistant pastor of a church, how he'd never been treated so shabbily by a business, and he'd be sure to tell everyone he knew how awful we were, that he was even considering a lawsuit against us for lack of confidentiality or something like that. He finished by saying that he wouldn't pay our bill." Harry shook his head as he relived the memory. "I haven't known what to do. He can sue me if he wants to." He laughed as if there were something amusing to his story. "And you know what the funniest thing is. When I saw him last Sunday morning, he shook my hand and greeted me like an old friend, asking me how business was going. I don't think he's ever realized that he was talking to my wife."

Leonard shook his head sadly. "I think you're right, Harry."

A silence followed as each man mulled over the situation. Leonard finally faced the fact that the church needed to dismiss Cole Odum immediately. Together they prayed, asking God to give Leonard the right words when he broke the news.

That night seemed to crawl by for Leonard as he thought about how to best approach Cole, but all too soon the blustery morning winds met him as he drove to work. The first item on the day's agenda was the staff meeting, so he would have a short reprieve before the appointed time. At the top of the list of items to be discussed that morning was the maintenance problem. Brother Steve explained his concern that maintenance wouldn't be able to handle the upcoming Christmas program. It was the spectacle of the year that people from all over Georgia flocked to see. He didn't want anything to go wrong. Brother Cole was peeved by the whole discussion, and Leonard wondered how he'd missed seeing the man's true character before. He asked for the maintenance problem to be tabled until the following week when he would hopefully have some good news to report.

After the meeting, Leonard knelt beside his couch to pray. He would eat later. Anxiety had killed his appetite. What he needed to do was unpleasant. It went against his peaceable nature.

Cole arrived at the scheduled time. There was a certain overbearing presence about the man that was intimidating, even to Leonard. Rising from his kneeling position with difficulty, he noticed a slight wearing in the carpet where his knees had been. Somehow this gave him a sense of comfort. The assistant pastor walked in with an arrogant expression on his face that Leonard had not encountered before. He seemed confident, almost cocky. Cole had asked for this conference, so Leonard would let him speak first. "Lanie said you wanted to see me."

Cole needed to know why Leonard had talked to Bill Tuesday evening, but it wouldn't be wise for him to ask directly. Instead he dissembled, something he did like a professional. Deceptively he asked his prepared question, one that should please Leonard. "I wanted to know if it would be all right with you if I took off Sunday, the seventeenth. I'm thinking about going to visit Greta."

Leonard frowned. This was a surprise. "Yes, that will be fine. Have a seat, Cole. I want to talk to you about Greta."

Cole sat down. He didn't want to talk about his wife and wished that he'd come up with another excuse for leaving that weekend.

"When I called Greta recently, I discovered that she has cancer."

A look of undisguised indignation flashed across Cole's face. He was tired of the pastor nosing into his personal business. With an effort he hid his anger. He needed to play the game just a couple more weeks. The job at Arrowhead looked better by the minute. "You see, Pastor, Greta didn't want anyone to know. I was trying to honor her request."

"I respect that, Cole, but you told me that you had called her when in fact you hadn't called her at all."

"I did," protested Cole. "Every time I called, no one answered." Cole felt an unraveling – as if his carefully laid plans were being eaten away by this capricious man. It was time to leave this church. This place was beginning to disgust him – and this oh, so honorable Leonard – the hypocrite – was becoming a thorn in his flesh. He would have his own church soon. The thought of that was extremely satisfying. A smug looked touched his face. He wouldn't have to tolerate this place much longer. Lifting his chin, he looked defiantly at Leonard. Enough was enough. "Anyway, I don't think it's any of your business."

Leonard shook his head. So this was the real Cole Odum.

"I want to know something," Cole continued, "What do you plan to do about the maintenance situation?"

Leonard squared his shoulders and in a resolute voice replied, "I've been reviewing the problems in maintenance. I've talked to both Bill and Sam recently." Without equivocating, he related his conversations with both men about the air conditioner incident.

"And you believed them over me?"

"How could I not? Everyone's stories agree but yours. I've decided to rehire Sam and place him as the maintenance supervisor."

"You do that and I'm leaving." Cole stood, darkness filling his eyes. He'd valued Leonard for a while but not anymore. He just about had a new job sewn up, and he would take it. He didn't need Leonard, and he didn't have to agree with every stupid thing that the man said. He was sick of buttering up this insipid man.

"Cole, Sam has agreed to come back. That decision has been made already."

Cole looked at Leonard long and hard. When he finally spoke, his words came out low and measured. "I'll work my last month here, and it'll be a month that you'll regret for the rest of your term as pastor."

"That won't be necessary." Leonard stood to face the man eye to eye. He knew Cole hoped to cow him with his threats. "You may leave today, and you don't need to come back."

"Oh, I'll be back all right. I can bring you down, Leonard. Just wait and see what happens this Sunday." Cole laughed – a hollow sound that sent ice down Leonard's spine. "Perhaps the church should know you better."

"What are you talking about?" Leonard felt a cold chill, as if he were talking to the devil himself.

"Just wait and see, Pastor Leonard," he chided, spitting out the word "Pastor" mockingly, then calmly walked out of the office, passing Lanie, who was coming in from her lunch break.

Leonard shut his door. His whole body shook. Struggling over to his chair, he sat down and looked out the window at the clouds as if he hoped to see Jesus in them, calling him home. Instead, the trees were bowing down to the wind as it mercilessly pushed them around.

Chapter 42

In quietness and in confidence shall be your strength.

-Isaiah 30:15

Saturday evening, with a feeling of satisfaction, Christine brought in the last boxes left from her day at the Pendergrass Flea Market. After expenses, she'd netted over four hundred dollars. Her garage sales hadn't made that much in the past. It was definitely God's blessing. With this money added to the income she'd made selling two of the quilts, there would be enough to pay off their property taxes and to buy a turkey for the holidays . Only three weeks till Christmas now. She would do her best to make it a happy time. For the past few days, Jonathan had been begging them to put up a tree, so after church tomorrow, they were planning on decorating a little cedar from their back yard.

The attic was clean now. Not one box was left. Christine had swept the floor and dusted away the cobwebs, but no angels or Jesus Nativity figurine had been found. She'd been so sure that they'd be up there. Even the journal said something about getting the angels out of the attic. Well, perhaps on Monday evening when they visited Mr. Robert, he could remember something that would help her to find them.

Sitting down with a cup of hot tea that Bill handed her, she drank it, enjoying the warmth that it gave. Theirs was a cozy home. She had missed it today.

"I looked up the scripture references on the last page of Nathaniel's journal," Bill told her.

"Oh, what did you find?"

"Not much. The first one is the same one that's in the Bible with the key in it. I got excited when I realized that, but the rest were kind of odd. I mean, they're all good verses, but they don't fit together in any way that I can tell. One verse was written down twice, and there were some verses in parenthesis that didn't exist."

Christine was too tired to give the subject much thought. "I want to look at them sometime, but right now all I can think about is taking a nice hot bath." Finishing her tea, she went to bathe off the grime that was part of the flea market and now a part of her. The warmth of the water felt good to her cold bones. Her feet hurt from hours of standing on the hard concrete floor, but all in all, she'd enjoyed her day. By the time she was dressed, the children were noisily playing. She could hear their cheerful laughter through the door. Walking into the living room, the smell of grilled cheese sandwiches and tomato soup met her along with three pajama-clad children. At that moment, she realized how full her life was. Sometimes it was easy to get bogged down in the everyday nitty-gritty details of existence and not appreciate her blessings.

After dinner, the family sat in front of the fireplace for their Christmas Advent story. Since it was the second day of December, they lit two of the candles on the advent log that Bill had made when Jonathan was a baby. He had drilled twenty-five holes into a cedar log, and Christine put a candle in each hole. Each night one candle was lit for each day of the month. The children enjoyed this tradition as much as their parents did. Christine sat back listening as Bill told part of the Christmas story. After this past year's occurrences, she realized that these peaceful family times were nothing to take for granted. By God's grace, Bill was here to lead the devotion and the singing. Later, as she snuggled under the covers, she wondered with anticipation what the next day would bring, the first Sunday of December.

Unfortunately Leonard was having trouble sleeping. Though his first advent sermon was ready, he feared he'd be unable to preach it. His mind, disturbed by the recent confrontation he'd had with Cole Odum, wouldn't rest. The final threat haunted his thoughts. As he lay reviewing over and over again how to defend himself, his own guilt from his past mistakes plagued him. He wasn't perfect. He was a sinner like the rest of them, yet somehow people expected him to be sinless. He needed to sleep. Sleep was elusive. He would begin to relax into slumber, then a thought would occur to him, and he'd find himself wide-awake, trying to mull it through. He felt the Lord requiring a lot of him lately. Finally, in the wee hours of the morning, out of pure exhaustion, he fell asleep.

Sunday morning dawned cold and frosty and did little to encourage Leonard's flagging spirits. Winter, with its icy blasts, had finally come to Georgia. The car was sluggish in getting started, but finally the engine turned over, roaring to life.

Driving into the parking lot, he saw Cole standing at the door. As usual, greeting the guests that were arriving. Leonard felt his stomach knot and his blood pressure rise as he walked over. "I thought I told you not to come."

"I thought I told you that I'd be here today." Cole seemed to enjoy taunting Leonard. Smiling more broadly, he continued greeting the church members.

Leonard walked to his office, feeling his strength wane into despair. His hope that God would keep his enemy away died. How would he be able to preach this morning? The spirit of tumult that he'd fought during the night engulfed him once again. *God is with you,* spoke the still, small voice in his heart. The Lord would fight this battle. Leonard knelt to pray, putting his spiritual armor in place. Time passed quickly, yet stood oddly still. Lately he'd spent hours in prayer, yet it felt like only minutes. Leaving his office, he went to the auditorium. People were beginning to enter. Brother Cole had already made his way to the platform and was sitting in his chair. The girl who had taken Greta's place began organizing her music. All was as usual.

Ann watched Cole uneasily from her seat. He sat in his velvet chair with an arrogant glint in his eyes. When he'd not come to work Friday, she'd breathed a little easier, taking this as a good sign, but here he was looking too comfortable and pleased with himself, whereas Leonard looked stiff, brittle even, as if he would break. She began to pray, praying earnestly for a spiritual warfare that was happening right before her eyes. Leonard sat in his chair, strain and weariness written on his face.

The organ began playing as the choir came in. Leonard felt his heart racing and skip a beat. He breathed deeply, feeling as he did a firm resoluteness take over his inner being. There were Hal and Rose Boxwell, and a few rows in front of them, Shirley and Harry Marls. They at least would have a partial understanding if anything untoward did happen. The singing began. It was the first week for Christmas carols which felt strangely incongruous with Leonard's sense of an approaching battle. At the finish of the second song, he rose to say the morning prayer. If it was different from usual, no one seemed to notice. Most fidgeted in their seats, probably thinking of things they had to do. The congregation sang again, announcements were given before the offering basket was passed. The sound of the piano and organ drowned out the murmurings of the congregation as the tithe was collected.

"Do you want to speak before I preach?" Leonard asked Cole as the two sat beside each other in their chairs. He wanted to get the inevitable over with. It would be hard to preach with his thinking about Cole Odum sitting there behind him.

Cole, startled by the question, felt smug satisfaction, pleased that Leonard was nervous. "You preach first." Let Leonard give his little Christmas sermon. Let him sweat while he does, then Cole would give a trenchant lowdown on the pastor that would cause him to look like dirt. After he finished, he would, with humble dignity, resign from his position – after all, Howard Barbin had assured him that his coming to preach at

Arrowhead First was simply a formality. The man had all but promised him the job. This would be a great way to leave this vapid place.

Leonard prayed as the choir stood to sing their special music. The melody settled like a balm over his troubled heart. A calmness surrounded him. No matter what happened, God was with him, holding him, keeping him – keeping His church, His children – safe.

The song ended. The choir sat. Time for Leonard to preach. He sat longer than usual, then slowly, like an elderly man rising from a wheel chair, he stood and walked to the podium.

"I came to bring you the first of four advent sermons...," he faltered, hesitating, looking out at the bored congregation. This was the sermon they expected. There may be a new twist on the advent story, but that would be all. Leonard stopped speaking, surveying the crowd. Behind him he heard Cole Odum move in his chair, reminding him of his presence. The long pause became almost palpable. People who had been gazing elsewhere turned to watch him. Those who were already paying attention leaned in a little closer, puzzling over the long wait.

Leonard felt words come from his heart to his throat. With an unsteady quaver in his voice, he began again. "I need to talk to you about something else. How many of you have ever read Hans Christian Anderson's *The Little Match Girl*?"

Surprised, confused, a few hands went up, then a few more.

"I have an Aunt Minnie. She's a little, tiny woman with the biggest heart you ever saw." Leonard's voice grew thick with the memory. "Every Christmas she would read my brother and me that story.

"Up the holler from my aunt lived a little girl named Trudy. Now Trudy was just a little, scrawny thing. She didn't talk much, at least not to me, but she loved to come down to visit my aunt. Her clothes must of come out of the church box. They were like three sizes too big for her. My aunt would take her ragged dresses and add lace to them and spruce them up, making Trudy happy.

"Well, one day I saw Trudy sneak some cornbread into the pocket of her jumper. I couldn't believe it. Here my aunt, who struggled to make ends meet, had been helping this mite of a girl, and she was stealing food from her. I was furious. I yelled out, "Why you thieving varmint." I was all of fifteen and thought I knew everything. I went to grab her and she turned to run, running right into my aunt.

"'Lenny you apologize to Trudy,' my aunt insisted.

"'But Aunt Minnie, she took some of your cornbread and stuffed it into her pockets. Look and see if she didn't,' I said, sure I was right.

"'I said you apologize, Lenny,' Aunt Minnie said, never checking the girl's pockets. I tried to defend myself, but my aunt got this look on her face that I knew meant business, and I apologized, not meaning a word of it. Wondering what was wrong with Aunt Minnie.

"Well, from that time on, whenever I came over to visit my aunt, Trudy, if she was there would scurry out the back door like a scared rabbit. I didn't care though. I still thought she was a thief. That year on Christmas Eve, we all went over to my aunt's house as usual. Now I tell you, my aunt could cook. We stuffed ourselves full of ham and green beans and fried tomatoes till we thought we'd all pop. Then we gathered 'round the big black stove in the kitchen while Aunt Minnie read us the story of *The Little Match Girl*. I kind of sat in the back, figuring now that I was fifteen, I 'bout knew that story by heart, I really didn't need to listen to it again. I just knew that as soon as she finished we'd eat all the pies that were sitting there waiting on us. I wanted a big old slice of that pecan pie, and if I didn't listen to the story, there was a chance I might miss getting my fair share.

"Well, Aunt Minnie, she read the story, and she kept looking at me. It kinda made me squirm, like she was checking to make sure I was really paying attention. Finally she finished, and my mouth started watering for the pie, but then she said that before we all had dessert that she had a job that needed to be done, and she told me to help her. She got out a box and put the left over ham and bread and vegetables in it. Then to my dismay, she put my pie in the box. I picked it up and followed her out the door, hoping maybe I was suppose to put it in my folk's car, but no, she walked right by the cars and started walking up a path through the woods. We climbed that dark mountain with only the moon to guide us. I thought we'd never get to the top. Finally, after what seemed hours, my arms aching from carrying that heavy box, we reached a little shack – what you might call a lean-to because it just looked like old boards leaning together, as if a big wind could blow it over.

"Aunt Minnie knocked on the door and an old woman answered. I guess she really wasn't very old, but at fifteen, she looked old to me, as if the cares of life had eaten away her youth and vitality. 'Oh, Miss Minnie,' she said. 'Please come in.' We did and there was Trudy reading a story to two little skinny children. I realized this rundown house was the place that Trudy lived, and it suddenly dawned on me that the girl had probably taken that cornbread that she had pocketed to her little brother and sister and to her mother. I must tell you I felt ashamed. We walked in and put that food down on the table, and Aunt Minnie said, "We done brought you some Christmas dinner. Don't know what I would do if I didn't have Trudy around to help me all the time. Wanted to return the favor.' Those children oohed and aahed as if this was the best feast they'd ever had, and the mother just started a bawling. Aunt Minnie patted her on the back and they went over to a corner to talk awhile. Trudy and I just kinda looked at each other and finally I told her I was sorry for yelling at her that one time. She kinda smiled at me, making me feel better. As Aunt Minnie and I headed back down the hill, she said, 'Lenny, don't you ever forget the story of *The Little Match Girl*. That sweet youngun' is our match girl. You understand, boy.'

"I did understand, and I think I grew up a little that day, desiring never to let my Aunt Minnie down again."

A tear slid down Leonard's cheek as he looked out past the heads of the congregation, forgetting they were there, past the church walls, back to his boyhood. His voice grew husky, a knot forming in his throat. "But I have let her down. I've violated Aunt Minnie's trust. I've violated God's trust." Lowering his eyes, he looked back at the congregation, remembering them again.

Walking out from behind the pulpit, he approached the crowd. "What would you do if the little match girl were sitting on our doorstep when you came into church this morning? What would you do if her eyes looked at you, begging for help? There are thousands of match girls. They're all over our city. They surround this church. What do you do to help them?"

His eyes shifted to the floor. "I'll tell you what I've done." He walked back to the podium. "Sunday after Sunday, I've looked away from them. I've stepped right over them and walked into this church. I made sure that the choir had bright, clean robes, ignoring the match girl's tatters. I've bought new carpet for the library, forgetting that she just needs a warm place to lay her head. And the grand gesture I've made is to give all I can to our insatiable building fund. The monster that eats our money. Because, after all, isn't it buildings that are important? Isn't that what God wants? Then I leave here. I walk out of this beautiful icon, and I step over the match girl. I walk by all her brothers and sisters and go sit in my warm, cozy car, patting myself on the back as I go home, convincing myself that I'm a virtuous man."

He stopped, looking out at the congregation, his eyes red rimmed, his voice quavering. "I've let down my Aunt Minnie. I've let down my Father in heaven. I've let you down, and finally, I've let down my Jesus who died for all the little match girls out there, not for buildings and robes and carpet." He looked quietly at his hands, unable to speak for a moment.

Cole looked out at the congregation, seeing thoughtful, sensitive faces. Tears slid down some of the women's cheeks. A couple of the men had their handkerchiefs out. How could he say what he'd planned now? Oh, Leonard was better at this game than Cole had given him credit for. Well, let it be that way. Perhaps some of them would be disgusted by him the way Cole was. He'd been the one to force the man's hand. Leonard was disgracing himself. Cole shook his head in annoyance. He wouldn't say anything today after all. There would be a better time later on.

"Now, Brother Cole has something to share with the church today."

Unexpectedly hearing his name, Cole glared at Leonard, shaking his head no.

Leonard, ignoring the anger in Cole's eyes, motioned for him to come forward. "Come on up, Brother Cole."

Leonard stood waiting. The entire congregation, eyeing him curiously, also waited. Reluctantly Cole rose from his seat, looking darkly at Leonard. The preacher's eyes glistened with tears – the weakling. He might just say something after all. He turned toward the congregation. Red-rimmed eyes stared back at him. It was downright ridiculous. "I felt I needed to tell you this morning," he began in a stiff voice. Earnest, expectant gazes stared at him. He hadn't prepared for this. He faltered, breathing out a puff of anger, of defeat. "I'm going to resign. I have a new church that wants me. I've decided to accept the appointment. Let's sing our final song." Cole disappeared off the stage, slipping out the side door.

A short pause followed as Brother Steve, caught off guard, stood and started singing. The choir soon joined him. Leonard sat down in his chair with his eyes shut praising God. As the song ended, the congregation began walking out. A few people came to the platform to tell Leonard how much he had inspired them, and then Ann walked up, took Leonard's hand and helped her fragile, tired husband down the steps and out to his car.

Chapter 43

Be alert and always keep on praying for all the saints.

-Eph 6:18 (NIV)

Monday afternoon, Cole walked to his office. Although he did not want to return, he wasn't about to leave his possessions as well as his important papers there. Margie, sitting at her desk, glanced up pleasantly with a smile that immediately evaporated when she saw him. "Good morning, Brother Cole," she spoke in an almost inaudible voice before looking back down at her work.

Grunting his annoyance at her diffidence, he went into his office to begin packing. Without a trace of guilt, he boxed the books that he'd had rebound in leather even though the church had paid the rebinding fee and many of the volumes weren't his. Finishing that task, he filled the brass trashcan with bric-a-brac from his desktop. All these things would look good at Arrowhead First Church where he'd soon be working. Taking his time, he made sure that he got everything. The church would have to re-buy the necessities if anyone was hired to replace him. That thought made a knot of bitterness grow in his stomach. He worked more furiously.

Afterwards, he looked carefully around – all that seemed to be left were the files in the cabinet. His important financial papers were there. They would be safe at home now that Greta was gone. Meticulously he began to place the folders in a box as if they were well-loved treasures. Opening the file of one of his stock portfolios, he couldn't resist the urge to get his calculator out of the trashcan where he'd stored it and add up how much money he had. Pulling out Greta's folder, he searched for the most recent statement to add in her trust fund money. Strange, he kept the sheets in order, but the last statement was not at the back where it should be. Pulling the sheets out, he went through them slowly, one by one. It was puzzling. It should be here. Perturbed, he began going through the other folders. Perhaps he'd misfiled it. The paper was not in any of them. Nothing else seemed to be missing except this most recent report. Could Greta have taken it? Would she know what it meant? He looked through the only other two folders remaining. One contained three copies of his will. It seemed to be in order. The other contained two copies of Greta's will. She must have taken one.

Cole felt his blood pressure rising. *Calm down*, he told himself, *she's not smart enough to know how to access the money.* Pulling out a letter from the trust fund, he telephoned the long distance number. When the woman answered, he explained in a confident voice that he had apparently lost the most recent statement of a trust fund that he and his wife had with them.

"Will you hold please." Cole waited, feeling his impatience rising.

"Yes, can I help you?"

A pugnacious tone touched his words as he repeated the problem. The woman asked his name and the account number which he curtly gave.

"Mr. Odum, we no longer hold that trust. It's been transferred into another account."

"What! How could that have happened? Someone must have taken our money," Cole sputtered.

"I have in the records all the verified paperwork." The woman sounded slightly nervous. "We have your wife's signature, and it's the same as on the account."

"Of course it's the same, you imbecile! They copied my wife's signature!"

"Will you hold please?" Cole waited a long time. He had to get this money back.

"Mr. Odum," a man's polished voice spoke over the line. "According to our records the money that was in your wife's trust has been put into a checking account that is in her name with her social security number. Have you talked with your wife to see if she moved her money?"

"It wasn't her money," Cole seethed. "It was our money."

"According to the restrictions made on the trust at the time of the initial deposit, it was only in Greta Odum's name. We placed the money in an account with that name on it. I think you should talk to your wife."

Cole slammed the phone down, stuffed the files into a box, and stormed into the outer office. "Get maintenance here right away," he bellowed. "Have them bring these boxes to my car." He shoved the outer office door open so hard that it thudded against the wall.

Margie picked up the walkie-talkie to ask someone from maintenance to come as soon as possible. Brother Dan opened his office door with a questioning look on his face. Margie shrugged her shoulders. She didn't know what Brother Cole's problem was. All she knew was that she was thankful the man was leaving.

Christine handed Mr. Robert the sugar cookies that she and the children had made that morning. Even though the icing and sprinkles had been put on haphazardly, and they weren't the prettiest cookies, they were the tastiest. The older man got all three children a cup of milk and sat down with them at the little kitchen table.

"We decorated our Christmas tree yesterday," Amanda mentioned between bites.

"It's a great big one this year. Before we could only get little trees 'cause we lived in a trailer that became a truck," added Jonathan.

"Your trailer became a truck, huh?" Mr. Robert repeated with amusement. His gruff voice didn't stifle the children's chatter one bit.

"Yeah, I asked Mommy how they did that. See, it always just sat there for us, but when the new people came and bought it, they turned it into a truck, and it went riding down the road."

"Oh, that's interesting."

"Uh-huh, I was kind of mad at Mommy for selling it when she knew it could be a truck. I've always wanted a truck, and I didn't know it could be one."

"But you like your new house, don't ya?" inquired Mr. Robert.

"Oh, yes," agreed Jonathan.

"We got stairs going to the attic. Daddy's gonna put a bedroom up there for me and Jonathan one day when he don't work no more." Amanda wasn't about to be left out of the conversation.

"He is, huh? You built some stairs, Bill?"

"Sure did. We'll have to bring you by sometime to look at them."

"I'd like that. When we built *Friedensheim*, that place you call a hall was more of a sitting room. That's why it's so big. We didn't believe in putting halls in houses much back then. Waste of space. We'd build a house and just add on a room here or there when another child was born." Robert pulled himself up on his walker and came into the living room to sit down.

As the discussion of the attic continued, Christine told the older man that she had been unable to find the angels and baby Jesus.

"We brought Nathaniel's journal with us, hoping you could help us understand some of this," Bill explained as he pulled the diary out from a large manila envelope where they had written down some specific entries to ask the older man about.

"I'll do my best to help you," Mr. Robert returned.

"On March 16, 1937, it says 'I put in an extra wall today. Don't think anyone will notice. Hope not. Only I know about it, and I'll keep it that way. I'm going to put the angels and Baby Jesus in there so they'll be safe. It's fun to have a secret place.'"

"An extra wall?" questioned Mr. Robert thoughtfully. "I helped

Nathaniel build most of that house. I don't remember any extra wall. Nathaniel did all the planning though, making the closets and everything like that, but an extra wall?" The older man sat puzzling over it. "Sounds like something he would do. I'm gonna have to think on this for awhile."

"Why do you think he'd build a secret place," Bill prodded, hoping to jog the older man's memory.

"Oh, goodness – Nathaniel was kind of the nervous type. Can't say I really blame him. His family came over here during World War One 'cause Germany was such a mess. They even changed their name. It was something like Schwartzenmuiller and they changed it to plain ol' Miller. Part of that was probably so we could all say it easier, but I think the real reason was 'cause people didn't trust Germans so much. When things started getting bad in Germany again, he started worrying. Wonder what he did with those Nativity pieces. He should have told me. I wish I'd asked him. I just thought they'd be easy to find." The older man looked concerned as he shook his head. "Anything else in that journal of his?"

"Let's see." Bill glanced at his notes on the manila envelope. "On December 22, 1976 he talks about it again. 'I put out the old Nativity tonight. Had to go up to the attic to get it – and then to my secret place.' I figure the secret place has to be in the attic."

"Sounds like it. Read on. Is there more?"

"No, after that he just talks about his friend, Marta, and her granddaughter."

"Marta!" the older man cried. "It tells you all about Marta then, does it? Read that part to me, Bill."

Bill obeyed. "'I ate lunch at Woolworth today. While I was there, Marta and her granddaughter came in to do some Christmas shopping. When Marta saw me, she asked if they could join me. Of course I said yes. It was like old times. Marta was as gracious as ever. I don't know if a better woman has ever walked this earth. God gave me a Christmas present just to sit and talk with her. We talked about our school days, and the grandchild listened with wide-eyed fascination. Somehow I felt that if I'd had children, I would have had one just like her.

"'I put out the old Nativity tonight. Had to go up to the attic to get it – and then to my secret place. I'm getting too old for this. The Nativity sure looks pretty though. Wish I had someone to pass it on to, like Marta's granddaughter. I don't dare give it to her. Marta would know it was me. So would Frank. Robert tells me Frank would get over it and not to worry about it. Frank don't think so good anymore anyway. I don't know. It's just not my way. I can write, but I can't talk. Wish I had me a little granddaughter.'"

"The baby Jesus just has to be up there somewhere," the elderly man concluded. "I bet Nathaniel hid it behind a board or something." He looked at Christine earnestly. "Tell me you won't stop looking for it, Christine. It's his gift to you. If only I knew where he'd put it."

Christine felt bad for the older man. He seemed confused, as if he were mixing her up with someone else. She didn't want to embarrass him, so she simply promised that she would keep looking.

He seemed tired suddenly, and Christine hoped they weren't overtaxing him. "I wish I could help you more. Don't stop looking. They have to be in the house somewhere. I know they are."

The elderly man appeared spent, as if some old memories had zapped his energy. The family left soon after, hoping they would be able to figure out the secret to their old house – not so much for themselves anymore, but for this older man. It seemed vital to him, as if he were delivering on a promise that wouldn't let him rest until it was finished.

It continued snowing lightly outside as Greta sat, huddled in a warm quilt, in her rocking chair, and looked out at the lopsided snowmen that had been so much fun to build that morning. In the glow of the evening moonlight, three little snowmen could be seen – one named David, one named Joseph, and one named Greta. The cold, fresh, December air had invigorated her and froze her at the same time. During the afternoon, Cindy had gone to her craft class, and Greta had cooked a big pot of chili for supper. When Barry came home from work, he'd built a fire and they'd eaten around the fireplace. The day had been a pleasant one.

Earlier Pastor Leonard had called to tell her that Cole had resigned and was apparently looking into another church. Where, he didn't know. She wondered a little absently about what would cause her husband to change jobs.

Cindy interrupted her thoughts. "Here, Mom. I made you some hot cocoa." She handed her a mug before sitting down to warm herself by the fire. "Thought we'd put the tree up tomorrow night."

"Oh, good. That'll be fun. I brought some ornaments from home."

Cindy had never asked Greta what happened to cause her to pack her things and come back a day early; however, effervescent Rose had filled in a few details. The fact that her father had once again apparently acted in an unseemly manner did nothing to endear him to Cindy. At the same time, she continued to nourish the hope that he would change, would realize what he was missing, would... oh, there were so many woulds – and it was

Christmas – a time for love, for forgiveness. Looking at her mother, she realized that she loved this woman with a strong, rather protective love. Almost the same way she loved her two boys. Her love radiated the warmth and contentment that she felt at having her mother near. In many ways Greta was her best friend.

Greta smiled at her daughter. She had grown into a beautiful woman of whom she could be proud – she was and always had been a special child.

"I've been wondering about something," Cindy broke the silence. "Do you think I should invite Daddy to join us for Christmas?"

"What do you want to do?"

In all honesty, Cindy didn't quite know what she wanted. Her emotions regarding this were confused. Truly, it would be easier to live without him and not talk to him again; however, she also wanted to get rid of old bitterness. She wanted to love this man who was her flesh and blood. She wanted him to love her. She wanted things that would probably never be. "I want to do what's right, and what's best. I think I need to invite him." This surprised her slightly.

"Honey, you might be disappointed. I'm pretty sure that he won't come."

"I know. I just think that if I invite him, I'll have done all that I can do. It'll help me to let go."

Greta understood.

They sat quietly gazing at the fire for a few minutes. "I'm glad that Rose and Hal are coming to visit us after Christmas." Cindy laughed softly. "When I first met Rose, I wondered how in the world you two ever got together. You're quiet – Rose is a talker. You're a private person – Rose tells everything. You both seemed to be such opposites, and yet there's a special kinship that I could see between you two."

Greta smiled thinking about herself and Rose. "Maybe we complete each other in some way. I always wanted to be more outgoing. Rose says she always wished she could be quieter. We're kind of like two puzzle pieces that were wandering out there in the world, and God fit us together. I liked Rose the first time I met her. I don't know what I would have done without her. All people should be blessed with a good friend like her and with a daughter like you." Greta smiled contentedly.

Cindy felt warm inside at the compliment. To have a mother who is also a friend is a unique blessing.

Cole stopped at a Chinese place to eat his dinner. The food was tasteless and eating by himself day after day at a restaurant was becoming tiresome. He shot angry glances at the table next to him where a family with three preschoolers didn't seem to know how to make their children behave. He had kept his own children silent. They had learned early not to speak unless they were spoken to, but this family seemed to encourage their children to talk. He ate hastily so that he could leave.

Arriving home, he first carried in the carton of important papers to put back in the file drawer of his desk. The other boxes he dumped next to the front door. Rifling through his mail, he saw that his *Money* magazine had come, and oh, good, what looked like a Christmas card from the Herrins. Tearing it open, he found a note inside instead of the usual check.

"Dear Brother Cole, I wanted you to know that for Christmas I gave the church's Charity Fund five thousand dollars in your name." Cole didn't even finish reading the letter. He cursed and threw it down. This had been an abominable day.

Moodily he lumbered over to his chair and sank down. The quiet house got on his nerves. Picking up the phone, he pressed Cindy's speed dial number. The phone rang three times before his daughter answered. "Cindy, let me speak to you mother."

Cindy felt herself stiffen at the sullen timber in her father's voice. "Just a minute, Dad." Putting the phone down, she walked to the boys' bedroom where her mother sat reading them a nighttime story. A happy scene of two contented children listening intently to their grandmother met her. Greta was doing so much better. Would her father upset her? A decision decided, Cindy walked back to the phone. "I'm sorry, Dad. She's busy. Would you like to leave a message?"

"I don't care if she is busy! Get her to the phone now!"

Taking a deep breath to control her nervousness, Cindy spoke with a quiet authority. "Would you like to leave a message?"

"I told you to get your mother."

"Would you like to leave a message?"

"Yeah. Tell your thieving mother to call me." The phone banged down.

With a trembling hand, afraid that she might cry, Cindy hung up her receiver. She wouldn't tell her mother that her father had called. If she could help it, he would never talk to Greta again. Somehow she would try to protect her mother from his harassment. A thought struck her. What if he called while she was at her craft class the next day? Maybe she shouldn't go. When she was here, she tended to answer the phone. But if she stayed home, her mother would know something was wrong. Perhaps she could switch the phone ringers off on all three telephones in the house before she left. Her mother's phone was usually turned off anyway since she took frequent naps.

Cindy slipped quietly into Greta's room. Good, the ringer was off. Yes, this would work. She would get the hammer dulcimer done as quickly as possible so that she could be at home from now on.

She sighed deeply and a single disheartened tear escaped her eye and ran down her cheek. Why did he have to be this way? No matter, whatever the problem, he wasn't going to upset her mother if she could help it.

Chapter 44

Thou shall keep them, O Lord.

The next day, Christine found herself reviewing Mr. Robert's words. One thing was certain – the angels simply weren't in the attic. That whole area was as clean or cleaner than any room in the house. The wooden floor had been swept thoroughly, and she'd even closely inspected the chimneys to see if she could find any loose bricks that something might be hidden behind.

Pulling out Nathaniel's journal, she read and reread the entries that she and Bill had marked. The way to the secret place just had to be in the attic. But where? Turning to the end of the diary, she glanced at the Bible verses. Bill had said the first verse matched the one in the Bible with the hidden key. Perhaps the key unlocked the secret place. Had she missed a keyhole somewhere up there? Looking at the clock – it was past four – she realized she would have at least fifteen minutes to search while the children finished their naps. Slipping quietly upstairs to make a more thorough search of the walls and floor, she hoped that this time she would find something.

In case her plans didn't work out, Greta hadn't mentioned her idea of a Christmas sleigh ride to her children, but now, while Cindy was at her craft class and the boys were happily watching cartoons, she thumbed through the yellow pages trying to decide who to call. Looking under Stables, she went into the kitchen and dialed the first number. The area around Asheville was still rural enough that there were many horse farms in the surrounding hills. No sleighs or carriages at the first number or the second. Slightly discouraged, Greta continued down the list. The third person she called suggested she get in touch with Gebhart's Stables. Encouraged, Greta dialed the number. Without any problems, Mr. Gebhart cheerfully arranged for their sleigh ride. If there was no snow, they would have a buggy ride instead. Either suited Greta. She was simply grateful that one more wish on her list seemed about to happen. Tonight she would tell the children so they could anticipate it.

Hanging up the phone, she noticed that the ringer was turned off.

Strange. She must have accidentally knocked it off. Greta pushed the tiny knob to the "on" position.

As Bill drove to the Tuesday evening prayer service, Christine told him about her unsuccessful search of the attic. "I looked at all the beams and even rapped on the roof, trying to find a false panel or something. I thought maybe there might be a keyhole up there someplace. There are so many knotholes and scratches – especially on the floor – that I might have missed something. I sure wish Mr. Robert had been able to help us."

"He may remember something yet," Bill offered. "He seemed disappointed that we haven't found the angels. He really wants you to have them, Christine."

"I know. Sometimes I think he confuses me with the granddaughter Nathaniel talks about in his journal. The way he said it was his gift to me."

"You ever go to Woolworth as a child?"

"Sure. Didn't you?"

"A few times. You ever go with your Grandmother?"

"Yeah," Christine smiled remembering. "We'd go there at Christmas time. It was kind of a tradition. We'd go shopping, then eat lunch at Woolworth."

"Maybe your grandmother is Nathaniel's Marta."

"But her name was Martha, not Marta."

"Maybe he had trouble spelling her name."

"Well, if he did, it was only Grandma Martha's name that he couldn't spell – and being he was so in love with the woman, I'm sure he would know how to spell her name," Christine argued.

"What was your grandfather's name?"

"Frank – now Bill, that's just a coincidence. There are millions of Franks in this world, especially back then. It was a popular name."

"I was just asking."

"Anyway – even if it was my grandmother Nathaniel was referring to – well, it's inconceivable! Think about it – we just happen to move into his house. Too coincidental if you ask me."

"Maybe so – but Donald Gresham approached me, asking me if I'd be interested in buying the house. Perhaps Mr. Robert orchestrated the whole thing. They sure gave us a good price on the place – maybe it was some of Nathaniel's Good Samaritanism rubbing off on the rest of the family."

"You really think it could be, Bill?"

Bill laughed lightly and sighed at the same time. "No, not really," he conceded a little unwillingly. "Donald wasn't nearly as good hearted a year ago as he is now, and he's the one who sold us *Friedensheim.*"

"Plus, my grandmother's name would have been misspelled throughout Nathaniel's journal." Christine gave a disappointed smile. "You were about to convince me, you know."

Bill smiled back contritely. "Sorry. I just find it intriguing that there are so many parallels, and Mr. Robert sure seemed to imply that the angels were meant for you."

"Probably because we bought the house."

"I suppose. I think he like us a lot."

"It's kind of a nice feeling. Like someone's out there looking out for us."

"Kind of like Nathaniel looking out for Marta," Bill teased.

"Bill! Give it up already," Christine laughed. "Let's talk about something else. Anything interesting happen at work today?"

"Sam turned in his resignation."

"So he did get the job at the church. I hope it goes well for him." Christine searched her husband's face. "How do you feel about it?"

"Good. It kinda bothered me when I heard everything was going downhill there. I felt bad for Larry."

"Well, it should go better for Sam since Brother Cole will be leaving soon."

"Sam says he's already left."

"Already?" Christine's eyes grew wide with surprise.

"Apparently so. Some of the maintenance staff told Sam that they'd carried out a lot of boxes for Brother Cole yesterday. They said he took everything, left the room bare. Some of the stuff was the church's too."

"Well, I certainly feel for the new church who gets him. I hope Pastor Leonard told them all about Brother Cole."

"I do, too. You remember the glowing report we got about Brother Cole from his previous church."

"Yeah, I never could understand that."

"Well, rumor has it now – I don't know if it's true or not – that he was fired from that church before he came to us. They didn't even tell us."

"I find that hard to believe. I mean, these are men of God that we're talking about. One of the most fundamental things is to tell the truth."

"Well, it's a rumor. I heard it from Sam, who heard it from Larry, who said that Brother Dan told him, but Brother Dan doesn't usually tell stuff like that. So it might not be true. Guess that's a good reason not to share rumors."

But the rumor was true. Larry had actually overheard Pastor Leonard tell

Dan this. Christine and Bill both determined to pray for their pastor to have the courage to tell the truth no matter the cost.

Cindy smiled with pleasure as she walked in the front door, a large package in her arms. "I got it done," she told her mother, showing her the hammer dulcimer.

"Oh, Cindy, it's beautiful," Greta said when she saw it. "Let's put it in my closet to hide it from Barry." The two giggled as they hid the gift, imagining Barry's delight on Christmas morning.

The phone began ringing.

"I'll get it," Cindy said before remembering that she'd turned the ringers off. She glanced at her mother who seemed undisturbed. Hopefully her father hadn't called while she was out. "Hello?" It was probably Barry calling to say he was on his way home.

"Cindy, I want to speak to your mother." Her father's authoritarian voice caused her heart to quicken. Glancing at Greta who had walked into the kitchen to get a cup of water, Cindy kept silent.

"I said, Let me talk to her," Cole demanded in an acerbic voice.

Greta was taking forever getting her water.

"Oh, Dad, it's you?" Cindy saw her mother's face blanch as she looked her way.

"Let me talk to her now, young lady."

"Thank you for returning my call."

"What are you talking about?"

"I just wanted to invite you to come here for Christmas if you're able."

"If you don't let me talk to her, I'll disown you for Christmas," he blustered.

"Will you be able to come?"

"No, I won't be coming. Now let me talk to your mother."

"Uh-huh," Cindy murmured as if she were listening to a conversation on the other end of the line.

"What do you mean, uh-huh?"

"Well, I'm sorry to hear that Dad. We'll miss you."

Cole was exasperated. "Are you going to let me talk to her or not?"

"No." Good. Greta had gone into the living room to help the boys settle a squabble. Cindy knew that she still might be listening though and intended to keep her side of the conversation light.

"Look, Cindy," Cole tried to sound more even tempered. His blustering ways weren't working. "I really need to talk to her. It's important."

"No." Greta walked back into the room. Time to get off the phone. "Bye, Dad. Talk to you later."

"Oh, no you won't. I'm moving and you won't know where to find me."

This caught her off guard. "Moving? Where?"

"If you must know, I'm going to pastor a large church in Columbus." Cole hadn't told anyone his good news, and even in spite of Cindy's contrariness, it was nice to brag on himself to someone.

"Really? Which one?" she asked.

He felt pleased that he'd gained her interest. "The one I did revival in last summer. Arrowhead First Church. They want me to become their new pastor."

"Congratulations, Dad."

"Thank you." Cole sounded sincere. It had been a few days since he'd talked to anyone and though he didn't recognize it, there was a deep loneliness in his soul that needed human contact from time to time. "And now, may I please speak to your mother?"

"Did you know that Mom was in the hospital?"

"Yes, I've started getting the bills to prove it."

Cindy wished her mother weren't listening so closely. "We were quite worried about her."

"Yeah, yeah, now let me talk to her. This phone call is costing me money."

"Good-bye, Dad," Cindy concluded, hanging up the phone.

Greta felt tight inside, but Cindy smiled reassuringly and seemed relaxed. "Dad won't be coming for Christmas. He said he's moving to Columbus to pastor a church down there."

"So he's going to move."

"I guess so." Cindy tried to seem nonchalant. "I better start supper. It's getting late. Hope you're not disappointed about Christmas, Mom."

"You mean about your Dad not being here? No, I'm just glad I'm here. Let me help you with supper."

"That's okay, you go and rest. You look kind of pale."

"I think I will." Greta did feel weak. She was tired a lot these days. Somehow realizing that Cole was as close as the other end of the phone made her feel defenseless, as if he'd penetrated her little sanctuary. She was surprised that he'd returned Cindy's phone call.

The Tuesday evening prayer service went smoothly. Thankfully Brother Cole didn't make an unscheduled appearance. Even though Leonard hadn't expected him to show up, he'd hoped the same thing on Sunday morning and been sadly disappointed. After the service, as he arrived home, he began to relax – even though unpleasant remembrances of Cole still often invaded his peace of mind.

Ann had other thoughts in her head. "I've been wondering how to plan Christmas. I need to tell Minnie exactly when we'll be there."

"Well, if you like, we can leave right after I preach the Christmas Eve morning sermon. There's no evening service," he paused, looking at Ann, noticing the resigned expression on her face. "Or you could leave a few days earlier. I could meet you there on Christmas Eve."

Immediately perking up, Ann gave him an impromptu hug. She missed her children and the grandchildren.

Grinning at her girlish excitement, he felt at that moment as if he would do anything for his Ann.

"We got a Christmas card from the Herrins," she commented a little later as she glanced through the mail.

Leonard opened the card and read a note from William telling him about his generous gift to the Charity Fund. He smiled. That was the kind of Christmas present he liked.

Judith lay cozily in her bed, reliving her pleasant day in her mind. This day had proved to be one of the nicest days she'd had in a long time. She had met Emma a second and then a third time at the grocery store. To her genuine surprise, she found that she liked this stout, sociable woman. On their third meeting, the two had exchanged phone numbers, and later Emma had called to invite her to lunch. Odd, only a few months ago she would have looked down her nose at a woman like this, and yet today, she'd actually gone to her home and had a wonderful time.

Something in Judith was curious about the easy-going, affable Emma. Plus, though it was painful to admit, she needed a friend. This was a woman that she could start over with, someone who didn't even have a television set. In amusement Emma had explained that there had been a time when her husband was a couch potato, and it drove her crazy, so she started praying that he would stop watching so much television, and the next thing she knew, lightning struck the antennae, damaging the set. Laughing, she'd said that she was learning to pray more carefully. Judith had laughed too and was thankful. Here was one person who didn't know all the ugly details of Donald's and her past.

The lunch had been simple but delicious. They'd eaten a spinach salad, and for dessert they'd had sour cream pound cake. Judith had gotten the recipes and planned to make them for Donald who was very enthusiastic about her developing culinary skills – something that was giving her a sense of accomplishment. Actually she was turning out to be a good cook. She wished that she'd gotten along better with Elsie and could ask the woman for some of her recipes.

Emma and she had eaten their lunch and talked about all sorts of things. Strange the way life was – if it hadn't been for the unfortunate way that Donald's business had gone, she wouldn't have ventured into Emma's little world. This woman was different from her past friends. She was genuine, real, a person who loved people and didn't seem to notice financial situations.

Today had been wonderfully pleasant. If Judith added up all the enjoyable days that she'd experienced during her life, today would be at the top of the list. Why? It had been such a simple day, nothing fancy, nothing extravagant. But there had been something. She didn't know what the something was, but she felt herself yearning for more days like this. She had told Emma little about herself, but that had been all right. At one point she'd mentioned her son, Michael, and Emma wistfully said that she'd so enjoyed her sons as little boys, but that now they lived far away and she missed seeing them. Judith had been quiet about Michael after that. Somehow, she didn't want this new friend to know about her poor relationship with her son.

Snuggling deep in the covers, she listened as a lone owl outside hooted – it was cold – she wished that she and Donald slept together so she'd have his warmth to share, but since she'd insisted on separate rooms years ago, that would be something that would probably not happen; however, Donald and she were getting along better. That was something else that Judith couldn't figure out. Donald seemed less stressed. He didn't talk about business, and she didn't ask. They were beginning to talk more about little things. It was almost as if they were strangers getting to know each other. Emma had invited them to the church down the road where she went. When Judith mentioned the idea to Donald, he surprisingly was very agreeable. She would consider it. She needed friends, true friends, and maybe Emma would prove to be one. Another owl answered the first one's call. Judith smiled as she fell asleep.

Chapter 45

A merry heart doeth good like a medicine.

-Proverbs 17:22

During the next few days, Leonard noticed that the church staff seemed especially cheerful. Perhaps it was because of the Christmas season, but he wondered about it. No one appeared to be the least upset or concerned by Brother Cole's recent decision to leave, and though Leonard had expected a barrage of questions, not one had been asked. The contented faces spoke more than any words could have. Leonard began to suspect that the staff knew more about Brother Cole than he'd ever been told, and that was something that troubled him. Somehow he would have to become more approachable.

For a start, he visited Margie's desk to find out how her husband was doing. She smiled, saying he was back at work again. The dark shadows that once saddened her eyes were gone. With pleasure, Leonard noted she looked more relaxed than she had for months.

Returning to his office, he decided to call Greta. From time to time, he liked to check on her. When Cindy answered the phone, she seemed relieved that he had called.

"Is something wrong?" He wondered if Greta had gotten worse.

"Oh, no. I'm just glad that you're not my father calling again."

"Cole's been calling your mother?" Perhaps that was a good sign.

"Yes, a couple of times, but I wouldn't let him talk to her. He's angry about something. I just don't think Mom needs that right now."

"Has she taken a turn for the worse?"

"No, not really...I mean...well...I don't know. I've noticed that she's been taking more of her pain medication, but she doesn't complain. She tires easily, but she's been that way for a while. It must be worse though because she sleeps a lot. She's napping right now as a matter of fact. I just don't want her talking to Dad." There was a short silence. Leonard wasn't sure how to respond, and Cindy suddenly felt embarrassed, as if she'd revealed too much of her family's personal struggle. She tried to redeem the conversation. "He's pretty happy about his new church position though. I guess you know all about him moving to Columbus to work at Arrowhead First. He's always wanted to pastor a large church."

KIMBERLY MILLER WENTWORTH

Leonard felt sick inside. So Cole wasn't dissembling. He did have another church. Of course, he could be lying to his daughter too, but it seemed unusual that he would go to so much trouble as to tell Cindy that he was moving. Leonard decided to change the subject. He would think about this later and decide what, if anything, he should do.

"Cindy, before I forget, I wanted to ask if I could stop by on Christmas Eve to visit your mother?" It was Ann's idea. They had looked at a map last night to check the roads that he could take to Tennessee, and they'd noticed that Asheville was right on the way.

"Really. That would be wonderful, Pastor Leonard. We'd love to see you."

Leonard explained that he was driving that way to meet his family and thought he'd just make a quick stop in to say hello; however, Cindy encouraged him to join them for an early supper which he agreed to. As he hung up the phone, he felt pleased. A joy had begun to penetrate the despondency that had tried to overtake his life.

Later that day, as Leonard walked into his house, he smelled the Christmas scent of pumpkin bread baking in the oven. The hot meal Ann had cooked helped warm his cold bones and cement the peace he felt returning to his life. Now that the cold December winter had come full force, warm food tasted extra delicious. As he ate, he told Ann about his call to Greta and what Cindy had said regarding Brother Cole being called to Arrowhead First Church.

"Oh, Leonard, do you think it's true?" Ann's quiet voice echoed his fears.

"I don't know, Ann. Unfortunately it has a ring of truth about it." Arrowhead had seemed impressed with Cole when they were there last summer. Leonard shook his head. "I was wondering if I should call and warn them, yet...I don't know... that seems like a bad idea, especially if there's the possibility that Cole's made up the whole thing."

"Don't churches usually ask for references before they hire someone? Surely they'll call you."

"That's true." Leonard was thoughtful. "I just don't want to stick my head in the sand anymore, but at the same time, I don't want to stick my nose in where it doesn't belong."

"Let's pray that if Cole Odum is actually being considered for another church, that someone will call you for a reference. It would seem unusual for them not to, but knowing Brother Cole, they might not."

"Well, if they call Angus Pember, hopefully this time they'll hear the truth."

"Who's Angus Pember?"

"He's the preacher at the church in Asheville where Cole worked before coming to us."

"Oh, the one that fired him but gave you such a glowing recommendation."

"Right."

"I didn't understand why the man did that."

"Apparently when he let Cole go, he promised to give him a good reference. I'm glad I didn't make any promises like that."

Ann was thoughtful for a moment. "I suppose Angus Pember must have felt a lot of pressure."

"Probably did. But even so it was wrong."

The two ate in silence. Each absorbed in their own thoughts. Leonard finally spoke up, smiling at Ann. "Enough of this deep thinking. Dinner is delicious." He stretched his arms. It had been a long day. One of many long days lately. "By the way, I told Greta's daughter that I'd be stopping by on Christmas Eve. She seemed pleased."

"I'm glad. Greta can use all the encouragement she can get. It'll make her feel special that you go out of your way for her like that." Ann stood, picking up her empty plate. "I've been thinking about the packing arrangements going up. I thought I'd carry the food and the grandchildren's presents with me, and I'd fill your car with the other gifts. You want to see what I got today?"

"Sure." Leonard ate his last bite of dinner before taking his plate to the sink and following her into the spare room.

"I probably spent too much. It's hard not to."

Ann pointed out camping equipment, a microwave oven, fishing rod and tackle box, and a C.D. stereo system, among other things. Leonard cringed at the price tags and thought to himself, "It's too much." Even though he didn't want to dampen his wife's enthusiasm or hurt her feelings, his sober countenance betrayed his thoughts.

Ann looked at her husband and felt herself deflate slightly. The blatant materialism in the room suddenly depressed her. "I know what you're thinking," she predicted, sitting down on the window seat. "I'm forgetting what Christmas is all about, letting it get too big. I was thinking about that on the way home today. It was fun while I was buying the gifts. But when I finished and looked at what all I'd bought – I don't know – I felt a little empty. It's as if I want to give my children a good Christmas, and each year

I compete with myself from the year before."

Leonard understood. "They're kind of hard to buy for, aren't they?"

"They really are," Ann agreed. "They already have everything. Remember how we struggled at their age to make ends meet? It isn't the same today."

"Well, in a way I'm glad they don't have to struggle like we did. But there are always struggles in life. I hope when theirs come, they're ready for the challenge."

Ann surveyed the stockpile of gifts. "I suppose I could take this stuff back," she sighed. The thought of much more shopping depressed her.

"I think the kids will love these gifts," Leonard said. "Why don't we give them these this year, but have a long talk with them about changes we might make in the future."

"And some of what God has been teaching us too," Ann added. "It's so easy to fall into old habits. I'll buy smaller things both physically and financially for the grandchildren. I don't want them having the same high expectations that our kids have. Also," the twinkle returned to her eyes, "I want you to have plenty of money on hand for when you see that next need. Now come, preacher boy, and help me wash the dishes."

Leonard smiled as a warm rush of love for Ann filled him. "I was about to say how much I thought of you until you put in the part about doing the dishes," he said, laughing as he followed her into the kitchen.

Chapter 46

The Lord shall guide thee continually and satisfy thy soul in drought.

-Isaiah 58:11

The next few days were a whirlwind of activity for Christine as she and the children made decorations and readied the house for Christmas. Using scraps of material and fringe, she made Amanda and Lauranna each a doll and Jonathan a teddy bear. Pleased with the final products, she anticipated seeing her children's joyful faces on Christmas morning. Thankfully she and Bill had not stressed Santa Claus since no large, white-bearded man would surprise the children with gifts this year. Blessedly, the little ones didn't have those expectations – this one simple present each should give them great pleasure.

Now, Bill was another problem. There was little she could make for him. She would have loved to have bought him a tool belt for his work – a sturdy leather one, but they were simply too expensive to even consider. Looking through the mismatched fabric she had left, she wished there were a piece strong enough to make a cloth tool belt, even though it wouldn't last as long as the leather kind. Laughing, she pictured the only sturdy material she had left – a bright pink corduroy – being made into a tool belt. Bill would probably wear it too – just to please her – but he'd never live it down at work. Well, God would continue to supply. Something would work out.

Christine's confidence in the Lord's provision had grown steadily during the past few months, a painful growth at times. Putting away her sewing box, she pulled out Nathaniel's journal. Often she came back to it, struggling to find something she'd missed. Turning to the Bible verses on the back page, she decided to look them up. Bill would be home early tonight because they were going to the Classic City's Christmas parade, so she didn't have much time, but she would use what time she had – and who knows – she might discover something.

Sitting on the floor in front of the coffee table with a pad of paper, she opened her King James Bible to the first verse Nathaniel referred to: Proverbs 17:8. *A gift is as a precious stone in the eyes of him that hath it: whithersoever it turneth, it prospereth.* Closing her eyes, she took a moment to pray for God's gift of wisdom.

The next verse was Deuteronomy 29:29 (1,2). She wrote out: *The secret*

326

things belong unto the Lord our God: but those things which are revealed belong unto us and to our children forever, that we may do all the words of this law. What a wonderful promise! Somehow she felt as if this was the encouragement she needed to continue. She would write out the verses in parenthesis later, assuming that it was a verse, if she had time.

The next verse was Genesis 24:23 (14). She wrote: *And said, Whose daughter art thou? tell me, I pray thee: is there room in thy father's house for us to lodge in?* This verse seemed incomplete by itself and didn't fit with the other verses.

Exodus 3:16 (1) was next. *Go, and gather the elders of Israel together, and say unto them, The Lord God of your fathers, the God of Abraham, of Isaac, and of Jacob, appeared unto me, saying, I have surely visited you, and seen that which is done to you in Egypt.* She wrote it out before looking up Genesis. 6:13 (22). *And God said unto Noah, The end of all flesh is come before me; for the earth is filled with violence through them; and, behold, I will destroy them with the earth.*

Luke 22:12 (8) was next. *And he shall shew you a large upper room furnished; there make ready.* Writing it down, she could see no connection between any of the verses. This was frustrating! Why would Nathaniel have bothered with this?

Next was I Kings 6:15 (16-19). *And he built the walls of the house within with boards of cedar, both the floor of the house and the walls of the ceiling; and he covered them on the inside with wood and covered the floor of the house with planks of fir.* Her hand was getting tired. Perhaps she was wasting her time – but then this was a verse about a house. Why though didn't he write I Kings 6:15-19. The emphasis was obviously on the verse outside of the parenthesis.

She continued – Numbers 35:5 (1-5): *And ye shall measure from without the city on the east side two thousand cubits, and on the south side two thousand cubits, and on the west side two thousand cubits, and on the north side two thousand cubits; and the city shall be in the midst: this shall be to them the suburbs of the cities.* All right! Verse five was mentioned two times! That didn't make sense. (1-5) must not mean verses. This confirmed her suspicion. It must be something else.

The next verse was II Chronicles 3:4 (7,8). *And the porch that was in the front of the house, the length of it was according to the breadth of the house, twenty cubits, and the height was an hundred and twenty: and he overlaid it within with pure gold.* There were a lot of measurement verses being used. It had to lead to the secret place.

Next, Hosea 13:3 (37). *Therefore they shall be as the morning cloud, and as the early dew that passeth away, as the chaff that is driven with the whirlwind, out of the floor, and as the smoke out of the chimney.* There was no Hosea 13:37 so her hunch that the numbers in parenthesis weren't verses must be correct. What then could they be? Words perhaps? The idea occurred to her. She counted out the words in Hosea 13:3 – sure enough, there were thirty-seven of them. She underlined chimney, the thirty-seventh word. Her heart quickened. This might work. Yes! It just might.

The final verse was mentioned two times, I Kings 6:3 (10-15) and I Kings 6:3 (23-28). She wrote it out. *And the porch before the temple of the house, twenty cubits was the length thereof, according to the breadth of the house; and ten cubits was the breadth thereof before the house.* Going back to the first verse to try out her theory, a sentence began to form. It wasn't grammatically correct, but it was indeed a sentence.

The door opened. Bill was home, and good grief – look at the time! Supper wasn't even started. If they didn't hurry, they'd be late for the parade. Reluctantly closing the journal, she hurried to the kitchen to warm up some leftovers.

The next few hours crawled by. Christine had never been so anxious for a parade to end. The children smiled, laughed, and cheered at the festive but garish floats, so it was all worth it for them, but the entire time, she was puzzling over her discovery and anticipating going home to hopefully find out what secrets were in their house.

Finally, they arrived home and put the sleepy children to bed. Christine showed Bill her notes. "Look, here's the first verse: Deuteronomy 29:29: *The secret things belong unto the Lord our God: but those things which are revealed belong unto us and to our children forever, that we may do all the words of this law.* Now see here where it says (1,2). Write down the first and second words."

"All right." Bill wrote: The secret.

"Now here's the next verse: Genesis 24: 23."

"And this time it has a fourteen beside it, so I write down the fourteenth word."

"Right."

Bill wrote: "The secret room." Starting to feel Christine's excitement, he exclaimed, "Christine, it tells us something about the secret room."

"I know. I don't exactly understand what it's saying, but this seems to work doesn't it?"

Bill continued, "Go" "Through" "Upper" "Floor of house" "Ye shall measure from" "the front" "chimney" "twenty cubits was the length thereof" "and ten cubits was the breadth."

"All right," Bill examined the message. "First, the Upper Floor must mean the attic. Shall we give it a try?"

Christine jumped up. "You get the measuring tape. I'll get the masking tape and flashlights." She dashed off.

Bill laughed as he got the tape measurer before joining Christine on the stairs. "He might be counting the downstairs as the Upper Floor, since we have that large crawl space underneath the house," he noted, as they walked up the steps.

"But the journal says that the angels were in the attic. Let's try there first." Christine felt certain there had to be something up there she'd missed.

At the top of the steps, she stopped as the wall of darkness met her. The moon hadn't risen yet to add any light to the pitch-black garret. Allowing Bill to go first, she saw the dim flashlight glow and heard his steady footfall. One of the bare bulbs blazed to life as Bill pulled the chain, spreading light and eerie shadows across the room. Christine shivered. It looked much different at night.

"All right, it says to measure from the front chimney. I'd say they're talking about this one near the road," Bill determined. "I think a cubit is about eighteen inches, so twenty would be," he paused, doing the math, "thirty feet," he eventually calculated. Walking toward the front of the house, he pulled the tape thirty feet forward. "I sure hope Nathaniel's cubit equals eighteen inches."

"I hope so too," Christine agreed as she put down a piece of the masking tape to mark the thirty feet.

"Now it says that ten cubits is the breadth, but which side do I measure from?" Bill wondered.

"Let's mark both, and then see if we can find anything."

They measured from one side. "This looks as if it would be over the dining room," Bill commented as he began to measure the other way. "And this looks like it would be in Jonathan's room. Maybe in the closet or the bathroom." He looked at Christine wide-eyed. "Jonathan's closet isn't very big, is it?"

"No, and neither is the bathroom."

Bill got down on his hands and knees to begin looking. Christine turned on the flashlight to give them more light and knelt down beside him. "Bill, it's almost as if I can see a line in the floor right here, but with so many scratches, it's hard to tell."

"Here's a large knot hole," Bill pointed out.

Christine stepped back, focusing the flashlight on the hole as Bill put three fingers in it and pulled upward. Slowly the floor came up, less than a quarter of an inch.

"It's moving!" Christine cried.

Bill gave a hearty pull as what appeared to be a trap door opened, groaning in protest.

They both stood a moment in awed silence as Christine let the flashlight play in the darkness below.

Bill spoke, breaking the stillness, trying to fathom this unusual discovery. "It's between the bathroom and Jonathan's closet. Who would have thought? There's a ladder." He smiled at her boyishly. "I'm going down."

Cautiously stepping on the ladder to test its stability, he slowly descended into the inky blackness. The flashlight dimly lit what appeared to be a light bulb. Reaching toward it, he felt a cord and pulled. The light cast an unearthly-looking glow into the room below.

Christine, anxiously watching from above, asked "What do you see?"

"It's pretty big. I don't see how I missed all this space before. I thought this was just a plumb wall for the bathroom. There's a few shelves with canning jars, and there's a chest." Bill tried to open it. "It seems to be locked."

"The key in the Bible! I bet it fits it!" Christine disappeared from the top.

Bill looked around. Grabbing one of the jars, he opened it. It was full of quarters – old quarters – silver quarters. Another jar held dimes, and one was full of silver dollars. There was a fortune down here.

Hearing a rattling above, he looked to see Christine starting down the ladder. She wanted to see this new part of her house for herself. At the bottom, she silently surveyed the small cubbyhole closet.

"This is neat, Bill. What's in all the jars? There must be at least a hundred of them."

"So far they seem to be filled with coins – silver coins."

Christine's mouth hung open. "You mean money – real live money!"

Bill laughed heartily, fully enjoying the moment. "I hope it's not alive."

They both bubbled over with merriment, letting in thoughts of large bills being paid off, of financial freedom, of God's riches blessing them. Then, as they quieted down, they remembered the chest, rich oak with large brass clasps and a small gold lock, sitting, waiting, to be opened.

Taking a deep breath to calm her excitement, Christine knelt down to put the key into the lock. It turned easily with a small click. Glancing at Bill expectantly, she lifted the right corner clasp while he lifted the left. With a silent prayer, she opened the heavy lid. Inside there was a large wooden box.

Carefully she pulled it opened. Fourteen of the most beautiful angels she had ever seen smiled up at her. They were carved from wood with gentle expressions touching their faces. They had been delicately painted with rich gold wings and lovely flowing dresses, each adorned in a different color. Each had a word on it, and together they read: May the Angels Lead And May God Bless The Ones Who Receive His Gift. With the fourteen angels, in the same wooden box was an exquisitely carved and beautifully painted baby Jesus wrapped in a blanket. Written on the blanket were the word's: God's Gift.

Together they looked at the baby Jesus - a symbol of God's greatest gift - the Christ child. Bill gave Christine a hug, feeling blessed beyond measure.

"Shall we take these to the living room, Christine?"

She nodded, shutting the wooden box and moving so Bill could pull it out. Deftly he picked up the angel box and started up the ladder. Christine's sudden intake of breath stopped him.

"What is it?" The look on her face worried him. "What's wrong?" He came back to her and looked into the trunk. There at the bottom of the chest was a picture of an eight-year-old Christine standing with her grandmother.

Early the next morning, Mr. Robert received an unexpected phone call from the Jamesons, asking if they could visit. Curious, he invited them to come over right away. An hour later, as they walked in, he immediately recognized the wooden box that Bill carried.

"So you found them, did you?" he cried, a big smile lighting up his craggy features.

Christine told how she'd finally figured out the whereabouts of the secret place from the Bible verses; then, Bill explained their late night adventure.

Mr. Robert began reminiscing. "I helped Nathaniel with those Bible verses too. He'd say 'Robert, you know where the word *secret* is in the Bible' and I'd search until I found it. I remember he wanted me to find the word *attic* , but I couldn't find it – so we settled for *upper floor.* He said it was a game he was playing to hide the angels. I'd forgotten that. That Nathaniel – he was almost too clever for his own good! Can I see them?"

Bill put the box on the coffee table in front of the older man's chair and opened it.

"I'd forgotten how pretty these are. It's too bad Frank wouldn't let Marta have them. Nathaniel didn't say much to me about it, but I'd seen how hard he worked on them. I knew it upset him. He didn't have to say anything to me. I knew." He looked at Christine. "I bet Nathaniel's up in heaven smiling down on us right now because you got your angels, Christine. He wanted you to have them. It was the last thing he told me."

"He told you he wanted *me* to have the angels?" Christine repeated.

"Yup. There he was in the hospital – sick as could be – and he told me to make sure that you got the angels. I told him I would, too. But then, after he died, I went through all his things and couldn't find them. Finally I decided I wanted you two to buy the house so you could find them for yourself. Took Donald forever to sell it to you, too. So long, in fact, that I decided to will it to you at my death. That would have been a surprise, wouldn't it?" Leaning back in his chair, his eyes glistened. "I've finally fulfilled his wish. It feels good."

Pulling out the picture of herself and her grandmother, she showed it to Mr. Robert. "Was my grandmother Nathaniel's Marta?" She had to ask. She had to be sure.

The older man looked surprised. "Why yes. Thought I told you that already."

"But her name was Martha, not Marta."

"Marta's German for Martha. Nathaniel tended to call everyone by their German names." Robert glanced over at Jonathan. "He'd have called Jon here 'Johann'. It was his way." Looking back at Christine, a sincerity touched his eyes. "He loved your grandmother. Even though he kept his distance, he would try to watch out for her."

"I know." Christine remembered the different accounts in the journal of how Nathaniel had cared for her grandmother and her mother and eventually for she herself. She remembered the stories her grandmother told of mysterious packages or money that would come just when it was needed – how God had given them a special angel who was watching out for them. Her heart felt full. There were no words to express the tremendous swelling in her being. Without a word, she hugged the older man.

Chapter 47

Every man's work shall be made manifest.

-I Corinthians 3:13

On the sixteenth of December, a cold, wet Saturday evening, Cole lay in the comfortable hotel room bed, reviewing in his mind the meeting he'd had with the search committee earlier in the day. He realized it had gone well, very well. He knew how to give the right answers, and he'd liked the encouragement that he'd received from the group. One woman had asked him about his conversion experience – a standard question that he'd expected. He'd given an exact date – people were impressed when he said Thursday, August 29, 1957 – which was actually the day he'd gotten his first expensive car. He talked about how changed he'd been even though there'd been no obvious sins in his life. How God had transformed his inner man. He mentioned the Sunday school teacher who had led him to salvation, though he didn't share that in reality this particular man had been obnoxious. Besides, this man always gave him a good reference since he thought he'd saved the sinful, arrogant Cole Odum. Cole chuckled as he briefly reflected on how he'd used this vain man over the years. He'd be pleased to hear that his convert would soon pastor one of the largest churches in Georgia.

When the food had come, he'd eaten heartily. He was hungry this time. Remembering a similar meeting with Pastor Leonard and that search committee – he'd been more nervous then – it had been harder to eat. But since he had pulled it off then, he knew that he could do it again. At the end, Howard Barbin had spoken to him privately, saying that a few on the committee would insist on reference checks but that he was sure Cole would have the job as soon as he was available to come. Cole asked him not to call Pastor Leonard. He would rather tell the pastor that he was leaving himself than have the man get a surprise phone call. Howard fully understood.

Sunday morning, Cole preached a brilliant sermon. It was one of his best, and he saved it for times when he wanted to impress others. After the morning service, there was a covered-dish luncheon so the church people could get to know him better. He realized that this was a good sign of their intentions to hire him. At three o'clock, he met with the deacons. The head deacon, Sidney Vaughdery, was difficult to impress. This bothered Cole slightly. He asked too many questions about Greta. Cole reluctantly explained that his wife would have liked to have joined him and was excited about the possibility of coming to this new church, but for health reasons, it was difficult for her to travel right now.

"Well, it's important that we meet your wife, Reverend Odum," Vaughdery insisted as if this was a mark against him.

"Indeed, I want you to meet her. Greta's a lovely woman. I know that you'll love her as much as I do. But right now she must stay in Asheville close to her doctor. We don't think she has much more time left." Cole sounded as if he were being strong, but at the same time this was tearing him up inside, a hard part to play; however he could tell by the silence that followed that he'd given a superb performance.

After the meeting adjourned, Howard Barbin walked Cole out to his car. "You should hear from us before Christmas," he asserted. "The deacons are meeting again tonight. Then we'll be presenting it to the church family for a vote on Wednesday. I know you'll be unanimously voted in."

"I feel God calling me to this church, Brother Howard. I know it's the right thing. There's a loving spirit about this place." Cole expressed his delight at the thought of working with Howard soon. He could see Howard's pleasure at his praise. Oh, this would be an easy church to pastor! That was certain.

Howard, joyful at Cole's obvious decision to pastor their church, asked him when he'd be able to move to Columbus.

"I need to give a couple weeks notice, but I've asked for some vacation time the first two weeks of January, so I can be available by January first if you'd want me that soon."

Howard was pleasantly surprised. Things were moving faster than he'd expected. Yes, they'd definitely like that, a new pastor for the new year. They couldn't ask for more. What a blessing from God – to have everything fall into place so easily.

Cole made the long drive home quite pleased with himself and his promising new job.

Monday morning, Reverend Angus Pember looked at the message marked urgent that asked him to call Sidney Vaughdery from Arrowhead First Church regarding a reference for Cole Odum. Angus put his head in his hands. Not long ago he'd had to answer to Pastor Leonard who had insisted upon knowing the complete truth about Cole Odum. The Reverend had finally confessed that the church had let the man go, but that he'd promised to give him a good reference. Pastor Leonard hadn't been too pleased by his duplicity and came just short of calling him a liar. The discussion had been unpleasant. He'd lost his temper, not because he was being accused unjustly, but because he saw himself as an honest, upright individual, and in this case, he hadn't been one. His defensiveness had caused him to be rude to Pastor Leonard, and both men had hung up the phone upset.

Now someone else was asking for a recommendation. This time he must tell the truth. In all honesty, if one were to dissect the character qualities of Angus Pember, he would be described as a loving, godly man – but also a fearful, somewhat weak person. If it hadn't been for his strong deacon body, Cole Odum wouldn't have been discharged from the church. Though in many ways Angus Pember was a good man and an excellent speaker, he was in truth a cowardly leader and thus at times a poor one.

Slowly he picked up his phone. As it was December 18th, who would know but that he was out for the Christmas holidays and didn't get the message. He hung up thinking the idea a good one and tried to busy himself, but the thought of the unmade call nagged at him. Finally, laying down his pencil, he picked up the phone. If he didn't call this man, he'd feel uncomfortable for a long time. Best to get it over with. Praying for courage, he dialed the number.

"Sidney Vaughdery, please." The secretary asked him to hold. Angus considered hanging up.

"Hello, Sidney Vaughdery speaking."

"Mr. Vaughdery, my name is Angus Pember. I have a message to call you."

"Yes, Reverend Pember, thank you for returning my call. I'm calling about a former employee of yours, Cole Odum. We're considering hiring him for pastor here, and we wanted to know more about him. He gave us your name for a reference. What can you tell me about the man?"

"Well, Cole Odum is an extremely hard worker, and he's dedicated." Keep it vague, even Pastor Leonard couldn't argue with this assessment.

"Can you tell me about his wife?"

"Oh, yes, Greta and I have been friends for a long time." Angus could warm up to the talk of Greta. "She's a wonderful woman, a quiet woman."

"Reverend Odum says that she's sick."

"Yes. She was in the hospital a while back, but she's been in church the past couple of weeks. I think she's doing better."

"Can you give me the number where she's staying, so I can reach her if necessary?"

"Certainly, just a moment." He put the man on hold and asked his secretary to get him Cindy's phone number. Then clicked him back on the line. "My secretary will have it for me in a minute."

"Tell me, Reverend Pember, why did Reverend Odum leave your employment?

Pember was quiet for a moment. He wanted to say because Cole had an excellent offer from a church in Georgia. He wanted to say because of church finances. He wanted to not tell the truth, but he wouldn't do that. "Because we let him go."

"Excuse me….Did you say you let him go?"

"Yes."

"Can you tell me why?"

"I'd rather not." Angus was relieved to be interrupted by his secretary coming in with Cindy's phone number. He gave it to Sidney. "Mr. Vaughdery, I'd suggest that you contact Pastor Leonard from Main Street First Church since Cole Odum just left their employment. He could give you more information on the man than I can."

"Did you say that he 'just left their employment'?" Sidney realized that his initial instincts about Cole Odum may have been right on target. He had insisted to Howard Barbin that he make the reference checks himself because his spirit felt an unexplainable disquiet about the man.

"That's my understanding."

"Well, thank you. I will contact Pastor Leonard. You've been very helpful, Reverend Pember. Thank you." Sidney hung up wondering how he would explain this to the other church members and Howard.

Lanie buzzed Leonard's office. "You have a call on line four from a Reverend Angus Pember."

Leonard was surprised. The last time the two had talked, he'd been abrupt with the man, and the Reverend hadn't been too friendly to him either. "Hello, Pastor Leonard here."

"Pastor Leonard, this is Angus Pember. You and I talked recently about the reference I gave you on Cole Odum."

"Yes, Reverend Pember. I remember."

"I want to tell you that I thought a lot about what you said. The last time we talked I said some things that I shouldn't have. I suppose I was embarrassed because I try to be a man of integrity. Pastor Leonard, I had a lot of excuses for my behavior, but I know now that they were just that: excuses. I preach about not excusing sin, but sometimes it's hard to see the sin in one's own life." This was a much humbler man than the one Leonard had talked to earlier. God was doing a lot of humbling lately. Leonard better than anyone could understand excuse making. The two began to have a congenial talk. Reverend Pember related his discussion with Sidney Vaughdery and the fact that Vaughdery would probably try to call Leonard in the near future.

"I was honest with this man," Reverend Pember said. "I didn't give him all the ugly details, but I didn't try to cover up the truth. Your words were the beginning of a chastening process that I seem to be going through. I'm having to look at myself and decide what I will stand for and what I won't, and though it won't help the grief that your church went through, I wanted you to know that your words have penetrated." The conversation ended on a pleasant note.

Less than an hour later, Sidney Vaughdery and Howard Barbin made a conference call to Leonard.

"First off, Pastor Leonard, I want you to know that anything you tell us will be held in strictest confidence," Sidney explained.

"All right."

Howard Barbin's uneasy voice came on the line. "We were very impressed by you and Brother Cole last summer during the revival, and we've been considering asking Brother Cole to become our new pastor. He asked us not to talk to you about this because he wants to tell you himself, but Sidney felt that we needed to contact you." Clearly Howard was uncomfortable with this.

"It's fine to talk to me. I've heard that Cole was considering your church. I'll answer any questions that you have."

This news caught Howard by surprise. It was only Monday morning.

"We need to know about your working relationship with Reverend Odum. How you feel he would do as a minister at our church," Sidney's businesslike voice came on the line. "My first question is: does Reverend Odum presently work at Main Street First Church?"

"No, he no longer works for us. We decided to let him go, but before I could tell him, he resigned."

The answer was clearly understood. He heard an intake of breath from one of the two men, then the voice of Howard Barbin exclaimed, "Pastor Leonard, why were you considering letting this man go?"

Leonard explained that there had been occasions when Brother Cole had lied to him, and as a result he had difficulty trusting the man. More questions were asked, and Leonard circumspectly described some of the circumstances that had led to his decision.

Howard had trouble reconciling his version of Brother Cole with the man that the pastor was describing. His trusting nature felt confused. He wanted to reject what he heard, yet something over the weekend had bothered him. "Can you tell us about his wife? He told me that she's sick with cancer."

"That's true. Greta was our pianist until recently when she became ill. She's now living with her daughter in North Carolina. Cole doesn't have much to do with her."

The silence was long. "You mean he doesn't visit her?"

"That's right. Not unless he's begun to recently. When she was in the hospital last month, he didn't know about it until I told him. She's a fine woman, too – one who deserves better treatment."

Howard had heard enough. His exalted opinion of Cole Odum sank quickly. His own wife had suffered with cancer and recovered. It had been a terrible time, but their relationship had grown deeper. He wouldn't have considered sending her off to live with one of their children during that difficult year. Pastor Leonard was speaking again, answering a question that Sidney had asked, but Howard didn't need to listen. He'd heard enough.

"Thank you, Pastor Leonard. We appreciate your honesty," Sidney expressed at the close of their conversation.

"I'm sorry I couldn't have been more encouraging."

Sadly Leonard hung up the phone. When he first became a Christian, he'd thought that if he loved people enough, they would accept Jesus and do what was right. This viewpoint wasn't necessarily wrong, but being a Christian was much harder than that. One needed to be willing to do what was right no matter what the cost. Leonard hated to speak ill of others, but deep within his heart, he knew that he'd done a difficult but right thing. There had been a spiritual battle for ownership of this church that for a time Leonard had been only vaguely aware of. With God's help, he would do whatever he could to prevent another church from suffering through what they had.

Sidney called the deacons and had the word passed around that the Wednesday night business meeting would be canceled until after the holidays. Howard Barbin called the search committee with the same words of cancellation. Sidney and Howard needed to meet at some later date to discuss how to best present this to the committee and the deacons. The search committee would start all over, and sometime after the holidays one of them would call Cole Odum to explain that he would not be hired. Neither wanted to do it, especially Howard, and Sidney suspected that the unpleasant duty would fall upon him. He wished that Howard hadn't been so positive toward the man. Howard wished the same thing.

Chapter 48

For my thoughts are not your thoughts, neither are your ways my ways, saith the Lord.

-Isaiah 55:8

By Christmas Eve morning a severe cold front had moved in, turning the already chilly weather even colder; however, as Leonard prepared for church, he had no time to watch the news or see what the weather would be like. Carrying his suitcases out to the already full car, he put them in the backseat. Ann had left a few days earlier with the grandchildren's and his aunt's gifts and enough food to feed the entire family for weeks. The other presents were in his car – the trunk crammed full. Even the backseat was heavily loaded. The church people had been especially generous this Christmas season, and on Friday, he'd placed a box piled high with all the goodies into the vehicle. Decorated with festive trimmings of red, green, and gold, they made an impressive display of abundance. He picked up the gifts he'd bought especially for Ann, an exquisite silver necklace and a sweet, porcelain Christmas ornament – an angel holding a lamb. Laying them on the passenger's seat next to him, he climbed into the car and drove the short distance to the church.

There was something special about having the last Christmas service on Christmas Eve. A blessed spirit seemed to envelope the entire church body. The Jamesons were there, Leonard noted. They looked happy as they talked to Mr. Robert Gresham and his son Donald. He saw Larry, Patricia, William, and Carol Herrin. Larry seemed satisfied with the way things had turned out, and Leonard was relieved that the transition had suited everyone so well. Sam and his wife, Cathy, could be seen in the alcove with their two boys. For the last couple of weeks, they'd been back in church, and the strained expression that he often saw on Cathy's face was no longer evident. Margie and her husband, Kevin, were turned around, talking pleasantly to Ben and Catherine Evans. As Leonard looked out over these people that he was privileged to shepherd, he felt a warmth toward them. The singing began, causing him to feel a joyous rapture as he relived the wonder of Christ's birth through song. When his time came, he spoke peacefully, reverently, softly about the gift that God had sent them - His Son - for Christmas.

After the service, the majority of the congregation came through the door where Leonard stood. There were more gifts. Among them was Miss Eleanor's famous homemade fudge and a decorative basket containing banana-nut bread from the Jamesons.

When the last family left with a chorus of "Merry Christmas," Leonard hurried out to his car to be on his way. The bitter cold met him as he walked through the parking lot, but the chill in the air couldn't take away the warmth he felt inside as he began driving toward Asheville.

The trip out of town proved difficult. It seemed that everyone had decided to do last minute shopping, and the traffic was fierce. One stoplight changed three times before he finally got through it, and the other lights seemed to stay red endlessly. When he eventually got out on the highway, the traveling was faster, but only for a short while. A tractor-trailer had stalled on I-85, and it took him over an hour to go only fifteen miles.

To add to Leonard's anxiety was the fact that even with the heat on high, a cold draft could be felt wafting through the car. On the radio, the announcer reported that the temperature would be dropping steadily as the day progressed. A snow advisory was in effect for the northeast Georgia mountains. *Well,* Leonard thought, *everyone says they like a white Christmas, but no one wants to drive in one.*

By the time he reached South Carolina, the weather report was less encouraging. The Blue Ridge Mountains could definitely expect snow during the night. Leonard would stop by Greta's and make a quick visit. He might not stay for supper if it looked as if the weather was worsening. A home-cooked meal would be nice, but he had at least an hour to two hours afterwards to complete his journey.

Arriving in Asheville much later than he'd planned, he reviewed Cindy's map. Heading north through town toward Black Mountain, he eventually found the Mountain Laurel Road. Thankful for the clear directions, he pulled into Cindy's driveway, realizing with relief that though it was cold, he'd seen no snow or sleet yet. A pleasant thing suddenly happened. The sun, which had been shadowed by heavy snow clouds, began to peek through and shine. As it was beginning to set, its bright rays made everything glimmer. Even though the weather was bitingly cold, Leonard felt reassured. Getting out of his car, he observed that the house, which was more like a cottage, was nestled into the side of a mountain. It had a beautiful view overlooking the valley. He still missed the mountains that he'd grown up in. A warm feeling of home nestled in his heart.

Seeing the front door open and a young woman beckoning him to hurry inside, he did just that. As the family welcomed him, Leonard noted that

Greta seemed more content than he'd ever seen her. Lines of unhappiness that used to mark her attractive face were gone.

Dinner was ready, and after he'd taken a moment to wash, they sat to eat. The warm, cozy house made the biting cold outside seem far away. Barry, whom Leonard had not talked to before, spoke about his job and love of music. They both discovered that they were from Tennessee and began telling old legends that they'd heard while growing up. The children listened in wonder as the men told their stories. Leonard relaxed, feeling at home with these people, letting the time slipped away unnoticed.

At a lull in the conversation, David spoke up. "We're going on a sleigh ride."

"Are you?" Leonard asked.

"Yeah, that is if it snows."

"If it doesn't snow, we get to ride a buggy instead," Joseph explained.

The thought of the weather reminded Leonard that he'd better leave. "This has been so pleasant, but I need to get on my way. I don't want to get caught in the middle of a snowstorm."

Although everyone agreed that it was wise for him to be on his way, Leonard found himself tarrying a little longer to talk and pray with Greta. It was hard to hurry off. He'd had such an agreeable time, and the cold outside was so uninviting, but when he heard one of the boys yelling that it was snowing, he hastily headed out the door, annoyed with himself for staying so long.

The sun had finished setting, turning the roads dark. The moon tried to shine through the clouds, and eerily lit the towns nestled in the mountain valleys as he drove past. He could tell there were many quaint little villages even in the moon's half-light. Snow began falling steadily, making it harder to see. Driving slowly, past a little town called Jupiter, past Mars Hill, he began climbing the steeper mountains. Unfortunately the snow had almost completely covered the road, causing him to have trouble seeing where it was.

"Lord, please help me," he asked over and over nervously. Christmas music played softly on the radio, contrasting to the tension Leonard felt. The mountain road wound back and forth. The steep embankment on his side of the highway looked dark and unwelcoming. His course was slow. The snow thickened. He could barely see as he gradually climbed the mountain. The terrain became steeper. He put the car in low gear, wishing he had chains on his tires. The wheels spun. Then graciously reconnected with the road. Again a front tire lost traction, sliding slightly. There, he was okay again.

Reaching the crest, he began to descend down the mountain. The car gained momentum. He pumped the brake – too hard. His wheels lost traction with the road, spinning. *Oh, dear God, help me!* He turned into the spin, willing himself to pump the brake softly, praying that he wouldn't slide off this mountain. Though it happened quickly, Leonard had the odd sensation of being in slow motion. The car finally stopped, half-on, half-off the road. With a breathed prayer of relief, he gently pressed the gas pedal. Oh great! The back tires spun. It had been foolish to stay so long at Greta's. Turning on his emergency flasher, he put on his coat, then climbed out of the warm vehicle into the icy coldness. With all his strength, he pushed the car. It wouldn't budge.

Getting back into the driver's seat – a panic tried to overtake him. "Lord, what am I going to do?" He would freeze if his car ran out of gas. Maybe if he could get warm enough, he could walk to a nearby house. He would wait awhile to see if anyone drove by. Surely someone would come by soon.

His feet were cold. He still had on his church shoes that were now wet with the melting snow. Reaching into the back seat, he hunted through his suitcase until he found his basketball shoes, a pair of sweat pants and a sweatshirt. He put the warm fleecy garments on over his church clothes, added an extra pair of socks and replaced his good shoes with his basketball shoes. Even though he now felt warmer, he wrapped his coat around himself. The thought of carbon monoxide poisoning worried him, but eventually he decided that the draft in the car told him that outside air was definitely leaking in. Fervently he begged God to allow someone kind to come by and help him.

Ben Langham drove cautiously through the furious storm toward home. He and Mary had gotten the good news the day before that his temporary job at the post office during the holiday season was going to become a permanent one. When he'd been laid off from the factory, the family had struggled through it all. It had been one of the most trying experiences of their marriage. Not nearly so bad as when little Randy had died, but they'd lost a lot. Even though he'd worked at many part-time jobs during the past eight months, they still hadn't had the money to pay the mortgage. The home, that they'd scrimped and saved to buy, had been repossessed by the bank. They had tried to sell it, but people didn't buy much on these old mountain roads. The huge down payment and all the equity that they'd put into it was now gone. The bank was having trouble selling it too, and Ben hoped that, with God's help, he could save enough to pay the delinquent payments and get their house back again. It was a beautiful place. Even though it only had three bedrooms, that was enough for their family. The two girls had slept in one room and the two boys in the other. It had been three boys, but now it was only two. This was their fourth Christmas without Randy, and yet, it still felt like their first one. The loss of their home was insignificant when he thought about Randy.

Aunt Rosella had been pleased with the cookies that Mary had made for her, but Ben wished he could have made the visit earlier in the day; however, there'd been no choice. He had promised Oscar, the old man that lived up the mountain from him, that he would help get his plumbing working again, and Oscar, bless his heart, had paid Ben twenty dollars for his trouble. He said he would have had to pay the plumber at the shop much more than that. Ben knew Oscar could hardly afford it. Hopefully his pipes wouldn't freeze again. Sometimes Ben was grateful for the little shack that they rented. It did, at least, have a button that they could press to get the pump to send water into the kitchen, but the best part was that he never had to worry about bathroom pipes freezing. They had an outhouse.

The blizzard was getting worse. Ice and snow continued to hit the windshield with no sign of relenting. Ahead of him a car was parked oddly in the road. It would be hit if it stayed like that. Stopping his truck, he got out. The car was dark and empty. Probably someone had already helped them. It was icy cold. The chill went right through his thin jacket, and with relief, he climbed back into his old truck again. About a quarter of a mile further down the road, he saw a man walking – slipping and sliding would describe it better. Stopping his truck, he rolled his window down, and yelled, "Hey, you need some help?"

The man looked a little nervous, but said a quick, "Yes." Ben opened the passenger door and told him to hop in.

"That your car back there?"

"Yes. It slid off the road. It's stuck. Thought I'd walk to the nearest house and get some help."

"Nearest house in these hills is about two miles. I can help get it unstuck for you." He began slowly backing his truck toward the car. "I'll hitch it to my truck. If it stays here, somebody might hit it." He stopped the pickup in front of the car and jumped out.

The man, who was enjoying the truck's warmth, forced himself to get out too. Realizing he didn't even know this Good Samaritan's name – he looked nice enough, but one can never tell – he awkwardly introduced himself. "By the way, I'm Leonard."

"Name's Ben. Nice to meet you, Leonard. Tough luck – getting stuck on Christmas Eve and all. Where ya headed?"

"Near Johnson City." Leonard watched Ben expertly attach the chain to the car and then to his truck. "Looks as if you know how to do this."

"Yeah, we often have bad weather up here in the mountains. I'm all the time getting people out. Been doing it since I learned to drive. My Daddy used to say to me that with my driving goes responsibility. One of those responsibilities is to help God's people whenever I can."

Leonard smiled. "Well this child of God sure does appreciate it." They got back into the warm truck, and Ben began driving slowly.

"The storm's suppose to get worse," Ben announced as the heavy snow continued to come down. "You might have to spend the night with us and wait this thing out. We just have us a small place, but you're welcome to stay if you like. It's kinda dangerous to go out in this weather."

"Thank you. I'm much obliged." Leonard felt himself slipping into the Tennessee accent that he'd been raised with. He felt better about this mountain man. "What were you doing out in this?"

The loquacious Ben told him in detail about visiting Aunt Rosella and how he'd meant to go earlier, but it had taken him a while to get Oscar's plumbing fixed. "You can meet Oscar if you want. My wife, Mary, is baking him some cookies right now for Christmas. Me or one of the young'uns will be going up there."

"Oh, how many children do you have?"

Ben hated that question. It was wrong to say five and pretend that they'd never had Randy. "We've had six, but one of my little boys went home to be with the Lord a few years back, so now we have five with us."

Leonard was quiet a moment. He didn't want to make this man relive his pain. "I'm sorry for the loss of your boy."

"Do you believe in heaven, Leonard?"

"Yes, I do." It'd been a long time since anyone had asked the pastor what he believed.

"Well, I do too, but when Randy got sick, I got mad at God – really mad. He was only five-years-old, and he was such a sweet little boy that I couldn't understand it. But it was like God gave us a little reassurance before He took him. We had another house at the time. It was real pretty with a big glass window in the living room that overlooked our backyard. We had this little birdbath back there, and all day long Randy kept asking us if we could see the man standing at the birdbath. I said, 'No son, there's no man there.' And he'd say, 'Yes Daddy. He's standing by the birdbath. He has on this white robe.' My wife said she didn't want to disappoint him, so she pretended to see him. I asked him what the man looked like, and he said that he had the most beautiful face – it was bright and shiny – and that the man was smiling at him and waving his hand for him to come. Then I knelt down beside my boy and hugged him. He was so little, and he said, 'Daddy, Mama, the man wants me to come and I need to go to him. Please don't be sad.' Mary said, 'It's okay, Honey,' and he shut his eyes, and he was gone. It was like a sign from God. I knew for sure that my boy was in heaven, that Jesus had taken him up there. I know I'll see him again one day. I'm glad that I have the Lord to depend on during the hard times."

Leonard was quiet, feeling moved by Ben's story. Usually he was so good with words, knowing the right thing to say to his congregation, but now he found himself wordless.

Ben hoped he hadn't overwhelmed this quiet Leonard fellow. Mary often said he tended to talk too much. He hadn't meant to tell Randy's story, but his son was still a part of him. Cautiously he turned down a driveway. "Here's my house. It isn't much, but we feel blessed to have a roof over our heads."

Leonard felt concern for this young man and his family. The place looked as if it was unlivable from the outside. Stepping out of the truck, Ben showed Leonard where the outhouse was. "We keep the seat inside. I'll show it to you when you come in. My oldest boy, Joey, got stuck on it a couple of weeks ago. We kept wondering where he was, and finally Mary went outside to try and find him, and she heard this weak little holler coming from the outhouse, and poor Joey was stuck to the seat, and the seat was stuck. I had to pry it off, and then he had to wear it into the house and let it heat up by the fire. He couldn't hardly sit down for a week. Don't tell him I told you. He's fifteen and gets embarrassed real easy." He opened the door to the shack. "Come on in."

Leonard walked into a tidy kitchen that had a sink, an old refrigerator and stove, and a few shelves on the wall that housed plates and cups. A table with benches was at one corner of the room. The living room, which was slightly larger, could be seen from the kitchen. It was sparsely furnished, with only a couch and a rocking chair, and contained a large wood stove. An old-fashioned-looking cradle sat in the far corner where a small baby slept. A few pictures hung on the wall. A sparsely decorated Christmas tree was next to a small window. Leonard had the impression that if Mary had more money, she'd have been good at decorating. It didn't look like a shack from the inside, but like a cozy little dwelling. There were two doors going off from the living room that apparently went to the two bedrooms. Somehow, the four older children all slept in one room.

Ben introduced his wife, Mary, an auburn haired woman with a quick smile. Though lines of hardship and fatigue touched her face, a youthful love for life could be seen echoing from her dark brown eyes. She seemed barely taken aback by the presence of a stranger in her home.

Charlie, Ben's five-year-old son came to meet Leonard. Like his father, he loved to talk, and Leonard soon learned all he could hope to know about the family from this blond, outgoing child – his daddy had just gotten a new job at the Post Office. They only found out about it yesterday. Mama was making cookies to celebrate. They hadn't had cookies for a long time because the "gredients" were too "spensive." Daddy lost his job last year, and they'd lost their house on Old Widow's Run, but now they were saving to buy it back again. He had a little sister now – Rebecca – she was asleep, but it was okay to be noisy. She could sleep through anything.

"Thanks, Charlie," Mary interrupted. "I think Leonard has now learned our whole family history in about five minutes. Go get your sisters and tell them the cookies are ready." Charlie ran toward a bedroom. "Leonard, would you like one. They're fresh out of the oven."

"I'd love one." It was delicious – chocolate chip.

"Now this is Leah," Ben introduced his pretty dark-haired daughter with a face much too serious for a twelve-year-old. "And this is Mary Lynn."

"I'm eight," offered Mary Lynn amiably with a ready smile that seemed permanently attached to her cherubic face.

"She just had a birthday," Charlie began again, but was interrupted by his mother asking him to give Leonard a chance to talk.

"Do you have any family, Leonard?"

"Yes. I was headed to see them when my car got stuck."

"Oh, I'm sure they'll be worrying about you if you don't show up," Mary said. Her eyes looked at Ben to help remedy this problem.

"The weather's awful, Mary," Ben pointed out. "We towed Leonard's car here. He'll have to spend the night."

"If I could just use your phone to let them know that I'm all right," Leonard began.

"We don't have no phone," Charlie told between mouthfuls of cookies.

"'Bout the closest one is in town at the restaurant, but they'd be closed now." Ben tried to think of a nearby place with a phone.

"There's the pay phone outside the bank, Ben. You should take him there. His family will be worried to death if you don't."

"You up to it, Leonard?" Ben asked, slightly concerned. Leonard looked older in the light than he'd thought he was when they were in the truck.

"Yes, if you don't mind, Ben. I'm sure my wife's wondering what happened to me."

"Okay, give me a minute to unhitch the car. Mary, where's Joey? He can help me." Ben started putting on his thin jacket.

"He's still up at Oscar's, giving him the cookies I made. He should be back any minute."

Ben walked outside while Leonard put back on his warm coat and gloves. A moment later, a dark-haired sturdily built teenage boy walked into the house, introducing himself as Joey. He told Leonard that all was ready, and Leonard went out to meet Ben at the truck. The drive to town was down into the valley, and the going was a little faster since they didn't have the car to pull behind them, but it was still slow travel. Leonard braced himself as he stepped out of the warm truck, into the frigid air, and phoned his anxious wife.

"Ann, it's Leonard."

"Thank goodness. I was so worried. Greta called me hours ago. Where are you?"

Leonard explained briefly what had happened.

"I'm just glad you're all right. You sure you can trust this family?"

Leonard looked at Ben sitting in the truck. "Yes, Ann, they're good people, but you wouldn't believe what little this family has to live in. They have five children and live in a tiny two-bedroom shack. I feel almost as if God sent me to them."

"Sounds as if God sent them to you, Leonard."

Leonard had to agree. It was too cold to talk for long, and he soon hung up with a forlorn feeling. He'd never been away from Ann on Christmas before.

Back at Ben's house, Leonard warmed up with a cup of strong coffee. He thought of the flavored coffees, that had been a gift from Margie, that were in his car and considered retrieving them, but he didn't want to offend anyone.

"Mama, do you think Santa Claus will bring me a train?" little Charlie asked.

"Charlie, the weather's so bad tonight that I don't think Santa can carry heavy stuff like trains," Mary answered kindly. There was a touch of sadness to her voice that Leonard didn't miss. Times had obviously been hard for this family.

"Should we even hang up our stockings?" Leah asked. She knew how difficult things had been.

"Course we should," Mary Lynn piped in. She wasn't sure if she believed in Santa Claus, but if there were any chance of his coming, she

348

wanted to make sure that her stocking was up.

"Yes, definitely hang up those stockings," Ben stated, "and then off to bed with you."

The children ran into their bedroom and returned a few minutes later with their handmade stockings that they placed on the little hooks where their coats usually hung.

"These are beautiful," Leonard said as Mary escorted the children to bed. He looked at the delicately crocheted top of one of the stockings.

"Mary made them. She's good with her hands. She helped out a lot the past few months by sewing for people."

Leonard noticed Mary come out of the children's room and quietly disappeared into her bedroom. She returned a few minutes later with two large bundles wrapped in plastic trash bags and put one under the tree. "I made two comforters. One for the boys' bed, and one for the girls'," she said, opening one of the bags, pulling out a comforter for Leonard. "You can use one tonight, Leonard. I don't have any extra blankets. I'm afraid that you'll have to sleep on the couch."

"Thank you, but that's much too pretty to use. I have a blanket in the car that I can get. You rewrap that to surprise your children. They'll love it."

Mary smiled, pleased by the compliment. She went to one of the two cupboards in the kitchen, and pulled out a bag of red-and-green wrapped hard candy. "I got these to put in their stockings, Ben. If I'd known for sure you were gonna get the post office job, I might have gotten more, but I didn't want to risk it otherwise." She began putting candy in each child's stocking.

"We were on food stamps for a while. It was kind of humiliating to Mary."

Even though Ben spoke softly, Mary overheard and came over to the table to drink some of her coffee. "People started treating us different. It's embarrassing. One day this lady behind me in line at the grocery store says to the checkout girl, 'I betcha she's got a Cadillac out in the parking lot.' I felt so ashamed. I didn't know what to say. I thought about not using the food stamps anymore, but then we wouldn't have had the money for electricity or for gas for the truck. I had to swallow my pride. I've told myself if we ever get beyond this, that I'm gonna be the nicest person to anyone that I see using food stamps and see if I can help them a bit myself."

Hard times and unkind words had tried to strip away this couple's dignity, and yet, to Leonard, they had more charity than many of the wealthiest members of his congregation. Something in him felt humbled.

A short time later, as Leonard went out to retrieve his blanket, pulling it off the boxes of gaily-wrapped gifts in the back seat, an idea struck him. Santa Claus might just make an unscheduled stop tonight.

Chapter 49

Glory to God in the highest, and on earth peace, good will toward men.

-Luke 2:14

As gently as possible, Leonard opened the door. Earlier Mary had moved the baby cradle with little Rebecca into her bedroom. Except for the sound of the wood crackling in the stove and Ben's snoring, the house lay quiet. Hopefully no one would be awakened and worried by his moving around. Outside the cold bit sharply through his coat. All the warmth that the daytime sun had brought had utterly vanished. Gently pulling the door to, he hurried to open the trunk of his car. The train was the first wrapped gift that he pulled out. Laying it on the stoop, he grabbed a second box – a large, square one – the stereo or possibly the microwave. Inside, he would sort it all out. Again he placed the package on the stoop. The cold stole his warmth. The snow made the ground slippery. Surely he wouldn't fall and end up waking the entire household. The tent was next. The big rectangular box made it obvious. After depositing it, he closed the trunk as softly as possible and opened the car door. It groaned faintly in the still night. Pulling out another large square box, and the long irregular gift that contained the fishing pole and tackle box, he tried to think how to best give these presents. There was a family of seven inside. He counted the packages – five. Back at the car, he put the two parcels that he'd meant to give to Ann in the box of goodies that had been given to him by various church members. Spotting Ann's gift to him lying on the seat, he grabbed it too before gently closing the car door. Now to get all this stuff inside before he froze.

Stealthily opening the kitchen door, the warm air met him like a gift. As softly as possible, he moved the boxes inside and shut the cold out. No one stirred. Except for, as before, the snoring that continued to interrupt the stillness and the faint crackle of the fire, the house seemed utterly silent. Every whisper of sound that Leonard made, he feared would wake someone. Searching through his pockets, he eventually found a pen. Thankfully Mary had left one small lamp burning as a nightlight so that he could see. He took the nametag off the train set and wrote on the Christmas wrap, "With Love, To Charlie." He wrote Joey's name on the tent and Leah's on the box containing the silver necklace. The stereo system was made out to Mary

Lynn. It was an odd gift to give an eight-year-old, but he had to work with what he had. He wrote Mary's name on the microwave's wrapping paper, the fishing rod was made out to Ben, and on the little Christmas ornament he wrote "To Baby Rebecca." Picking up his gift from Ann, he took off the tag, and wrote "To Leonard." With painstaking care, he tiptoed into the living room and placed each gift under the tree. That done, he smiled at his handiwork and slipped back into the kitchen to neatly arranged the confections, pastries, nuts, fruit, breads, and delicacies in the middle of the dining room table. With a sigh of relief that he hadn't been caught, he took off his coat and lay on the lumpy couch. Satisfaction engulfed him and a contented smile rested on his face. Cuddling under the blanket, he felt suddenly extremely tired and soon fell into a dreamless sleep.

Christmas morning comes early when one has youngsters in the house. Leonard was awakened by the sound of Charlie gasping, and then shouting, "Mama, Daddy, Santa Claus came! Santa Claus came!"

Leonard peered over his blanket to observe with satisfaction Charlie happily running between the two bedrooms. One by one, he saw the expressions of disbelief written across the children's faces as they came into the room. Ben walked in with a sleepy expression that quickly changed to one of almost childlike wonder as his eyes widened, and he surveyed the gifts. He looked at Leonard who shrugged as if to say, "I have no idea how it all got here."

"Mary, get out here! You've got to see this!"

"Give me a second. I'm almost dressed," she called back. Upon spying the bounty, her mouth formed an "Oh" of astonishment, and she gave Leonard the same look that Ben had.

Leonard again shrugged his shoulders. "I didn't hear anything."

"I heard him. I heard him. I thought it was you, Leonard, going to the outhouse, but it must've been him," Charlie cried as he rushed to the pile. "Look, what does it say, Leah? Read it. This one starts with a C. That must be for me, right?"

Leah looked. "Yes, it says "To Charlie'."

"Can I open it, Mama?"

Mary sat down on the couch. Though she smiled, tears were in her eyes. "Sure, Charlie, go ahead."

Charlie carefully removed the wrapping paper, which surprised Leonard. His children and grandchildren tended to rip off the Christmas wrap so fast that Ann would try to slow them down.

"I'm gonna save this paper. It's too pretty to mess up. Will you help me Leah, so I don't tear it?" Leah helped, and the train set slowly appeared. Charlie looked at his mother and father with delight dancing in his big, brown eyes. "Santa knew just what I wanted. It's the most beautiful train in the whole world."

Leonard felt a flood of joy that was so tremendous he was afraid he might let his secret out. He heard a noise next to him and looked at Mary. She was crying. "Mary, are you okay?" he asked, worried that he might have offended her.

"I'm better than okay. God answered my prayer. I didn't expect Him to do it or know how He would, but I asked Him for a train for Charlie. I'd looked all through the stores, but they were so expensive. I've been praying for one, and now – God let him have one. Thank you, Leonard."

"Don't thank me. It was definitely God. I didn't buy it." That was true. Ann had bought it.

"Is there a present for me?" Mary Lynn asked with a restraint unusual for her tender years.

"Right here." Joey moved the large box toward her. "You want me to help you with the paper so that you can save it."

Mary Lynn nodded. Carefully she and Joey unwrapped the stereo system. "Wow," the young girl declared, stars dancing in her eyes. "Look – here are some Christmas tapes with it, too. Can we hook it up now, Daddy?"

"Sure," Ben agreed with a smile.

"Now you can listen to music again, Mary Lynn," Charlie said, then whispered to Leonard in a confidential tone, "Mary Lynn loves music. She's the best singer in our family. Someday she's probably gonna be famous."

Minutes later, Christmas music penetrated the small house.

"Here's one for you, Daddy," Leah said, reading the message. "'To Ben. Your generosity is an inspiration to all.'"

Ben eyed Leonard again. Grinning, the young man unwrapped the fishing rod and tackle box. "How did you know that I liked to fish?" he asked with genuine awe in his voice.

"I prayed that God would get you a fishing rod, Daddy, since yours got broke, and you had to tape it back together, and it don't work so good now," Charlie confided. "I guess God told Santa."

Ben tousled Charlie's hair lovingly as Joey opened the tent. Though he was a sturdily built lad who looked older than his fifteen years, suddenly the little boy seemed to spring out of him. He looked at the tent wordlessly and then at his father, tears springing into the young man's eyes. Ben moved closer to his son, putting an arm around his shoulder. Together they examined the tent and began discussing when they'd go camping.

"Joey had to sell his tent to the pawn shop when we were trying to save our old house," Charlie murmured to Leonard. "It made him real sad. He and Daddy love to go camping."

Leonard wondered briefly how hard the losing of their beloved home had been to this family. His thoughts were interrupted by Mary Lynn.

"Leonard, here's one for you."

Charlie noticed Mary's and Ben's look of surprise. "Santa knew that Leonard was here. He wouldn't leave him out."

Leonard grinned and opened the gift from Ann, hoping it wasn't too extravagant. Inside was a beautiful forest green sweater. "Just what I need to be warm for Christmas," he said merrily.

"Mama, this one's for you." Leah pushed the big box toward her mother.

"For me," she smiled at Leonard, then opened the package with the same care that the children had taken. "A microwave oven," she whispered in disbelief, looking at Leonard.

"Mama, you said just yesterday that you wished you had one and look now you do." Charlie could hardly contain himself.

"Are you an angel, Leonard?" Mary asked seriously. She was beginning to wonder.

"Oh no, I'm very human," he confessed, thinking of the Christmases he'd spent many dollars overindulging his family.

"Here's a tiny one. What does it say, Leah?" Charlie asked, handing over the small gift.

"To Baby Rebecca."

"Let Leah open it since she didn't get anything," Charlie suggested. Leonard looked and could barely see Leah's gift underneath the comforters that Mary had made. He considered speaking up, but being afraid he would give himself away, he kept quiet.

"Oh! It's a little Christmas ornament, with the date on it, for Rebecca's first Christmas."

Mary contemplated Leonard. "I just don't see how you could have known – such perfect things."

"I really don't know how that happened. God moves in mysterious ways." Leonard had been afraid that the gifts would seem odd to this family, but somehow they had been perfect.

Charlie buried his face underneath the cedar limbs of the Christmas tree and pulled out one of the large plastic bags. "What's this say?"

"It says to the Langham boys," Leah read.

Joey pulled out the other bag. "Here's one for the girls."

Charlie opened the boys' bag. "Look Joey. Isn't it beautiful? Thank you, Mama."

"I love it, Mama," Leah stated appreciatively as Mary Lynn hugged her mother. Charlie crawled under the tree again, and Leonard felt relieved as he pulled out the gift for Leah.

"Look! Look! One more! This must be yours, Leah."

Leah, who had seemed unbothered by the absence of a present, suddenly appeared very pleased as a smile spread across her face. She carefully opened it. "Oh, Mama. It's beautiful."

Mary picked the necklace up gently. "It says here that it's made of sterling silver. You must take good care of it."

"Oh, I will, Mama. I'm gonna save it for special occasions like when I get married."

Leonard looked at the sweet young lady's face, touched by her words. He felt a surge of warmth and thanked God silently for the moment. His inner spirit stirred to the point of overflowing – his cup ran over.

For the Jamesons, Christmas Day was the happiest of all in a procession of pleasant days. After they'd shared their gifts with each other, Bill lit all twenty-five candles on the advent log and began telling the Christmas story from beginning to end. Christine felt content as she watched her husband. Only a few scars remained to reveal the accident. God had protected him and given her a special gift that could never be store bought. She would praise Him for whatever amount of time He gave them together. Looking at the Nativity, complete with angels and Baby Jesus, she felt a contented glow. She understood why they were special to Nathaniel and now to her. Sighing deeply, she realized they told the story of what Christmas was truly about – God's gift of His son.

Greta and her family gathered in the family room after the afternoon meal to sing Christmas carols. They sang heartily while Barry played his hammer dulcimer and Greta played the piano. Prettier music could only be heard in heaven. After the singing, the ladies went to the kitchen to wash the dishes together while the men sat watching a football game. A happy confession was made by one of Greta's daughters-in-law that indeed, she was expecting – due in late July.

Greta sighed inwardly as she walked to her room to take a much needed nap. She would have to revise her list. She wanted to live at least long enough to see whether she would have another grandson or a granddaughter.

Sinking into her bed, she realized that she felt so tired today, probably because of all the activities. Tomorrow, if the weather cleared as it was supposed to, Rose and Hal would be coming. She wanted to rest so that she'd have energy to enjoy her friends.

The pain that seemed to sap her energy and yet often kept her from sleep hit her. She took one of her pills before she lay down. She smiled as she eyed the Hummel Nativity that she'd given to Cindy. Her dear daughter had put it on the dresser for her to enjoy. A picture of Cole flashed across her mind's eye. "I hope he's okay," she thought wistfully.

Cole didn't want to admit it to himself, but he was concerned about the job at Arrowhead. Howard Barbin had been so positive about his coming and had said that he would contact him before Christmas, yet no call had come. Finally Cole had left a message with Barbin's secretary, asking for the man to call him as soon as possible, even if it were over the holidays, but the phone remained silent. Probably everything was delayed because of Christmas. It did tend to get in the way of business. Even so, it would seem that Barbin should have returned his call.

As the day progressed, Cole thought about Greta and his children and wondered what they were doing. He hadn't bothered to send gifts or contact them. In spite of his seeming unconcern, he'd gotten a gift from Greta. It was a C.D. of her music. He had played it almost continuously since receiving it. She was talented, and he felt proud that it was his wife who could play so well. Also, another elusive feeling that he kept carefully tucked into the corners of his mind kept trying to escape today, probably because it was Christmas.

Taking another bite of his microwave dinner, he changed the television channel to see what else was on. *It's A Wonderful Life* came on the screen. Tommyrot! He pressed the remote control. The end of *A Christmas Carol* was playing. He watched as Scrooge began to change his ways. What was so wrong with the old Scrooge anyway? He was simply a good businessman. Just a bunch of sentimental fools, he thought as he flicked the television off and finished his meal to the last measures of Greta playing *O Holy Night*. The fragile emotion of loneliness slipped out of its corner for a brief moment. Shaking his head, he shoved it back into the recesses of his mind where it belonged.

Donald opened the door to his house uncertainly. When he'd left to go eat dinner with Michael and Nancy, Judith had screamed at him that he was an ungrateful husband and didn't care about her. He encouraged her to come, but she'd adamantly refused. The television was on as he walked in. Judith sat in front of it, petting the stray gray cat that had recently taken up permanent residence at their home. By the one lit lamp in the room, he could tell that she'd been crying.

"Nancy sent some leftovers. Can I fix you a plate?"

"Yes, thank you," she responded almost meekly.

Walking into the kitchen, he arranged the meat, stuffing, bread, and vegetables on a plate, and then on a saucer put a piece of pumpkin pie. Judith loved pumpkin pie. He brought it to her, placing the meal on the coffee table. She ate quietly for a few minutes. "This is good," she said in the same small voice. "Did you have fun?"

Odd, Judith didn't tend to ask him questions nor was she so tentative in her speech. "Yes, it was nice seeing everyone."

"I wish that I'd gone," she mumbled almost inaudibly. It was the closest to an apology for her morning outburst as she would come. She had examined her life during the long, lonely day and didn't like what she saw or where it was going. She knew that she needed to change in some way, but she didn't know how.

"I wish you'd have come, too," Donald replied.

"I was thinking, Donald. I need someone to talk to," she paused, and he waited for her to continue. "I need some advice. I've been considering going to see a Christian therapist that I heard about. Do you think we'd have the money for such a thing?"

"Yes." Some way he would make sure that they had the money for such a thing. His proud wife even considering getting help was a miracle. "Do you want me to go with you?"

"Maybe eventually, but just me at first. I've got some sorting out to do."

Donald knew how painful sorting out could be. He touched his wife's hand and gave it a small pat. The gesture would have brought ridicule before, but it didn't this time.

"I have a little gift for you." He pulled a small box out of his pocket.

"Oh," she smiled, and Donald felt a warmth toward her that he hadn't felt in years.

Inside the box was an ornate ring with her birthstone in it. She owned many rings, but this one felt extra special. She knew he had sacrificed to buy it. It was beginning to dawn on her that he had made many sacrifices in the past year. "It's beautiful. Thank you. I got you something, too." She gave the

357

cat a final pat before putting him down on the floor. Leaving the room, she returned shortly with a wrapped package of specially flavored coffee. There had been little money this year, and she hadn't known what to get him. She felt almost embarrassed.

He opened it eagerly. "My favorite coffee," he exclaimed graciously. That was Donald - gracious. Judith could learn from him if she allowed herself to.

They held hands and quietly watched the ending of *The Christmas Carol*. The story was about change, real change that touched other people's lives. Perhaps that could be Judith's story as well.

Ben waited in the warm truck while Leonard talked on the phone. Aunt Minnie answered first and told him all that he was missing. Surprisingly Leonard didn't feel left out. Instead he felt as if he'd been honored by God to be a human type of angel. It still amazed him how the gifts that Ann had bought were so perfect for this mountain family that he'd happened upon.

"Christmas isn't the same without you," was the first thing that Ann said. "I listened to the weather report. It's supposed to start clearing up this afternoon."

"Good. I'll leave as soon as I can. Ann, I have something I need to tell you and ask you to tell the children."

Ann hesitated. "Sure, Leonard. Is something wrong?"

"Oh no, everything's fine. I've just had the most amazing Christmas of my life, but I may disappoint you all. I gave the children's gifts and yours, too, to this family. You see, they had nothing for Christmas, and I...." He heard the sound of crying or was it laughter on the other end of the line. "Ann?"

"Oh, Leonard, I don't care about those gifts. Last night I was so worried about you. It kind of puts things in perspective. I don't think the children will mind either. I was just realizing what a big turn around we've had this year. I think it's wonderful. The children and I had a long talk last night about some of the things that you and I have been going through the last couple of months. I think we all realize that Christmas should be more a time of giving to others than for getting for ourselves. Our Christmas present will be to hear all about your Christmas morning. I'd like to meet your family. Maybe we can go home that way, and you can introduce them to me."

"That would be great, and Ann," Leonard paused, looking at Ben in the truck, "I think I know what God wants us to do with that money from

William Herrin, and perhaps some of our own." He would somehow help this young family to get their house back. "I'll tell you about it when I see you."

"I can't wait. Sounds as if you've had quite an adventure."

"I have. I really have. I love you, Ann."

"And I love you, Leonard. Oh, and Merry Christmas."

"Merry Christmas."

Leonard hung up the phone as the sun peeked out from behind the clouds, turning the snow-covered world into a field of diamonds. In the distance church bells began to ring. The soft, warm melody touched his ears and went straight to his heart. Leonard thought he'd never seen a more perfect day. As he sent his gratitude heavenward, he imagined that he heard a melodious voice softly whispering in his ear, "Peace on earth. Good will to men."

* * *